Praise for Rod Duncan's previous novels,
Backlash and *Breakbeat*:

'An action-stuffed tale of crime, intrigue and murder' *Zoo Weekly*

'This pacy tale of life in the inner city shows that modern British crime fiction is alive and kicking over the traces' Mike Ripley, *Birmingham Post*

'A fast-moving, gripping detective story. The plot twists, turns and thickens in a most satisfying way, engaging the reader from start to finish' *India Weekly*

'Written with confidence, skill and sheer page-turning compulsion, this is what contemporary British crime fiction should be: unafraid to ask difficult questions of our society, knowing the answers are never truly black and white' Martyn Waites

'A cracking good read ... intelligent yet accessible' *UK Baha'i Review*

'The pages turn at a rapid pace ... An impressive debut' *Big Issue*

D0242784

By the same author

BACKLASH
BREAKBEAT

Born in Wales, Rod Duncan now lives in Leicester with his wife and children.

His debut, *Backlash*, was shortlisted for the John Creasey Award for the best first crime novel of 2003.

BURNOUT

Rod Duncan

POCKET
BOOKS

LONDON • SYDNEY • NEW YORK • TORONTO

First published in Great Britain by Simon & Schuster, 2005
This edition first published by Pocket Books, 2005
An imprint of Simon & Schuster UK
A Viacom company

1 3 5 7 9 10 8 6 4 2

Simon & Schuster UK Ltd
Africa House
64–78 Kingsway
London WC2B 6AH

www.simonsays.co.uk

Simon & Schuster Australia
Sydney

A CIP catalogue record for this book
is available from the British Library

ISBN 0 7434 5021 3

Typeset by M Rules
Printed and bound in Great Britain by
Bookmarque Ltd, Croydon, Surrey

One must judge of search by the standard of the Majnún* of Love.

from a story of Leila and Majnún told by
Bahá'u'lláh in *The Seven Valleys*

* Literally, the name Majnún means 'insane'.

PART ONE

Chapter 1

The third package arrives during the night – a manila Jiffy bag with the shadow of a fold line down the middle from its forced passage through the narrow letterbox. It lies on the carpet until six fifty-five, when Frank comes downstairs for breakfast. It has landed with his name facing upwards – printed in deliberate, marker-pen capitals. There is no address. No stamp.

He isn't about to make the same mistakes as before, so he doesn't open it there in the hallway. Not even the study feels safe. So he lifts it from the floor, holding it away from his body, and carries it out of the house and down the path, past the display of bonsai trees, all the way to the far end of the garden. He steps into the shed and presses his back against the door. Creosote and cut grass smells prickle in his nostrils. He looks down at the package to examine it again and sees that his hands are shaking.

'Damn.'

He would have been more in control if this had happened a few years ago – when his confidence and strength were still growing. Back then there was no need to tint his hair. And the bags under his eyes used to recede whenever he had the chance to repay the sleep debt he'd accumulated through back-to-back shifts.

Frank closes his eyes and takes a deep breath. He lets it

out slowly, then holds a hand up in front of his face. It is steady now. The calm has started to return.

He goes to a workbench under the cobwebbed window, selects a modelling knife and runs the blade along the side of the Jiffy bag, scoring the paper layer but not letting it puncture anything critical inside. He repeats the move, deepening the incision, forming a slit down the length of the bag. Then he splays out the edges, probing for wires or batteries, finding none. More confident now, he starts to tease open the inner layer of bubble-wrap padding, stroking the cut wider and deeper with the point of the knife.

There is something loose and heavy in there. He can feel it shift when he tips the bag. So he gets his eyes down to the level of the work surface and peers inside. It isn't razor blades this time, or faeces. Nothing like before. He sees a black object – smooth plastic, by the look of it. He lifts the Jiffy bag and out it slides.

Inexplicably, his tormentor has sent him a mobile phone.

The first thing that comes into his mind is the memory of a news story from a few years back – a Hammas leader assassinated with a mobile that had been packed with plastic explosive. Frank picks the phone up. He weighs it in his hand, then turns it over and searches the screws for signs of burring. Nothing seems to have been tampered with. He eases the body open, examining the battery unit and sim card. Everything looks mundane.

But he's seen enough of the dark recesses of society over the past twenty years to know that character doesn't change. A drug addict is still a drug addict, even if he or she has been clean for six months. A killer is still a killer after he's served his term. That doesn't mean that people can't be given a second chance. There's always redemption. But he knows he'd be a fool to trust them not to revert to type.

Now this man – he's assuming he's dealing with a man – sends Jiffy bags twice in the last three months, both designed to distress or injure. And now he sends a seemingly benign object. There will be a trick to it. A trap of some kind. Frank thinks about disposing of the phone – dropping it in a bin somewhere on his way to work. But this time the man has tried to do something different, something clever. And in taking that extra step he might have made a mistake. There is no way that Frank can go to the proper authorities with this problem. But if he could just discover the man's identity, he might have a chance of sorting it out for himself.

He lays the mobile on the desk and takes another deep breath to steady his nerves. Then, using the end of a ruler, he presses down on the power button. He stands back as words appear on the tiny screen. The phone is registering itself on the network. It chimes a single note. He steps forward, examines the display more closely, and sees a picture of an envelope. Using his finger this time, he presses the RECEIVE CALL button, expecting to hear a recording of his enemy's voice, hoping for the certainty that that would give him. Instead a text message appears.

He reads it twice before realizing that he must have missed something about the package. Picking up the Jiffy bag again, he feels inside and draws out a black and white photograph. An image of a Ford and an Audi parked in a lay-by. A group of men in late 1980's-style suits stand between the cars. Frank examines the faces. Eight people from the past. And in the midst of them Frank sees his own younger self.

It is now that he really understands what is happening and the kind of choices he is going to have to make.

His own face in the picture is so much like the others that

it makes him shiver. All are conspicuously confident and full of self-congratulation. Even without the clothing styles and car models to go by, he would still recognize the age the picture came from. It reeks of forced optimism.

A movement through the window catches his attention. His wife is standing by the side door of the house, scanning the garden. She calls his name.

'Frank. Your breakfast is on the table.'

He waves to her through the glass. She smiles as she sees him, and then beckons.

For a moment he doesn't respond. He slips the phone and photograph back in the Jiffy bag.

'Is everything all right?' she calls.

'Yes, love. Everything's fine.'

Frank doesn't want to keep secrets from his family. Secrets aren't healthy in any relationship. But Julie knew what she was taking on when she married him – his character, the nature of his work. There were times when he'd return home in the early hours of the morning, physically and emotionally drained. Most of the others told their wives the details of what went on. But it never felt seemly to Frank to burden her in that way.

She never begged to be told. He was grateful for that.

Their marriage was a fortress, and the unsaid things were no more than a crack in the plaster of the outer wall. Time passed, and the secrets didn't go away. But they became invisible, like any blemish seen every day for twenty years.

Julie is looking at him now, over the breakfast things. Their daughter gets up, still chewing, a slice of toast and marmalade in one hand. With a flick of the other hand she signals her goodbye, a gesture slick with teenage nonchalance.

'Have a good day, dear,' Julie calls after her.

'Sure.'

The front door slams.

Frank finishes his coffee. He feels his wife's hand on his arm. She is probing him with her eyes.

'I'm sorry,' he says. 'I'm a bit preoccupied.'

'You need to relax,' she says.

Frank puts on the same smile that he always wears to cover moments like this. 'I'll be fine.'

'You could spend more time with your trees,' she says.

'I've been busy.'

'Or a class. They do yoga in the village,' she tells him. 'Wednesday evenings. I could book you in.'

Frank gets up and carries his plate across to the dishwasher. 'I'll think about it.'

'Perhaps a holiday soon?'

Frank nods. 'You're right. I know it. It's just that we've got a rush on at work. But after that . . .'

This morning, he gets into his uniform jacket without looking into the mirror. He has the car keys in one hand and his briefcase in the other as he descends the stairs. Julie is waiting for him in the hall. He makes a smile. She busies herself, brushing his shoulder with her hand, straightening his tie. He bends forward to kiss her cheek, but she turns his head and presses her lips to his.

'I don't need to know,' she says. 'The details, I mean. But if you did ever want to talk about it . . .'

He hugs her, but finds that he can't relax into her body. It's been a long time since she has reacted to him like this. But this secret is different from the others. When he has kept things from his family before it was out of a sense of duty. Protecting their feelings. And the need for professional confidentiality. This time it is from fear. He kisses the back of her neck, aware as he does so of the Jiffy bag inside his briefcase and the photograph inside that.

'I love you,' he says.

Julie steps back, out of the hug. 'I know.'

The secret gnaws at his mind as he drives down the Glenfield Road towards the city. If Julie can sense that something is going wrong, then perhaps his children will too. He wouldn't do anything that would risk their well-being. As for people outside the family – he is more confident about this. He has always been able to cover his anxieties, to hide his real feelings. It's been part of the job. He could have been a professional poker player – if he didn't despise the idea of gambling.

Frank finds himself driving in through the main entrance and into the work car park. He pulls up in his slot, knowing that his mind has been drifting. He turns off the engine and steels himself for the things he will have to face in the next few hours. It is a well-practised routine, clicking over from Frank the husband and father into Superintendent Frank Shakespeare of the Leicestershire Constabulary. The change takes no time at all.

It's a busy morning. A consultant talks to him about what he'd like to see in a proposed new national police computer system. There is a meeting to work through the interim departmental budgets. He has a pile of letters to read and papers to sign. It is past eleven before he has a chance to send his secretary off for her morning break.

Alone for the first time in the day, he opens the briefcase and gets out the mobile. He rests his finger on the button that will recall the message to the screen. He whispers the words 'God help me', then presses.

£10,000. Used notes. Monday noon. Be ready or I publish.

He's searching for any clue that he might have missed on the first reading. The money isn't a fundamental problem. He could pay. But blackmail is a habit people never give up once they've started. It might take six months, a year, ten years, but there would be another demand eventually.

Asking for used notes could be a sign that the blackmailer is experienced in these things – or just that he has watched enough television crime dramas to pick up the right phrases. Frank looks at the last sentence. His children seem to send text messages to their friends all the time. They would have shortened the word 'Be' to a single letter 'B'. That suggests the blackmailer isn't young enough to be part of the texting generation.

There is a movement in the corridor outside. Frank Shakespeare posts the mobile back into his briefcase and snaps the catches closed. The knock on the door is soft but precise.

'Come.'

One of his inspectors puts her head around the door. Marjorie Akanbai – known as Mo. Head of the community policing team for the Waterfields area of the city.

'You left a message for me,' she says.

'Yes. Yes.'

Frank wrests his thinking away from the blackmailer and on to the officer standing in front of his desk. She is a mixed-race woman. Early thirties. A fast-tracker. Destined for the top, he guesses. He doesn't grudge her the fact that she will go higher than him because of her ethnicity. Twenty years ago it would have been the other way around.

'It's about the multiculturalism conference,' he says.

She purses her lips slightly. He knows she doesn't like tokenism. She's told him that on more than one occasion.

'We need a display,' he says. 'Something on your community policing projects. The graphics people have photos already. But they'll need numbers as well. Anything that looks good.'

She nods slowly, as if deciding whether she is going to go along with the request. 'Yes, sir.'

'That's all,' he says.

She flashes him a smile. 'Right.'

She's on her way out when he thinks of something else. 'Mo . . .'

She looks back through the door.

'. . . do you know anything about mobile phone networks?'

'Try me,' she says.

'When did you last buy a mobile?'

She narrows her eyes, as if suspecting a trick question. 'A couple of months back.'

'You gave your name and address, right, when you bought it?'

'Sure.'

'So if you called someone . . . it would be traceable back to you?'

'I guess so . . .'

Frank nods slowly. 'Thanks, Mo.'

'. . . theoretically . . .'

'Great.' He gestures towards the door with his hand, dismissing her.

'But,' she says, 'if I didn't want to be traced . . .' She scratches at her scalp.

'What?'

'It's just that no one checked who I was. I could have given someone else's name and address.'

'They saw your credit card, didn't they?'

'But if I'd paid cash . . .'

Frank thinks about his own mobile, which Julie bought him over a year ago. 'If you gave someone else's address,' he says, 'you wouldn't get the phone bill. You'd be cut off. End of story.'

'Not with pay-as-you-go. There are no bills. You just go into the supermarket, hand over the cash and they top the phone up for you. The only way to trace it is through the location of the transmitters that pick up the phone's signal.'

'How accurate is that?'

Mo is still standing in the doorway. She folds her arms. 'This sounds more like CID work.'

'Humour me.'

'Well, I'm not an expert . . .'

'Spit it out, woman.'

'It depends on how closely the transmitters are spaced,' she says. 'Out in the countryside they're few and far between. You'd be lucky to place any call closer than a quarter of a mile either way. In the city you might pin it down to a couple of streets.'

'What's the procedure,' he asks, 'if we want to get that kind of information?'

She shakes her head. 'I've never had to do it. I think we have liaison people in the companies that run the telephone networks. We tell them the number we're interested in. They feed it into the computer and keep a watch out for any calls.'

There's a kind of half-smile on her face, as if she is secretly pleased that she knew something he didn't. 'Why the questions?'

'Perhaps I'm going for a promotion,' he tells her. 'Mugging up on detection methods.'

She laughs at the joke. He likes that in her. The quick

mind. The vein of dark humour. He points to the door. 'Now bugger off and get some work done.'

Without trust, love is nothing. Frank knows this. When God instructed that Isaac be sacrificed on the altar, Abraham didn't question it. He loved God. And trust was part of that. He knew that it would work out right in the end. The marriage between two people has to be the same. With trust, there is nothing it can't withstand.

What Frank can't fathom – what he is thinking about now as he shifts his position in the bed – is the question of where trust ends. A lie would do it for sure. Or an act of unfaithfulness. The unsaid, though – this is different. What information to volunteer. Julie wouldn't expect every little detail from him. It wouldn't be loving to say what he thought at every stage. 'You're putting on weight' or 'Inspector Akanbai has a beautiful figure'. Those things are true, but saying them would do no good to anyone. They are only part of the truth. Julie is the same age as himself. They have both fattened out a little over the years. But it isn't important. As for Mo, any man who claims not to notice beauty must be lying. But Frank would never act on that attraction, even if there were an opportunity.

So it is right to keep some knowledge locked away. The problem comes when the importance of that knowledge starts to grow. Like with the hate mail. At one point the withholding of that information was a mercy. An envelope packed with excrement. Julie didn't need to know about that. And it was too trivial to involve the police. Then the second package arrived. Razor blades. A deep gash on his finger. That was more serious. It was only the printed message that stopped him from reporting it: *Frank Shakespeare, the bent copper.*

The change from mercy to deceit passed without him noticing.

Frank moves his leg across the bed towards Julie's warmth. She stirs, sighs, mumbles something.

'Are you awake?' he whispers, knowing that she is not.

'Mmm?'

'I love you,' he says.

'Love you too.'

She turns and puts an arm over his body as if gathering him to her, but with no strength in the movement. He turns to her, kisses her mouth. In the grey pre-dawn light he can see the look of contentment on her face.

He kisses her again, more urgently this time. But she has already slipped back into sleep. Her breath deepens. He knows that if he hugs her or speaks to her she might wake up. They might make love. Then he could know that everything was right between them.

Her mouth has dropped open slightly and her breath is ebbing and flowing in a purring half-snore. He eases himself out from under her enfolding arm, back into the place where he was lying a few moments before. The sheets have cooled. He studies her. There are wrinkles radiating from the corners of the eyes and mouth. 'Smile lines' she calls them – though he has never been sure that sorrow doesn't leave the same traces. If a forensic expert was being questioned under oath, could he testify to the happiness or sadness of a life by examining the marks on the skin?

He gets up, careful not to make his movement shift the mattress. He carries his clothes through to the bathroom and dresses. Civvies today. A jacket and trousers. No tie. He doesn't know where he is going to have to go. Too formal might be conspicuous. Or too informal. He slips the blackmailer's mobile into an inside pocket.

He's booked the day as time off in lieu – though he hasn't told this to Julie. He steps back into the bedroom and removes the uniform he would have been wearing. He doesn't think she usually looks in his side of the wardrobe, but he isn't sure enough to take the risk. He will put it in the boot of the car. Take it with him. Going downstairs, he places his feet silently.

The clock in the kitchen tells him it is ten past five. He feels a sudden, intense surge of loneliness mixed with a strange sense of excitement. This is the day when it can all be resolved. The day when he will be able to cast off the burden. If he can just finish it, he won't need any more lies.

His stomach isn't ready for toast. His insides are feeling too tightly wound. He takes a banana from the fruit bowl and peels it as he waits for the kettle to boil.

'Dad?'

He wheels to see his son standing in the doorway, rubbing the corner of one eye. The boy is thirteen, but still sweet enough in the privacy of the family. 'Jem. You should be asleep.'

'I heard a noise.'

Frank gets another mug from the cupboard. 'Have a cup of tea. Take it back to bed. You could read a book or something.'

'Why are you in those clothes, Dad?'

'We're doing a special thing at work,' Frank tells him.

Jem nods as he shuffles over. He hugs Frank.

Then the mobile chimes. A single note.

'What's that?' his son asks.

'Nothing. A text message, maybe.'

'Cool. You going to read it, then?'

'Later.'

*

By the time Frank reaches the third building society, he feels that he should be more relaxed than he is. Practice is not helping.

He manages to smile at the cashier as she leafs through the bundle of notes, keeping his poker face.

'. . . four-fifty, five, five-fifty . . .'

Frank and his wife have joint accounts. And they've been careful over the years, consulting on any major purchase. The result is that they have been able to pay off the mortgage ten years early and put away a tidy sum in low-risk securities. She trusts him, he believes. The reason they go through the bank statements so carefully together is to keep an eye on expenditure. She's not miserly, though she'd be certain to query any withdrawal of over £200.

Tax-free investments are different. Individual savings accounts. One name per account. Frank has three of these, containing a total of £17,000 and change. It is into these that he now dips.

There is something vaguely unseemly about withdrawing so much money in cash, but so far it hasn't raised any eyebrows. He's got a response ready, but no one has asked him why he's doing it.

'. . . eight-fifty, nine, nine-fifty, three thousand.'

The cashier taps the edge of the bundle on to the counter, straightening it, then slides it towards him. 'Going on holiday?'

'I'm buying a car,' he says, too quickly.

'Something nice?'

'Yes.' He clicks open the catches on his briefcase and slips the bundle of notes inside, next to the ones he collected earlier. 'Thank you.'

His heart is beating fast as he strides past the clock tower towards the shopping centre where he left his car. The surprise is that part of him is actually enjoying this. He hadn't noticed it to this point because he'd been so focused on the task in hand. But now he's all prepared.

He's the only person in the lift up to the roof level. He turns and looks in the polished metal, examining his reflection. He should be miserable or angry. Perhaps scared. Instead he is feeling a kind of elation. Someone is trying to blackmail him. And he intends to find that person. It is a battle of wills – something he hasn't felt in years.

Sitting in the car, he arranges things as this morning's text message instructed him to. Ten thousand pounds in used notes, all wrapped in a bath towel, which is in turn put inside a plastic carrier bag. Frank is still waiting to be contacted for the final details of where to take it, but he is guessing that it will be a sports facility of some kind.

He watches the dashboard clock tick forward towards noon. The second hand is on its final pass around the face when the phone trills. A picture of an envelope has appeared again on the display. He clicks to read the message. Eight words.

Cossington St swimming baths. Bring a pound coin.

He feels another adrenalin shot entering his bloodstream, and with it a sense of returning control. His guess was right. He is starting to be able to predict the actions of the blackmailer. He will win.

He finds a place to park on Rendell Road. There's a row of red-brick palisade-terraced houses on his left. On his right is the flat, grass expanse of the recreation ground. There are small heaps of cooked rice and lentils on the grass here – leftover food for the birds to eat.

The further he gets with this undertaking, the more certain he is that his tormentor has made a mistake. This whole area of town is so dominated by Asians that any white face is conspicuous. All the people Frank can think of that might have taken the photograph are white or black. They were the kind of people he was dealing with back then.

He sees a woman in a bright green sari sweeping dust out of her front door. And further ahead is a group of elderly men strolling along the edge of the grass. The Cossington Street baths are in view already, up at the end of the road. He starts walking towards them.

There is a sudden explosion of whirring to his left. He jolts around, ready to fight, ready to run. But the sound is the wing beats of hundreds of feral pigeons, which have launched themselves from the grass. They climb and wheel around in the air. A dog is running across to the place from where they took off. It curves its run, bringing it back in a great loop to the edge of the grass and away. The birds circle once more before dropping back to the ground.

Frank tries to refocus. He scans the area again. All the people he can see are Asian, except for a man walking towards the doors of the sports centre. Frank speeds up, breaking into a run when the man disappears inside. It takes him perhaps thirty seconds to reach the doors. He steadies himself, breathes deeply, then steps inside.

The air is thick with swimming bath moisture and chlorine. In the distance he can hear the squeal and splash of children in the water. The man he was following is directly ahead, walking through another door, a sports bag slung over his shoulder. He is white, but perhaps a few years too young to be the person Frank is looking for. The blackmail photograph was taken more than a decade ago.

Frank casts around for some kind of clue. He pats down his pockets and locates the mobile phone. The envelope icon is on the screen again, though he didn't hear it ring. He clicks to read the message.

Go to sauna. Remove out-of-order sign. Lock bag in. Drop key by Bridge Road war memorial.

The door that the white man has just walked through is labelled SAUNA. Frank steps towards it, but the lady behind the reception desk calls him back.

'You have to pay first.'

Frank dips into his pocket and slides a £5 note across the counter. She shakes her head.

'And you need to be a member.'

'Hell. How much?'

'You'll need passport photographs and . . .'

'Look . . .' he bends forward and whispers across the desk. 'I'm a police officer.'

The woman shifts her weight on her chair. 'I really don't know . . .'

Frank can feel the pressure building behind his eyes. 'It's bloody urgent!'

She looks at the papers stuck to the wall next to her, as if that is going to provide some kind of answer. She's reaching for the phone, but Frank has given up waiting.

'I'll be right back,' he says. 'Don't call anyone.' Then he hurries past the desk and pushes through the sauna room door before she can complain.

Inside is a second door, and through that is a changing room with benches around the walls and a row of metal lockers. Opposite is another entrance, through which the white man is walking, a towel wrapped around his waist like a sarong. From further in, Frank can hear the sound of a shower turning on followed by a man crying out, then laughing.

He scans the room. And then he sees it – there's a sheet of lined paper taped to the door of the top locker on the left. Someone has written the words OUT OF ORDER on it in marker pen.

Frank doesn't have gloves with him or any other kind of scene-of-crime protection gear. He guesses that most of the evidence will be in the tape itself and perhaps in the middle of the paper. So he takes an edge of the sheet and pulls gently, increasing the force until the whole thing starts to peel away from the metal. Laying it on the bench, he opens his briefcase and takes out the carrier bag, complete with towel and money. This he stuffs into the locker.

Now the purpose of the extra pound becomes clear. He puts the coin in the slot in the door, locks the locker and the key comes free. Finally, he lays the sheet of paper in his briefcase and clips it shut.

Frank is driving across town to Bridge Road. He can feel the locker key in his trouser pocket pressed up against his leg. While he has that, he still has possession of the money. And he's not planning on giving it up without a fight.

This area of town is far more racially mixed than Cossington Street. Asians, blacks, whites and various mixtures. The blackmailer is going to be harder to spot here. The shops are a mixture as well: fruit and veg, furniture, international telephone shops, sweet marts. Frank turns down Bridge Road and sees the war memorial. It isn't big – a stone plinth with a metal plaque inscribed with the names of the dead. It stands in a children's playground, the whole area of which is surrounded by high metal railings. The only access is through a cast-iron gate.

Frank sees now how clever the blackmailer has been in choosing this place. There is nowhere here to hide. An open play area with narrow roads around it, overlooked by terraced houses. He can hear a radio in the distance, blaring out Leicester Sound FM. He looks around and sees that it is lying on the pavement outside one of the houses. Two builders are standing there, leaning against a white van. Frank drives past the war memorial, circles the block and comes around for a second sweep before deciding to park in a side street and approach on foot.

There is a group of white kids behind the climbing frame, playing around with a box of matches. Two Muslim women push their toddlers on the baby swings. Over on the grass at the far side, two more Asian kids are playing cricket with a milk crate for stumps. Frank walks into the playground, over-aware of how strange it must look for a middle-aged white man to be strolling around in here – especially if anyone noticed him circling the block before. He goes slowly, hands in his pockets, feeling the key, sauntering across the width of the playground. When Frank is sure that there isn't anyone else hiding there, and that there is no other entry point, he circles back to the war memorial itself. He stands, pretending to read the inscription. The locker key is in his hand now. His fingers open and it drops into the grass. Then he walks away. The iron gate creaks behind him as it closes on its spring.

He's across the road, heading for the builders, who are unloading bags of plaster from the back of the van. They're both white. Neither can be more than twenty.

'Is the boss around?' he asks.

'He's at the other site, init.' The man points over his shoulder with a thumb.

Frank nods. 'I'll wait for him inside, then.' Then he steps through the door, not giving them time to object.

The house is a shell. Bare brick and floorboards covered in grit and concrete dust. A complete renovation job. Frank climbs the stairs, trying not to make it look as if he is rushing. He steps through to the empty front room and looks out of the window. He is directly above the playground gate. The perfect place to keep wat...

He looks down at the grass in front of the war memorial but can't see the key. At thirty metres distant, it is going to be hard to see. He knows that, but still feels panic rising from his stomach. He puts a hand on the wall to steady himself. He's only had his back turned on the scene for a minute. There's no one running away. The key must still be there. He takes a deep breath and lets it out through his nose. He looks again at the grass in front of the war memorial. Then he sees it – just a glint of metal in the sunlight. He takes another deep breath. His heart rate is slowing. But when he takes his hand off the wall and looks at it, he sees that it is still trembling.

Time passes slowly after that. He keeps the area of grass where the key lies in his sight. And he waits. The mothers cajole their toddlers into pushchairs and wheel them out of the playground, passing another group of Asian boys on their way in to join the cricket game. People walk along the pavement below the window. Children and old people stroll. Others march with purpose, towards appointments perhaps, or waiting chores. A black soft-top BMW catches his eye. A gangster car, complete with boom box loud enough to set the glass rattling in the window. It moves slowly, and Frank readies himself to charge down the stairs and intercept, but it shows no sign of stopping. He watches it turn the corner and roll out of sight.

Two flies have found their way into the room and are darting around with maddening urgency. He swipes them away with his hand but makes no contact. His shirt is sticking to the skin under his arms.

There's a tramp shuffling down the pavement next to the railings. He's got a long coat on in spite of the heat, and a battered trilby on his head. Frank watches the man's slow progress.

A fly lands on the back of Frank's hand. He tries to squash it, but it's too quick for him. He grabs and misses as it buzzes overhead. The playground gate clangs and Frank's attention snaps back to the war memorial. The tramp has moved inside and is making his way towards one of the litterbins. He reaches down into it, pulls out a beer can, shakes it and drops it back. Then he's moving again, circling around to the next bin and then on towards the war memorial. Frank can feel his heart rate start to climb again. To this point, he hasn't been able to see the man's face at all. It's been shielded by the brim of his hat.

When it comes, the tramp's movement is so quick that it seems to belie his earlier shuffling. He stoops and one hand dips into the grass. In a blink, the locker key is gone.

And Frank is running, taking the steps three and four at a time. He thuds down on to the ground floor, sprints the corridor. He's in the sunshine and across the road in five bounds. He crashes the gate. The tramp starts at the sound. But he's too late to go out the way he came in. Instead he starts to run for the far corner of the playground.

Frank is after him, gaining with each footfall. The tramp flings his carrier bag down to the floor. He's heading for a gap in the railings. Frank vaults the spilled junk. He's dimly aware of children running out of his path. He launches himself into a diving rugby tackle. The tramp lands heavily. He's squirming and struggling to free himself, but Frank has a firm grip. Children are screaming.

'Let go!' the man shouts. He's still got the key in his clenched fist.

Frank can smell him now. Tobacco and piss and stale beer and body odour. He draws back his fist. 'Give it!'

The man's bloodshot face crumples and he starts to weep.

He has only broken stumps where teeth should be. He opens his hand, letting the key drop on to the ground.

'Didn't know it was yours. Didn't know. Let me go.'

Frank looks at his face. There's something terribly wrong. He's not looking at a disguise. This isn't the man who bought mobile phones and sent text messages. Everyone in the playground is staring. A child is wailing in the distance. Frank snatches the key, picks himself up and runs for his car.

He drives, feeling the sting, knowing he's been played for a fool.

He marches into the Cossinton Street sports centre, past the receptionist, ignoring her complaints, and into the sauna changing room. He already knows what he is going to find. The locker in which he placed the bag of money is open, the metal door scratched and bent as if it has been prised open. He reaches inside, needing to feel the empty space, knowing that the instruction to go to Bridge Road had one purpose only – to get him out of the way.

A man in Leisure Department uniform steps through into the room. 'You're the policeman who was here before?'

'These lockers . . .' Frank begins.

The man looks at the damage and sucks air over his teeth. 'If you've lost something, you're not the first.' He points to a printed disclaimer on the wall. 'You leave stuff here at your own risk. It wasn't valuable, I hope.'

Frank drops on to the bench. He grips the key, feeling the bite as it presses into his skin, but no amount of pain is enough.

Chapter 2

It was when Tami's boss first saw her car that he started calling her his kitsch princess. It is a Fiat – hot pink with dirty brown eruptions of rust on the bodywork above the sills. He used to hit on younger women – that's what the other girls in the factory said. But after seeing her leopard-pattern fur-fabric seat covers, the fact that she was thirty-three seemed to fade from his mind. Since then, he's taken to standing very close to her whenever he strolls across the factory floor for a chat. If he gets any closer and if it's on the wrong day, she's afraid she might lash out. Then it'll be back to the JobCentre with an even blacker mark against her name.

She's sitting in her car now, staring at the dashboard, thinking about bacon, lettuce and tomatoes and feeling slightly queasy. The alarm clock woke her at eleven thirty p.m. That was ten minutes ago. The only thing that got her up was the knowledge that she'll get a break after tonight's late shift.

Some kind of joy.

Since staggering out of bed, her main achievements have been to pull on some clothes, reheat an old mug of coffee in the microwave and scald her tongue. She also wrestled a brush through her blonde hair in an attempt to gather a ponytail, but gave up when she reached a particularly difficult knot.

She turns the key in the ignition now. The engine fires first time, so she whispers a silent thank you. Then she kangaroos out on to the road and away towards the industrial estate. She's still not got back into the habit of driving.

The only parking spaces on site are reserved for the managerial staff. The rest of them – the bread-and-butter brigade – have to take their chances where they can find them. The first ones to arrive on shift can usually find spaces just outside the factory. Being late, Tami has to drive back down the road a way before finding a slot. She says goodbye to the many furry animals and plastic Mr Men that dangle in the car and then hurries off down the pavement.

There's a man up ahead – a suit standing under a streetlight, with his hands in his trouser pockets. The industrial estate is right at the edge of the red-light district, so Tami has a pretty shrewd idea what it is he's waiting for. She lets her hand slip into the open top of her bag and finds the reassuring smoothness of her rape alarm. Keeping her head up and her back straight, she advances, only stepping out on to the road to pass him at the last moment.

'Tami?'

She doesn't break step as he calls her name, though her mind is knocked off balance. There's a whir of possibilities in her head.

'Tami Steel? It is you, isn't it?'

He's walking along beside her, his slow stride easily keeping pace with the pounding of her shorter legs. She's got the factory door in her sight, and it suddenly clicks in her head that this man must be a new shift manager or something. She leaves the rape alarm in her bag and, to disguise the movement, pulls out a tissue and dabs it to her mouth.

'There was an accident,' she lies. 'On the inner ring road. The traffic was jammed for ages. I'll make the time up, though.'

He looks nonplussed for a moment, then says: 'I'm not from work.'

She stops and turns towards him. He must be in his forties. Brown hair. Bags of loose skin under the eyes. Now she comes to look at him properly, he does seem vaguely familiar. She feels the sweat starting to cool on her forehead.

'How do you know me?'

'Through your husband,' he says.

'Jack?'

'Yes.'

'You're a friend of Jack's?'

He nods.

She looks into his eyes for a moment longer, wondering how this man thinks he can come along and say what he has just said and get away with it. It must be Jack himself who arranged this. That's the only explanation she can come up with. Her husband sent him.

Something clicks in her head. She takes a half-step forward and snaps her knee up between his legs. The contact makes no sound, but the effect is instant. He folds – first bending double, then tumbling sideways, ending in a foetal position on the pavement. There is a fraction of a second in which she can't believe what she has just done. Then she jumps over him and runs for it. He hasn't cried out, but behind her she hears the wheezing sound as he tries to fill his lungs with air.

The smell of hot bacon fat is the first thing that hits her as she hurries inside. It makes her feel instantly unclean, reminding her of the accumulated taint that she fancies must remain on her skin and in her hair from two months of working in the factory.

Tami is the last person on shift tonight; all the others are already in their aprons and caps and setting to work, so it is certain she is going to be stuck with the least popular job for the next eight hours – baby-sitting the machine that sticks the cellophane tops on the triangular plastic boxes.

It sounds easy – watching the BLT sandwiches trundling along the line. Minimum concentration required. But the result of nodding off for a moment can be catastrophic. Sometimes a sandwich comes down the line without a box and there are a couple of seconds to dart out a hand and pull it off the belt. This is one of the ways the other workers find to keep the machine's baby-sitter on her toes. It doesn't matter whose fault it is – the baby-sitter always gets the blame when the line has to stop. And it's her who has to wipe the inevitable mess of mayonnaise and crushed bread from the heat-sealing rollers.

But responsibility isn't the main reason the job is unpopular. The machine is at the edge of the room, adjacent to the loading bay. That puts it too far away from the preparation benches. The baby-sitter is outside the gossip loop – just able to hear her name mentioned above the dull grumble of the rollers, not close enough to defend herself.

But tonight this arrangement suits Tami fine. She watches the line of bread triangles approaching, passing, being sealed in. She listens to the hypnotic rhythm of the machine. And she forces her mind back into the past.

She thinks of the man outside, picturing him in her mind. She is certain now that she has seen him before. She never forgets a face, so the vagueness of the memory tells her that it was a long time ago. That makes sense – because the man said he was a friend of her husband's.

She pictures the guests at the parties they used to go to, flicking through the rogues' gallery in her mind. Mostly they were white men. Twenties to forties. More money than taste. The time of the sheepskin coat and the glitzy watch had passed already, though this crowd hadn't seemed to notice. They made money where they could and didn't mind if other people knew it. They were proud to buy crap and sell it as glitter. They admired each other for it. Maggie's reign was over, but they hadn't noticed.

And the women – they were bimbos who seemed to believe that the only reason mink was out of fashion was because poorer people were jealous. Not that Tami could sneer. She went along with it. She remembers the feeling of fur brushing against her skin.

'Hello, Tami.'

The voice of the manager breaks her trance. She looks up from the sandwich line.

'Hello, Mr Lloyd.'

'Call me Steve,' he says, as he always does.

Tami notes that the chatter of conversation on the preparation tables has died down. They'll have much more to gossip about if Mr Lloyd steps any closer. She angles her body away from him, reducing her sense of claustrophobia, but not lessening the oppressive smell of his Lynx aftershave.

'How's my princess today?'

'Fine,' she says.

'Something hold you up again this evening?'

'Stuff,' she says, the irritation making her voice sound prickly.

'Hey. It's not me that minds. But let's not make a habit of it, right? Set off earlier next time.' He pats her shoulder and then leaves his hand resting over her bra strap for a moment, the fingers stroking. 'I marked you down as on time.'

She can feel the pressure rising inside her. A few more seconds of this and a valve will blow. So she sidesteps away from his touch and turns to look back at him.

'I need to pee,' she says. 'Mind the machine for me?'

He sucks air over his teeth, as if searching for the right way to turn her request down without ruining his chat-up chances. She flashes a quick smile and hurries away before he has time to get the words in order.

The toilets still smell of bleach from their last cleaning. She stands in the cubicle and fishes a stick of nicotine gum out of her pocket. She lets out a long sigh. Getting laid off isn't an option she can afford. Even with all the overtime she's been putting in, it's going to be a couple of months before she can save up enough to buy a sofa for the flat. And, more important, she needs to get that vital first reference.

She relaxes, feeling the nicotine start to work. High on the wall above the cistern is a narrow window of bobbled glass. It occurs to Tami that this side of the building should look out on the road where she kneed Jack's friend. She puts the cover down on the toilet and stands on it. It takes her three tries to open the stiff catch. Night air reaches in through the gap, warm and moist. Tami scans the scene outside. Sodium light and parked cars. The road is empty.

She thinks about the man again. Her chewing slows. She gets a flicker of an image of him in her mind – not as he was tonight. This must have been years ago. There were no bags under his eyes. He was lighter, too – a sharper angle between his neck and his chin. Her chewing speeds up again. She forces herself to concentrate, to catch the image and hold it.

Now she's got it – the place where she saw the man. It was in the courtroom. He was sitting right next to Jack.

It was the very last time she saw her husband outside prison. He was looking handsome as always – though cast in a tragic light. His skin had been getting greyer every day the trial progressed. Now the jury were about to deliver their verdict. She remembers him looking down at the floor, ashamed – as well he might be. The foreman of the jury stood.

'Guilty.'

There was no cry of shock or surprise from the gallery. Everyone must have known that this was going to be the outcome. The judge spoke about the seriousness of the crime. Drug trafficking. A cancer, eating into society's heart. She remembers looking around the court, wondering where this society was that he was speaking about. Then came the sentence – fourteen years in prison. She felt too numb to take in the magnitude of what she was hearing. But others must have understood. An example was being set. A warning to others not to make the same mistake. She felt the shock whisper through the court like a spreading ripple. The man standing next to Tami put his hand on her arm. She remembers his touch. It wasn't unkind.

'Come on,' he said. And then he led her away, down to the cells to begin her sentence.

Tami knows she should feel good about the way she dealt with Jack's friend. It's a sign that she can take care of herself. She can make her own decisions. And she does feel a kind of high from it. But it has also left her jumpy. Her mind skips around from one memory to the next, making it impossible to concentrate on work.

She doesn't like the person she has become since Jack's

betrayal. But she wouldn't for anything go back to the naive, trusting girl she'd been when she married him. The place she came from, the things he did, these are all a part of who she is now. Trying to forget or undo the damage would be like self-mutilation.

She watches the last of the night's sandwich boxes trundling through the machine, then presses the button to cut the power. Somehow it has become morning outside. Low sunlight streams through the few windows. The other workers finished a few minutes ago. They're away already, changed and heading for the exit, fumbling for cigarettes and dreaming of bed. The factory isn't running a morning shift, so the place will be empty until mid-afternoon when the next load of bread-and-butter men shuffle inside.

She stretches, takes off the hair guard and scratches her scalp. God, but it's been a long night. She's walking across to the changing area, untying her apron, when Mr Lloyd, the production manager, intercepts her.

'Are you doing anything later?' he asks.

'I'm dead beat,' she says. And it's true.

'Then a coffee perhaps? Perk you up a bit.'

Tami hangs up her apron and takes her bag out of the locker. She doesn't want to be mean to him, or seem ungrateful. Nor does she want to raise his hopes. It's not that he's ever been unpleasant to her – not intentionally. And he's not bad looking – dark hair, dark eyes. He is the type who spends money caring for his appearance – which would be a good thing, except for the way it makes him assume he must be irresistible to women.

He walks with her to the door, then clicks through the bank of light switches on the wall and turns the key in the alarm system. Tami hesitates, suddenly worried that Jack's friend might have returned. He's not directly outside – she can

see that from where she's standing. But he could be waiting by
her car. And he must be sore after what she did to him.

'Anything wrong?' Mr Lloyd asks.

She steps out. 'No. It's just . . .'

He locks the door behind them. 'You can tell me.'

'. . . there was a man here last night. He bothered me.
I . . .'

'I knew it!' he says. 'I'm strongly empathetic when it
comes to women's feelings.'

Tami isn't in the mood to come back with obvious jokes.
She scans the road up towards where she parked last night.
There are plenty of places where the man could be hiding –
in the bushes, behind the burger bar van, perhaps in one of
the other cars.

'Mr Lloyd . . .'

'Steve,' he corrects her. 'Come on, I'll walk you to your
car.'

He puts a hand on the small of her back and steers her
along the pavement away from the factory. 'It's going to be
a beautiful day,' he says. 'When are you on shift again?'

'The day after tomorrow.'

'Then we've time enough to enjoy the sunshine. You can
sleep later.'

Tami's pink Fiat is in sight now. There is no sign of Jack's
friend. She begins to lose the tension that's been gripping
her stomach. She lengthens her stride, pulling away from
Mr Lloyd's touch.

'We could go into town – have breakfast together.' He
says this as if it is a suggestive joke.

Tami has her keys in her hand. She opens her mouth to
give him a polite refusal but then sees a sheet of folded
paper tucked under her windscreen wiper. She plucks it out
and turns so she can read it away from his gaze.

We need to talk about your husband. Don't try to pull the same trick next time. I will contact you.

Tami crumples the note into her pocket. She gets a sudden fear that the man could have found out where she lives. It wouldn't be too difficult. And the flat is a creaky old place, all too easy to break into. She could lean a chair against the door – but he might force the window while she slept.

'Well?' says her boss.

She turns back towards him. 'It's nothing.'

'I mean breakfast. How about it?'

'I . . .'

'Go on. Live a little.'

They're sitting in a swish new breakfast bar on Churchgate. Mr Lloyd – she doesn't want to start thinking of him as Steve – is chatting to the waiter. It seems they know each other from somewhere. Jack was like that. He knew everyone. When they ate out, it was always at the best table.

'Chosen yet?' Mr Lloyd asks.

'Espresso.'

'And some breakfast, surely. The bacon sandwiches are excellent. My treat.'

Any form of sandwich, let alone bacon, is the last thing she wants to see in front of her after seven nights on the production line. She shakes her head, but he has turned away already and is placing the order. Strangely, she finds his insensitivity comforting. It gives her another reason to turn him down when he asks her back to his place – which he is sure to do.

Another problem about Jack, aside from him being a heartless bastard, was that he was too damned attentive. Too perfect. When he turned on the charm, it was as if every fibre of his being was there, ready to do whatever it was that would please her. Some men become the centre of attention when they walk into a room. But with Jack, he had this way of making the room disappear and all the voices fade into the background. No man she has met since has measured up to that standard.

The espresso arrives.

'So,' Mr Lloyd says, 'how is life treating you?'

Tami watches her spoon move through the foam as she stirs. 'I'm surviving,' she says.

'How about your family – your husband and kids?'

'Who said I was married?'

'Are you?'

'No.'

When she looks up, she's shocked to see a quiet smile on his face.

He reaches out and puts his hand on hers. 'You don't have to lie to me. I'm cool with it – however you arrange your life.'

She pulls her hand away. 'I . . .'

'The note from your windscreen,' he explains.

'It was private!'

'I only saw a few words – something about your husband.'

'It's not like you think,' she says.

'Divorced?'

'He's not my husband any more.'

'That's not really an answer.'

'And this isn't really any of your . . . business.' She's quite pleased with herself for managing to hold the profanity back. It's another sign that she's starting to get back in control of her life.

He smiles at her. 'Like I said – I'm cool with it.'

She manages to hold herself back again, long enough for the waiter to arrive with two plates of sandwiches. She'd been planning to make an excuse and push it to one side. But just to remind herself how much of a nauseous pig Mr Lloyd really is, she picks hers up and takes a large bite. With any luck she'll have to go to the ladies' room and throw it all up again and she will be able to picture him in her mind as she does it.

'Good, huh?' he says.

And the most stomach-churning thing is that he's absolutely right. The sandwich is unlike anything she's seen in the factory. Even calling it a sandwich seems something of an insult. The bread is warm and has that just-baked smell. The butter is starting to run. The tomatoes are sweet, the lettuce has a hint of peppery bitterness and the bacon is full of its own delicious flavour, hardly salty at all.

She takes another bite.

'I tell you what would be great to follow this – a ripe honeydew melon. And you know – I've got one waiting in my fridge at home.'

Even with melon to tempt her, Tami knows that going back with Steve would be a very bad idea. She consents to let him pay the bill and then politely disengages. His face drops when she steps back away from him, but she's had men try out the wounded puppy act before and she's pretty much immune to it. She knows he'll be smiling as soon as she turns away, boasting to his friends about how close he got to bedding her.

She walks back to the factory, which is quiet now, then picks up her car and drives across town to the flat. It is in a red-brick Victorian building. Her first key unlocks the communal outside door at street level. She then climbs a narrow and dimly lit staircase to a landing where she needs a second key to unlock her personal front door.

A couple of paces down a passageway and she steps into the biggest room in the flat. There is a bulky old arm-chair here, a high-backed dining chair, some stained coffee tables and a magazine rack. The most that can be said of the bedroom is that a single bed fits in it. There is also a shower room and a kitchenette. The flat is whitewashed throughout, but she has brought some colour into the place by draping purple, green and gold sari fabric between nails hammered into the walls. She has also put up some of her own pictures.

She gets a momentary pang as she steps towards the bedroom – the fear that Jack's friend might be hiding somewhere. But it isn't rational. The real issue eating away at her is the memory of Jack himself.

She first met him in Leicester market. She'd got a summer job selling hot drinks to the traders. He was calling out the prices on his dad's fruit and veg stall. *Best bananas. Twenty pence a pound. Best bananas.* Even when she was way off down by Rosa's kiosk on Cheapside, she'd still be able to pick out his voice from the others.

She was getting grief from her own parents that summer. They couldn't seem to understand that she was growing up. She was seventeen when Jack asked her out. He was twenty-three. He had a car and a terraced house of his own. That was back when house prices were going up so fast that no one who wasn't already on the property ladder had any chance of buying. Her parents rented.

Instead of going back to school after the holidays she started working with Jack on the market stall. She watched him charming the housewives who came to buy. But he saved the real magic for her. Or that's the way she saw it at the time.

His family, she quickly discovered, had other business interests – some of which existed on the ragged outer fringe of legality. But the police didn't seem that interested. The crimes didn't hurt anyone so far as she could make out. Mostly it was buying and selling. Not all the designer labels were genuine, and it wasn't always clear where the goods came from. She didn't understand and she didn't pry. The family weren't going to be filthy rich but they had a good income, which they spent easily – and not just on themselves. They helped out people in trouble, and the only ones who hated them were the loan sharks whose business they undermined.

Tami and Jack got married as soon as she turned eighteen.

Her parents didn't come, of course. She was reconciled to that. But hundreds of other people did – local politicians, businessmen, people she'd seen but never spoken to. And there were some of her ex-school friends – wide-eyed and jealous as hell. It felt as if she was marrying into royalty. The guests lined up to shake Jack's hand, kiss her on the cheeks and place their gifts on the pile in a corner of the hall. Silver wrapping and blue and white and pink ribbons. It looked like a photograph from a magazine.

The parties didn't stop. There was a stack of invitations waiting when they came back from their honeymoon. More events than they could possibly get to. She had money to spend on new clothes. Jack made out that he would do anything for her. And she believed him. If he'd only been a bastard from the start, she could have forgotten him and still been herself. But he'd had an angel's smile.

All through the trial, he poured out his affection and concern. And when they put her in prison, he still found ways of helping her – sending a stream of letters, visiting twice a month, bringing things to make life more comfortable. The shock of entering the prison system still pushed her to the edge. But she didn't crack.

It happened after she'd been inside eleven and a half months. His visits had been getting less frequent, but she'd put that down to the increased distance since she'd been moved up north. And though the letters were as loving as ever, they didn't come anything like as often as they had at the start. Still, she hadn't suspected anything.

Then one day there was an envelope addressed in Jack's handwriting but with a letter from his father inside. Jack had been seeing another woman. It was a stupid thing to do. They hadn't been careful and now the woman was pregnant and intending to keep the child. She was moving up to Glasgow to start a new life, and Jack was going to follow her. The letter said that she should try not to think badly of the boy. Few relationships survive such a long separation. She would have to get over it and there would be money waiting to support her when she was released. He promised her that. The family wouldn't turn their back on her, she would have a home, whatever Jack chose to do.

That was the day of her first suicide attempt.

Tami wakes in the armchair in her flat, fully clothed. Her neck is stiff and she feels as if she's been drugged. She stumbles to the kitchen and turns the kettle on. She splashes cold water on her face while she waits. It's one in the afternoon by the clock on the cooker. She must have been asleep for a couple of hours.

It's only when the doorbell rings that she remembers her appointment with the probation officer. A home visit.

Somehow in her mind she had placed it as happening tomorrow.

'Coming.'

She reties her ponytail as she walks into the hall. The bell rings again.

'I'm coming!'

She removes the chain and opens the door. She stands frozen for a fraction of a second, made stupid by the shock of it. There is a man smiling at her from the communal landing just outside her door. The man from last night.

Then she's moving, slamming the door closed, but he has his foot in the way already. There's a juddering impact. She is pushing with her body, putting her weight into it.

'I'm not going to hurt you Tami.'

'Get out!'

He has his arm inside now and he's trying to squeeze his shoulder after it. She wedges her own foot between the ground and the base of the door, stopping the gap from opening any wider. There's a sharp crack of breaking wood then the force from the other side stops.

When he speaks, his voice is quiet. 'I need to talk to you.'

'Then talk.'

'It's private. I need to come inside.'

'No way!'

'Do you want me to break the door down?'

'I've got my mobile in my hand,' she lies. 'I'm going to call the police.'

There's a long pause. She looks down at the toe of his shoe, which is still wedged in place. Black leather with a high shine.

'I'm starting to dial.'

'OK,' he says. 'OK. If I can't come in, you come out. We can walk down the street in full public view. You'll be safe.'

Tami hesitates.

He twists his foot free and pulls it back. The door closes. 'I'll go and wait for you on the street,' he says. 'But if you don't come down in five minutes . . .'

She hears his footsteps moving away down the stairs. The street-level door slams.

Tami knows that this man isn't going to give up. She has few choices. She could call the police as she threatened. But the thought of them coming into her flat is even more unnerving than facing up to Jack's friend. Or she could talk to him and hope that afterwards he will leave. There is a third option – going back to Jack's family and asking for their help – but that is something she hasn't been willing to do until now.

She fetches her bag from the living room. Talking to the man is the easiest option. It will take a couple of minutes of her time, and then it will be over and she can go back to putting her life together again.

It is when she opens the door to leave that she knows she's been tricked. He's on the landing, and this time he doesn't mess around. He's through into her hallway, bundling her in front of him.

'I'm not going to hurt you,' he says again.

And it strikes Tami that this is what men always say when they're about to do just that.

She is sitting in the armchair with her handbag clutched to her chest, her arms folded over it. He's already searched through the flat. Now he is standing in the middle of the room, looking down at her.

'Where is Jack?' he asks.

She shouts back at him: 'Who are you?'

'That doesn't matter.'

'It matters to me.'

He takes a deep breath. 'Frank,' he says.

'Frank Shakespeare?' The name pops into her head from somewhere.

His smile wavers for a moment, but he nods.

'You're a policeman, right? An inspector or something.'

'Superintendent,' he says. 'Look, I just need to find your husband, then I'll be away and you won't have to see me again.'

Tami is about to tell him that she hasn't a clue where Jack is and that she doesn't care. She feels the words inside her, pressing to come out. But when she speaks, it is to say: 'Why do you want him?'

'I'm a friend.'

She manages a laugh.

He puts his hands in his pockets. 'We had business together a few years ago. There are still some things to straighten out.'

'Then why not ask his old man?'

Frank Shakespeare wets his lips before answering. 'Your father-in-law is dead.'

'Shit.'

'You didn't know?'

She doesn't want to give away any information, but she finds herself shaking her head. 'No.'

'You weren't close, then.'

That's not completely true, but she doesn't correct him.

'When did you last see Jack?' he asks.

'Nine years ago.'

'In prison?'

She nods. 'What about you?'

'Same sort of time,' he says.

Tami tightens her grip on the handbag. 'Then ask

someone else. His brothers, his sister, the other market traders.'

Frank shakes his head. 'I have already. All that they tell me is that he upped and left nine years ago. I can't find anyone who's seen him since. He's disappeared.'

Chapter 3

Superintendent Kringman retired years ago. He moved out to Spain and bought a villa. There was some gossip at the time – questions about how he could afford a place with a swimming pool. But then he came back, and the word was that he'd been scammed on the deal and lost half his savings.

It seems that he still has some friends in the police force. A couple of names are mentioned when Frank asks around. But when he approaches those officers, they shake their heads. They don't want to speak about him. If they know his address, they aren't saying.

Frank waits until his secretary goes for her coffee break and then walks over to the finance department. This part of the building could be any kind of office. Filing cabinets, computer monitors, a water cooler in the corner. No uniforms. All the staff are civilians. It is a different culture that doesn't always mesh perfectly with the rest of the force. But there is one lady here with whom Frank is on friendly terms. He has known her for years. She must be close to retirement – though he's never asked about her age and it is difficult to be sure. She doesn't seem to wear make-up but her high cheekbones and animated face make her attractive nonetheless.

Frank tells her what he needs. She gives him an *I'm not*

supposed to do this, but . . . smile and phones through to someone who clearly has access to the personnel database. He watches her pull an envelope from the bin and, with the receiver wedged between her shoulder and ear, copy out a number.

He knows this is his reward for being prompt with his paperwork over the last five years. And for smiling at her. Treating her as a human being.

'Thank you,' he says.

She folds the envelope with the address on the inside and passes it to him. 'Don't make a habit of it.'

He doesn't take the envelope out of his pocket until he is back in his own office with the door closed. He sits at his desk with it in his hand, still folded. He closes his eyes and tries to remember the feeling of being in control of events. It used to be his norm – part of his reason for being a police officer. There was a satisfaction in doing the job properly. Being a service to society.

He remembers a day six months ago when everything went as it should. There'd been a disagreement brewing between two different teams of officers. He'd been aware of it for a couple of weeks. He waited until the right moment – just before it came to a head – and then brought them together. He talked them through it, made them understand where the dynamic was going wrong. Everyone went away happy. That was a good day.

Frank opens his eyes and unfolds the envelope. The number has a Leicester area code. He keys it into his phone and listens to the ringing tone.

'Hello?' A woman's voice. Sounding too young to be the retired officer's wife.

'I'm trying to get in touch with Superintendent Kringman.'

She laughs. 'It's a while since he's been called that.'

'Is he there?'

'He's doing some painting right now. He won't come through.'

'Tell him it's important.'

'You're a police officer on some terribly important business, right?'

Frank doesn't answer.

'I can always tell,' she says.

'He's been approached before?'

'Only every year or so. They want to know about old cases he worked on. But he never sees them.'

'Try for me. Tell him it's Frank Shakespeare.'

She sighs. 'You're all the same, you know. Goal-orientated beyond any kind of self-awareness. You think you're the first one who's said something like that?'

'Please.'

'Well don't hold your breath.' There's a soft clunk, as if the receiver is being laid on a table. Then silence.

He waits, wondering if she's going to bother coming back at all. He could work backwards from the phone number to get Kringman's address. He could drive around to the old man's house and try doorstepping him. Even if the old man wouldn't discuss the matter, he might drop a careless phrase or give something away in his body language.

Frank hears the receiver being picked up again.

'Did you work with him?' she asks. Her tone of voice has changed from brusque to curious.

'A long time ago,' Frank says. 'Will he come to the phone?'

'No. He says you'll have to come round here. He'll only talk to you face to face.' And then she tells him the address. It's in Glenfield – a couple of hundred yards from Frank's own house.

*

It looks as if it was one of the original 1950s bungalows, though it must have been extended several times. There are dormer windows projecting from the roof, the connecting double garage looks huge and new, and down the side Frank can see the edge of a large conservatory projecting into the back garden.

He rings the bell and waits.

The woman who opens the door looks to be in her thirties. She is small, with mousy hair tied back, and she has a thin, determined face.

'You're the policeman, right?'

Frank isn't wearing his uniform. 'Is he in?'

Her mouth presses into a downward-curving line. She steps back.

There's thick carpet on the hall floor and a barometer and a mirror on opposite walls. Frank breathes in the smell of frying tomatoes. 'I haven't seen Superintendent Kringman in a long time,' he says. 'Is his wife . . .?'

'Dead,' the woman says.

'I'm sorry.'

'You don't have to pretend,' she says. 'We're not stupid.'

Frank looks over her shoulder into a large living room. He can see the conservatory beyond.

The woman isn't making any move to allow him further into the house. 'I want to know what's going on,' she says.

'What's your relationship to the superintendent?'

'Have you any idea how much you policemen all sound alike? It's like some kind of self-parody.'

'Please.'

'I'm his daughter.'

'Do you live here with him?'

'What is this?' she snaps. 'Are you investigating him – is that it?'

'No. I'm sorry.'

'Then why the questions?'

The truth is, Frank doesn't need to know these details, but he's been out of touch with the superintendent – his one-time senior officer – for so long that he doesn't know where to start. He did bump into the man once after he retired. It was in Marks & Spencer on Fosse Park. They had nothing to say to each other. It was embarrassing.

'I'm sorry,' he says again.

'Why do you want to see him?' she asks.

'I . . . can't tell you.'

'You can't and he won't.'

'But he did agree to see me?'

'Yes.' She says the word as if it is an accusation, proof of some conspiracy.

The double garage isn't full of the usual lawnmowers and junk. Nor would there be any room for a car. Standing in the middle is a huge tabletop, perhaps three metres by four, on which a hilly landscape has been constructed. Papier-mâché, Frank guesses. There are forests, houses and a painted river. A model steam train is working its way along a track, over a viaduct. He watches it disappear into a tunnel. The scene is so unexpected that it takes Frank a couple of seconds to realise that there is a cut-out square in the centre of the landscape, in which Superintendent Kringman, retired, stands, a small paintbrush in his hand.

'Excuse me if I don't come out to shake your hand,' he says. 'These days it's a major operation crawling through.' He gestures to a strip of carpet under the table. 'As for standing up again . . .' He shakes his head.

'Should I come in?'

'No.'

Kringman's hair has receded to the point where the little that remains, clinging to the sides of his head above the ears, only serves to emphasize his baldness. He still has a couple of centimetres on Frank in height, but there seems to be less of him in the shoulders and face. He rests his paintbrush in a jam jar of clear liquid. Then he picks up the model building he was working on and places it with a group of others next to a goods yard.

'There's not enough room in here for two,' he says.

The model train has emerged from the other end of the tunnel and is now curving around the side of the table nearest Frank and beginning its return journey towards a rural station. It pulls in and stops.

'It's very impressive,' Frank says.

'Don't patronize me.'

Frank resists the impulse to deny it.

Kringman pulls a scowl. 'Annie doesn't like you being here. She thinks you're disturbing me.'

'Am I?'

'Apparently so. She's had the blood-pressure monitor on my arm again this morning. She keeps a graph, you know. Systolic and diastolic pressures. Now she's threatening to call the doctor. I keep telling her that high blood pressure is the only thing that keeps me standing.'

'It's been a long time,' Frank says.

'So?'

'It's good to see you, that's all.'

'If that really is all, then you may as well go because the feeling isn't mutual.'

There isn't any subtle way to approach this, so Frank says: 'Someone sent me a package. He didn't give a name, but there was a photograph inside.'

'How much did he ask for?'

'I'm sorry?'

'I got one too, Franky my boy. And a mobile phone with a text message waiting. He wanted £10,000 from me. Said he'd go public if I didn't pay up. I assume that's what you've come about.'

'What did you do?'

'The same as you, I guess. I sent him a message back, telling him to publish and be damned.'

Frank smiles to cover the shock of the revelation, but he can feel himself being examined by the other man.

'You paid, didn't you,' Kringman says.

'I had to.'

'Idiot. He'll ask for more.'

'He might not.' Frank hates himself for denying what he knows is the truth. But admitting that he's been a fool would be even worse.

'They always come back,' Kringman says, as if to himself.

'I thought I could catch him. And I was close . . .'

'But he got away with your money?'

'I got his fingerprints,' Frank says. 'On some tape he used to stick up a notice.'

'He got away with your money and his prints aren't on file. Right? Otherwise you wouldn't be here.'

Frank nods.

Annic arrives, bearing a tray with two half-pint glasses and two beer bottles. She puts it down on a workbench that runs along the side wall of the garage. There is a clink and hiss as she removes a top and pours. She hands the glass to Frank.

'Real beer for you,' Kringman says. 'Gnats' pee for me.'

'Alcohol free,' she says.

'She doesn't drink it herself, you note.'

'I don't drink beer at all. Anyway, you could have half a glass of red wine if you wanted.'

She fills the second glass and reaches across the landscape table, placing it next to the track, opposite a model of a brick water tower. Kringman doesn't pick it up.

'Will you be staying for lunch?' she asks.

'No he won't,' says Kringman.

Frank shakes his head. 'Just a few more minutes.'

Annie's mouth thins even more. She leaves the garage, closing the door with a bang, just loud enough to convey annoyance but not so loud as to be unambiguously rude.

'She hates all this,' says Kringman.

Frank isn't sure if he means the train layout or the secret conversation or both.

'You really don't care if the blackmailer publishes?' he asks.

'Of course I care. It would be difficult if it came out. But what can I do? Even if I wanted to pay, all my money is tied up in property. The only chance is to make it look as if I can't give a toss.'

'It might be difficult for you,' Frank says. 'For me it would be bloody devastating. I'd lose my job. I had to pay.'

Kringman shakes his head but doesn't explain why he disagrees. 'Are you still married, Franky, my boy?'

'Yes.'

'Julie, wasn't it? What does she think about it?'

'Did you tell Anne?' Frank asks.

'She's my daughter, not my wife.'

'If your wife was . . .'

'Alive?' Kringman suggests. 'Would I have told her? We'll never know, will we.'

Frank looks down at the garage floor. 'I'm sorry.'

Kringman snorts. 'Sure.' He tweaks a control knob on the table in front of him, but the train doesn't move. He tries again.

'Damn Jinty, playing up again.'

He lifts the engine, upends it and inspects the underside. Then he takes a cotton wool bud from a pot on the table, dips the end in a bottle of meths and starts working it around the front wheels. Frank watches. There is a fierce concentration about the way the man works, as if he is using the activity to cover his feelings.

'Do you have any idea who it is?' Frank asks.

Kringman places the engine on the track and pushes it back so the coupling engages with the rolling stock. He twists the control knob again, and this time the train pulls out of the station once more. The small electric motor hums quietly, and the wheels make a low rumble as they pass over the track.

'No,' Kringman says at last. 'No idea.' He picks up his beer glass and sips. 'But if I wanted to find out, I'd start asking why it's happening now. Like you said, it's been a long time. Have you started looking up the people in the photograph?'

'And their relatives. Yes. You're one of them, of course. That's why I'm here.'

Kringman doesn't seem to react to the challenge in Frank's statement. 'Have any of your suspects had a recent change in circumstances?' he asks.

Frank nods. 'But, so far as I can work out, it's just the one.'

'Then that's your man.'

'It isn't a man.'

Tami is tidying up the flat. She's piled the magazines under the bed. *Bella* and *Fiction Feast*. She's even borrowed the vacuum cleaner from downstairs and given the carpet a quick going over. The windows are open, and the curtains are shifting in the breeze.

None of this is logical. An air freshener and a clean flat shouldn't make any difference to her probation officer. But life on the outside is still such a new experience that she can't trust the system not to change its mind.

The doorbell rings. Tami checks herself in the mirror one more time before opening up.

Miss Quick is older than Tami by a few years. There are strands of grey in her long black hair. And although she wears formal clothes – a pale green trouser suit today – there are hints that she is not quite the model of orthodoxy that she first appeared to be. The earrings, for example – small silver parrots. Tami wonders if she wears them deliberately to make her clients feel that she isn't part of the system that put them away. She comes in, carrying a brown leather briefcase in one hand.

'Hello, Tami.'

'Hello.'

They shake hands. Safe and formal.

'You've got the flat looking nice.'

'Thank you.'

'Hanging saris. That *is* a good idea.'

Again: 'Thank you.'

Miss Quick points to one of the paintings on the wall – a nautilus shell. 'Is that one of yours?'

'Yes.'

The teacher in prison told Tami it was a good example of naive art. She took that to mean that it was badly painted. She keeps it up anyway because of the colours it brings to the room – bright oranges, yellows and deep blues.

The probation officer walks up to the picture. 'You should do more.' Then she continues around the room, doing a complete circuit before sitting herself in the high-backed dining chair.

'Would you like some tea, Miss Quick?'

'I think it would be better if you called me Karen now.'

So the name is Karen Quick. Tami doesn't ask why things should change. Nor does she want to become too relaxed with a woman whom she sees as representing the prison system.

'And the tea?' She has an urge to reach for the packet of nicotine gum on top of the gas fire, but resists.

Miss Quick smiles. 'Later, perhaps.'

Tami perches herself on the front edge of the armchair, matching her visitor's upright posture.

'How is everything going?' the probation officer asks.

'Fine.' The word comes out fast and false-sounding in Tami's ears.

'What about the job?'

'It's fine.'

'And how about friends or family – have you got in touch with anyone from before?'

'No.'

Miss Quick smiles sadly. 'It would be a good idea, you know. You need to start building up a life – something that's more than having a flat and a job. You're going to have to relearn legitimate ways of loosening up. Have you been to the pub since getting out?'

'I'm not drinking,' Tami says, though she's sure she said that at the last interview. She's waiting for the probation officer to get out some papers, to start ticking boxes, to get the interview over with. But the briefcase remains on the floor.

'Did you see that new sitcom on the BBC last night?'

Tami tries to think what this might have to do with her case. 'I would have been asleep,' she says. Then adds: 'I work nights.'

'It was really funny. I think they're showing it again on Tuesday – on digital.'

Tami just nods. She doesn't have a digital decoder. In fact, she doubts that there could be a decoder that would work with her old black and white portable.

'What was the last TV programme you saw?' Miss Quick asks.

'Why does it matter?'

'Help me here, Tami. I'm trying to make conversation.'

'Why?'

'If I'm to help you, I need to get to know where your life is coming from right now.'

'*Countdown*,' Tami says.

'I'm sorry?'

'The last programme I watched. It was *Countdown*.'

Miss Quick nods and beams a smile of encouragement. 'How about that cup of tea?'

Tami fusses over a couple of mugs in the kitchen. She'd cleaned them before, but now notices a hint of a tannin ring on the unchipped one. She can hear the other woman walking around her living room again. The urge for a nicotine hit is stronger now, but the only gum is in the other room. She looks at the small fridge under the work surface.

'I do like these colours, Tami.'

'Thanks.'

'I used to live not far from here.'

'Never!' The word slips out. Too familiar.

But Miss Quick just laughs gently. 'When I started out. The job doesn't pay as much as you think.'

'Was the place . . . the same as now?' Tami asks. She's beginning to relax in spite of herself.

'It was worse.'

'It couldn't be!'

'The working girls actually put red lights in their windows. Can you imagine that? There were kerb crawlers all times of day. I got propositioned more times than I can remember.'

'The kerb crawlers haven't gone.'

'And there were men on the street corners selling hard drugs.'

Tami doesn't respond to this. She finds she is gripping the teaspoon unnaturally hard. Miss Quick wanders into the kitchen. She puts a hand on Tami's shoulder. Tami jumps as if the touch were a hot iron.

'You're going to have to trust me. I'm on your side. I'm here to help you. What you've been through takes time to get over. Who was it who said that living in prison was the second hardest thing in the world?' She picks up her mug of tea and walks back to the living room.

Tami follows.

'You're doing really well. Everything you've achieved so far. I'm proud of you. I wish that all my cases were as determined to make it work as you are.'

Tami wants to cry now. She feels the prickling in the corners of her eyes.

'Has anyone tried to sell you drugs yet?'

'No.'

'They will, you know.'

Tami gulps a breath. 'I didn't do the things they said . . .'

'It's not my job to say whether you were guilty or innocent. I can only go by what the court said. But . . .'

'I didn't do it!' She is crying now.

'I was going to say that you wouldn't have been the first woman sent down for something her husband did.'

'You believe me?'

'What I believe isn't the point. You admitted to the parole board that you'd been drug trafficking.'

'I lied to get out.'

'Saying you're innocent doesn't necessarily have a bearing on whether they let you out. It is your risk of re-offending. And you did test positive for heroin when you were inside.'

Tami weeps into her hands. After a while the flood of self-pity starts to ebb and she becomes aware of herself again and how foolish she must look. And then she starts to worry that she's exposed too much of herself.

'For what it's worth, I am inclined to believe you,' Miss Quick says. 'Lots of people have gone into the prison system clean and come out with a drug habit. But I can't say any of this in public. And neither can you. You're out now. That's all that matters. You've got to let it go or you'll never be able to rebuild your life. Feelings of injustice are natural, but they don't do you any good. Your job is learning how to make choices for yourself again – not just to react to the choices the system makes for you.

'I'm going to leave you now. But I want you to do something for me. Call up an old friend – someone from before you got married. Go for a pizza together, or to a movie. And if anyone tries to sell you drugs, you run to the nearest phone and call me. You've got my number.'

Miss Quick picks up her bag and moves off towards the door. Tami follows, still clutching her tea.

'Any questions?' the probation officer asks.

'You said living in prison was the second hardest thing.'

'It's true.'

'What's the hardest?'

Miss Quick smiles, as if grateful that Tami finally went for the bait she laid. 'Trying to live on the outside again,' she says. She steps forward, gives Tami a stiff hug and walks out through the door and away.

The probation officer's last move was so unexpected that Tami had no time to react. She stands behind the door for a long time before sleepwalking back into the kitchen. She opens the small fridge, reaches behind a loaf of sliced white bread and pulls out a pickle jar. She unscrews the top and empties the contents on to the work surface. A syringe, a single hypodermic needle in a sealed, plastic packet. And a small packet of golden-brown crystals. The crystals shift as she presses with her finger. Then she puts the objects back into their hiding place, closes the fridge and leaves the kitchen, walking fast to the front door, putting as much distance between herself and her flat as she can.

She's got her bag and her car keys, but she doesn't know where she's going to go. None of her school friends would remember her now, even if she could find them. And her family have told her never to come back. She gets a flash memory of her mother, standing on the seafront at Skeggy, clutching her coat collar, hair whipped back in the wind. She can see it clearly in her mind's eye, but it feels distant, as if it was part of a documentary about someone else's life. Or a memory of a photograph of something she never experienced.

As for the people she got to know after she was married – they were all Jack's friends before they were hers.

She drives her pink Fiat up the hill to the Victoria Park roundabout then turns left on to London Road, heading out of town towards Oadby. She does know where this road is taking her. The only way she can justify not turning back now is by telling herself that she will turn back later in the journey. It is a lie, of course.

It's been ten years since she last came down this way. There are some new buildings. A couple of landmarks have gone, but she doesn't need to look at the map. She turns off into the residential streets. A left. A right. Another right. She pulls up fifty metres short of the house, still telling herself she can go home, not believing it any more.

She doesn't want them to see the car, though she isn't sure why that should be because she isn't answerable to them any more. Not having any friends means she isn't answerable to anyone. She sits behind the steering wheel, listening to the sound of a lawnmower trundling back and forth in one of the nearby gardens. If the number of four-by-fours parked on the road was anything to go by, this street must be home to a community of rainforest explorers. But that would be to ignore the BMWs and Audis. She wonders if she should put a notice in the window of her car just to say it isn't a wreck and it hasn't been dumped.

A new thought occurs to her as she walks down the pavement – that they might have upped and left. They'd only just bought this house when Tami was sent to prison. It wouldn't be a surprise if they sold up after Jack's old man died. Not to go back to the St John's estate, of course.

She's in front of the house now – looking for clues. It's a detached residence, painted white with a black criss-cross of mock timbers. The double garage has the same medieval appearance. There's a silver Rover parked on the wide gravel drive. The front door is new to her – a white plastic job with a glass inset panel, complete with diamond-pattern leading.

The lawnmower motor chugs to a stop.

She walks up the drive and rings the bell. It has the same chime as she remembers. The world has changed. She has become a different person. But she's now sure that Jack's family are still here. There's a noise inside. Footsteps in the hall. A movement through the dimpled glass. The door opens. A woman stares out at her – chestnut hair without a hint of grey, but skin deeply lined and tanned. The lipstick is too pink for her complexion.

'Vera?'

The woman narrows her eyes, then widens them.

'Vera – it is you, isn't it?' Tami holds out her hand towards Jack's mother.

Vera seems frozen. Seeing her daughter-in-law on the doorstep after so long must hit her strongly. Tami imagines the surge of emotions. Memories. Guilt from the way her son acted. She waits for Vera to take her hand, for the attempted apologies to begin.

Vera takes a deep breath and opens her mouth. 'You've got a cheek turning up here!' She spits the words out as if they taste bitter.

Tami is too taken aback to respond at first, and Vera is just getting going.

'You whore!'

'I . . .'

'The way you treated us! How dare you . . .'

'What do you mean?'

Vera brings back her arm as if to slap Tami across the face. The hand balls into a fist, the knuckles white, then the tension drops out of her. The arm goes slack and falls to her side. She turns her head away, but not before Tami sees the tears running.

'Go.'

Tami steps up, pushing Vera back into the hall. 'Not until you tell me what that was all about!'

Vera flees back into the house with Tami stalking after her. She's so focused on her mother-in-law that she hardly registers the weirdness of being in this house again. It's like wading into the thick syrup of a dream, where she knows what she is about to see just before she sees it. The curl of the oak-effect banister rail, the framed photograph of Filbert Street on the wall, the brown tiles on the kitchen floor. It is here, in the kitchen, that she corners Vera.

'It's me that's been pissed on!' Tami shouts. '*He* left *me*. I'm the one who's been . . .'

'How can you say that?'

'Because it's true!'

'You're the one who told him to get lost. In a letter! You couldn't even tell him to his face.'

They're staring at each other. Tami becomes aware of herself, of the fact that she is shouting. She closes her mouth, runs the fingers of two hands back through her hair. Vera actually believes what she is saying. This is the truth that hits Tami harder than anything. Her mother-in-law thinks that it was her who dumped Jack. Tami takes a deep breath, pulls out a chair at the breakfast bar and sits. 'Make me a cup of tea,' she says.

She watches Vera sleepwalk to the kettle. The cups are kept in two cupboards above the work surface. One for the mugs the family use, the other for china brought out for visitors. It was only after she and Jack got engaged that Tami had been able to drink out of a mug in this house. She watches Vera's hand reach up, then hesitate before reaching for the door of the cupboard with the china. Two cups come out and two saucers and a teapot. But she doesn't bring out the sugar bowl.

Tami doesn't get up and move into the lounge, so Vera has to sit facing her across the breakfast bar. They both sip. It is Earl Grey, which always tastes to Tami like weak tea mixed with a drop of lemon washing-up liquid. She manages not to pull a sour face. The china clinks quietly.

'Tell me about John,' Tami says.

Vera busies her hands, arranging the teaspoon in her saucer. 'It was a heart attack,' she says. 'Years ago now.'

'How many?'

'Eight. No. Nine.' Vera touches the wooden door of a cupboard, as if the action might ward off some evil.

'I only heard a couple of days ago,' Tami says. 'I'm sorry.'

Vera looks up for a moment, as if to check her expression. 'He had it coming. The doctor gave him enough warnings.'

'That doesn't make it any easier.'

'No.'

Tami knows that the longer she leaves the question, the harder it is going to be to ask. The silence is so tangible between them that it's all she can do to clear her throat.

'What did Jack tell you?' she asks.

'What did . . .?'

'What did he tell you to make you think I'd treated him badly?'

'You found someone else.'

'I was in prison – how could I?'

'It was an old boyfriend. He visited you.'

'Jack was my first.'

'You wouldn't let my son see you again.'

Tami's wrists are itching. She has an urge to turn them so Vera can see the scars. She wants to be able to dip in to the surging emotion that washed over her that night, after she got the letter. She wants to be able to immerse herself in it, to know that it was really real, not some construct of her imagination. She searches her feelings, but can find only a void, a sealed-off place, where the events of that night must be.

She can remember the facts, of course. This isn't amnesia. She didn't show the letter to anyone. No one knew. She wasn't considered a high suicide risk, so it was only by fortune that they got to her in time. Or maybe through her own inefficiency. Or her cowardice – that she didn't cut deeply enough. They said it was a cry for help, but that wasn't true. It was a leap towards oblivion. A failed leap.

'I did want to see him,' she whispers.

'You were going to get a divorce.'

'Jack told you this?'

'He was too broken up about it. He . . . he went up to Scotland to get away from everything.'

'Who told you?'

'You can't talk your way out of what you did, Tami. John told me everything.'

John. She pictures him in her mind. John the father-in-law. The patriarch of the family. The market trader who knew everyone and everything that was going on. The man who ate steak and chips like there was no tomorrow. Until there wasn't a tomorrow. The man who wrote to Tami in prison telling her that Jack had found another woman and had gone off to Glasgow to start a new life.

She wants to explain to Vera. But what could she say – that John and Jack were both lying to her? That way leads to a slanging match. She'd get nothing more out of her mother-in-law if she tried that. So she says: 'There was no one else.'

Vera brushes this off. 'I don't want to talk about it.' Then she adds: 'Why did you come here? Is it money?'

That pricks under Tami's skin. 'It's a bit late to start thinking about that now!'

'I can give you a few hundred. But don't come back for more.'

Tami stands. 'I don't want your filthy money! Give me Jack's phone number and I'm out of here.'

'I can't.'

'You must. You owe me that.'

Vera shakes her head. She looks scared, perhaps bewildered. 'He's gone,' she says. 'Disappeared. I had one letter after he left, then nothing more. You drove my son away.'

Chapter 4

Frank is following all the leads he has. The phone that the blackmailer called from is registered to the same address as the one that he sent with the photograph. Frank checks it out and finds a Somali family living there. The house is owned by an Indian man who lives two doors away. None of them were even in the country when the blackmail photograph was taken.

He then asks around and finds someone who tells him about a man called Ricky, who apparently works for one of the mobile phone networks and takes on occasional 'free-lance' jobs.

'Do you have his number?' Frank asks.

'You don't call Ricky. He calls you.'

'When?'

'When he's ready. I'll tell him you're interested.'

By Thursday lunchtime there has been no call from Ricky, and Frank realizes that he will have to cast his net wider.

He walks down the corridor and looks in at the Community Relations office. The secretary, Leah, is here, fingers clattering over the keyboard, headphones on and her foot working the treadle for the audiotyping tape recorder. She doesn't seem to hear him come in behind her. Other than that, the outer office is empty. There is a glass-sided partition office in the corner. Mo Akanbai is sitting there in front of her own computer. She seems to be gazing at the wall. Her hands rest on the edge of the desk, perfectly still.

Frank taps on her door. She starts, standing abruptly with a smile that appears too fulsome to be genuine.

'I was thinking about a letter,' she says.

'That's good. Better to think first and write later.'

Mo's features are a beguiling mixture of the black and white races. On skin tone alone you night mistake her for southern European. But her hair and nose carry hints of African features. He's not sure if she is half and half or some other combination. He has never felt comfortable to ask.

He parks himself on the corner of her desk and nods. 'Is everything going well?'

'Fine.' Though she speaks the word in a cheerful enough voice, her expression seems more closed than usual. It is as if she is hiding some emotion.

'Work?' he asks.

'All under control.'

'How is your mother? I haven't seen her since last summer.'

'She's doing well, thank you. Building her life up again.'

'That's good.'

He knows that Mo is waiting for him to come to the point. But the truth is that he doesn't have a particular point to raise. He just wants to reassure himself that she wasn't suspicious about his questions the other day. Like she'd told him, tracing the location of mobile phone calls should be a job for CID rather than uniform.

'What about the data for the multiculturalism conference?'

'All done,' she says. 'I've passed it on to graphics. They're going to put together something visual. It'll look good.'

'Good. Good.'

'Is there anything else?'

Frank gets off the desk and shakes his head. 'We need to talk from time to time,' he says. 'That's all. I value your work. If I had half a dozen like you, there's no limit to what we might be able to achieve.'

Her hands are still resting on the desk. 'That's it?'

'Yes. And to say that I'll be out of the office for an hour this afternoon. Some local politician needs his feathers smoothing. You know how it is. I'll be back later though. If you need anything.'

'Thank you,' she says. And it seems to Frank as if she probably means it.

Things turn out differently from Frank's plans. To start with, the politician, Bill Arnica, turns out to be rather harder to contact than he had imagined. The number in Frank's personal address book no longer works. Not that this should be a surprise. It has been several years since they last spoke.

He tries directory enquiries – but they have no record of a Bill Arnica. Which means he must be ex-directory. Frank's next call is to one of the man's businesses. He keys in the number out of Yellow Pages. The phone on the other end rings twice before it is answered.

'Arnica Properties,' chimes a woman's voice.

'I'd like to speak to Bill Arnica.'

'What's your name please?'

'Frank . . .' he hesitates, then adds: '. . . Shakespeare.'

'Mr Shakespeare? What is it concerning?'

'Just tell him my name.'

'Please hold.'

Frank is expecting Vivaldi. Instead he gets Leicester Sound FM – the end of a track by U2 and the beginning of a sale announcement from a local car showroom. Then it cuts off and Frank hears a thud in the background that might be a door slamming shut.

'Shakespeare?' It's Arnica's voice, unmistakably shrill, just like the way he sounds on the television. It is at once irritatingly insistent and unforgettable.

'I need to talk,' Frank says.

'Obviously.'

'But not like this.'

'Then why phone in the first place?'

'Just to make contact.'

'You could have come to the office.'

'I don't think that's a good idea.'

'Well, I don't have time for prissy guessing games.'

There's a click as the line cuts back to Leicester Sound FM. It's still on the same advert.

Frank swears under his breath. Arnica's trademark rudeness has made him a gift for the media over the years. They never seem to be able to get enough of the man.

Frank is moving to put the phone down when he hears the voice of the receptionist.

'Mr Shakespeare?'

'I'm still here.'

'Mr Arnica wanted to make sure you knew the details.'

'I'm sorry?'

'Do you know the St John's community centre? It runs from seven till nine. He says there's usually a bit of a queue, so best bring a book or something.'

'What runs from seven till nine?'

'The surgery, of course.'

Frank does not now need to leave the station in the afternoon. But he has already set up the time, made his excuses, cancelled appointments. So he goes out anyway, telling himself that it looks less suspicious this way. He drives to a multi-storey car park, then walks to Bishop Street. He is in uniform, but that doesn't seem to bother anyone in the reference library.

He gives them his request and ten minutes later is sitting at a desk in a quiet corner, leafing through a pile of newspaper cuttings about the man himself. Bill Arnica. Most things have been said about the man at one time or another. The record is shot through with contradictions and accusations of all kinds, but there haven't been any libel cases. Bill Arnica has not until now been a litigious man.

He rose to prominence as a militant union rep back in the late 1970s. The earliest picture that Frank manages to find is of Bill marshalling the pickets in front of a clothing factory. There is a fire in an oil drum and there is Bill, pointing with one finger to the side. The set of his body, angled slightly forward, makes him look like a figure in a Soviet propaganda poster. It was at around that time that he was put forward – or, according to other newspapers, he put himself forward – to stand for the city council. That was in the St John's estate, a ward so red in those days that they would have elected a dining room chair so long as it had the official Labour Party candidacy.

So Bill served the community – or, in other versions of the story, he served himself – for nine years in that capacity before having a serious run-in with the party. When the next election came around he stood as an independent socialist, and such was the local feeling – or the degree of intimidation, or the level of corruption, or the anti-party sentiment, or the personal charisma, or concern about local issues, or the fact that the official candidate had less charisma than a dining chair, or various combinations of these, depending on the commentator – that he clung on to his seat in the council.

Then emerged Bill Arnica the businessman. He started buying up property in and around the St John's estate. Dividing houses into flats. Converting buildings into shops. Using his knowledge of the planning system and of local developments to good effect – or making corrupt use of his influence, depending on which paper was telling the story.

Frank skips to a bunch of cuttings from the time just before Tami went into prison. It looked like Arnica was going to lose his seat on the city council. Local support was leaching away. He threw accusations of corruption at the woman who was standing against him. She threw accusations back. It was a bloody fight, and the papers loved it. Arnica won by fewer than a hundred votes.

Frank's fingers walk through the remaining cuttings. There is little coverage of the election that finally lost Arnica his seat. A couple of column inches in the local paper. The fight was over.

Much of this information Frank already knew. But by the time he packs up to leave the library, he has fleshed it out with specific dates and pictures. And although Bill Arnica is the last man he would choose to sit next to at a dinner party, Frank has a grudging admiration for what he has achieved.

Things are never as simple as the media like to make out. Everyone makes compromises. That is the way things happen in the real world. If he could take a microscope to the lives of a hundred successful people, Frank is sure he would find ninety-nine examples where the morality of the case could be argued in more than one direction. And as for the hundredth example, that would be someone whose success came from chance rather than graft. A lottery winner perhaps.

Not like the men in the blackmail photograph. Frank

pictures it in his mind. His own younger self standing with Jack and John Steel on one side and Superintendent Kringman on the other. Next along the line from John, and standing a little way apart, was the militant firebrand himself, Bill Arnica.

Getting away in the afternoon was easy. The lies he told were small. He felt a rush of excitement but no guilty aftertaste. Concealing the truth from Julie is infinitely harder. She knows there is something happening below the surface. He can see it in her eyes as he tells her he has to slip out for an hour.

'Why now?'

'This is the only time I could see him.'

'Who?'

'It's work,' he tells her. 'I'm sorry.'

He can still see her face in his mind as he drives away. He decides that after he's seen Arnica he'll stop off in the twenty-four hour Tesco at Beaumont Leys. They sell flowers. And chocolate. He'll make it up to her somehow.

He parks his car as near the front of the community centre as he can find a place. Directly under a streetlight. It is also in view of the security camera on the wall, so he feels fairly confident that it will still be there when he comes out. He spent his first few years in the force policing St John's. It was never an easy area. But better then than now.

There are already a few people sitting on plastic seats in the waiting room: a girl of perhaps sixteen, wearing tight cotton trousers and a thin top that stops above her navel – perfectly showing off the state of her pregnancy; next to her a man in his twenties with a skinhead haircut, wearing shorts and a running vest. Opposite them is an elderly woman with a sheaf of official-looking documents on her lap. Housing Benefit claim forms by the look of them. She is working the edge of the papers between her thumbs and fingers. The man in the vest looks at Frank's shoes, then at his face.

'You from the council, or what?'

Frank shakes his head and looks around, taking in the doors to the gents and ladies and another, wider, for the disabled. There is a fourth closed door with a sheet of printed paper taped to it at eye height. *Bill Arnica. Surgery.* His photograph is on the right-hand side of the words. Not smiling, even for his mug shot to be taken. Frank wonders if anyone would recognize the man with a happy expression on his face.

'If you're waiting for him, you better get in line,' says the man in the vest.

Then the door opens and Bill Arnica himself glares out – just like the photograph image.

'You,' he says, nodding towards Frank.

Frank can feel the anger being directed towards him by the skinhead and the teenager. Ignoring them, he follows Arnica through and closes the door behind him. The room has a plastic-coated desk with a utilitarian swivel chair on one side, in which Arnica sits, and two brown soft chairs on the other. Frank chooses the one with the fewer cigarette burn holes. He finds himself uncomfortably low, looking up at the other man.

'Well?' Arnica demands. 'What's brought you out of the woodwork?'

'I've not been hiding,' Frank says.

'Not hiding, no. I've seen you in the papers. Pressing the flesh with the great and the good. But I haven't seen you face to face in ten years.'

'Different circles.'

'That's crap!'

Frank has managed to keep smiling, but he is repelled by the other man. He looks away.

'You know why you made it to superintendent?' Arnica asks. 'It's because you'll pretend to like anyone if it'll get you another inch up the shitty pole.'

Frank knows this is hypocrisy. Of all the men in the blackmail photograph, Arnica was the most ambitious. He fought battles for power and influence with each of the others. He never had the charisma of Jack or John Steel, and it always seemed to Frank as if Arnica was jealous of the way people turned to them for help instead of him. As for all the work with the poor of the St John's estate, Frank has a grudging admiration for it – though whether it is done to honour a socialist ideal or for some selfish motive he can't decide.

'You know why there are people out there?' Arnica asks. 'You know why they queue behind that door? It's because I never claimed to be nothing but what I am. I never said a thing I don't believe. And they know I'll help them if they can be helped at all.'

'You're not on the council any more,' Frank says, knowing he's stating the obvious. 'So why all this surgery business?'

'Just because they changed the wards around to squeeze me out doesn't mean the people don't have problems.'

'They've got other councillors to help them now.'

'Who do nothing but sit on their arses and claim fat expenses cheques for things they've never done. You know that as well as I, Franky-bloody-establishment-man-Shakespeare.'

The longer the conversation goes on, the more Frank feels himself getting wound up and the less he wants to raise the real subject of his visit. He knows all about Arnica's temper and impatience, so he is pretty sure the man is going to throw him out at any minute if he doesn't get to the point. In fact, he is surprised it hasn't happened already. 'We've come a long way,' he says, 'since the 90s.'

'You think so? Look out that window and tell me we've made progress. The streets are seething. Can't you feel it, man?'

'I mean us. You and me. In different ways.'

Arnica blows air through his lips and looks as if he is about to swear. But then he just shakes his head.

'Do you remember the 90s, Bill?'

'What is this? A quiz?'

'Just a civil question.'

'One that you wouldn't ask on the phone this afternoon?'

Frank is really expecting Arnica to crack at this point. But the other man is still holding back. And there's something behind his aggressive expression that seems out of place. Almost a nervousness. A waiting for the question to be asked.

'Why did you let me in first just now?' Frank asks.

'You're wearing a suit. You sitting out there would scare off half the people who come to see me. Now spit out whatever it is you've come to ask. Or walk and let me get on with helping people.'

Frank feels desperate to get it all out in the open, but some instinct is telling him to hold back. He's had to trust his instinct in all his years as policeman. It hasn't always been right. But he chooses to follow it still. He pulls himself out of the chair.

'I don't want to waste any more of your time, Bill,' he says. 'If you're so busy.'

Bill is on his feet as well. 'Don't be a cretin, Shakespeare.'

'Your work's too important. I shouldn't have come.'

'Fuck off, man! Just tell me why you're sodding here!'

Frank draws a deep breath and says in a level voice what his instinct is now shouting inside his head: 'The blackmail letters, Bill. You've got to tell me all about them. How many have you received? Have you paid? You've got to tell me everything.'

Arnica tightens his already-balled fists. 'Fuck!' He whispers. 'How did you find out?'

Eddie Piper is one of the faces that Tami sees in her mind when she closes her eyes and thinks back to those days. He was at all the parties that Jack took her to. Sometimes as a guest. Sometimes a doorman. He was the man to buy things from at prices below even what the wholesalers could manage. A gadget would hardly be in the shops before he was selling one second-hand.

Tami stands on the road in front of the place where Eddie used to live. It is a pleasant semi in a row of similarly pleasant houses. Small front lawns all nicely trimmed. It is early evening and sweet scent is rising from the flower borders. Roses and lavender. The low bushes are alive with bees.

The front door opens and a middle-aged woman looks out. A neat woman to match the neat property. 'It's you, isn't it?' she says. 'You're Jack Steel's wife.'

Tami walks through the gate and up the path. Now she looks more closely, she recognizes the woman's face. 'Mrs Piper?' The hairstyle has changed. It used to be shoulder length and tightly permed. Now it is straight and cut shorter, cropped into a neat line at the back.

'I saw you through the window,' Mrs Piper says. 'It is Tami, isn't it?'

'I wanted to speak to your husband.'

The woman's eyes flick down for a moment, as if she's deciding what to say. 'It's not so simple. I could . . . I could phone. He'd come over if he knew you were here. But I've got guests coming.'

'You and he?'

She shakes her head. 'It's just for a few months. To see how we get on.'

'I'm sorry.'

'No. Don't be. It's all for the good. Really.'

Tami sits in the lounge while Mrs Piper makes the phone call in another room. Her voice is muffled by its passage through the connecting wall, but the tone is unmistakably assertive. The carriage clock on the mantelpiece ticks quietly. The second hand travels around the face three times. Mrs Piper's voice has become more pleading now. Softer. Then Tami can't hear it any more. She waits ten minutes, gazing at the Artex ceiling. Then another ten.

She has just made an agreement with herself not to wait beyond a further five minutes without going to find out what is happening when Mrs Piper comes back into the room. Her face looks fresh, as if make-up has been freshly applied. She is carrying a tray with cups and a china teapot.

'Sugar?' she asks.

'No. Thank you.' She accepts the cup from Mrs Piper's hands and the rattle of china stops.

Mrs Piper clicks a sweetener into her own cup. 'I haven't seen you since . . . you know.'

'I was only released three months ago.'

'Oh. I thought . . .'

'I served ten years.'

'But it was serious, I suppose. Drug trafficking, right?'

'I didn't do it.'

Mrs Piper hasn't made much eye contact through this exchange but now she sneaks a glance. 'No?'

'They planted a kilo of heroin in the boot of my car.'

'Who?' When Tami doesn't answer, Mrs Piper makes an apologetic coughing noise. 'Of course, you don't know. It's all been so long I've forgotten the details. I . . . I don't mix with the same people these days. You understand.'

There is a rattle at the front door. A key in the lock. Then the doorbell rings.

When Mrs Piper comes back into the front room, it is with a man behind her. But for the introduction, Tami might not have recognized him.

'This is Eddie.'

Tami stands, shocked into silence. He grins at her. The bulk is still there in his arms and chest from when he used to lift weights, but the definition has gone, the finely sculpted edges are smeared out. And, most shocking of all, the angles of his face and neck have been submerged in a tide of fat.

He gestures to his stained T-shirt and jeans. 'Sorry about this. I was helping a friend. Cleaning up and stuff. Came back home soon as I got the call.'

Tami manages to say: 'Thanks.'

'So, you're out.'

'Yes.'

'It's . . . been a long time.'

'Yes.'

'You haven't changed. I mean, not much.'

Tami feels a pressure to fire back the automatic return compliment. But it would be so obviously untrue that she finds herself unable to say anything.

After a couple of seconds of silence, Mrs Piper coughs. 'You two have a lot to talk about. I'd better . . . You know.' The door closes behind her.

Eddie gestures for Tami to sit, as if feeling he ought to be the one playing host. But there is no conviction in his body language. She sits anyway and watches him place himself on a chair facing her.

The shock of seeing him like this is wearing off now and she feels once again the question that has brought her so painfully back here. 'What can you tell me about Jack – about what happened to him?'

He puffs air through his cheeks. 'That? Woah. That was years ago. I'm . . . I'm sorry.'

'Tell me.'

'I didn't know or anything. Hell of a shock. Must've been for you, too. A shock, I mean.'

Tami is sitting forward in her chair. In her head she is screaming at him to spit out whatever he knows. To confirm the fact that her husband left her for another woman so that she can get back to the task of salvaging a life from the ruins of her past. She says: 'What happened to him?'

'You don't know?'

'Just tell me.'

'He disappeared.'

Tami feels her insides puckering up. 'When?'

'Way back.' Eddie's forehead is wrinkled with puzzlement. 'Not seen him . . . must be nine years. Went off with that . . . with that Scottish bird. She was pregnant. He had to follow. I'm sorry.'

The relief washing through Tami's body is so complete and sudden that she feels faint. There is a rattling of china, which stops when Eddie takes the cup and saucer out of her hand. She hadn't noticed him leave his chair. He stands in front of her, biting on his podgy lower lip. 'I'm really sorry. I thought . . . I thought . . .'

'It's OK. I just needed to hear it from someone else.' She

takes her cup back from him and gulps down the contents.

Eddie retreats to his chair. 'Why are you asking this?'

'I did know what happened. But someone said something. It got me confused.'

'Gossip. Shouldn't listen to it.'

Tami doesn't want to have to explain that it wasn't gossip. The truth is still too confusing. So she says: 'Yes. You're right.'

'Who was it told you?'

'It's not important.'

'Yeah, it is. Coz people got motives, right? If someone's spreading shit, you want to know why.'

Tami's first reaction is to brush the suggestion away. Which she starts to do. 'You're right, Eddie.' Then the thought comes to her that what he has said is *exactly* right. Shakespeare told her that Jack disappeared. He must have had a reason.

Eddie is frowning. She follows his eyes to a line of small framed photographs on the mantelpiece. Four family groups, two on either side of the carriage clock. They are Mrs Piper's relations, to judge from the facial resemblance. The one in the middle shows Eddie as he used to be, standing between two women who could be his wife's sisters.

'What do you know about the policeman, Superintendent Shakespeare?'

His eyes click back to hers. 'Don't have nothing to do with that man. He's bad news.'

'Jack knew him, right?'

'I guess. We all knew him – if you know what I mean.'

She doesn't. 'When was this?'

'The good old days. You and Jack were together. His old man was alive. Red Owen was there. And Bill Arnica. You know . . .?'

'Jack never told me much.'

'But you knew about the business, right?'

She shakes her head.

'You must have. You put the heroin in your car, for Christ's sake.'

'No. It wasn't me.'

'Jack, then?'

'He was never dealing heroin, if that's what you're saying. He hated the stuff.'

'Yeah. But there was evidence, right? Your fingerprints. And some hair, wasn't there?'

'It wasn't me.'

Eddie gets up and paces across to the door. 'Did he tell you about the agreement or not?' When he turns to face her again she sees a frown of concentration rippling the fat on his forehead.

'I need you to tell me what you know.'

He shakes his head. 'If you weren't in on it . . .'

'I just spent ten years inside for something I didn't do. Now you tell me what was going on!'

Eddie paces back the other way across the room, ending up by the mantelpiece. 'You just got to know that the cops Shakespeare and Kringman were both in on it. They're both crooked, OK? You got to understand that.' He's fiddling with the edge of one of the picture frames as he speaks. 'But the agreement is all finished now. There's no point in stirring it up. The only thing that counts is that Jack was one of the good guys. Forget the rest.'

'Tell me, for pity's sake!'

'You don't need to know.'

'Please.'

'It's not safe for you if I tell it. I'm sorry.'

The door opens and Mrs Piper steps back into her front

room. Eddie snatches his hand back from the picture frame as if it has just burned him.

'Is everything all right?' his wife asks.

'Yes,' says Eddie.

'Only I'm expecting guests. They'll be here in a few minutes . . .'

Tami feels their eyes on her. She stands. Mrs Piper is ushering her to the door. She feels dazed by Eddie's partial revelation. She wants time to digest what she has learned, but the moment is slipping from her. She steps out on to the path.

'Goodbye,' says Mrs Piper.

Tami turns for one last try. She speaks over the woman's shoulder to where Eddie hovers in the hallway. 'What did she look like – the woman Jack went off with?'

He shrugs. 'She was a good-looker. Beautiful, I guess.'

'Tall? Short? Blonde? What?'

'I . . . I can't say.'

'Can't or won't?'

'I never met her. It was all real quick. He didn't turn up at the pub one night and that was it. They said she was beautiful, though.'

'They? Who told you about her?'

'Oh, everyone knew. It was no secret or anything.'

'How did they know? How can you be sure it was true?'

'It was true all right. Had to be. Jack's old man was the one that told us. And he was as straight as a snooker cue.'

Chapter 5

Frank and Julie are at home watching the film *Gladiator*. It was her choice. He's lost count of the number of times they have seen it together, but she never seems to get tired of it and she always weeps at the end.

They've reached the scene where Oliver Reed is threatening Omid Djalili when the phone rings. Frank clicks the DVD on to hold.

'I'll get it,' she says, then hurries out into the hall.

He can't hear what she's saying through the door. He doesn't need to. There is something heavy about the tone of her voice as well as the quality of the silence in between her words. He knows the relaxing evening is over.

She comes back in, her face creased with worry. 'There's been some trouble. It's on the news. They need you down at the station.'

He grabs the other remote control and flicks through the channels. There are pictures of burning buildings and crowds throwing stones. It seems more like a movie scene than news footage. But the news anchor's voiceover announces that the riot is happening right now in inner-city Leicester. This is live.

The speedometer touches seventy as he motors down the Groby Road, racing towards the city. He breaks hard, puts his hand on the horn and runs the red lights at the Fosse Road junction, then he's accelerating across Frog Island, past the mills and on to the inner ring road.

The initial message said that he was needed in the station, but it feels as if he might do more good on the street. Not many of the other officers will be old enough to remember the riots in 1981. He experienced them directly, using his shield to fend off flying bottles on the front line with the other constables.

So he gets on the radio, finds out who is in command, tells them he's driving to Waterfields. They tell him to approach from the Majestic Park end to bring him in from behind the police lines.

They're regrouping when he gets there, forming a line two deep across the width of the road. Frank finds the commanding officer, an inspector ten years his junior. The man is out of his depth, trying to make decisions on the run, missing the obvious.

'Send another squad fifty paces behind,' Frank shouts.

'I don't have enough men!'

'Then don't send this line in. They'll get surrounded.'

'I can't just leave it!'

'You've got no choice.'

Then Frank runs to the nearest van and starts trying to raise someone who can get enough reinforcements sent in so they can try to stop it spreading.

A quarter of a mile away, Tami is pushing the armchair up behind her door. She heard the outside door being kicked in a few seconds ago. There are men's voices in the hallway downstairs.

She grabs for the light switch, throws the flat into darkness. There is an explosion of breaking glass in the living room, the thump of a brick landing on the floor. She runs to the kitchen, pulls a big vegetable knife from the draining board and flattens herself against the wall.

She hears a woman's scream outside, above the shouts of the riot. Another car alarm starts to shriek. There is a growing light in the room, yellow-red flickering from a fire out on the street below. She dare not go to the window to see what is burning. She can smell the fire already, smoke and fumes drifting in through the broken window. Burning rubber or plastic. Her eyes are stinging.

She gets up on the work unit in the kitchen and tries to release the catch of the window. But it can't have been opened since the last time the flat was decorated. Hard paint seals the gap.

Then there is a new sound. The sudden whoop of a police siren out at the front. The voice of the crowd shifts from exultant to angry. People are running. More glass breaking. Bottles landing in the road perhaps. And now a loudspeaker. A man's voice, commanding, crackling with amplification. *Clear the road. Go back to your homes. Clear the road.*

The smell of burning is stronger now. She clambers off the worktop and runs through the flat to the bathroom. Another window. She grips the catch hard but it won't move either. There is an extractor fan mounted in the middle of the glass. She clicks it on but the air doesn't clear.

Frank Shakespeare is moving along behind the line of advancing police officers. He's scanning the houses on either side of the road, the side streets, doors leading to walkways. Part of his mind is telling him that he was in this road recently, out of uniform. He pushes that thought back.

A bottle lands in the road in front of him, then another one. The line of police officers speeds up to a fast walk. The bulk of the mob ahead of them is starting to retreat. But the hard cases are still at it, darting forward to hurl missiles, then jumping back and becoming part of the anonymous mass.

The police advance turns into a slow run and the mob are scattering. He can see a knot of them regrouping behind a burning car in the road fifty metres ahead. If they could only snatch a couple of those men, the rest might disperse. There are two Tactical Support Unit vans coming up behind.

The advance stops and the line breaks to make room for the vans to pass. Frank watches them accelerate towards the burning barricade. They give a burst of siren, trying to frighten the crowd back further. Then someone is on the megaphone: *Clear the road. Go back to your homes. Clear the road.*

Another three bottles land in quick succession, but the mob are moving back, running full tilt, and the vans are skirting the burning car and giving chase. This bit of the battle is over.

He's right outside Tami's flat. He sees that her door has been kicked in, along with several others on this stretch of road. Most of the windows are broken. There's no time to look in, but if she is there she's going to be really shaken up. He feels some kind of obligation to her. He signals to the officer in charge that he's going in, then he runs, pushing the broken door back and pounding up the stairs.

'Tami?'

There's no answer.

'Tami, are you all right?'

Again no answer. He presses his ear to the door and holds his breath, listening. After a moment he gives up, pulls away and runs back down the stairs to join his comrades.

*

Behind the chair that blocks the door, Tami stands, the knuckles of her hand pressed into her mouth. She listens to Frank Shakespeare's heavy footfalls going back down the stairs and away. And she wishes he didn't do what he just did. The boundary between the good guys and the bad guys is blurred enough for her already.

Chapter 6

Frank looks out to where Inspector Akanbai is waiting.
'Mo, I want you in my office now!'

'Yes, sir.'

She doesn't make a move to come inside.

'Now!'

He's been getting a talking to from the chief constable this morning, in front of a whole cluster of other senior officers. He's not sure why it was that they had to congregate in his office. Possibly because he was the first in this morning. In fact, he didn't make it home at all.

The chief constable gives him a nod and walks from the room. The other officers follow like rats after the Pied Piper.

The trouble is, last night's riot was triggered by a stupid mistake made by a couple of beat police officers. They were waiting outside the Waterfields Youth Club, looking for drug dealers. They did a stop and search on two Asian men and turned up a couple of substantial knives. Frank isn't sure whether the constables knew about the arrangement the police have with the Sikh community. It's not even certain whether the two Asians were wearing their turbans at the time. And the blades themselves were rather longer and more functional than the usual ceremonial item that members of the Sikh faith are obliged to carry by religious

law. But even with all that uncertainty, the officers should
have had the sense to know they were on dangerous ground.

Frank looks at Mo Akanbai. 'Didn't you teach them
anything? We're supposed to have an understanding with
the Sikh community.'

In his fist he holds a half-empty cup of coffee from the
vending machine in the corridor. He drains it into his
mouth. It's cold and tastes of Styrofoam.

'Sir . . .' Mo begins.

'They're talking about seven million in damage,' he tells
her.

She nods, as if accepting the blame. Then she says: 'The
race awareness training scheme would have been good.'

Frank runs a hand back through his hair. He knows
exactly what Mo is talking about. A couple of months back
she put in a request for all the officers who might have any
contact with Waterfields and its inhabitants to be put
through a professionally run training course. He'd refused it.
There wasn't anything spare in the budget. Money again.
That reminds him of his own financial troubles – his
personal bank accounts all but emptied by the blackmailer.

'Well, it's a proper balls-up,' he says, 'in more ways than
one.'

'Yes, sir.'

He is being unfair to his junior officer. He is aware of that.
But the stress of the riot and its aftermath, combined with
the stress of the blackmail, which he is no closer to
resolving, has pushed him towards the edge of what he is
able to cope with. It's been a long night and he knows there
will be a long day of mending fences ahead. Mo is right to
throw some of the blame back in his direction. He softens
his voice.

'The business community need to know we're on the

case. But we don't want too many uniforms out there. Don't want it to look like . . . well . . .'

'An occupying army,' Mo suggests.

Frank drops the Styrofoam cup in the bin. 'Balance,' he says. 'That's what we're after.'

'Yes, sir.'

'I want you out there, Mo. I want more officers with your—' he wants to say with your sensitivity, but that sounds too patronizing. '—with your connections. Get some snapshots done for the *Crusader*.'

'Yes, sir.'

'Police talk to local people. Smiles and handshakes. That sort of thing.'

He watches her leave the office, knowing he handled the interview badly. He was too hard on her, though he thinks she probably appreciated the way he brought her into his confidence at the end.

The phone rings on his desk. He jerks the receiver out of the cradle.

'Yes?'

'I'm trying to reach Frank Shakespeare.' It's a quiet voice – male, but effeminate.

'Superintendent Shakespeare here.'

'This is Ricky.'

Frank can't think of anyone by that name.

'From the phone company,' Ricky adds. 'I was told you wanted to speak to me.'

'From the . . .?' The memory comes back to Frank, and with it a lurching anxiety. 'You shouldn't call me here. It's . . .'

'Untraceable. Don't worry. Discretion assured. You wanted to find the location of a mobile phone?'

'Is it possible?'

'Surely.'

'And can you do it?'

Ricky laughs. 'If you give me the number. But the phone has to be turned on and registered to the network.'

Frank pulls a sheet of paper from his pocket and reads the number out. 'Do you need anything else?'

'Four hundred pounds.'

'I . . . That's too much.'

'Really?' He sounds disappointed.

'Two hundred.'

'Three hundred?'

'Two hundred and fifty.'

Ricky sighs. 'Very well. I'll call you when there's news.'

'Hello. Mr Lloyd? This is Tami. I'm just phoning in so you know why I'm missing the shift. You heard about the riot?'

She hears her manager clearing his throat on the other end of the line. 'I saw the news,' he says.

'It was right outside my door. They turned a car over in the street.'

'I'm sorry,' he says.

'You'll still pay me though. Right?'

'All the others managed to get here.'

'But the police told us to stay indoors!'

His voice drops to little more than a whisper. 'I'm sorry, Tami. It sounds unfair, I know. But there's nothing I can do.'

'I need the money!'

'Look,' he says. 'There's still half the shift left. Come in now. I'll add something when I mark your time card.'

'I can't leave the house. The outside door's smashed. I've got a window broken.'

'It's an upstairs flat,' he reasons. 'No one can get in.'

She finds that she is breathing too fast. She closes her eyes.

'Tami,' he says. 'I can't get them to pay you if you don't

turn up at all. Come in and let me buy you breakfast afterwards. You can tell me all about it. Or I can come back to your
place and you can show me.'

She cuts the connection. Her mobile tells her there is
only another seventy-five pence worth of calls before she'll
have to buy a top-up card. She throws it on to the mattress
then presses her face into the pillow.

She doesn't feel comfortable getting undressed. The
violence of the riot having spilled into her flat has made the
place seem somehow less private. She pulls the quilt over
her and tries to fall asleep, but finds it too hot. She pushes
the covers on to the floor, but then feels too exposed. After
an hour of shifting around on the small bed, she gets up,
turns on all the lights, uses the toilet, then makes herself a
cup of tea. She goes towards the fridge to search for something to snack on, but then pulls away at the last moment
and goes and washes her face instead.

Most of the broken glass is in fragments large enough to
pick up. Tami places them one by one on to the bottom of the
metal wastepaper bin. The smaller pieces she sweeps into a
dustpan, where they lie like hundreds of tiny diamonds. She
will have to wear shoes around the house for a few weeks to be
on the safe side. Next she extracts the angry teeth remaining
in the window frame, pulling them by hand, jiggling each
one free and placing it in the bin. A sheet of thick cardboard
serves to cover the hole. She tapes it in place, then carries all
the sharp and broken things to the bins outside at the back.

The light is growing steadily. The sky has changed
through shades of grey to palest blue. She goes back inside
and surveys her work. It is good. Lying on the bed again, she
does feel tired enough to sleep. She hopes it will be for a
long time. Oblivion is her greatest solace.

*

It is a noise that makes her eyes jolt open. She looks at the clock on the bedside table, expecting it to be mid-morning. But the hands have moved only a fraction from when she lay down. She can't have been out for five minutes.

The noise comes again. A creak from the stairs. With the outside door smashed, anyone could have wandered in from the street. She sits up and starts to rub some wakefulness into her face. But a knock at the door stops her dead.

'Hello?'

It is a woman's voice. Somehow familiar.

Tami creeps to the door.

'Who is it?'

'It's me. Open up.'

The woman on the landing is Rita. She is leaning with one shoulder against the wall, a black holdall and a supermarket carrier bag on the carpet, a raincoat over her arm and a fag between her lips. She's wearing a pink leather jacket, which has almost as many wrinkles and creases as her face.

'Gonna invite me in?' she says, a grin starting to spread.

'Your hair,' Tami says.

'Had it done after I got out.'

'Blonde,' Tami stutters. 'I didn't recognize you.'

'Good, huh? Are you going to let me in or what?'

'It's just that . . . my probation officer . . .'

'Doesn't want you meeting up with your pals from inside. Yeah, yeah.' Rita hefts her shoulder off the wall, picks up her bags and steps forward. 'Fuck that for a laugh.'

Tami finds herself giving way as the woman carries her things inside and slams the door closed with one foot.

'I had a hell of a job tracking you down,' Rita says. 'I could murder a cup of tea. Or a beer if you've got one.'

'Tea,' Tami says.

'Make it strong then. There's a doll.'

Tami fidgets with the mugs while she waits for the kettle to boil. She can hear Rita moving around in the living room. The floorboard creaks. The TV comes on. A flick-through of channels. Random switching. Volume up. Volume down. It clicks off again.

She pours the boiling water, dunks the teabags with a fork.

'How long you had this place?' Rita calls.

'Three months.'

The woman whistles in appreciation. 'Doing well. What about money?'

'I've got a job. It's nothing.'

'Are you straight, then?'

Tami opens the fridge to get the milk. She takes a deep breath of the chill air, staring at the pickle jar. Then she closes the fridge. 'I've been clean for two years.'

She carries the mugs back into the living room and finds Rita looking through the pile of envelopes on the table. They are all business letters: a gas bill, Housing Benefit claim forms, letters from the probation service. But the sense of intrusion makes her stomach feel as if it is shrivelling to the size of a prune. 'Here,' she says, holding out a mug.

Rita grins at her. 'You're really doing it, eh. Really going straight.'

'I'm trying.'

'And your probation officer's OK?'

'She wants to help,' Tami says. 'What about yours?'

'He's a bastard. But stupid, too. Told him I had to go see my aunt in Leicester and he didn't even check up on it or anything. It'll just be for a couple of days, then I'm back to Brighton and out of your hair.'

'You want to stay?'

Rita sits herself on the chair and leans back. For a moment it looks as if she is going to get angry. Then she shakes her head and smiles. 'You should see your face, girl!'

'I'm sorry. It's just the shock.'

Rita starts to giggle and then to laugh out loud. 'For a moment there I thought you were gonna throw me out on the street.'

'My probation officer . . .'

'Won't find out. A couple of nights is all I need. I'm too old to do tricks on the street, Tami. Hell. I know it's hard for you – being reminded of it all – but I got nowhere else to go.'

Tami is standing in the middle of the room, clutching her mug. She watches the other woman get up and step towards her. Rita takes the mug out of her hand and places it on the table. Then she takes Tami's hand and rotates it so the wrist is facing up. She pushes back the sleeve and Tami feels the other woman's finger tracing the scars.

'Me coming here makes you remember,' Rita says. 'That's why it looked like you were sucking a lemon when you saw me outside your door. But I can't go and sleep in a doorway – not after that riot. Too dangerous tonight. I'd be raped and killed.' Her breath smells of tobacco. 'You couldn't live with that. Could you, Tami?'

The first thing that Rita does, after she has sloughed off the pink leather jacket, is unpack all her stuff in a corner of the living room. Clothes mostly, and piles of cheap jewellery. Tami watches the chaos expanding as the carrier bag contents spill out on the carpet of her recently tidied room. Make-up. A set of white towels – the kind that hotels and guesthouses use. Two glass ashtrays. The creeping sense of powerlessness is making Tami feel nauseous.

Rita moves over to the sink in the kitchenette and starts

to freshen herself up. Water on the face, around the back of the neck, under the armpits.

'I need some kip, Tami.'

'OK.'

'I'll bunk down on your bed, OK?'

'OK.'

Tami watches, paralysed, as the other woman kicks off her heels and stretches out.

'Wake me in a couple of hours.' Rita coughs once, flashes a smile, then turns over to face the wall and lies still. Her breathing slows, almost immediately falling into a sleep pattern. And still Tami stands watching.

She remembers the day she met Rita. In fact, she remembers the exact moment. It was in the learning suite in her second prison. She'd been inside for two months and they'd just moved her up north. The initial shocked denial was beginning to turn into a more pragmatic sense of resignation. She was getting by. Living a day at a time had worn her down. She was starting to look forward to things. Setting goals for the week – just like the chaplain had suggested. So she signed up to study towards two GCSE qualifications. English and maths. If she managed those, there would be other opportunities. There might be art lessons if a teacher became available.

She sat at a desk with the textbook in front of her. She'd learned enough on the market stall to make the simple calculations easy enough. But this was going to take her into subjects such as algebra, which she'd only known as a name before. She was looking down at the page, at the lines of letters and numbers. And a voice behind her said: 'You've taken my Biro.'

She turned around and saw one of the other prisoners staring needles at her. This was someone she'd managed to avoid but had heard about. Joy was her name. A sinewy woman with rose tattoos on her upper arms and eyes disconcertingly far apart – as if there was something slightly wrong with the way her face was put together, though not enough so that it would be obvious.

'Give it back.'

'I didn't take anything,' Tami said. But she was already beyond the point of no return.

'Are you calling me a liar?'

'No.'

'Then give – it – back!'

On that last word 'back' at the moment it hit the end, Joy's hand struck out, grabbing the pen from Tami's hand, and in the same movement stabbing the ballpoint upwards towards her face. It happened so fast that there was no pain. Just the sickening feeling of the tip embedded in her cheek, the pen still hanging there. Tami reached up and eased it out. She could hear herself screaming. Somehow she'd got to her feet and the bloody pen was clasped in her hand like a dagger. And then she was moving forward, drawing her hand back to lunge. And Joy was grinning at her, as if this was exactly what she wanted – which it probably was. Tami would have been no match for her in strength or fighting cunning.

That's when Rita stepped into the gap between them. Her hair was short in those days and jet black. But the wrinkles were the same. The weathered skin. The tan that could only have come out of a bottle – there was no other opportunity to catch the sun in that holiday camp.

'Sit fucking down!' Rita shouted.

Tami stopped dead.

Joy lunged again, pushing Rita out of the way. And then the warders came rushing in. Tami found that she was still screaming.

Tami told the full story to the governor. But Rita was still carted off to a cell in solitary along with the real instigator of the fight. And Tami found herself in the sickroom with stitches in her face, a sore buttock from a tetanus jab and a couple of pills in a plastic beaker, which the doctor said were tranquillizers and would stop her shaking. She took them. It was two days before she pulled herself properly back to the real world and got her eyes to focus again. But the doctor was right about the shaking. It had stopped.

The other inmates steered clear of Tami after that. Probably because they knew the fight would be resumed after Joy was out of solitary. The woman had re-established herself as someone to be respected. No one wanted to be near the scene when that happened. No one except Rita.

She was out after three days. She went straight to Tami and told her that next time she shouldn't say anything. Leave it to the screws to sort out what had happened. But don't grass up another prisoner. Even if it happened to be Joy. This was the beginning of Tami's real education. Rita took charge, told her what to do and what not to do, which of the other prisoners to trust and which of the warders to go to for help.

Rita's family came from Eastern Europe somewhere, though she herself had been brought up on a council estate in Reading. She'd been in and out of care homes since she was twelve and knew how things worked in the real world.

Joy was out by now and making her presence felt. The fight seemed to have given her extra leverage with the others. People gave way to her. Even the warders – though this was such a subtle thing that Tami would not have seen it without Rita pointing it out.

Tami finds herself in her own flat, standing in the kitchenette, her hands in the sink, rubbing a scouring pad around the lip of a mug, trying to scratch away the print of Rita's cherry lipstick. The mark fades. Then it has gone. She rinses with cold water and upturns the mug on the draining board. Her back and legs feel clammy with sweat.

Realizing it is morning already, she clicks the light off. There is a pressure inside her skull that must come from all the lost sleep. All she wants to do is curl up somewhere and close her eyes. But the bed is occupied. *Her* bed, she reminds herself. Her own flat. With her own keys to lock and unlock the front door. She doesn't want to walk out and leave the woman in control of her things, her own space. But she feels so claustrophobic now that she has no choice. It's walk or explode.

She straps her watch to her wrist and picks up the keys. Twenty minutes should be safe. Rita won't have woken up in that time. She scrawls a 'back soon' note on an old envelope and balances it on top of the kettle – just in case. Then she picks up her purse and leaves, using the key to stop the lock making a click as she closes the door.

None of the signs of damage that Tami sees on the street would have been so shocking in themselves. It is the cumulative impression of chaos they convey that touches her as she walks. Broken windows. Kicked in doors. Two burned-out cars. The remnants of a barricade across the middle of the road, including the metal frame of a bed, a smashed bicycle. A couple of road signs. Car tyres melted and charred.

It is seven in the morning already, but there are few people on the street. The emptiness is eerie. She comes to a junction and chooses the road that seems less touched by the riot. Some of the businesses here have escaped. A Muslim shopkeeper hefts a box of apples from the back of a van and lays it with more boxes of fruit and vegetables on the pavement.

Tami looks into her purse and finds a £5 note. Money she has earned.

Carrying a bag of apples, she makes her way through the terraced streets, turning left, then right then left again. There is nothing to see here. No objective in her choices except as a token proof of her capacity to make decisions for herself. She carries on the random journey and comes to a corner park that she doesn't remember seeing before. There is a wooden bench here, a wastebin, a crab apple tree and a rowan. She sits and selects the greenest of the apples, polishes it on her jeans, then takes a bite. She looks at the iron railings as she chews. There is a curled and yellowed sheet of newspaper caught in the undergrowth beneath it. She checks her watch. She's only been out of the flat ten minutes. She takes another bite of apple, wondering why she chose the least appetizing one to start with. Perhaps it is habit. Saving the treat. Leaving something to look forward to. She tries to relax into enjoying the juice of it in her mouth. Concentrating on the 'now'. But after ten years living on deferred gratification, it is hard to taste it at all.

Instead she thinks about the woman sleeping in her bed. Rita. The woman who saved her life. How many times was it? It depends how she calculates it. Joy could have killed her only once. But there were many occasions when it might have happened. Times when Tami would feel Rita's hand on her arm, guiding her towards the protection of a security camera or into the view of one of the tougher warders. She would look around, and there would be Joy approaching with a couple of her hangers-on.

The impression Tami has is that Joy's attempts to break her neck were an almost daily occurrence. But when she really fixes them in her mind and counts, she can remember only four narrowly missed assaults over a period of three months. It was the fear that was constant.

It may have started with Joy wanting to demonstrate her power for everyone else to see. One fellow prisoner crippled would win a certain kind of respect from the other two hundred and thirty. Or it could have been Tami's refusal to have anything to do with drugs – Joy's main business venture on the inside. Or perhaps it was that Joy came from Leicester and took a dim view of people from her home town. Or any one of another hundred possible motives. But every failed attempt at making Tami suffer seemed to be taken by Joy as a personal slight. The reasons mounted. There must have come a point where the original motivation was so dwarfed by everything that had happened since as to become irrelevant.

Midway through the afternoon and the civilian staff are getting fidgety, looking at their watches. It is the usual Friday-afternoon psychology. But from where Frank is sitting there doesn't seem to be any prospect of getting home. The riots are bad enough. But now it is emerging that half the criminals in the East Midlands must have taken the opportunity to make hay while the forces in blue were stretched out across the streets of Waterfields being pelted with broken bottles. As well as the petty stuff, there was a major theft of designer clothing from a factory and a race hate attack against the Dean Street Mosque.

The only good thing is that Frank hasn't had time to worry about the blackmail photograph. He tries to cheer himself with the thought that the blackmailer might have been caught up in the riots in some way.

Frank rubs his hands over his face, wondering what he should do next. All the officers under his command have their instructions now. He needs to call a few people on the phone – do a bit of reassuring and smoothing of feathers.

He flicks through his address book and pulls out the numbers of the contacts he wants to try. The first is the *Crusader*, the local paper. But the PA he gets through to says that there's not much possibility of speaking to the editor in the next two or three hours.

Then comes the question: 'What shall I tell him that it is concerning?'

'The . . . disturbance last night.'

'The riot, you mean?'

'Well, if the editor does become available, could you get him to call me, please?'

'Perhaps you'd like to speak to the crime correspondent?'

Frank shudders. 'No. No, thank you.'

He cuts the call and moves on through the list of people who need talking to. None of them is available. He starts to think that perhaps they are all talking to each other about the inefficiency and insensitivity of the police force.

He puts the phone down and closes the address book. He reaches across the desk to where his coffee should be, then remembers he's finished it. There are already five empty Styrofoam cups in the bottom of the bin, so he shouldn't really go back into the corridor and get another one out of the machine. He holds his hand out in front of him. The tremor will recede once he gets enough sleep.

Sleep. That's what he really needs.

His desk phone rings. That probably means more trouble. But he picks up anyway. It's Mo Akanbai's voice on the other end of the line. She was at the Dean Street Mosque this morning when the race hate crime was discovered. The prayer hall was desecrated. The accounts he has heard make it sound pretty horrible. A butchered pig. Blood everywhere.

She is probably shaken up, though she'd never admit it.

'Mo,' he says. 'Heard you had some trouble this morning.'

'Yes, sir. And there's going to be more.'

There is a knock on Frank's office door. His secretary is hovering there, hands clasped in front of her.

'Hold on . . .' Frank says into the phone.

The secretary looks at her watch. 'I've done the letters. If there isn't anything else . . .?'

He nods and she hurries away, as if she thinks he might change his mind.

'Sorry about that, Mo. You were saying?'

'The Muslim community, sir . . .'

'You should know that it's going to be very different tonight. We're prepared. There's going to be low-key surveillance of all the flash-points. And we'll have support units in place. We can be in there and breaking up trouble before it has a chance to get going.'

'This is something different, sir. The Muslim community. They're outraged by what happened today. Rightly so.'

He clears his throat. 'Mo . . .'

'They need to know we're taking it seriously.' She sounds stressed.

'It must have been very . . . well, upsetting for them,' Frank says. 'You too. But it's out of our jurisdiction. We've got to hand this one over to Race Crime. It's CID's property from here on.'

'Sir. If the Muslim community don't think we're serious . . . I'm just worried that some of them might try to take the law into their own hands.'

Frank really doesn't want to be dealing with this kind of inter-departmental jealousy. He tries to think of something to say that will make her feel less sore about losing what she clearly thinks of as her own case.

Then the phone in his pocket starts ringing. 'Hold on a moment,' he says, putting his fingers over the mouthpiece and pulling out the mobile.

'Yes?'

'Mr Shakespeare?' It's the voice of Ricky from the phone company. Sounding soft and breathy. 'I thought you'd like to know, the phone switched on half an hour ago. It made a very brief call – probably a text message – and then switched off again.'

'Where was he?'

'I'm sorry. He may be on to you. He was in the middle of Victoria Park. Bye now,' Ricky breathes. Then the phone cuts.

Frank uncovers the mouthpiece of the desk phone. 'Sorry about that, Mo.'

'Sir, I think . . .'

'It's out of our hands,' he says. All he wants to do now is get her off the line. But his mind won't come fully back from the blackmailer. Frank knows he should have asked what number the call was made to. He needs to disengage from Mo and dismiss her. He also needs to sound normal, but he can't get his mind to focus. 'I expect the Race Crime Unit will . . . when they get around to it . . . they'll want to interview you.'

He knows he needs to change the subject or he'll never be able to get her off the phone. 'Mo,' he says. 'Everything that happened . . . Have you made an appointment with the counsellor?'

'I . . . no. No need.'

'Good. Now, this afternoon. Start to make arrangements with the schools. We'll need people out doing the Monday-morning assemblies. Find out where that kid . . . the one who ran out in front of the fire engine . . .'

'Roddy Wellan, sir.'

'Indeed. Find out which school he goes to.' His words are starting to flow now. His breathing is coming easier. He glances at the mobile in his briefcase.

'What about the Dean Street Mosque?' she asks.

'And the *Crusader*, Mo. Had those pictures taken yet?'

'I . . . no. But I think . . .'

'It's important. Take Sergeant Patel with you. Try to get someone prominent . . . one of the local community leaders. A handshake outside the Afro-Caribbean Centre. It's the symbolism we're after.'

He hears her take a deep breath. 'It's Friday . . .'

'I'll twist some arms, try to get your picture in the Saturday edition.'

'I mean the mosques, sir. They'll be full tonight after sunset. That means crowds of Muslim men. Thousands. All angry.'

'We are prepared, inspector. Everything that can be done is being done.'

'Yes, sir.'

'Steer clear of Dean Street, inspector.'

He hangs up before she can get in another protest.

He feels over-aware of his heartbeat, of its heaviness, of the slight irregularities in its rhythm. He pulls the blackmailer's Nokia from his briefcase and clicks it on. It connects to the network. The screen display has the flashing mail icon. *You have 1 message waiting. Read message now?* He presses the button and the words scroll.

Thanks for the 10,000.
Same again by Thursday.

Tami tries to go back to the flat but as she walks down the street towards the front door a feeling of dread begins to build inside her. It is as if she is walking back towards the prison. By the time she is halfway there, the anxiety of having Rita loose in the flat is less than the distress she gets from imagining herself talking to the woman again. So she turns around and walks into the city centre. She walks for a long time. It is evening before she can bring herself to go back home again.

The outside door has not been mended. This is no surprise. She steps over a fat binbag that has somehow found its way inside, then climbs the stairs to her own door. It is ajar. She feels an involuntary surge of anger. She's worked hard for the little she has. Trying to hold things together. Rita just swans into her life, then swans out of the flat without even bothering to close the door behind her. It would have locked automatically.

Tami reaches her hand out to push her way inside, but then feels the first emotion draw back and a second one wash forward to replace it. Fear. In the time the door has been open, anyone could have entered. They could be waiting for her. They could have listened to her coming up the stairs from the street and be listening to her breathing right at this moment.

She bends her knees, lowering the shopping towards the ground. The plastic bags crinkle as they touch the carpet. Tins of food clank against each other. She lets go and stands. Her fingers touch the door, pushing it open. She can see Rita's pink leather jacket hanging on a peg in the corridor. She steps over the threshold, intensely aware that every movement makes a sound. Fabric touching on fabric. The breath flowing in and out of her mouth. She is halfway to the living room now and already knows that something is wrong. The magazines that she neatly piled next to the gas fire have been scattered over the floor in front of her.

The chair is upended, four legs pointing up and across the room.

Another step and her view widens, taking in the whole room. The place has been ransacked. Every object turned over. She steps again and hears the crack of something breaking under her foot. A plastic spoon. There are tea towels here as well.

The kitchenette. Tami's gaze snaps through the doorway to the fridge under the work surface. It is closed, though several of the cupboards are open. She steps between her scattered possessions, picks her way across the room, over boxes of economy teabags and tins of beans. She stoops and opens the fridge. The chill air rolls out over her. Right at the back, the pickle jar remains untouched. Exactly where she left it. She reaches out a hand and feels the cold glass.

It's only now she becomes aware that her skin is covered in a film of sweat. The fine hairs on her arms are standing. She feels the cool start to work its way into her.

Her flat has been searched by someone, though she can't think what anyone could want from her. She has nothing here of value.

She remembers the warders in prison picking through her belongings, searching for drugs. That was just humiliating. But there she knew what was happening. Here she feels defiled and frightened. Suddenly she remembers the front door, which she left open ready for a quick exit. She hurries back and slams it closed, clicking the catch into the lock position. The living room and kitchenette are secure. She checks the bathroom and then the bedroom. Again, everything is closed. Whoever it was that desecrated her space must have entered and exited through the front door.

It is as she is pushing the biggest chair up the corridor to use as a barricade that she hears the noise. It's like a sigh. On the edge of audibility. She snaps her head around, looking back into the room. It was so faint that it could easily have come from the street outside – but there was something about it that felt close. She holds her breath. A second later she hears it again. A gasped breath.

If she tries to pull the chair away from the door again, she is going to have to turn her back on the room. So she steps forward instead, putting her head to the corner where the passage meets the living room. The sound comes a third time. It is no louder than before, but now she knows what she is looking for, she can tell that it is coming from the bedroom.

She steps towards it. Advancing across the floor. Not letting her eyes shift from the edge of the bed, knowing that the sound is coming from behind it. She stoops and picks up a wooden stool, holding it by two legs, ready to swing it like a club.

'Come out!' she says, her voice sounding shrill to her own ears.

Another sigh. A shifting and scraping sound, as if something is dragging across the carpet.

'Now!' she shouts.

She is at the bottom of the bed. Tensed. Taking a final sidestep. Edging around to see an arm, then a body curled up in a foetal position. Rita, opening her mouth to gasp like a fish drowning in air.

Tami never did a first-aid course, but she knows that the sound of whimpering must mean that Rita is breathing. And there is no sign of blood. Tami runs her hands over her friend's body, though she doesn't know what she is looking for.

Rita recoils with each touch – as if Tami's fingers are hot irons.

'What happened?'

No answer.

Tami hauls her friend on to the bed. Rita screws her eyes tight closed, as if the light is attacking her. Her clothes are soaked in sweat. Her face is bluey-white.

'I'll get a doctor.'

'No.'

Rita is moving her head from side to side.

'What's wrong?'

'My head.'

'You want aspirin?'

'Codeine,' Rita whispers.

There is a chemist's shop around the corner from Tami's flat. The pharmacist is an Asian man. He tells her they don't sell codeine any more because it is addictive – but there is a drug with a little of it in, mixed with other pain killers.

'What do you want it for?' he asks.

'A friend.'

He sucks his lower lip for a moment. 'Why does she want it?'

'A migraine,' Tami tells him.

He nods slowly, then takes a packet from the shelf behind him. 'Read the instructions. No more than four doses a day.'

She starts running back to the flat, clutching the box in her hand. Then she slows to a walk. She lets her breathing slow as well. She climbs the stairs, thinking of Rita's transformation. Tami has seen the same symptoms before, though never so strong or with such a sudden onset.

Rita is still on the bed, in the same position. She seems asleep, but when Tami runs a hand over her forehead the eyes open.

'It's heroin, right?' Tami asks.

Rita tries to grab the box of pills. 'Please.'

'When did you last use?'

'So sorry . . .'

'When?'

'Two days.'

Tami slides the blister pack out of the box and pops two pills into the palm of her hand. She can see Rita's watery eyes on them, the pupils dilated unnaturally wide. 'What were you looking for when you searched the flat?'

Rita snivels, reaches for the pills. 'I'll die . . .'

'Tell me and I'll give them to you.'

Rita's face crumples. She screws her eyes closed as if she is going to burst into tears. Then they snap open, full of anger. 'Fucking whore! I saved your life! You fucking, fucking bitch!' Droplets of phlegm spit from her mouth with each word.

'And now I'm saving you. So answer me.'

Rita's eyes are closed again and she is sobbing, shivering. 'Needed money,' she wails. 'Need it so bad. You don't know. Just one more shot. I'll tell you. Please. Please. Please.'

Tami wants to give her the painkillers, but there is something in Rita's words that holds her back. 'What will you tell me?'

'Everything. The whole story.'

'Start speaking.'

Rita sniffs and runs a hand under her nose. Her arm is covered in goosebumps. 'Was looking for money,' she says. 'That's all. Please help me.'

There is more to come. Tami can feel it. Her own skin is tightening across her forehead and chest. She holds the pills out – just beyond Rita's grasp.

'Didn't mean it,' Rita wails. 'Wasn't my fault. I was in prison. He told me to keep it secret.'

'Who?'

Rita starts pulling herself across the bed, grasping handfuls of quilt, as if she might topple over otherwise. Her eyes are fixed on the pills. Tami stands and backs away.

'I'll give them to you. But first tell me the rest. Were you working for someone? Is that it?'

Rita cringes at the words, shakes her head, collapses back to the bed, weeping again. And in the midst of the sobs Tami hears the name that she could not have guessed – though she instantly knows it is true.

'Jack.'

Tami echoes the name, her voice a croaking whisper. 'Jack.'

Rita is shivering worse than before. The sheen of sweat on her arms catches the light from the bedroom window.

'What did you do for Jack?'

No answer. There doesn't need to be one. Tami already knows. The name from Rita's mouth has uncorked the obvious truth.

'He paid you to protect me in prison.'

Rita begins crawling along the bed again. She suddenly appears to Tami like some unhuman creature. She feels disgust flooding through her. All she wants to do is throw the pills down on the quilt and run.

'What was Jack doing all that time?' she asks.

Rita's dilated pupils blaze again. She lunges forward, scrambling across on to the floor, spitting and swearing. Tami turns and runs into the living room. She wants to put the spilled coffee table between them, but her foot lands on a magazine and she slips. The impact with the floor knocks the breath out of her. Then Rita is on her back, scratching and pulling at the hand that holds the pills. Tami feels her fingers being prised apart. She throws her weight to the left and rolls, spilling the other woman on to the floor. Then she scrambles away, preparing for the next onslaught. But the fury has drained from Rita's body. She curls up where she lies.

'I hurt so bad. Please help me.'

Tami is still winded but she knows this is the only chance she will get to ask the question. She draws as deep a breath as she can manage. 'What was . . . what was Jack doing . . . when I was in prison?'

Rita looks up, agony on her face. And Tami suddenly sees her as human again. She holds out the pills and watches Rita hungrily grab them and stuff them into her mouth.

The painkillers can't start working for half an hour at least, but Rita seems to relax as soon as she swallows. She curls up on the floor again and closes her eyes, spilling tears across her face. It seems as if she is withdrawing into herself again, but when she speaks it is strangely lucid.

'He was hunting,' she whispers.

'Hunting what? Hunting who?'

'The one who framed you. It was like he was insane.'

PART TWO

I see him like he's in a fog. Jack. My own Jack. Backed up against a wall. His hands are feeling the rough brick behind him. I am standing by his shoulder. And though his face is turned away from me, I know his dark hair must be sticking to his forehead. There will be droplets of water beading on his eyelashes. His pupils will be dilated. And if he would only turn his head, I would be able to see them. Circles of perfect black.

He is waiting for someone. Or hiding from danger. Or chasing his fantasy. In my dream, all I know is the dread he feels. I am inside his eyes. I am riding the quickening fear that thunders through his arteries.

Then he is running away and I am calling, begging him to stop. It is as if he never betrayed me. As if I really want him back. It is my favourite nightmare.

It is my scream that wakes me.

Chapter 7

The fifth of May, 1988. Cold air but bright. Dexy's Midnight Runners playing on the car radio. Superintendent Kringman smoking his third since they pulled into the lay-by. Frank tried winding down his window, but the super complained that he was getting hay fever from all the long grass on the road verges. A thread of blue-grey smoke drifted across next to the windscreen, back-lit by the sun.

'Are you nervous?' the superintendent asked.

'No.'

'Well, you're a fool then, Shakespeare.'

Frank had learned that silence was the safest response to most situations where he didn't know what to say. All he had to do was project a hint of swagger and people would assume he knew more than he did. But not too much confidence or they would challenge him. Try to knock him off his perch. No one liked a smartarse.

'Well?' Kringman demanded. 'What are you smiling about?'

Frank kept his eyes on the road ahead and the same passive amusement on his face. And inside he chewed over what the superintendent had said. He knew that some of the men they were dealing with were dangerous. A couple of them might have killed before – though only one had served time for it. But at a meeting like this, he didn't think there was any chance of things getting badly out of hand. They all knew each other too well for that.

'You think I'm wrong,' Kringman said, speaking into the silence. 'You think it's just about guns.' Then he looked at his watch and stubbed his cigarette out in the ashtray. 'It's time.'

Frank fired up the engine, suddenly uncertain. He rolled the car out of the lay-by and eased down on the accelerator. The road was busy with bank holiday traffic and they were quickly at the back of a queue, stuck behind a caravan and a couple of drivers who seemed content to dawdle along enjoying the rolling hills of Charnwood.

Frank's eyes flicked to the digital clock on the dashboard. They were already five minutes late. He edged out into the middle of the road and dropped the car into third gear, preparing to overtake. There was nothing coming, so he upped the revs and hopped out, quickly passing the first and second cars. Perversely, this was the moment the driver hauling the caravan decided to speed up, pulling away from the queue. Frank was still accelerating, but the race was eating up the road between him and the blind bend a hundred metres ahead. He pressed his foot into the metal and started to inch past the caravan and the Volvo that was pulling it. That was when a lorry rounded the bend, horn blasting. Frank willed his car to go faster. He didn't know if he was past the Volvo, but he pulled in anyway. The lorry's horn Doppler-shifted, and the car was sent rocking as it crossed into the slipstream. The Volvo driver – who from Frank's point of view had caused the near accident – was flashing his headlights and waving his fist.

Kringman snorted a laugh. 'Dangerous,' he said.

Frank put his foot hard on the brake, bringing the speedometer needle down to thirty. He could see the Volvo driver in the mirror, one finger raised. He wound down the window and reached for the police light to put on the roof. He wanted to make the man sweat.

'No,' Kringman said.

Frank took a deep breath. 'We're late already. Five minutes more won't hurt.'

'We're exactly late enough.'

'People like that should roast in hell.'

'He probably will.'

Frank bit down on his youthful anger and eased his foot on to the accelerator, pulling away. The Volvo driver was still flashing his lights behind them. Frank rounded the bend and once again he had an empty road in the rear-view.

They arrived at the lay-by rendezvous nine minutes and fifty seconds after the time the meeting was scheduled to start. Frank walked level with his superintendent as they approached the group of men. He knew all the faces well enough. But after three months of individual meetings, it was the first time he had seen them all together. They made a curious assemblage.

Bill Arnica stood scowling in the middle. The centre of attention, as usual. That was the way he seemed to like things. Perhaps that was why he had gone into local politics way back when. He was the kind of person who had been in his post so long that no one would think of voting for anyone else. Kringman had told him it was because that seat in the local council chamber had worn to Arnica's shape. No other arse would fit.

On the left of him stood Eddie Piper, nightclub security consultant, one-time amateur boxing champion. He was there because of his work as a surprisingly light-fingered entrepreneur.

On the right was Owen. Tall and thin with his coppery

hair tied back in a ponytail. Jeans and T-shirt. Quick eyes, always jumping from face to face. Red Owen, they called him. He was the man who knew the price of everything. Also its value. Or at least how much each individual would be prepared to sacrifice to get it. Buying and selling was his business. Discretion always assured.

And to his right, standing at just enough distance to show that he did not belong to the same club as the other three, was the man they called Bird's Eye – because he looked like the sea captain from the fish finger advert. White beard, blue blazer. Everything but the jolly smile. Bird's Eye was a real businessman. The kind who could declare his earnings to the tax man. He was in the cash loan and repossession business so, even though he was widely hated, the economy of the St John's estate couldn't really have functioned without him.

Kringman advanced towards them, shaking Bill Arnica's hand first, then working around the group. Frank followed in the same order, ending up with Bird's Eye.

'Where are the others?' the captain asked.

'Late,' Superintendent Kringman answered. 'But that's good. It gives us a chance to get some things straight.'

He had their attention. Frank could see the body language, everyone angling themselves towards the superintendent, edging forward to close the distance.

'We all know what needs to happen,' Kringman said.

Bill Arnica nodded. 'It's for the good of the city.'

'You can drop the political speeches,' Kringman said. 'In present company, at least.'

'I do what I do for the good of St John's. And I don't give a shit for what you think about that, Superintendent holier-than-bloody-thou Kringman.'

Bird's Eye coughed into his fist. 'This isn't helping. We've all got our reasons. Let's just be happy we're on the same team for once. There's no other way to keep hard drugs out of the St John's estate. That's all that matters. We don't have to pretend to like each other.'

That's when the last two vehicles pulled up. A shining black Mercedes and a white van, onto the dirty side panel of which someone had finger-painted the words: *I Wish My Bird Was This Dirty.*

Gabriel got out of the Mercedes. He was a Russian, people said – though no one seemed sure. Jack and John Steel emerged from the van. They nodded greetings. Most people shook hands with most, though Frank noted that Arnica avoided contact with either of the Steels. The hardest grip was Gabriel's. Frank felt the bones in his hand grind against each other. In the width of the man's chest he could see what he thought might have been the bulge of a shoulder holster. So much for Kringman saying the danger wouldn't be from guns.

'So,' said Gabriel. He was smiling, though he must have understood that the meeting had been called for the purpose of controlling his activities, and the activities of others like him. 'You are all happy for this, yes? Then it is good.'

Bill Arnica didn't reflect Gabriel's smile. But then he was never the baby-kissing type of politician. He always said he loved society, but he never hid his distaste for the people who made it up. 'You get out of St John's,' he said. 'That's the only thing that'll make me happy.'

'I don't get out,' said Gabriel. 'I sell other things instead. Hashish is still good. This is the agreement.'

'But no heroin or crack,' said Kringman. 'Between us, we'll know if anyone starts. And if someone does break the rule we'll all turn on him. We'll crush him.' He twisted his heel into the ground as he spoke, making loose chippings of gravel crackle and scratch against the tarmac.

John Steel wasn't smiling either. He was the nearest thing the group had to an honest broker. He wasn't directly involved in the drug trade. And he certainly wasn't involved in law enforcement. Jack was standing just behind and to one side of his father. He fixed Gabriel with his eyes. 'I know why I want this,' he said. 'But why do you?'

'You don't trust me?'

'Give me a reason to trust.'

'I tell you then,' Gabriel said. 'I do business in every city. And the police hunt me everywhere. Like a dog. But here . . . here I will be safe. Because you and you—' he pointed to Kringman and Frank '—will tell me if they come looking. So here the Russian dog can hide.'

'We'll be watching,' John said.

'Now you understand me,' Gabriel said. 'But tell me this – why turn off the tap? You make the junkies go crazy with this agreement. They will die for smack.'

'Then they can be crazy in someone else's city,' Arnica said, jabbing his finger towards Gabriel's chest.

'Shakespeare!'

The chief constable's voice jerks Frank back into the present. He finds himself standing in a corridor in the police station. Daydreaming. He silently berates himself for letting his guard slip. Dawn is coming up after a second long night of violence on the streets. He is physically and mentally exhausted.

'Shakespeare!'

Frank fixes a smile in place and turns to face his boss.

'Sir?'

'We need a word.'

The chief is always abrupt. But this sounds worse than usual. Frank follows him into one of the small side offices off the main corridor. During the week it is occupied by a civilian accountant, but at this time on Saturday morning it's a good place to talk with no danger of being interrupted.

'Door,' the chief says.

Frank closes it behind him and waits for whatever roasting he's about to get.

The chief bares his sharp, white teeth. 'I need your angle on the riot.'

Frank shakes his head. There is no way to articulate the despair he feels about the events of the night. A pitched battle between the police and a usually law-abiding section of the community. 'There was a racist crime,' he says, knowing his words are a horrible understatement for the desecration of the Dean Street Mosque. 'And there were troublemakers from out of town. If it had been just the local community, it wouldn't have happened like that. And I don't think it'll happen again.'

Saying more isn't going to explain the events of the night away, so Frank closes his mouth.

After a pause the chief says: 'We've got trouble.' He points his finger heavenwards. There must have been a phone call from the Home Secretary's office.

'It's a balls-up,' Frank agrees.

'There'll be suspensions.'

The chief seems to be waiting for a response, so Frank says: 'We could start an inquiry. That would give us enough time to let things quieten down. It'll all look . . . well, not so bad once a year's past. Assuming mistakes were made, that is.'

'Were they?'

'Maybe,' he says, though the answer should be *yes*. A catalogue of small errors combined to make something that could easily look like one very big mistake. 'Could we handle the inquiry ourselves?' Frank asks.

'It's out of our hands. Might be another force. Or a judge. Trouble either way.'

'I'm sorry.'

The chief shakes his head. 'Don't be. Not for me. I'm not going to be left holding the pearl-handled revolver. This city needs me. Remember that.'

There is a long pause, during which it sinks in to Frank's mind that the chief never uses sarcasm and therefore he is being serious. He really believes that saving his own hide is going to be a virtuous act. And there's no doubt that the man is well capable of protecting himself.

They haven't broken eye contact yet, and Frank doesn't want to be the one to flinch first. When he can't hold it any more, he says: 'Why are you telling me this, sir?'

'Give you time to think. Who's it going to be? I'll dump you if I have to, Shakespeare. But give me another name and I'll think about it.'

The chief gives the briefest of nods, then marches to the door and out. Frank stands, listening to the heel clicks receding. A door swings at the end of the corridor and all is quiet. He remains in the empty office for a long time after that, his mind hopping through the permutations of his future. None of them looks good. He wonders how many other people the chief has had the same conversation with, and what his real motives are. It seems unlikely that the man is just trying to be decent. Perhaps it is that he knows who he doesn't want to lose and is giving his favourites a chance to find a way out.

There is an echo in that thought of the chief's own brassy claim. Does the Leicestershire Constabulary really need Superintendent Frank Shakespeare?

He waits until there is no sound of movement from the corridor, then leaves the small office himself, closing the door quietly behind him. He needs time and space to think things through. But he knows he doesn't have access to either of those luxuries.

He slows as he walks, coming to a stop next to a rack of wall-mounted pigeonholes. His secretary usually empties his for him after the post arrives in the morning. But he sees a slip of paper waiting. It must be internal. He takes it out and unfolds it.

> *Thanks for listening to my warning about tension in the Muslim community – i.e. the danger they might believe that the police are not following their case seriously enough and so take the law into their own hands. I will leave the matter to the Race Crime Unit as you have instructed, though I must admit that I'd prefer Community Relations to be involved.*

His eye skims to the bottom of the page. It is signed Mo Akanbai. He thinks back, trying to work out what the memo is really about. There was a conversation with Mo. She phoned him before the second riot. He can't remember what they talked about – he'd been distracted at the time.

Instead of heading back to his own office, he turns around and walks to the Community Relations Unit. Mo might be there – even though it is the weekend. But the room is empty.

When things are going well, office politics is directed towards the need to be seen, to be prominent, to have your name on every report. But when there is trouble the process is instantly reversed.

Frank finds that he is standing next to Mo's filing cabinet. The key is in the lock. He has an impulse to turn it, to look through her papers and search for evidence of the inspector protecting herself. Or evidence that might implicate her. Not that he would necessarily use it – but it would be good to know what was there.

The lift winches hum in the distance, breaking the silence. Feeling himself starting to blush, he walks across the room to her partitioned-off office. He sits in her chair and swivels it from side to side. The room smells of her. He still has the memo in his hand. He raises it to his nose and inhales but can smell only copier paper.

Thanks for listening to my warning . . .

The phrases she has used in the memo make his lack of action sound particularly damning. She is being oh-so-helpful. By implication, he is the blockage that has stopped her good advice from getting through. This kind of document would become evidence in any inquiry.

It suddenly occurs to him that she might have put this memo in his pigeonhole during the night – after the riot started. It could be a ploy to save herself from blame, dropping him in the mire in the process. He gets up and walks back to the filing cabinet. The top drawer rolls open with a low rumble. His fingers walk through the suspension files. The labels read like a who's who of community groups in Leicester. NGOs. The voluntary sector. Religious organizations from Bahá'i to Zoroastrian. He pushes it closed and tries the next drawer down. This is dominated by internal paperwork. Measurable outcomes. Mission statements. Fat files stuffed with wasted time. Almost at the back he finds a very thin one labelled RIOT. Inside are three sheets of paper – official memos that Mo would have received, instructing her on what not to say to reporters. There is nothing else.

The rearmost file in the drawer is labelled JOB. There is more in this one. He opens it and finds Mo's letter of employment. A copy of her contract. Copies of other correspondence relating to small changes in the duties she was being asked to perform. And, tucked away in the middle, a copy of her memo to Frank. He pulls it out, compares the identical sheets, then folds them both away in his pocket, closes the filing cabinet and hurries from the room.

Sometimes Tami thinks that when she is asleep she is outside time. It is as if one part of her is simultaneously dipped into all her past and future life. And when she wakes suddenly – as she has done now – it takes her a few seconds to understand which part of her life she has fallen back into. Until her memory clicks in.

She reaches out her left hand, feeling for the wall of her prison cell, finding only air. And then her right hand is groping across the bedclothes, searching for the warmth of another person but finding only the edge of the quilt that she is lying on, and beyond that the rough texture of worn carpet.

The ambiguity is abruptly resolved and her awareness slams back into the present. She is lying in the dark on the floor of her living room, looking up at the ceiling. There is a moment – a fraction of a second – when she is aware of some searing loss. But then her mind sharpens further and it is forgotten like the tail end of a bad dream.

She listens to the silence, trying to detect Rita's breathing. She tilts her head and holds her own breath but the only sound is the regular tick-tick-tick of the small alarm clock. She gets up and treads to the door of the bedroom. The quilt is thrown back. There is a bar of dull orange from the streetlight outside the window. It lies across the pillow and up the head of the bed on to the wall.

Rita has gone.

*

When Tami wakes the next time, it is morning. Rita is standing over her with a mug in each hand. The snarling, spitting animal of the night before has been replaced by a sleepy-looking woman. She knows that her friend must have got a fix of something during the night. If not heroin, then perhaps codeine or methadone.

She takes a mug. 'Thanks.'

'Thought you were gunna sleep for ever,' Rita says.

Tami clambers off the floor and hauls herself into an armchair. The tea is sweet. She had given up sugar since coming out of prison, but it feels good to have the extra kick this morning.

Rita is looking around the room. 'You got any money? I'll go and buy us some food.'

Tami sips from her mug. 'Got your appetite back, then?'

'I guess.'

Tami doesn't believe this. 'There's no need to go out. I've got eggs in the fridge.'

Rita walks to the window and looks down. 'I'm no good at cooking,' she says. 'Out of practice. You know.'

Tami does know. She was the same when she first came out. Struggling to relearn things that were automatic before she was sent down. Simple things like buying toothpaste and paying bills. None of them would have been any problem on their own, but because they came all together she felt as if she was being submerged.

'I'll fix breakfast,' she says.

Two eggs are frying in the pan and four slices of bread are heating under the gas grill. Rita is sitting in the living room, blowing her cigarette smoke out of the open window.

Tami, chewing a stick of nicotine gum, puts the margarine on the work surface. She has the fridge door half-closed when a suspicion starts niggling at her. She stops, crouches, reaches inside, pulls out the pickle jar and unscrews the top. Just to check. The syringe and hypodermic needle are still in their sealed bags. She touches the clingfilm-wrapped packet of brown crystals, then replaces it, pushing the jar right to the back of the shelf.

'Who did Jack think it was that framed me?' she asks, speaking the words as lightly as she can manage.

'Why do you want to know?'

'Wouldn't you?'

'Depends if knowing was gunna get me killed.'

Tami pushes the eggs around the frying pan, wondering if Rita has just fed her a clue. Her first thought is of the killer she knew in prison. Joy was from Leicester. There could easily have been a connection between her and the people Jack knew. But the woman was already on the inside when the package of heroin was found in Tami's car. There is no way she could have been involved in the framing. Then she starts to search her memory of Jack's associates. Men like Red Owen and Eddie Piper. She didn't know them well enough to say what they might be capable of.

'Look,' Rita says, flicking the end of her cigarette out of the window, 'he never told me what he found. I just know he was crazy with it all. He was doing dangerous stuff, and he didn't want you to know. Said you'd make him stop.'

'Then how come he told you?'

'He wanted me to look after you. I said I wouldn't do it unless he told me why. There had to be a reason, right? No one gets worked up like that without a reason. So he told me he was after this bloke who'd set you up. And the closer he got, the more dangerous it was.'

'Dangerous for him?'

'Dangerous for you, sweetie.'

Tami watches through the doorway as Rita lights up another cigarette.

'So it was someone on the outside who could do stuff on the inside?'

'I'm not playing twenty questions,' Rita snaps.

A sudden, piercing alarm makes Tami jump. She looks up to the smoke detector above her head. The toast is burning. She yanks the grill pan out. There is an angry hiss of steam as she drops it on to the wet draining board. Then she flaps a tea towel in the air, trying to clear the smoke. The alarm stops as abruptly as it started.

Rita hasn't moved from the chair. 'It's easy to get burned,' she says.

They eat their breakfast in silence, sitting in the living room, plates balanced on knees. Tami finishes first. She watches Rita picking at her food.

'It's a man Jack was tracking?' Tami asks. 'You did say *he*.'

Rita glares at her for a moment, then goes back to the yolk of her egg – which is all she seems to be interested in eating.

Tami tries again. 'Is the man in Leicester?'

No answer.

'The law? A policeman?'

'I'm not even going there,' Rita says.

'Then he did tell you a name?' Tami can see the cornered animal in the other woman's eyes, in the pressure of her jaw thinning the lips to pale lines. 'I need to know.'

'He's a killer,' Rita shouts. 'You don't need to know nothing more than that.' She jumps out of her chair, spilling the breakfast plate on to the carpet, running from the room. The front door slams and footsteps hammer away down the stairs.

Tami gets down on her knees and starts picking the pieces of toast and egg white from the thin carpet. She thinks about a killer she met once. Long ago. And the more she thinks about him, the more likely it seems that he could have been involved in some way. If it wasn't him who framed her, he might still know what Jack was up to. And if it *was* him, then things will be resolved. One way or another.

Mid-morning and the caffeine isn't working. More coffee only seems to be making Frank feel jumpy and paranoid. When the phone chirps, his hand is on it before the first ring is over. He forces himself not to snatch the receiver. He doesn't want his jerky edginess to show.

'Yes?'

There is a moment of silence on the other end of the line. Then: 'Are you all right?' It is his wife, speaking in a small voice, which tells him that he must have barked into the receiver in spite of all his efforts.

'I'm fine.' Then he swallows his bravado. 'No. Not fine. But safe. It's been another bad night.'

'Yes.'

'You saw the news?'

Again: 'Yes.' A difficult pause. Then she says: 'Are you coming home soon?'

'It . . . it's hard right now. Later, maybe . . .'

'Something arrived for you,' she says.

Suddenly he knows that this isn't simply a call to check up on his safety after the riots. 'What is it?'

'It came through the letterbox. There isn't a stamp.'

He takes a breath, trying to make his voice sound calm. 'You'd best put it in my study. I'll deal with it when . . .'

'Frank . . .' There is a tremor in her voice. 'You need to come now.'

There's no way he should be leaving his post this morning. It is his duty to fight through the layers of fatigue, to come out punching the air, springing on his heels, ready to inspire the officers under his command. That's what the others are doing. It's as if the station is an ants' nest that has been stirred up with a big stick. No one is walking. The corridors are full of people bumping shoulders as they dash from one emergency to another. It's not just the hundreds of organizations that are phoning about the riot – the media, the Asian Business Forum, the city council, the fire department. There are individuals as well, people who have given up on the already jammed switchboard, people who are prepared to queue up out of the front doors and down along the street, waiting for a chance to report their particular tragedy. Cars trashed, windows broken, personal injuries, houses and livelihoods left as burned-out shells.

There aren't enough people in the police station this morning to do all the jobs that absolutely need doing. Frank knows that leaving will look like a betrayal of the whole team, even though he's worked longer and harder than any of them. But he has no choice now. He gathers a sheaf of papers from his desk and marches out of the office and down the corridor towards the exit, head bent forward, rushing like everyone else. No one stops to ask what job he is hurrying to. He motors out of the car park with determination, going somewhere important. A couple of constables stand to attention as he passes.

There was a risk with each delivery that the blackmailer's packages could have been picked up by Julie. A small risk, because Frank's name was printed on the front of each. By the tone of her voice on the telephone, he knows that his wife has somehow seen inside this one. Perhaps it caught a sharp corner of the letterbox and ripped open. Or maybe his name was obscured in some way.

He is thinking all this as he hurries up the path from his car. He gets out his key and aims it for the lock. The door opens. Julie is standing inside, looking at him.

'Frank . . .'

He's trying to place the expression on her face. Guilt, perhaps. He puts on his own emotion-covering smile. 'Are you all right?'

'What's happening, Frank?'

He eases her back and steps inside. 'Where's the package?'

She glances into the kitchen. He walks through and sees a Jiffy bag on the table. This one is cream rather than manila, as the others had been. The flap is open. Julie slips past him and busies herself with a cup and a jar of coffee.

He wants to take the envelope away, to look through it in private. But that would make the situation even worse. So he sits and lifts it. It is similar in weight to the package that contained the mobile phone. But this one feels as if it contains two objects. He turns it over and sees writing in marker pen. But this time it is one word only. *Shakespeare*. As if the blackmailer had meant for this to happen, for Julie to open it and discover her husband's betrayal.

'I love you,' she says suddenly. 'Whatever this is about.'

Frank tips the bag and the contents slide out on to the table: held together with elastic bands, two thick piles of fresh £20 notes. At this point, Frank can feel something in his head click over into a different mode of working. He turns the first pile with a single finger, then the second one. He gets his head low and inhales. There is a definite smell of cigarette smoke here – something he didn't notice with the other packages. The piles of notes appear to be of the same size. He picks up the first one and starts to count.

Julie places a mug of coffee on the table next to him. 'If you knew what this was about, you'd tell me, wouldn't you?'

He glances at her and nods.

There are two hundred and fifty notes in the first bundle. He puts it down and moves on to the second.

'I've never pried into your business. But this isn't the same. It's coming through my front door. Into my house.'

'I'm sorry.'

'The children might have seen it.'

'I'm really sorry.'

'I don't want sorry! I want to know what's going on!'

'So do I, love. Believe me.'

'You're telling me you can't even guess what it's about?'

He shakes his head again. He is slowing in his count as he gets towards the end. He can already guess the number of notes. He flips over the last one. Five hundred new £20 notes: £10,000. Exactly the amount he paid to the blackmailer.

'Frank?'

He puts on a smile that he hopes will hide the turmoil of questions inside him. 'I have absolutely no idea,' he says. 'Not a clue.'

Chapter 8

There is no address for Gabriel. All Tami knows is that when he visits London he stays at the Midland Green hotel. That's what she found out by ringing around some names from the old days. Acquaintances of people who were once her friends. That and the fact that Gabriel is in London now.

She wonders, as she prepares for her trip, if travelling down to see him is proof that she is making her own choices at last, or if the real choice would be to not go. It can't be both. She's felt her heart rate kick at each of the moments when she could have backed out – just before buying the A to Z of London, just before booking the cheap-day return at the National Express office in St Margaret's Bus Station. It kicks again now as she steps up into the coach that will take her down the motorway to the capital.

The Gabriels of this world are dangerous to disturb. She met enough of their victims on the inside. It's not possible to cold-call a man like that without there being some kind of repercussion. If she walks into his presence, she will be putting herself beyond any law. He could kill her or rape her or both, and that would be an end to it as far as he was concerned.

She watches the motorway embankments blur past and the horizon drift. Between them is a landscape of pylons and scattered agricultural buildings. Fields of green and bright yellow. Watching them makes the nervous nausea strengthen in her stomach and chest. But she has to keep looking, because when she closes her eyes the madness of what she is doing becomes more obvious.

She met Gabriel only once. It was at a party in Birmingham. Jack had been invited. She was tagging along. A couple of hundred people in a stuffy room. The buffet had been stripped by the time they got there and the pay-bar was charging over the odds.

Jack had business to do. Him and another man had gone into a huddle next to the door. But before he left her, he pointed out a couple of men on the other side of the room. One was large – though not out of proportion. He wore a leather jacket even in that heat. His arm was over the shoulder of the other man – a much smaller figure, dressed in tight jeans and a flouncy shirt.

'Gabriel,' Jack said, pointing first to the bigger of the two. 'The other one is Max. They're both Russians. Drug dealers. Best keep clear.'

She'd got herself a half-pint of sweet cider and a packet of crisps and then moved over to a corner so she wouldn't get jostled.

But Gabriel had obviously seen her. She watched him walking towards her across the room, easing his way like a plough through heavy soil, not hurrying, but neither seeming to notice or be deflected by anything in his path. His blue eyes were on her from the start, his face scrunched slightly as if he'd been peeling onions and was just about to cry.

'I am Gabriel,' he said, his voice not as deep as she would have imagined for a man of his size.

'Tami,' she said.

He engulfed her hand. She felt over-aware of the wall behind her.

He let go and took a shot from his glass. She assumed it must be vodka, but when he leaned forward and spoke again she could smell the gin fumes on his breath.

'Are you really Russian?' she asked, surprised by her own boldness.

He shrugged. 'You want me to be?'

'I was just curious.'

He nodded, as if the matter was closed. 'If you want anything, I am the man.'

'Thanks.'

'A beautiful girl must be with someone, yes?'

She pointed past Gabriel's chest to where her husband was standing on the far side of the room.

'Ah. You are Jack's.'

She felt caught between agreeing and objecting.

'Is he good for you?' Gabriel asked.

'Yes.'

'If he stops being good for you, you come to me. I can do anything.'

The words themselves would have sounded like the boast of a spoiled child. But they were spoken with such matter-of-fact ease that Tami felt appalled.

Then he took her hand again and kissed it. *'Salute.'*

She watched him walk away, cutting an easy line towards the door. When he got there, she saw him turn and look back at her, nod once, then leave. Even though her body was sticky with the sweat of the room, she felt her skin tighten into goose flesh.

It was a terrible party. The only people who bothered to stay were the ones who had travelled a long way to get there and felt some commitment to remain for an hour or so at least. And the ones who were already so drunk that they didn't notice the bar prices. The mood was flat and the men pestering. She'd smoked her way through the last of her cigarettes by the time Jack returned, with his business friend following close behind.

'What's eating you?' he asked.

'I was bored. That's all.'

'I'll make it up to you,' he said. 'Let's have one drink all together, then I'll take you somewhere nice for a meal.'

So Jack bought another round and they toasted each other. He told stories about characters on the market. And when it was time to go, Tami was surprised to find that she'd been enjoying herself. The party didn't look so pitiful any more. She was holding Jack's hand as he led her through the crowded room towards the door. And then someone outside screamed.

Jack was the first out of the room. By the time she reached the fire escape stairs there were half a dozen people ahead of her. She had to press through them to get to the front. Several were already turning, pushing back up the stairs the way they'd come, panic in their faces.

The first thing she saw when she got to the front was that the outside door was swinging open. Then she saw Jack, kneeling next to some sacking rags. And then she saw the blood – pooling in a rough depression and in the hole in the concrete floor where the door bolt would be anchored. It was Jack who pulled away the rags. But they all saw the body at the same time. Max, the smaller of the Russian drug dealers – if Russian they were. His flouncy shirt was ripped open down the front, revealing a stab wound just under the solar plexus, and a long, upward-curving cut across the stomach from which a loop of intestine had slipped free.

The people at the front of the crush – the ones who had

seen it – turned en-masse, trying to get back up the stairs. The people just behind them must have felt the pressing surge because they, too, wheeled and ran. It was a stampede. All knew that it was better not to give the West Midlands Constabulary the chance to question them. It was that kind of guest list.

Of course, it must have been Gabriel who killed Max. That's what Jack said. Or one of Gabriel's people. And there may have been some kind of justice in the killing. By all accounts, Max hadn't been a saint. Disputes were common among the dealers. And they were usually settled through acts of violence.

The police questioned her and Jack and the other half-dozen individuals who were left in the bar. All the others had fled. But there was nothing to be done. The hunting knife that had killed Max was eventually found in a dustbin a couple of hundred metres away. Clean of fingerprints. A single stab wound had punctured Max's heart and killed him. The disembowelling slice across the stomach had apparently come after the heart had stopped pumping. Probably just for show, one of the detectives said.

The coach is coming into the capital now. Everything is bigger here than in Leicester. The width of the streets, the height of the buildings on either side. Greyer, too. As if centuries of grime have so ingrained themselves into the fabric of the place that no amount of cleaning could ever get it out.

From Victoria Coach Station she walks to the tube and from there rides along the District Line to East Putney. It's hot everywhere – in the underground, on the streets. An unrelenting, dusty heat. She rubs her forehead with her fingers. She can feel the place where her skin has started to flake, as if all the sweating has dried her out. Or perhaps it is the stress of the last few days. The sudden knowledge of a gaping void in what she knows about her own past.

The Midland Green turns out to be a hotel offering single rooms at £200 a night exclusive of VAT. For that price, Tami thinks the place should be more luxurious. Functional is the most flattering word that she can find for it. She enters through the revolving doors, into a dark lobby that smells of wood polish. The woman behind the reception desk is wearing a red jacket that has to be too hot for this weather. The fan attached to the wall behind her looks as if it was made some time in the 1960s. It clicks as it sweeps from side to side.

Tami stands waiting. The lift winches hum. Lights go on behind the numbers, switching in sequence from seven to one and then to G for the ground floor. The steel doors slide open, but there is no one inside. They remain open for a couple of seconds then close again. The receptionist puts down the telephone she's been nodding into. 'Can I help?'

'I want to talk to a man. He's staying here. I . . .'

'He has given you his room phone number?'

Tami shakes her head. 'But I just need a quick word.'

'It's not me, you understand. It's management policy. There were complaints before, you see.'

'I do know him.'

The receptionist smiles briefly and slides a pad of paper across the desk. 'Then he'll be delighted to receive a message from you.'

'You can tell me if he's in, though?'

'I'm sorry.'

Tami can detect no sincerity in the other woman's words. Knowing that argument never helps in this kind of situation, she takes the chained pen from the desk and writes: *We met in Birmingham. You said I could come to you for help. I need help now.* She prints her mobile number at the bottom and then rips the sheet free and folds it. Then another thought comes to her, so she unfolds it and adds: *It was the night Max died.*

'Who should I pass it to?' the receptionist asks.

'He's foreign.'

'We have many foreigners.'

'The name's Gabriel. I think he's Russian.'

The receptionist nods again, takes the note and slips it into a pigeonhole on the wall behind the desk. The number under the box is 523.

Tami retreats through the revolving doors. She crosses the bright and baking street to a café opposite the hotel. Soft drinks from bottles at a couple of pounds a glass. At first she has to content herself with a table at the back, but after half an hour a window seat comes vacant so she takes up position with another diet coke in front of her, watching.

The window seats seem popular in this place. There are three other tables next to the glass and all are occupied – even when the rest of the room empties towards mid-afternoon.

The waiter works his way across the room, wiping tables, then stops near her, hovering.

'Another drink?' He has a Scandinavian accent.

'I'm fine.'

He doesn't leave. 'Then may I take your glass?'

'Sure.'

He labours, vigorously wiping her tabletop.

The man at the next table raises a hand. There's a £5 note between his fingers. 'I'll buy the lady a drink. Whatever she's having.'

The waiter nods to him, takes the money and sweeps away, back to the counter.

'You didn't need to,' Tami says.

'You were hogging a table,' the man says.

She looks around the almost-empty room.

'It's a prime location. That's what you're paying for.'

She takes the hand he offers. 'Thanks.'

He beams at her. 'Bruce,' he says.

The diet coke arrives.

Bruce is a pleasant-looking man. Mid-thirties, she thinks. His hair is very short. Half a centimetre shorter and it would be a skinhead cut. He wears his shirt collar open.

'What brings you to the big city?' he asks.

'I might live here.'

He smiles again instead of challenging her further.

'Sightseeing,' she says.

'Well, you picked a hot day for it.'

Tami looks back out to the street. A black cab has pulled up in front of the Midland Green hotel. A couple get out and push through the revolving doors.

'What about you?' she asks.

'What about me?'

'Are you a tourist?'

'I live here.'

She picks up the glass. If she has too much she'll be hopping to the toilet all afternoon. But having the drink there on the table makes her nervous. As if someone else is going to come along and take it. Or spill it deliberately. It's an impulse that she is consciously trying to unlearn. She takes a small sip and puts the glass down again.

Bruce is stirring his espresso with a teaspoon. He gazes out into the sunshine. 'I love sitting here. There's so much to see.'

'Yes.'

'But it's not what I'd call sightseeing.'

She opens her mouth to answer, not yet knowing what she is going to say. But then her phone trills.

Panic: that is her first reaction. Her heart is thudding. She fumbles in her bag, stands, feeling that she has to get further away from Bruce before she takes Gabriel's call.

She turns her back to him and presses the RECEIVE CALL button. 'Hello?' She can't keep the tremor from her voice.

There's a static-filled pause, then the voice of Miss Quick, the probation officer. 'Tami, is that you? Are you all right?'

'Yes ... Yes, of course. I ...' Her mind is racing to readjust.

'Where are you? I called round at your flat.'

Tami retreats towards the door, putting another three paces between herself and Bruce.

'I'm in London.'

A pause, then: 'You should have told me you were going to travel out of Leicester. It's a condition of your probation. What are you doing?'

'I'm sorry ...' There is a churning surge of emotion rising inside her now – the irrational fear that she might be sent back to prison because she has broken the rules. The most terrifying part of it is the unexpected knowledge that the return of walls and locks and rules would be a relief. Without them she is naked.

'Listen, Tami.' Miss Quick's voice is calm and assertive. 'I'm not going to get you in trouble. Just tell me what you're doing.'

'Drinking a coke.'

'Alone?'

'I just wanted to get out,' she says, finding that the lie flows more easily than the truth did.

'When are you coming back?'

'Tonight. The eight-thirty bus.'

'Very well.' There's a decisive clip to the probation officer's words. 'Tell me what you're going to do this afternoon.'

'A museum?' Tami tries.

'Which one?'

'Um . . .'

'Try the Natural History Museum. South Kensington Tube Station.'

'OK.'

'And Tami – stay clear of people selling drugs. Don't go near them. No pubs or clubs. You know the kind of places that are dangerous for you.'

'Thank you,' she says.

The beads of condensation on Tami's glass have begun to coalesce and run by the time she gets back to her seat. A small pool of water has formed around its base. She takes a sip and looks out across the road to the hotel doorway.

'Husband? Bruce asks.

'Sorry?'

'On the phone. You looked guilty. He might not like you chatting with a man like me.'

'I . . . no.'

'Your boss, then?'

She rounds on him. 'I don't even know you! Why do you think I'm going to answer?'

He's a creep, she's decided. Chancing his luck. It feels good to have raised her voice to him. But her sudden waspishness doesn't even seem to have penetrated his skin. He continues to grin at her.

'A beautiful woman. A sunny afternoon. Can you blame me?'

'It's not right!'

'Don't tell me I'm the first.'

Bruce's persistence is unnerving. Something about it feels wrong. Being this close to him is starting to make her uncomfortable. There's an intensity about the man that reminds her of stories of stalkers. Obsessive people who search through rubbish bags, trying to get their fingers on personal objects.

'Do you mind if I join you,' he says.

She does mind. And he looks as if he is going to move across to her table. But then she catches a movement on the periphery of her vision. She turns to look through the window and sees a large man in shirtsleeves striding across the road away from her. And even though it's been more than ten years, and she's seeing him from the back, she knows it's Gabriel. She remembers his movement more than anything else – how he walked with purpose and everything gave way around him. Back then it was people. Now it is cars. They slow to let him through. He reaches the pavement, then climbs the steps and vanishes into the darkness of the hotel.

She finds that she is standing, the glass still in her hand. Bruce looks from her to the street and back. She sits, flustered. She gulps the rest of her drink. She wants to get her mobile out – to check that she didn't mistakenly turn it off. But she is too aware of Bruce examining her.

'You didn't tell me your name,' he says.

'You're right. I didn't.'

She's walking towards the door.

'I'm Bruce,' he calls out after. 'See you round.'

The door closes behind her. She steps to the edge of the pavement and waits for a gap in the traffic. But it doesn't part for her as easily as it did for Gabriel. She takes her moment and skips across, speeding and slowing, trying to ignore the beeps of car horns. On the other side, she risks a last look back to the café. Bruce is there, sitting in the seat she was occupying a moment ago. She sees him pick up her empty glass and a shudder travels down her back.

The lobby is dark and cool after the street. The same receptionist is behind the desk in her red jacket. Tami catches her eye.

'Did you give him the message?'

'I'm not allowed to give out . . .'

'Personal information,' Tami completes the sentence for her. She knows that spilling her irritation would make things much harder. She takes a breath and forms her facial muscles into a kind of a smile. She looks at the pigeonholes on the wall behind the other woman. Number 523 is empty. 'Can I wait here?' She gestures to the soft seats near the parlour palm in the corner.

'So long as you don't bother the customers.'

Tami sits, clasping her mobile phone in her lap, watching the signal strength bar on the display, and the battery charge indicator – now on low.

There are clocks labelled London, Tokyo, New York and Los Angeles on the wall behind the desk. She is keeping an eye on these as well. Once every minute the long hands click forward. But the moment of the movement is different for each clock. The wait between each tick forward is excruciating. She tells herself that she will stay where she is until half-past before making a move. Though she is still undecided as to what the move should be. To go or to stay. She knows Gabriel's room number. If she could get past the receptionist, she could go to his door and knock.

The London clock clicks forward to twenty-five minutes past. The mercury is rising inside her head. She moves her shoulders downwards in an impression of relaxation. But the muscles are still rigid. She waits for the Tokyo clock to click. The air in the lobby feels depleted in oxygen. She fills her lungs.

She is gripping her mobile too tightly for comfort. But when it chimes, her muscles jolt and she almost spills it off her lap.

She stabs the RECEIVE CALL button. 'Hello?'

A pause. 'Tami?' It's Miss Quick again.

Tami holds the phone away from her mouth so she can catch breath without the probation officer hearing.

'Tami?'

'Yes,' she says.

'Where are you now?'

'Going to the museum.'

'Heading for South Kensington tube station?'

'Yes.'

'What line are you on?'

Panic. She doesn't know which line goes to South Kensington. 'I meant that I'm heading out of the tube.'

'You're walking? That's why your voice sounded strange?'

'Yes,' Tami says again. 'But I've stopped now.'

'You are in the subway between the station and the museum?'

Tami is about to say yes – but then it hits her that it might be a trick question. There is no signal under ground. She is being cross-examined and it's not going to be long before she breaks. 'I've just come up the steps,' she says.

There's a pause, which Tami thinks is going to end with another question, a knife blade working into the cracks in her story. So she says: 'Thanks for looking after me.'

Miss Quick flusters for a moment. 'You know . . . it is my job . . . so long as you're not lost. That's all. I just want you to be safe.'

After the call is over, Tami stares at the mobile. She *is* lost. More now than at any time since she was released. She still doesn't know if the things she is doing are the result of her own volition or if they're just a reaction to a series of bizarre events. If she could have a moment of calm, she might be able to make a real creative choice, which would prove her freedom – at least to herself. But the situation that confronts her is so detached from anything within her experience that she has no idea if her responses are logical or crazy. At least crazy would be coming from herself. Logical might just be like a cog in a clock mechanism, moving in regular steps, free to move – but only in that one direction.

She hears a click and looks up. London has reached half-past the hour. The receptionist is busy talking on the phone, looking down at some papers on the desk. There is a pen in her hand.

Tami gets up and slips across the lobby, heart thudding, trying to make her footfalls on the stone floor as light as possible. She steps into the open lift and presses the button. The doors rumble closed behind her and the nervous tension starts edging into nausea. Her legs and arms feel jittery with more energy than she knows what to do with. She hears the lift winches hum through the metal walls and feels the heaviness as she starts to climb. Then the thought hits her of Miss Quick phoning, just as she is starting to talk to Gabriel, so she clicks the phone off and slips it back into her handbag.

The doors rumble open and she's in the empty corridor of the fifth floor, counting the room numbers. This part of the hotel is chill with air-conditioning. She can smell the acrid tang of cigarette smoke. She reaches into her bag for the nicotine gum, but there is none left.

Room 523 is right at the end, around two corners. There

is a DO NOT DISTURB sign hanging from the door handle. She backs off, around the corner again, and stands with her shoulders resting on the wall and a hand on her chest, trying to get enough oxygen into her lungs so she won't feel faint any more.

She knows that if she hesitates again she will just walk away. After that there won't be any coming back. She pushes herself off the wall and steps forward. She doesn't let her eyes drop to the door handle this time. She touches her knuckle against the wood. Three gentle knocks – a sound too slight to wake him if he is asleep. She holds her head close to the door and listens to the silence. Perhaps it is because nothing bad has happened to her that she feels able to knock again – louder this time.

On the third knock the door is snatched open. A hand grabs her wrist and pulls her inside. She feels her shoulder being wrenched by the sharpness of the movement. But it's only when the door closes behind her that panic hits. There's no time for logic or words. She opens her mouth and draws breath but a hand is clamped over her face, stopping the breath from escaping. She tries to scream through his fingers. It comes out as a muffled shout. She tries to bite, but can't reach his flesh. His body is pressed hard into her back. There isn't the strength in her to pull free.

She's being forced against the wall, face first. Her mouth is still covered and his other hand is feeling down her body. He probes with his fingers, up her thighs, right to the crotch. The terror inside her flips to anger. She raises her foot then slams it down and backwards. She feels the contact – her heel raking across his shin. She's never done it better, but he doesn't stop.

She feels herself being turned. Then she is looking into his face. It is Gabriel. There was never a doubt. That same scrunched expression as if he is about to cry. But there is no emotion in his eyes.

He slips his hand off her mouth, and she thinks she's going to get a chance to call for help. But before she can draw breath, he has her neck in his grip, fingers on one side, thumb on the other. He isn't throttling her yet, but she is aware of the pressure on her arteries, and the fact that her windpipe is completely within his grip.

He is examining her body with his eyes and his free hand, feeling down her front, over her breasts, her stomach, her legs. Ungentle. He is searching. For a weapon, perhaps. It's only now, as she has time for conscious thought, that the animal panic starts to turn into a sickening consciousness of the fragility of her position. That he can do whatever he wants, and all without breaking into sweat. Casually.

He puts the first finger of his free hand up to his lips and makes a shush sound. Then he pulls her bag from her shoulder and steps half a pace back. Her hand goes up to her neck, covering the place where his has just been. This is the first moment that she could realistically attempt to escape. But she doesn't. She watches him upend her bag and shake the contents on to the bed. Loose change. Keys. Cigarette lighter. Two ultra-thin sanitary towels in their packets. He picks up her rape alarm, examines it, drops it on the pile, then pulls out the return portion of her coach ticket. He frowns as he reads, then he nods, as if satisfied. But still he searches, feeling around inside the empty bag, probing the lining with his fingers.

At last he throws it down and looks at her again. He is pointing to the bedside table. She follows his finger with her eye and sees a sheet of paper with a crease mark down the middle. It is her own message to him written earlier in the afternoon. She nods.

He sits on the edge of the bed and starts scooping the scattered evidence of who she is back into the bag. All but the mobile.

A minute later she is striding down the corridor in front of him, the bag over her shoulder. This is another moment when she could run. All she'd lose would be her mobile phone – which is still on the bed in his room. Again she balances the risks of action and inaction in her mind, wondering if this is what people mean by freedom.

He ushers her through a set of double doors to a back stairwell. This they climb together, all the way up to the top, where another set of doors issue out on to a small balcony – perhaps two paces wide. It is a narrow place, running the length of the building, sandwiched between a low sandstone parapet to the front and a brick wall to the back, above which she can see the slate roof sloping upwards all the way to the ridge tiles.

'Who sent you?' he asks.

She's so struck by the sound of his voice after the prolonged silence that she can't think of an answer. It seems to her that perhaps his Eastern European accent is slightly more pronounced than it was when she met him before – though this seems unlikely.

'The police. Yes?'

'No.'

'I don't believe you.'

'I need your help,' she says.

'Then why you talk to the police?'

'You know who I am?'

'Of course. You are Jack's woman. Birmingham – yes? You think I forget so easy?'

'I don't know.' She shuffles back and puts a steadying

hand on the parapet. Nine storeys below, a car horn beeps.

Gabriel takes a slightly crushed cigarette packet from his trouser pocket. She watches him light up. 'They bug my room,' he says.

'You know what happened to me?' she asks.

'Before? Sure. They caught you dealing smack, right?'

'I didn't.'

'You went away how many years?'

'Ten.'

He whistles, nodding.

'And now you're out, you need work?'

'No.'

'You want drugs?'

'No!'

He leans back on the wall of the building, watching her. She feels suddenly exposed. 'I want to ask you about Jack.'

Gabriel narrows his eyes and shifts his head to one side, as if it's the cloud of smoke in front of his face that's bothering him.

'You make trouble for me. The note – stupid to put Max's name. The girl downstairs – she passes everything to them before she gives to me. So they read it and they think: *Max – who is this Max that died?* And then they look at the files and think: *Here's an unsolved murder that maybe we can stick on that man Gabriel.*'

'I needed to get your attention.'

'For what? Because you can't keep track of your man?'

'Why do you think I can't?'

Gabriel folds his arms. 'It's dangerous game. Jack knew it. Same with all of us. When a man disappear, you maybe feel sorry. But this business – it's like a war. People die.'

'He's not dead.'

'No?' Gabriel examines the tip of his cigarette.

'I don't believe it. There'd be a body. Or someone would know.'

'There are ways,' Gabriel says. 'Like if I wanted to kill you . . .' He steps towards her. She's so fixed on his eyes that she doesn't see the hand moving until it is too late to avoid it. It happens fast, like a snake striking at a mouse. His fingers are around her wrist, gripping hard. '. . . I could throw you over the edge. Right now. One move.' He is pulling her arm out over the parapet, forcing her body weight to shift after it. Struggling makes no difference. 'Easy for me, yes?'

Then he lets go and she stumbles back towards safety, throwing herself down on to the ground. If she could grab chunks of the concrete floor in her hands and hold on to them, she would.

Gabriel speaks into her vertigo: 'Difficult questions when they find your body, yes? I don't do it like that. If I want you dead, I do it when you don't think I'm there. When you sleep, maybe. Give you an overdose. Maybe they find you in bed. Maybe find you in the gutter. Either way they think they know what happen. Or there are ways to get rid of your pretty body. Easy if you know them.'

The things he is telling her feel familiar. Horrific threats casually spoken. She looks up at his face and for a moment it is as if she is back in prison, looking into Joy's eyes. The prison bully. Somehow that helps.

'If you could do it so easily,' she says, 'I'd be crazy to come and see you. Right?'

'Or stupid, maybe.'

'Or desperate.'

Gabriel nods. 'Maybe.'

'So desperate that I could do anything.'

'What is the point?'

'The point is, desperate people are trouble. You could kill me but you don't want to have to do it. You just want me gone.'

He shrugs. 'Then go.'

'First tell me about the business you had with Jack. Did he buy heroin?'

'Not Jack. Not from me.'

'Then what?'

Gabriel narrows his eyes further, making him look as if the tears are only seconds away. 'I tell you and you go?'

'I promise.'

'Jack hate me making money this way. All his business is to stop me selling in Leicester. He is on the other side in the war. So they make a big agreement. The pigs and all the little crooks. They have no more smack in St John's. No more heroin. And the pigs make it easy for other things. E, hashish, khat – no one will make trouble on this. This is the business I had with Jack. Jack and his dad make this agreement so all the crooks, all the police, everyone goes to them. With the agreement they are kings of St John's.'

'Shakespeare – was he part of it?'

He nods. 'Maybe.'

'Who else?'

'You make promise. I answer the question. You go now.'

'Please!'

'No more names.' Suddenly his eyes flare up with anger. 'You think I'm crazy to be careful like this? Paranoid?'

She manages to shake her head.

'There are bugs in my room,' he says. 'Always. And they send people to me with bugs on their body. In their bag. In their mobile.'

In spite of her tension, Tami says: 'Then why do you stay here?'

'Better stay where they can see you. This way I can watch them watching me. When I slip away, I know I'm safe to do anything. Come. Look down here.' She crawls forward again, her head level with the top of the parapet, and she looks over the edge, following the line of Gabriel's arm with her eye, down to the street level, to the buildings on the opposite side.

'See that café?'

She sees it. The same place she was sitting earlier.

'A policeman sit there all day, watch for me. See who come and who go.'

Which is when Tami gets a flash image in her mind – a memory of seeing Bruce, the creep, moving over to sit where she had been sitting, picking up the glass she had been drinking out of, the glass with her fingerprints on the surface. She shivers.

'Who runs the agreement now Jack's gone?' she asks.

'No one. It is finished ten years. All gone.'

'Why did it finish? Did you break it?'

She senses him shifting his position. His body tenses up, and it seems as if she has pushed too far. Then he starts laughing again. Huge laughter this time. Laughter such as only a man of Gabriel's size and intensity could generate.

'What?'

He wipes his eye. 'You think I break this agreement. You know nothing.'

'Then tell me! Who was it?'

'You broke it. The smack was in your car. Or maybe it was Jack. Now go. Go back to Leicester. Be happy you are free. Be happy you are alive.'

When Frank tried to leave the house earlier, Julie stood in the door, barring the way. She demanded to know how many hours' sleep he'd had in the last two days. The truth was he hadn't slept at all. But he didn't feel like admitting it, so he mumbled something about getting a couple of power-naps in while he was at the station. She marched him upstairs, pulled the curtains and told him to get into bed. Then she lay next to him, pressed herself close and rubbed her fingers over his back, working on the knots of tight muscles near the base of his spine. It felt as if she meant them to make love. He started to relax.

Then he was asleep.

He didn't wake until the evening.

He is now standing in the hall, trying to figure out what to do. He hears the paperboy stuffing the *Crusader* through the letterbox. He pulls it through. For a moment it surprises him to see the word 'Saturday' printed at the top of the page. That means it has only been twenty-four hours since the second blackmail demand arrived. He unfolds the paper. There is a large photograph of Mo Akanbai on the front page and an article about police mishandling of the riots. He starts reading but can't finish it. The feeling of guilt is crumpling up his insides. So he pulls his mind away and thinks about the £10,000.

He calls into the house: 'I'm just going out.'

Julie appears from behind the kitchen doorway. 'Where to?'

'Nowhere. Just a walk.' He doesn't think she believes him. 'It'll freshen me up,' he says.

It is a perfect evening in Glenfield. The air is still warm. The sky has paled to a duck-egg blue near the horizon. The towering poplar trees are motionless silhouettes. He walks away from the house, trying to look relaxed, knowing Julie will be watching him from the window. He only speeds up once he is around the corner.

It takes him three minutes of brisk walking to reach Superintendent Kringman's house. He rings the bell and waits. There is a movement behind the dimpled glass, someone approaching, dressed in a yellow top. Then the door opens. Kringman's daughter is standing inside. She doesn't look pleased to see him.

'Can I come in?' Frank asks.

'You didn't make an appointment.'

'I just need to see him. A couple of minutes . . .'

She closes the door before he can get his foot in the gap. He sees the yellow splash receding back into the house. He hammers on the woodwork, but she has gone already. He pounds until his fist starts to throb, then he presses his thumb on the bell button. He keeps jabbing at it, listening to the jangle of chimes. It is perhaps a minute before he sees the next movement. Different colours behind the glass this time. Darker.

It is Kringman, wearing a greenish tweed jacket that must be too heavy for this weather. His scowl is even more angry than it was on Frank's last visit. 'You upset her,' he says.

'It's urgent.'

'It always is.'

'Can I come inside?'

'No.'

'But this . . .'

'Is oh-so important that you can trample all over me and my daughter. It doesn't work that way, Franky.'

'I need answers.'

'So?'

'I won't go until I get them.' Frank drops his voice. 'This is private. Please help me.'

Kringman's shoulders drop. He takes a deep breath and shuffles out, across the path and on to the small lawn. It doesn't seem to bother him that he is wearing slippers. Frank follows him away from the house towards the low front wall of the garden where a line of rose bushes are blooming.

'You got another blackmail demand, right?' Kringman says, his voice loud. 'Well, so did I. The only difference is that you're panicking about it. You think the sky's falling on your head.'

'Keep your voice down. Please.'

'You think people are listening?' Kringman says, louder this time. 'You think they care about you and your little problems? Relax. What's the worst that can happen?'

'I did get another blackmail demand,' Frank whispers. 'You're right. But that's not why I'm here. Someone sent me a package.'

Kringman is looking away from Frank. He cups a pink rose in one hand. He doesn't show any signs of interest, or even that he has heard.

'It's different this time,' Frank says. 'It's—' he drops his voice still further '—it's money. Ten grand in new notes.'

'You say that like it's a bad thing.'

'It could look like . . . like corruption.'

Kringman plucks the rose, lifts it to his face and inhales. 'I used to be able to bend down to these bushes. Take time to stop on life's highway and smell the roses. That's what they say. Now I have to kill the thing if I want to get my face close enough.'

'Superintendent?'

'What?'

'I think someone is trying to trap me.'

'Convenient, though. Ten grand, just when you need it. And it's in cash – so no one will know. No difficult-to-explain bank statements. You should be pleased, Franky.

Bet you've been on your knees in church praying for this to happen.'

There's a touch of a smile on Kringman's face. Frank only sees it for a fraction of a second before it is gone. But it is enough. 'What do you know about this?'

'Why panic when that god of yours answers your prayers?' The smile is more definite now. Taunting.

'Who sent it to me?'

'You always were a tight-arsed bastard, Franky. That's why you never made any real friends in the force. Never understood the way the world really works.'

'Who sent it to me?'

'Can't say.'

'For Christ's sake, tell me!'

Kringman tuts. 'Shouldn't take the name of your lord in vain.'

'Then tell me what you can.'

Kringman places the pink rose in Frank's hand. 'I put the word around that you were short of ten thousand, that you'd be *grateful* for help. I'm sorry I did it now.'

'Who did you tell?'

'I whispered it in someone's ear. An old contact. A friendly face from the old days. He used to send me presents like the one he's just sent to you.'

'For what?'

'Advice and information. But I can't get about like I used to. I'm not allowed to go drinking with the boys. I don't have any information to sell. So I pass the baton to you. You should be thanking me.'

Frank feels unsteady on his feet. The blood seems to have drained from his head. He knew Kringman used to bend the rules but had no idea the corruption went this far. 'What does he want from me?'

'He'll let you know soon enough. But don't worry. Ten thousand doesn't buy a lot of time from a superintendent.' He turns and starts shuffling back to the house in his slippered feet. 'Smell the roses, Franky,' he says. 'Smell them while you can.'

Chapter 9

Instead of heading back home to Julie, Frank strolls on around the block, mobile phone pressed to his ear. He can think of only one face from the old days who might be described as friendly and would be likely to have access to ten grand. And that person also happens to be one of the people in the blackmail photograph.

'Hello. Shakespeare here. I wonder if you could do a search for me on the computer . . . Yes, I know what it's been like . . . I wouldn't ask if it wasn't urgent . . . Thanks. I'm really grateful. The surname is Owen. *Red* Owen, they used to call him. I can't give you a proper first name.'

Frank folds away the phone and strolls on, heading around the block on the long route back towards his house. It is almost dark now. A fox lopes across the road fifty metres ahead, out in the open for a couple of seconds, then back into the cover of the bushes.

Frank always used to think of Red Owen as a bit of a fox. A Welsh fox with a quick mind and clever eyes. He was in on the agreement because of his work. He ran a fencing operation in St John's. Everyone who was on drugs came to him to ship their bent goods. He was like the *Financial Times* of the socially excluded. He could quote a price for anything from amphetamines to video recorders, and tell them how many points the item had gone up or down in

the last month. It was as if he was reading all the information from tables in his head.

Owen should have been against the agreement. It was
never in his interest to have the drug supply cut. Half his
business came from junkies – people who needed to keep
stealing in order to feed their habits. The other half came from
the people who bought bent goods to replace the stuff they'd
had stolen. People in St John's couldn't afford insurance. And
they certainly couldn't afford to pay shop prices.

The thing was, the police knew what Owen did and
where he lived. They knew where his lockups were. With a
search warrant and a couple of officers, they could have had
him out of circulation. He'd had three previous convictions,
so one more would have had him put away for years. That
made him vulnerable. *Amenable to pressure*, as Kringman
used to say.

But getting rid of Red Owen wouldn't have solved the
drug problem in St John's. It might have put one network
out of action. But within a month others would have started
to take over. Nature abhors a vacuum, they say. So does
crime. The new fences would be people unknown to the
police. Harder to manage.

That's why Red Owen was included in the agreement. It
was why he chose to cooperate. And the agreement was
probably the reason he eventually moved out of St John's,
heading south to the bright lights of a bigger city. Owen was
never poor. But judging by the man's past ambitions, he
might well be rich enough now to spend £10,000 on buying
influence with the police.

Frank has completed his circuit of the block and is almost
home when the mobile trills. Owen's details were on the
computer. He thanks the operator and copies the address
and phone number on to the palm of his hand with a Biro.

Inexplicably, Owen is back in Leicester.

Frank gets out his keys and climbs into the car. Then, as quietly as he can manage, he reverses out onto the road and pulls away.

The address proves to be a pleasant semi-detached house in a pleasant suburb to the south of the city. Suburban living for a man who was once the ultimate urban criminal. It seems unlikely. Driving along the road, Frank doesn't see anything extraordinary about the place. Nothing flashy. Privet hedges and net curtains. Number 92 – supposedly Owen's address – is a modest property. Frank studies it for a few minutes before getting out of his car and straightening his shirt. There is a blue Toyota in the carport and, on the drive in front of it, one of the new VW Beetles, also blue. He steps across the block paving and rings the bell.

The thing he doesn't expect to see when the door opens is a girl standing just inside, ten or eleven years old, long dark hair and dark eyes. She is wearing Bart Simpson pyjamas and holding a music CD in her hand. She calls back into the house without looking away from him: 'Mum. Dad. There's a man to see you.'

Frank tries a smile and gets a rather uncertain one back from the girl. A woman comes up behind her. Mid-thirties. Dark hair, like the child. A pleasant, rosy complexion.

'Can I help you?'

'I'm . . . it may be I've got the wrong address. I'm looking for Owen.'

'I'm Mrs Owen.'

'We used to call him Red Owen. His hair . . . It's been a few years.'

'Sergeant Shakespeare?'

Frank turns to see a man approaching from the direction

of the carport. His hair is cropped very short now. Under the streetlight it seems blond rather than red.

'Hell's bells, Owen, you're wearing a suit.'

The woman in the doorway has both eyebrows raised so high that they have disappeared under her fringe. 'Darling?'

'I'll explain later,' Owen tells her. Then he catches Frank's arm and leads him away around the corner of the house and into the carport. When they are in the deepest shadow he stops.

'How is it you found me?'

'Were you hiding?'

'No. It's not like that any more.'

Frank surveys the other man as best he can. The white shirt shimmers ghost-like in the gloom. 'What's with the clothes? A change of image?'

'I'm not in the business now. Not for years.'

'Then what are you doing back in Leicester?'

'It's where my wife was born and brought up.'

Frank is chuckling now in spite of the stress he feels. Owen balls his fists. 'What?'

'You look like an accountant. I'm sorry.'

'And what is it that's wrong with accountants?'

'Don't tell me . . .'

Owen turns away, as if looking for an escape route.

'You *are* an accountant?'

'Keep the noise down,' Owen pleads. 'I've been through . . . a change. The old life is gone. Completely.'

'Been to Damascus recently?'

'I'm sorry?'

The Pauline reference clearly means nothing to Owen, so Frank guesses it wasn't a religious conversion. 'What changed you?'

'You're a policeman. You should be pleased.'

'I'm a policeman, so I don't believe in fairy stories. What happened to the long-haired entrepreneur?'

'He found a better way to live. That's all.'

'He?'

'It's not me any more – the man you're talking about.'

'Who was he, then? Where did he go?'

'I've changed. No one can think that's a bad thing.'

'Except all the junkies on the St John's estate?'

'Officer . . .'

'I'm off duty. Call me Frank.'

'You have to go.'

'When you've given me some answers.'

'You said you were off duty. That means this isn't official and I don't have to talk to you.'

'You *could* say that . . .'

Owen opens his mouth, and it looks for a moment as if he is going to refuse. Then he closes it again.

'Did Superintendent Kringman talk to you?' Frank asks.

'Kringman? No.'

'Are you sure?'

'I didn't even know he was still alive.'

Frank digests this information. Then he tries a new approach: 'You remember the agreement?'

'I can't talk about it. Not here.'

'Then let's go inside.'

Owen rubs a hand over his forehead. 'I never told my wife all the . . . all the details. She knows that I had a difficult background. That's all. I never told her what I used to do.'

'Just say I'm a friend from the old days.'

'You would never lie to your wife,' Owen says. 'It's not right that you ask it of me.'

Frank screws his eyes tightly closed for a moment. 'You don't have to lie. I'll do the talking.'

Owen's wife seems to accept Frank's story – that they used to be drinking partners. She leaves them in the lounge with a teapot and milk jug on a tray and fine china cups in their hands.

Frank manages to wait until the door closes before letting his chuckle escape.

'What?'

'Your house, Owen. A bit of a change from the way you used to slum it in the old days.'

'So?'

'It's funny, man.'

'Is that what's brought you here – to have a laugh at me?'

'You remember that day,' Frank says, 'when the agreement was fixed?'

'That's years ago. It's gone.'

'Fourteen years. And someone remembers.'

He tells Owen about the blackmail letter, about Kringman and Bill Arnica being sent the same package. And as he speaks he watches for any kind of reaction – recognition, fear, guilt. Surprise tinted with anxiety creeps over Owen's face like a troubled dawn.

'Have you ever seen a photograph like that?'

Owen is blinking rapidly. 'No. Never. I . . .' He shakes his head.

'Do you remember what was on the other side of the road? Where could the photographer have stood?'

'Nothing. We were alone. My God – if this came out . . .'

'No one's written to you?' Frank presses.

'I can't help. I'm sorry.'

'You see where I'm coming from? Nine people in the photograph. Nine who knew the meeting was going to happen. Only nine people who could've fixed it for the photograph to be taken. Of those, two are dead. One went missing years ago. Three have been blackmailed. That leaves three. Gabriel, Eddie Piper and you.'

Owen's teacup rattles in the saucer. He quickly steadies it with his other hand, then raises it to his mouth and drinks, swallowing heavily.

'Nothing to say?' Frank asks.

'It's not me. Like I said, I've changed. Everything's changed. I wouldn't risk all this.'

'Not for £30,000? Bollocks!'

'Thirty?'

'Ten thousand from each of us. Kringman, Arnica and me.'

Owen screws his eyes closed. 'I have a job already.'

Frank watches him for a few seconds before asking his next question. 'How come you got out of the business?'

'You are joking. Don't you think this way is better?'

'Better? Yes. Easier? No.'

'I didn't want to stop,' Owen says. 'It was the agreement that gave me the push. The addicts were leaving, and London looked to be a better bet. But it didn't work for me.'

'So you took an accountancy course? Just like that?'

'I was unemployed. The Jobcentre told me that I needed training.' Owen raises his hands, as if to ask what else he could have done in the circumstances.

'So now your money problems are over?'

Owen nods, though Frank notes that the man's eyes haven't left the carpet for the last minute and a pink flush has risen in his face. 'When are they going to let Jack's wife out of prison?' he asks.

'They released her already,' Frank says. 'It's been three months now.'

Owen's eyes flick up to Frank's face and then back down to the floor. He doesn't ask any more questions after that.

*

Behind St Margaret's Bus Station. Late in the evening. Diesel exhaust and a scatter of people waiting under the street-lights to meet the National Express service from London. Miss Quick is standing slightly apart from the others. She raises a hand to chest height and gives a tiny wave.

Tami feels herself beginning to blush. Perhaps it is the feeling of guilt. Or maybe the irrational fear that other people will somehow be able to see that she is a convicted criminal – only allowed to walk the streets under licence.

'How did you enjoy it?' Miss Quick asks.

'You didn't have to meet me.'

'It's late. I thought it best to make sure you were safe.'

Tami knows she is being checked out. Partly, this is comforting – the feeling that there are still rules that she has to follow and doors she isn't allowed to go through. But there is another emotion here – because forbidden things used to be behind locked doors. Now the doors are unlocked. Breaking rules has become possible again after so many years inside.

Miss Quick is smiling – but the expression looks forced. 'Did you see the Rosetta Stone?' she asks.

'The what?'

'The Rosetta Stone – in the museum?'

Tami shakes her head. She's hoping this is the correct answer to what has to be another trick question. The gamble pays off.

Miss Quick's smile suddenly broadens and relaxes. 'It doesn't matter,' she says. 'Perhaps that was the British Museum after all. I've got the car. I'll drive you home.'

Tami sits in the passenger seat, allowing herself to relax into the experience of being driven, of not being asked to make choices. The probation officer keeps her speed just under thirty miles per hour, accelerating smoothly away when the traffic lights turn green. And finally slowing to a stop right in front of Tami's front door.

The people opposite Tami's flat have their front door open. Two of them sit shoulder to shoulder on the step, smoking and laughing. Three more stand, leaning on walls and lamppost. All have cans of lager in their hands. It looks like it's going to be a loud night.

Miss Quick pulls on the handbrake. 'Well,' she says, 'here we are. Is there any chance of a cup of tea before I go?'

Tami wants to get rid of her probation officer. Under the woman's scrutiny she feels off balance and flustered. But to refuse would suggest that she has something to hide.

'I . . . I think the milk's off,' she says.

'I can drink it black.'

'And my shift starts soon. I'll need to rush.'

The probation officer looks alarmed. 'When do you sleep?'

'I'll . . . I'll sleep tomorrow. It's OK.'

'Well, I won't stay very long.' Miss Quick is already unclipping her seatbelt. Tami gets out of the car. She fidgets with her keys. Gabriel said that he deliberately puts himself under scrutiny so that when he slips away he knows he isn't being watched. She doesn't have any such confidence.

She is aware of how cramped and stuffy the stairway is as the probation officer follows her up to her front door. It is only as she puts the key in the lock that she remembers Rita – the drug-addicted ex-offender, the one person she definitely shouldn't be associating with.

She holds her panic down and unlocks the door, thinking fast. She steps inside, scuffing her feet to make noise, trying to warn Rita that something is different. 'Come in, Miss Quick,' she says, projecting her voice into the flat.

But there are no answering words from inside. No noise

of occupancy. Her flatmate must be out. On the streets somewhere. Selling or buying or both.

It always feels airless when the house has been locked
up all day. Especially in the summer. The kitchen bin. The
drains. Last night's take-away. Everything leaves a trace.
But as Tami steps down the corridor, she finds herself
sniffing for a smell that she can't quite place among the
others.

She hurries into the living room, picks up mugs, tidies a
magazine away from where it lay on the floor. Rita's things
are all in the bedroom.

'I do like the picture,' Miss Quick says. She is looking at
Tami's brightly coloured nautilus painting.

'Thanks.'

'Did you take an art class when you were in prison?'

Tami nods.

'You like Van Gogh?'

'Sorry?'

'Van Gogh, the painter. Your style reminds me of his
work. It's the way you use colours.'

Tami hurries out to the kitchen and clicks on the kettle.
The unfamiliar smell is stronger here. For a moment she
thinks it is something she has smelled before. There is a hint
of a memory attached to it. But as she tries to bring it into
her conscious mind, it slips away and is gone.

She opens the fridge and sniffs inside, pulling out a box
of eggs, then putting them back. All seems fresh. She looks
in the cupboard under the sink and peers down the side of
the cooker. It's not an unpleasant smell. In another person's
house she wouldn't think anything of it. It's just that it
doesn't belong here.

The kettle boils. She throws teabags into a couple of mugs
and pours the water.

Miss Quick steps into the kitchen. 'You look preoccupied with something,' she says.

'Thought I smelled something.'

'You shouldn't worry, Tami. Your flat has been locked up all day. Look . . .' She steps over to the window and starts wrestling with the catch.

'Don't bother. It doesn't work.'

But then, with a quiet click, the catch moves and the window opens – the window that Tami knows for certain was sealed shut with layers of paint.

Chapter 10

Sunday morning. It's been a long night on the production line for Tami. She's been standing by the aluminium-topped table, assembling sandwiches with the others, drifting in and out of sleep, fingers working on automatic. There were a couple of conversations going on in other languages. A group of three African men speaking French. Four Afghans, with faces that look almost Chinese, talking in their own language; she doesn't know what it's called. She does catch occasional words in English mixed in with their conversation, and the names of Man United and Real Madrid football players.

The whites around the production table are all women, and they're all younger than Tami. When they talk it is in low voices with their faces angled away from her, so she can never hear more than a couple of words. It's her they're talking about, of course. Her and the production manager, Steve Lloyd.

By six in the morning she has her second or third wind. She forces her mind to sharpen up, taking in the detail of her surroundings, of the other workers, trying to follow their conversations. Apparently, a group of them went out clubbing a couple of days back. There was a bloke they all fancied but couldn't get to talk to. And they are planning on going again next time they have an evening off, hoping to meet him again. But the snippet that is most interesting to Tami is that Mr Lloyd has recently gone cold on one of them. She wonders how hot he was before.

She looks back over her shoulder and sees him standing near the loading bay, watching her. He waves. She catches the word 'cow' from one of the whispered conversations. She attempts a smile in his direction. After all, it's not his fault that things are like they are. He beckons to her with a finger. She wants to ignore it, but he doesn't look as if he's going to give in. So she wipes her hands and turns her back on the bitches. It feels like a long walk to where he is standing.

'Are you all right?' he asks.

She doesn't feel like answering that, so she says: 'It was Hannah, wasn't it?'

'I'm sorry?'

'An affair or something?'

He shakes his head and deepens his smile. 'We had a meal together. It was nothing.'

'Did you sleep with her?'

'Look – if she's giving you trouble, I can do something about it. OK?'

'That's not the point.'

'Princess. I'm not seeing anyone else right now.'

'Hannah thinks you're seeing me.'

'I really like you, Tami. I only wish you'd let me show you how much.'

'It's not a good time.'

'That's why you need my friendship.'

Tami can feel her tension level rising. 'The shift's almost done. I'd better go back.'

'One thing before you go. I do want to take you out. A meal. Please. My treat.'

She looks up to his face. For a moment she thinks she can see real longing in him, then it's gone. 'Like you did for Hannah?' she asks.

His shoulders drop a fraction.

'I really have to go,' she says.

The English conversation stops as she walks back to the table. The girls look at each other, exchanging nods. There's a sudden, harsh clanging from an electric bell mounted on the wall. The others start to leave. One of the Afghans smiles at her before he turns to go. She is left on her own, clearing up her table space.

She glances towards Mr Lloyd, but he has his back to her now.

It's five minutes later as she walks towards the door that he approaches her again. They're the last two in the building. He seems embarrassed – which isn't his usual style.

'I meant it,' he says. 'A meal. Or if you're not comfortable with that, how about we just go shopping together or something? We could go now.'

'It's Sunday,' she says. 'The shops won't open for hours.'

'Breakfast, then.'

'I'm . . . busy.'

'That's better than last time. At least you're not heading straight back to bed.'

Bed. Now she has the opportunity, going back to sleep would seem like a criminal waste of precious time. 'I've got something to do,' she says.

'Then let me help you.'

'It's not your kind of thing.'

'It doesn't matter. I'll be your taxi service. I've got a nice car – not that there's anything wrong with yours.'

She laughs in spite of herself. He's locking the factory

door behind them, so she can't see his reaction. 'You're terrible,' she says.

It feels strange, to have stepped out into the natural light again after eight hours under neon. It was night when the shift started. Now the sunlight is strong – even though it is early. She shields her eyes with her hand and looks towards where she parked, a couple of hundred metres up the road.

He pats the bonnet of a silver-grey BMW. 'At least let me drive you to your car.'

She finds herself walking around to the passenger side. The door opens with a satisfying click, unlike the tin-can sounds that her Fiat makes. The seat is more comfortable than anything in her flat. It hugs her as she sits back into it.

She knows he's going to try to get her to go home with him again. The thought is exciting and disturbing at the same time. The temptation to hand control of her actions to another person. His insistent persuasion perhaps absolving her of the need to make the decision for herself.

'Where to, madam?'

'To my car.'

For once he doesn't complain, which surprises her. He turns the key and the engine thrums into life, powerful yet quiet, like the growl of a panther. Suddenly, the thought of firing up her pink Fiat doesn't feel so attractive. He would be watching, of course, listening to the badly balanced spin-dryer that passes for an engine.

Steve Lloyd eases his foot off the clutch and rolls them up the street, smooth as syrup, then slows again to stop without the brakes even squeaking.

'Door-to-door service,' he says.

Tami feels unaccountably flustered. 'Thanks.'

She gets out, still waiting for him to proposition her. She closes the door. Another exquisite clunk. The window hums down, and she sees him looking up at her. He's definitely going to ask now. All he wants is to get inside her knickers, to bed another of the girls on the sandwich line, to cut another notch on the bedpost.

'I'll be going, then,' she says.

'Tami . . .'

'What?'

He smiles. 'I really like you, that's all.'

Then the window hums up and he drives away, the crackling of loose chippings under the wheels louder than the purring engine.

There was no way she could have gone with Steve and no way she could have let him come with her. If he found out he would say she was crazy. What Tami is doing feels reasonable so long as she doesn't try to explain it. But it stops making sense as soon as she puts the plan into words in her head.

It started with the knowledge that Superintendent Shakespeare was involved in some way with Jack and John. An illegal agreement long ago. Suddenly there was a deeper significance to the way the policeman came and questioned her, unofficially and in private.

After she left Gabriel she started wandering around the streets. There were hours left before her bus back to Leicester. If she hadn't come across a library she might have dropped the idea. But Shakespeare's name kept repeating in her mind, as if Jack was calling it out to her. She went inside, presented herself to the librarian and asked if there was any way that she could track down a person. An individual living in Leicester.

'What person?' the man asked.

'Someone I knew.'

She fielded a few difficult questions after that. Why did she want to do it? What kind of information was she looking for? And who exactly was it she was trying to trace?

'It's private,' she told him.

First they tried the phone directory, but he wasn't listed. 'Ex-directory,' the librarian said. 'I don't know what else to suggest.'

'But I really want to find him.'

The man puffed out his cheeks. 'I suppose you could try the Internet. Friends Reunited, perhaps – if you were at school together. Or one of the search engines.'

He led her to a computer and showed her how to get online and access the search site Google.com.

She pointed to a box on the screen. 'I just type his name in here?'

'And then click GO.'

He was still standing just behind her. 'Thank you,' she said. At which point he finally took the hint and walked back to the desk.

Typing with two fingers, she entered the name *Frank Shakespeare*. There was a pause and then the screen changed. A notice telling her that it had found 354,000 possible references related to her search. Then she remembered something from an IT class she'd taken in prison. She retyped the words, this time using quotation marks around the name *"Frank Shakespeare"*. That cut it down to 605 possible references. An improvement – but it would still take her hours to search through them all. Many people in the world must be sharing the same name, but she didn't think high-ranking police officers would be common among them. She typed *"Superintendent Frank Shakespeare"* in the box and clicked GO once more. This time only three page references came up. The first two were police websites – which she was sure wouldn't let her know his home address. The third belonged to an Anglican church just outside Leicester. She clicked the link and found herself looking at a picture of the man himself – shaking hands with a woman who was wearing a clerical dog collar. *Superintendent Frank Shakespeare, stalwart member of the congregation, is thanked for his help organizing the Youth Away Day.*

There was even a map on the site, complete with the times of services.

The church looks old. Weathered, grey stones, tinted malachite-green where the lightning conductor touches them. She tilts her head back, following the line up the high wall and on to the spire, right to the pinnacle where it is silhouetted against the brilliant blue of the sky. Looking at it makes her feel dizzy, so she starts wandering through the graveyard, killing time.

From inside the church she can hear triumphal organ music. It sounds and feels very distant. She wanders between the stones, reading the dates and inscriptions. *Sarah, loyal wife of William Joseph b. 1832. Departed this life 3 December 1871.* And next to that stone, William Joseph himself. Date of death 1875. She reads along the line. Children who died in infancy. Husbands and wives buried together. Then a stone with the husband's details and a space left blank, presumably for the wife. Tami wonders whether she found love again. Perhaps she shares another man's grave.

Her mind drifts back to Steve Lloyd. She has found herself worrying over the last couple of days that perhaps she has been judging him unfairly. Just because he is such a good-looker and so smooth and attentive, it doesn't necessarily mean that he is after nothing more than a quick roll between the sheets. She doesn't have a good track record when it comes to judging men. One hundred per cent failure rate.

One out of one. Jack.

Someone told her once that eyes are windows on the soul – that you can tell the truth about someone if you just look deeply enough. But when she looked into Jack's eyes, all she could tell was that her feet were being pulled from beneath her by a powerful riptide. Inescapable. It wasn't fair that any man should have eyes like that, more blue than the ocean.

She remembers his hands. Beautiful hands. A fine gold hoop on his ring finger. It had been his grandfather's. Eighteen carat. And on the little finger of his right hand, a cheap silvery ring that she'd bought him from a market stall that first summer. It was shaped like a snake swallowing its own tail. It had a single red eye.

The organ music from the church gets suddenly louder as the doors open. The congregation is beginning to emerge. The vicar stands in the porch, shaking hands with people as they leave. Tami steps back and crouches down, shielding herself from view behind one of the larger headstones. If someone asks, she is going to say that she is searching for one of her ancestors.

Members of the congregation are milling around in the sunshine, chatting to each other. They are all white and look middle class. All seem contented. And then she sees the man she has been waiting for. Superintendent Frank Shakespeare, wearing a jacket and tie in spite of the heat. He's holding hands with a woman of a similar age, presumably his wife. With their free hands they wave to another couple in the crowd – who respond, mirroring the gesture. Tami watches as Shakespeare and his wife walk away down the path towards the road. Only when they are out of sight does she get up and follow.

*

Frank follows Julie into the cool of the house and inhales the smell of roasting chicken. She is stepping towards the kitchen, but he catches her hand and draws her back.

'What?'

Instead of answering, he kisses her.

'I've got to baste the bird,' she says. Then she pulls free.

He watches her for a moment. Things weren't good between them last night. She didn't press him about the unexplained package of money. Nor did she ask about where he went on his walk after he left the house. But the questions were there. He could see them behind her eyes.

So this morning he got up early and made her breakfast in bed. He hasn't done that in years. It's not that he doesn't care for her. The attention he is giving her now is completely sincere, an expression of his love. He would do it more, but the requirements and responsibilities of living usually get in the way.

Julie is the most important thing in his life. More so than the children even – though he would never say that out loud. His love for her came first. It is for her benefit, as well as the children's, that he is covering up the problems of the past. Not for himself.

He hears her opening the oven, the metallic sound of the roasting dish sliding out. The children are both out at the houses of friends, but she still prepares the full meal. She always goes the extra mile, and he loves her for it.

'Can I do anything?' he calls.

She comes to the kitchen doorway. 'Relax for me. That's all. Go and look at your bonsai trees.'

Then she is gone.

He sighs, steps into his study. Compartmentalizing is the only way he can manage all the parts of his complex life. He closes the door and clicks his mind over onto the problem of the blackmailer.

The change is as quick as turning the key to unlock the desk.

His meeting with Jack's wife proved more difficult than he had imagined it would. She'd been unaware of quite how thoroughly her husband had disappeared all those years ago. The most disturbing part was when she started to weep in front of him. He asked more questions but she couldn't or wouldn't say anything.

After the physical pain she'd inflicted when she kneed him between the legs, he hadn't felt too bad about pushing his way into her flat. He'd assumed she would still be in touch with Jack, that she was just like any other small-time criminal. The tears threw him off balance.

He opens his desk drawer and pulls out the blackmail photograph. Nine people standing in a loose arc in a traffic lay-by. In the picture Frank is standing next to Jack. Jack is perhaps twenty-two and Frank a few years older. Jack must still be in his thirties now – assuming he is still alive. John is next to Jack. They were never far from each other.

On the other side of Frank stands Superintendent Kringman. And next to him is Red Owen the fence, a roll-up in his mouth as it always was in those days. There would have been enough evidence to put Owen away if it had been collated. But somehow none of the police officers bothered to make the effort. It had seemed strange to Frank – then just a sergeant. He hadn't understood the dynamics of crime on an estate like St John's. It's always going on, and the best place to get evidence is from the person who receives the stolen goods.

Next to Owen stands Eddie Piper, the housebreaker and nightclub bouncer. Eddie wasn't one of the ones who broke into houses on the estate itself. People who did that were the hopeless cases. Drug addicts and kids excluded from school. Eddie was a professional. He dressed well enough to walk around middle-class suburbs without raising anyone's suspicions. He chose the houses carefully and sparingly. Never two from the same street. He was another one who kept good relations with the police. He even got paid as an informant.

Frank looks around the other faces. Gabriel the Russian, Bill Arnica the politician, Bird's Eye the businessman. Nine people, each thinking they were invulnerable. And a tenth man, somehow standing on the other side of the road without being seen. The man holding the camera.

Frank closes his eyes and thinks back to that day, trying to remember the layout, trying to get a picture of what was on the other side of the road. Perhaps a hedge through which someone poked a long lens. But he can't bring the picture back into his mind.

'Lunch is ready, darling.'

He closes the box file as he looks up. Julie is smiling at him from the doorway, untying the strings of her cornflower apron. There is a smudge of white on her shoulder. No one could compare with her. The Mo Akanbais of this world may be quick-minded and beautiful – but they could never compete with the loving care that Julie gives him.

'You're an angel,' he says.

She casts her eyes down, just like she used to do when they first met. Somehow she still looks like the blushing maid he asked out to a dance twenty years ago.

He touches his own shoulder with a hand. 'You've got flour on your dress.'

She sees the mark and flashes him a grin, touching her upper teeth on her lower lip. 'Come on. It'll get cold.'

He gets up and follows her from the room.

'The children won't be back until this evening,' she says. 'That gives us all afternoon to ourselves.'

Frank gets a flash image of the blackmail photograph in his mind. A thought comes to him. 'We can go for a drive.'

'I suppose so.'

'Out towards Bradgate Park.'

'If you want.'

'It'll be lovely.'

It only occurs to him at this point that there is a look of disappointment in her eyes.

They drive out of Glenfield along the A50, through Groby and then turn right towards Bradgate. There are huge oaks here, in the borders of the fields. And stone walls. Frank remembers the meeting place being up in this area somewhere – but can't figure out which road it must have been on.

Julie is sitting quietly in the passenger seat. She seems to be concentrating on the scenery out of the side window. Frank turns off down a smaller side road. He knows it's wrong immediately. He stops and reverses.

'Are we going somewhere in particular?' Julie asks.

'Yes and no.'

She hasn't turned towards him.

'There was somewhere I came once,' he explains. 'I wanted to see it again.'

'Somewhere you came with me?'

'No.'

'With someone else?'

'It was a long time ago. And it wasn't like that.'

The road is climbing here, through a tunnel of overhanging branches. A green canopy. The dappling sunlight flickers past as they drive.

'You don't have to go so fast,' she says.

He pulls his foot up a fraction until the speedometer needle has dropped by ten miles per hour. 'Better?'

She hasn't replied half a second later when he sees the lay-by. He has to brake hard to stop in time and pull in.

'Frank!'

'Sorry.'

He gets out of the car and looks around. It is definitely the place. The slope of the road clinches it – though he hadn't remembered until this moment. He looks down at the ground, as if there might be clues still remaining after all these years. There is a line in the tarmac – a scar from some road maintenance work in the past. He's fairly sure it is shown in the photograph. It feels strange that a small detail like that should remain.

'Is this where we were going?' Julie asks.

'We can go on to Bradgate Park in a minute,' he tells her.

He walks to the other side of the road and looks back at the car. Julie is still sitting in it, arms crossed. He steps to the right, lining up the hedge with a tree in the background, trying to duplicate the image in the photograph. He might have expected the hedge to be taller now, or shorter, but it is just the same. If the photograph had been taken in the city, he feels sure there would be differences: new developments, new road signs. But it seems that things don't change so fast in the countryside.

He can hear engine noise approaching. He steps back to the edge of the road. Three cars pass in quick succession, no more than a flash of colour. Blue and green and pink.

It occurs to Frank that he gets a better match to the photograph image, now he's pressed up hard against the hawthorn behind him, and that perhaps the photograph was taken through the hedge. He turns to look at it. It is thick and very dense. It is hard to imagine anyone being able to work a camera lens between the branches.

He crosses the road again and slips back into the driver's seat.

'Sorry about that,' he says. 'I just needed to see.'

'Who was it?' Julie asks.

The question snaps Frank back on to his guard. He turns the key in the ignition, firing the engine. 'Who was what?'

'The person you brought here.'

Following Superintendent Frank Shakespeare and his wife proves much harder than Tami had imagined it would be. It's nothing like the movies. To start with, she's in the wrong car. The Fiat doesn't have enough acceleration. And it's the wrong colour.

None of which seemed like a problem when she bought the thing. She'd been out of prison a month, and it had hit her that she wasn't going to get work unless she could travel. And then she saw it parked by the roadside with a FOR SALE note stuck in the back window. It was the fact that it was so different from every other car that attracted her to it. The furry animals and Mister Men dangling from the inside of the windows. Buying it was a deliberate statement to herself that she could do whatever she wanted and that she no longer needed to blend in. She paid the £200 asking price on the condition that the ornaments would be included.

But to blend in is something that she would at this moment love to be able to do. She's following the superintendent's car along a road out into the countryside. She sees him indicating right, heading up into the hills. Now she has to hold well back to avoid being seen. He keeps disappearing around bends and over ridges, and she has to wait anxious seconds before catching a view of him again.

Then he suddenly slows and she finds herself getting too close.

She drops back and he disappears once more, over the hilltop. She puts her foot to the floor, trying to catch up. But there is no sign of him over the other side. She races on, the engine whining in protest.

She sees him at the last moment, reversing out of a side road. There's no way to stop without making it obvious, so she carries on past him, watching him in the rear-view mirror. He's started driving up the road behind her. She drops her speed, letting him get closer. But just as he is getting to the right distance, he pulls abruptly into a lay-by. Within two seconds he's out of sight behind her. She stops. The car rocks slightly with the uneven beat of the engine.

She is trying to work out what the policeman is doing. The erratic driving makes his Sunday afternoon in the countryside look like a search for something. But he's not in uniform and his wife is with him – which means this isn't police business. And that brings her back to Shakespeare's questioning of her about Jack.

She finds a farm track to reverse into, then heads back the way she came. There are two other cars in front of her now, Sunday-afternoon dawdlers. She sits tight behind them and watches for the lay-by. Shakespeare's car is still parked there. She gets a view of Shakespeare's wife in the passenger seat as she approaches. As she passes she sees the super-intendent out of his car, flattened against the hedge.

Tami turns the car again and starts back towards the lay-by. Slowly this time. She feels a sense of frustration. She has never been good at subterfuge. Unlike with Gabriel, she isn't facing a dangerous criminal. She can see Shakespeare's car up ahead. She slows further.

And then she makes a snap decision. It may be the wrong

thing to do, but for the first time in many years she feels sure that it is really her own choice. She hits the brake and turns the steering wheel left, taking her car in so that it stops just in front of the policeman's.

She gets out and marches directly back. The hedge is reflected in his windscreen so she can't see what's happening inside until she gets level with the side window and bends down.

He is in the driver's seat. His wife sits next to him.

'Hi,' Tami says. 'I thought it was you. Coincidence, huh?'

She has no idea what he will say or do. All she is hoping is for her unexpected appearance to shake something out of his tree. She catches a moment of shock in his face, followed by the same, veiled smile that he wore when he was questioning her in her flat. But it's his wife's face that makes the biggest impression. Because after a moment of silence, her mouth thins to a line. She folds her arms and stares out of the front window. Shoulders like steel rods.

Chapter 11

Tami recognizes the face of the man but doesn't know his name. He was a friend of Jack's: that is the only thing she is sure of. She remembers seeing him in a pub once, the White Ox perhaps. He had long red hair and wore a denim jacket. Now he is in a suit. The hair is still red, but short-cropped.

'Are you Tami?' he asks.

'What do you want?'

'To talk to you about your husband.'

'Then talk.'

'It can't be out here.'

Tami folds her arms, keeping her elbows wide, filling the doorway as best she can. Rita is in the bedroom. She might or might not be asleep. Whatever Owen has to say, Tami doesn't want the woman knowing.

Owen's eyes plead. 'It's very private, what I have to say.'

'So whisper.'

He drops his voice. 'No one told me you were out. I would have come sooner.'

'What did you want me to do – take out an advert?'

'Your friends might have said something. Word gets around. That's the usual way.'

'I don't have friends.'

This statement seems to embarrass the man further. He scrapes the sole of one shoe across the carpet.

'So why are you here?' she asks. 'Someone send you?'

He nods.

'Then spit it out!'

He looks up and meets her eyes for the first time. 'Jack.'

Tami was in a car crash once. This is the same. There is no physical damage, but she has a sense that her body has just been hit by something and part of her – some connecting cable in her mind – has been jolted out of place. She doesn't feel any different from the way she did a moment before. She's not shaking or crying or shouting at him. But there is a sense that these emotions exist somewhere inside her and aren't getting through.

She finds herself being guided inside the flat. He is steering her by the elbow, manoeuvring her into her own living room. She should resent this. But lacking the feelings she would normally channel into lashing out at him, she just goes where he directs. When the big armchair is behind her, she sits.

'Tea, isn't it?' he says. 'That's the thing. I'll get the kettle on.'

'What?'

'It's the shock, you see. You've gone white.'

Some resentment spills through into her awareness. 'Stop pissing around and tell me where he is!'

'Jack? I don't know.'

'You said you had a message.'

'He told me to find you when you got out.'

'So you did see him!'

'It was a long time ago. I'm sorry. It must have been . . . nine years. It was the week before Christmas. You were in prison. He told me that if anything happened to him, that I should find you when you got out. And . . . and here I am.'

Tami opens her mouth to speak, but the words don't

seem important enough to give breath to, so she closes it again.

Owen glances around the flat. He seems unsure of what to do next. Tami feels as if she is shouting at him to give her the message, though she isn't making any sound.

He clears his throat. 'Jack wanted you to know about the man who was threatening you. In case . . . well, in case the worst happened. He was going to meet whoever it was – that was the plan. Up in Glasgow. My guess is he was thinking it would be dangerous. That's why he told me to give you this.'

She sees Owen take an envelope from his inside jacket pocket. He hesitates, then passes it to her. Her name on the outside is written in Jack's unmistakable hand.

Dear Tami,
I'm sorry for all the trouble that's been dumped on you.
I've done my best to sort it. But it's got worse the more
I've done. I'm going to Scotland today and it'll be fixed
one way or the other. I'm giving this letter to Dad to
hand to you if things go wrong. He'll explain.
* I love you.*
* Jack*

In a different pen at the bottom of the page, looking as if it was hurriedly written: *Dad is out of town. I'm leaving this with Red Owen.* And below that, scrawled in pencil, is an address in Glasgow.

Frank feels old now. But then they are all old – the men who hammered out the agreement. That's what the decades do. It's not the wrinkles or grey hair that are so consuming. They accumulate by increments. You can measure extra pounds on the bathroom scales. Differences of degree. But the change of direction from progress to decay – this is absolute. The passing from one life into another.

Frank has watched this happening to himself and has found some comfort in the thought that perhaps accumulating wisdom acts as a counterbalance to decreasing strength and stamina. In himself he can believe this. But then Eddie Piper opens the door to him and stands blinking in the sunshine and the illusion vanishes. It takes a few seconds for Frank to even recognize the shambling heap Eddie has become. The stained T-shirt does nothing to hide the way his stomach now hangs over his belt. If the man had been given the wisdom of Solomon in the intervening years, it still wouldn't make up for what he's lost.

Eddie blinks rapidly. 'Sergeant Shakespeare?'

'It's superintendent,' Frank says.

'Superintendent.'

'But call me Frank.'

Eddie leaves his jaw hanging slack, as if he, too, can't believe what the years have done. 'I guess you'd better come in.'

Frank last saw him around the same time he lost contact with Bill Arnica. Back then the man used to work out three times a week. Four, sometimes. Running mostly, plus sessions working on free weights down at St Margaret's sports centre. He had the kind of body that an anatomy student could use to revise muscle groups. Biceps. Triceps. Pectorals. Deltoids. And he spent money on clothes so that he could show off all the work he'd put in. He smoked, of course. But everyone smoked back then. And if he drank a few pints, it never seemed to put an ounce of fat on his body.

This isn't the house where Eddie used to live. A few

phone calls have already yielded the fact that this place is rented. The old house is held in his wife's name. The rest of the story was an easy guess. And looking at the way Eddie has run to seed, Frank feels confident that his guess is correct.

Eddie's rented house has everything it would take to look good. The living room contains a grey leather three-piece suite, resting on a soft, deep-blue carpet. There is a wide-screen TV and a new-looking nest of occasional tables. It would be like a picture from a furniture catalogue if someone were first to clear the take-away cartons from the floor, the beer glasses, the scatter of newspapers. Curiously, the glass ashtray looks to have been wiped clean.

'It's been a long time,' Frank says.

Eddie lets out an embarrassed laugh. 'The place probably looks a bit of a tip. I . . .'

'It doesn't matter.'

'It does. I'm sorry. I've changed to working nights and it's thrown me a bit. I don't usually . . . you know . . .' He sweeps a hand around, indicating the state of the room.

'What about Paula?' Frank asks.

'She . . . you know. She thought . . . and me too . . . that it'd be the best thing if we . . .'

'I'm sorry,' Frank says. And he means it. He used to get on well with Eddie and his young wife. They were a couple that everyone wanted to be with.

'And we're still friends,' Eddie says. 'Which is brilliant.'

'Yes.'

'I could wash a couple of glasses,' he says. 'There's beer. Or . . . or I guess you're on duty . . . There's some blackcurrant.'

'I'm not on duty. This is a private matter.'

Eddie stops, as if reassessing. A suspicion of confidence

comes into his posture, adding a couple of centimetres to his height. 'You sit, then. I'll get the beer.' He gathers a cluster of glasses from the floor near the armchair and heads out of the room. Frank follows him through a small dining room and into a kitchen at the back of the house.

Eddie moves enough dirty plates from the sink to make it possible for him to get the beer glasses under the tap. Frank stands in the doorway, arms crossed, watching the other man work. Letting him stew for a few seconds. Eddie keeps glancing at him. The light from the window shows up the sweat on his forehead and upper lip.

It isn't that Frank wants Eddie to suffer. But this is like any police interview. It has to start with the suspect off balance. If the questioner can keep him that way, all the better. If the suspect gets too confident, then extracting information becomes hard and slow.

'What job are you on, Eddie?'

'Now?'

'You said you work nights.'

'Yeah. It's uh . . . down the industrial estate.'

'A factory?'

'Yes.'

'The clothing industry?'

'Something like that. Yeah.'

Frank is glad of the resistance in Eddie's answers. The more evasive the man gets, the closer they are getting to interesting information. It is like a game of hunt the thimble with the person who hid the thing saying *warmer* or *colder* to guide the seekers in.

'Does the work pay well?'

Eddie is wiping the glasses on a limp tea towel. 'You know how it is,' he says. 'Overtime helps.'

There's a slight brightening in Eddie's voice, so Frank

decides to double back. 'The factory you work at – tell me about it.'

'It's . . . uh, you know . . . knitwear. Like you said.'

'They run a night shift?'

Eddie levers a bottle opener with a practised snap of the wrist and tosses the cap towards the bin. It bounces off an empty bean can and skits on to the floor. He pours, tilting the glass, his forehead creased with concentration.

'Eddie?' Frank prompts.

'Yeah?'

'You haven't answered.'

'Answered what?'

'I can check up all this detail from other people if you want. But it's much better if it comes from you. Don't you think?'

Eddie's shoulders slump. He seems to grow shorter and, in profile, his stomach bulges further, submerging his belt.

'Don't. It'd finish me. Please.'

'Then tell me.'

'I . . . I had to go round begging for work – door to door. And no one's hiring. It's humiliating, you know? Had to take what they gave me.'

'You're a security guard?'

'I didn't mean it to go like that.'

Frank wants to laugh, but he clenches his jaw muscles and holds his gaze steady. 'They asked about previous convictions, of course.'

'I couldn't tell them . . .'

'You couldn't tell them that they were employing the most prolific burglar out of the whole of the St John's estate to look after night-time security. No. I can imagine.'

'You're making it sound . . .'

'What?'

'I'm going straight.'

'You can't tell me you haven't been tempted, Eddie. All that gear lying around. Only you in charge.'

'Shit, Frank. Please don't tell. I'm holding it together. But if I lost the job . . .'

He is mumbling now. It sounds as if he is on the edge of tears. That's not something Frank wants to see.

'No one needs to know.'

'Haven't done a house in seven years.'

'Sure.'

'I mean it, Frank. It's the truth.'

And the strange thing is, it really sounds as if he is being sincere. But for someone like Eddie, there isn't usually any way out. The rewards of breaking and entering are just too generous. Choosing a harder, more honest path is never easy. And for a professional like Eddie, there is no reason why he couldn't keep it up for years without being caught.

'How long has Paula been gone?'

'Five months. No. Six.'

'Didn't she like you going straight?'

Eddie doesn't answer. He's pouring his own beer now. In a hurry. Letting it slop out into the glass. He gulps some through the foam. Three long swallows, then he pours the rest of the bottle in.

'I'm not going to make things worse for you,' Frank says. 'I just want to ask some questions about the old days, OK?'

Eddie nods. 'The old days.'

'Gabriel – you remember him?'

'The Russian? Yeah.'

'And Arnica? What do you know about them?'

'Old Billy Arnica's done all right.' Eddie brightens slightly – as if he can see the possibility of escape.

'John and Jack Steel?'

'John was the best,' Eddie says. 'None like him any more. You could trust him, even though he was on our side of the fence, you know?' His voice is starting to come alive. There is a touch of a smile on his face as he mentions the father and son.

'What happened to Jack?'

Eddie shrugs, and just for a moment Frank thinks he sees the veils closing behind the man's eyes.

'What does that mean?'

'It means I haven't seen him.'

'Since when?'

'Since he went off to Glasgow, following that bird he got pregnant. And then his father kicked the bucket – and Jack wasn't even there at the funeral. You wonder how he could get like that.'

'You have children?' Frank asks, suddenly curious.

'We . . . couldn't.'

'Your fault or hers?'

Eddie shrinks again but doesn't answer.

Frank hates himself for what he is putting Eddie through. Sometimes it's worth giving the tree a shake, just to see what falls out. But he knows this is cruel. Desperation is driving him, that's what he tells himself. There are only four days left until he has to pay the blackmailer again. He has £10,000 but doesn't know where from or what he will be expected to do for it.

'Who was there at John's funeral?' he asks.

'Everyone. The family, of course. I'll not forget Vera's face. She looked so white. And Bill Arnica and all that crowd.'

'Gabriel?'

Eddie shakes his head. 'He was never one of us.'

'Owen?'

'Red Owen? Yeah. He was there, all right. It was one of the

last times I saw him. He went away after that. London, wasn't it? Or Watford. Somewhere south, anyway. God, but I haven't seen him in years. He was moving up to the big time. Going places. He'll be in prison now. That or the House of Lords.'

Eddie grins at his own joke. But when Frank doesn't respond he takes a gulp of beer.

'Anyone else there?'

'The usual crowd. Not you, though.'

Frank takes a breath. 'John Steel was a criminal. There was an anti-corruption drive in the force. It was difficult.'

'Old Kringman made it,' Eddie says.

'He was retiring. They couldn't touch him.'

Frank takes a first sip of his beer. It is warm.

'Why you asking about Jack?' Eddie asks.

'He's missing.'

'Sure. But why now? He's been gone years.'

'Now's as good a time as any,' Frank says. And again he gets the momentary sense that things are being concealed behind the other man's eyes.

Sunday night in the factory. Tami is preparing a tub of sandwich filling, reading the instructions from a plastic-laminated recipe on the wall behind the table. One measure of cooked prawns, five measures of mayonnaise.

She is thinking about the letter from Jack. It isn't evidence that he was faithful to her. Only that he had other things going on – things she did not know about. She still can't believe that his father would have lied to her about something as serious as there being another woman. She feels as if the letter Owen gave her should have changed everything. But the only difference it has made is to increase her uncertainty. She has no idea how to use the information.

She unscrews the mustard jar and measures out a generous spoonful to add to the mix. Then she takes a stainless-steel stirrer and begins working the mixture around in the tub.

One of the other girls calls to her from the sandwich preparation tables: 'Get a move on!'

Tami pretends not to hear. She slows down her mixing. She likes this task. It is agreeably physical. And it is easier to think over here, away from the spiteful chatter. She turns the mixture, enjoying the heavy slop sound as it folds over on to itself.

'You're not avoiding me, are you?' Steve's voice comes from very close behind her, making her jump. It is soft and intimate.

'I'm busy,' she says, not managing to keep the fluster from her voice.

He chuckles.

'And please don't creep up on me like that.'

'Sorry, princess.' He puts a hand on her shoulder and starts working the muscle with small circular movements of his fingertips. 'I'm not making you nervous, am I?'

'A little.'

'We can't have that.'

His hand moves up to her neck. Part of her wants to relax into his touch because he is good at what he is doing. But she knows all the other girls will be watching and she can't let her guard drop.

'I hope you're not mad at me for the other day,' he whispers.

'For what?' She can't think of which of his indiscretions he could be referring to.

'When I drove you to your car and then didn't take you home.'

'Oh.'

'Mmm? Sorry if I left you frustrated.'

The prawn mayonnaise is well mixed now, but she continues to fold it over.

'Mr Lloyd . . .'

'Steve,' he says.

'Steve . . . please stop.'

He chuckles again. 'Am I putting you off?'

She nods.

He lets his fingers trail down to the small of her back before pulling his hand away. 'I had a word with the boss,' he says, 'about you being absent for your shift the other day. I told him you had problems because of the riot, persuaded him to let it pass this time.'

'Thank you.'

'I stuck my neck out for you, princess.'

She tries to swallow but the movement gets caught somewhere in her throat.

'Let me drive you home after the shift.' He is so close to her as he whispers this that she can feel the warmth of his breath on her ear.

'Need to sleep.'

'Then sleep afterwards.'

'Too tired.'

'We're starting a morning shift on Tuesday,' he tells her. 'I put your name down. That gives you twenty-four hours to get as much sleep as you want before you're on again.'

She turns to face him. 'Don't I get a choice which shift I work?'

'I'm going to be managing it,' he says. 'It'll give us more time together.'

Tami wants to tell him off for assuming so much. But she knows that part of what he says is true. He has been protecting her. And the shift change does give her twenty-four hours. That might be enough time to do something about the information Red Owen gave her.

He lifts his hand to her forehead and tucks a loose strand back into her hairnet. 'What about it, then – after work? You can show me how grateful you are.'

'I . . .'

'Or are you still playing hard to get?'

One of the girls shouts from the preparation table. 'Get a move on with that prawn mayonnaise!'

'I have to go,' Tami says. 'I'm sorry.'

The phone wakes Frank.

'Franky, boy?' It's Kringman's voice.

Frank blinks to clear his vision. He looks at the bedside clock. 'Speaking.'

'You've been having trouble with racists.'

For a moment the compartmentalization in Frank's mind starts to break down. Racists and riots – this is the problem of his work. The chief constable looking for a scapegoat. Mo Akanbai and her memo. But Kringman – he is concerned with the blackmail photograph. 'I don't understand.'

'I have a name for you,' Kringman says.

'What are you talking about?'

'Go and see Vince,' Kringman says. 'Go now. Go alone.'

'It's not my case,' Frank says. 'The Race Crime Unit is in charge.' But the retired superintendent has already hung up.

There is only one Vince that Frank knows of who could have anything to do with the desecration of the Dean Street Mosque. Vince the Prince, he is called. He's been around for as long as Frank can remember, fixing things on the St John's estate. He's not the kind who will ever make it to be a major criminal. There is no business strategy about the man. What motivates him is the thirst for a kind of tribal power. He's not a person that Frank would choose to visit. Especially not on his own. Going is a risk. But not going is a risk also. Kringman may be corrupt, but he is uniquely well connected.

It is half-past eleven when Frank pulls up his car at Vince's address. It's an ex-council house on a sink estate. There is nothing to recommend it. The lights are on downstairs. The door opens before Frank can knock.

Vince the Prince is standing there in a vest and shorts. His well-muscled arms are hanging by his sides. 'Yeah?'

'Superintendent Shakespeare,' Frank says. 'May I come in?'

Vince steps back with a flourish of the arm and the curl of a cruel smile. 'Be my guest.'

The cleanliness of the house surprises Frank. New-looking carpet. Bright, silvery door handles. He can see the flicker of television light from the front room. The volume is low. Vince leads him into the kitchen and closes the door behind them. There is a faint smell of fish and chips here, but not a cup or plate is out of place. The stainless-steel draining board gleams. The only thing on the work surface is a folded newspaper.

Frank hasn't got a plan, except to press straight on with the most direct kind of questioning. If Vince was connected with the race hate crime, then he might get a reaction of some sort. 'You've heard about the Dean Street mosque?' he asks.

'Sure.'

'I've been told it was you that did it.'

Vince chuckles. 'You've come here to say that?'

'Was it you?'

Vince opens the fridge and retrieves two bottles of American beer. He pulls the tops and starts pouring. 'That's not why you're here,' he says.

'I'm on duty,' Frank tells him. 'I can't drink that.'

'No, you're not and, yes, you can.' Vince puts a glass in his hand.

Frank can feel his heartbeat. It has that over-heavy, irregular feel that it gets at moments of the highest stress. 'I'm here,' he says, 'to question you about the . . .'

'You're here,' Vince cuts in, 'because Kringman told you to come. You're here to get your instructions. And to drink to our business deal. I gave you ten grand. You get to feed me the information I need.'

Frank takes a swallow of beer, trying to cover his shock.

'Got a problem with that?' Vince asks.

'I . . . need to think.'

'Kringman said you'd do it.'

'How did he know you had . . . work?'

'He's too old to do it any more. That's why.'

Frank absorbs this, keeping his poker smile in place. His facial muscles feel like lead. 'How long was he helping you?'

'That's between him and me.'

Frank swallows more beer. He'd been praying that the criminal who provided the money wouldn't contact him for another few days. A little time was all he needed. Four more days. He could have used the money as bait to trap the blackmailer, then returned it unused. Now he is being forced to choose between two impossible options. 'What information do you want?'

Vince's eyes play over Frank. He tilts his head like a terrier examining a mouse hole. 'Information. If they're planning on arresting me. Or doing a search. Anything like that. And there's something else.'

He reaches for the paper on the work surface. It is the *Crusader*. He unfolds it on the front page and points to Mo Akanbai's picture. 'What do you know about this woman?'

'I've seen her a couple of times,' Frank says. 'That's all. She doesn't work with me.' He swallows some more beer.

Vince nods. 'I want information on her as well.'

'I understand.'

'You've got my money. You try and double-cross me and I'll take you down. Understand that.'

Frank's mind is reeling. The irregular beat of his heart is getting worse. He wants to bluff it out, to give himself time to think. 'It's late,' he says. 'I have to go home.'

Vince finishes his drink. He examines the empty glass in his hand. 'You haven't said if we've got a deal.'

'Yes.' Frank says. 'Of course.'

Vince smiles. 'Good choice,' he says.

Chapter 12

The idea starts like this: Vince the Prince wants harm to come to someone. That someone is Inspector Mo Akanbai. Frank knows her well enough to guess that she won't lie low and let the storm blow over. At the same time, the chief constable is looking for officers to take the heat over the handling of the riot. Frank decides to sleep on it. His mind motors all night and sleep doesn't happen. It is around three in the morning when the pieces of the puzzle come together. By dawn he has devised a possible plan. He can't see why it wouldn't work, but it seems crazy nonetheless.

If Mo could be suspended – temporarily – then she'd be out of the firing line, away from any danger that Vince might want to throw at her. An officer like Mo isn't going to be down for long. She is too good. Too ambitious. Too politically necessary to be thrown out. So all he needs to do is to give her a little push. She'll stumble. Everyone will end up better off. Her included. And Frank wouldn't have to admit that he's holding money from a known racist criminal.

The idea is still there in his head when he gets into the police station five hours later. He marches to his office, pulls the papers out of the in-tray and drops himself into his chair. Then he sees it – a memo sitting on top of the pile. It is from the chief constable. Handwritten.

*Been a complaint about Akanbai. Probably nothing. Bad
timing though. Complaints and Discipline will want to
talk to her. It's about her conduct after the riot. Thought
you should know.*

Frank sits, staring at the sheet of paper. Suddenly his idea
doesn't seem so implausible. If Complaints and Discipline
are going to be looking into her case anyway, all he would
need to do would be to give a tiny extra push. And it would
be for her safety. To get her out of the way for a few months.
His head feels so full of fatigue that everything seems slightly
unreal – from his plan to the solid desk in front of him.

The first step should be easy to take. He tells himself that
he can always back out later.

He dials Mo's number. She picks up on the third ring. She
always does.

'Inspector Akanbai,' she says. Bright and efficient.

'Mo. How are you fixed for this evening?'

'I . . . was planning on finishing off some paperwork, sir.'

The 'sir' sounds overemphasized, and it occurs to him
that his question might have sounded like a proposition. So
he says: 'There's a meeting at the Walkers Stadium.
Preparation for the multiculturalism conference. I can't go
myself.'

The words come out smoothly, and for a fraction of a
second he worries that he finds it too easy to lie. 'I'd like you
to go instead of me. Represent the constabulary. The reports
are printed out already. No problem, is there?'

There is a short pause before she says: 'No.'

He gives her the details and hangs up.

Tami gets off the train in Glasgow Central Station and her
first thought – quite unexpected – is the sudden fear that she

might see Jack walking down the platform towards her. This was to be his new home city in the version of the story that she has lived with for the longest. That was one of the bricks in the foundation when she started to rebuild her life all those years ago. Even if she now thinks it might have been a lie, the image of him living here is buried deeply inside her.

But he isn't on the platform. Nor does she see him when she walks out on to the street, though her eye jumps ahead, scanning the faces of the people walking towards her and the backs of the heads of those who are walking away.

The city feels big in the same way that London felt big. It is a question of scale. Terraces of high buildings on either side of wide streets. A sense that there will be more of the place around the next corner and the next and on for further than she could walk.

It takes her ten minutes to get properly lost. She stands at a corner, trying to read the street names. But even having identified the intersection in her map book, she can't work out which direction she should take to get her closer to the address that Jack had scrawled on the letter. She feels a sense of panic building in her chest. It was crazy enough to have come all this way on a hunch. She should be getting some sleep during her time off, not chasing ghosts. And more stupid still – she is disobeying her probation officer. Miss Quick told her not to leave Leicester again without informing her first.

Tami could still turn around and retrace her steps. It can't be so hard to find the station again. Take the next train back south. Ashamed but not damaged.

'Are you lost or what?'

She turns to see an elderly man with a big smile and chipped front teeth. Inexplicably, his accent is Australian.

'You've had your nose in the A to Z for the last five minutes.'

'I know where I am,' she tells him. 'But not which way the map should point.'

'Depends on where you're heading.'

She doesn't think that can be correct, but she nods anyway.

'And where are you trying to go?'

She takes the letter, folds it over so that only the address is showing and holds it up for him to see. He takes it from her hand and she starts to panic.

'Please . . .'

But he doesn't seem to be listening to her. He holds the paper close to his face. 'The eyes aren't what they used to be.'

She catches hold of the corner, and tries to get it from him. 'Please can I . . .'

'I know the street,' he says, releasing the paper at last. He strokes his chin with one leathery finger, then points back the way she has just come.

'You want down there. Second right. Then straight on to the end of the street and make a left. That'll take you there, all right.' He tilts his head for a moment. 'Better I go along with you, eh?'

She would refuse, but he has already started to walk. 'First time I ever came here, some bloke I didn't know from Adam walked me across between the stations because I didn't know the way. That's why I settled here. It's a great town.'

He continues to speak about his life as he walks along the pavement. She hurries to keep up with his easy stride.

'Nowhere else in the wide world people will go so far out of their way to help you as here. You're thinking it's a rough city. True enough for parts of it. Like this street you're going to now.'

'Bad?'

'Not so much in the daytime. And not so bad as it used to be – from what they say.'

They turn a corner and Tami sees the street name that she has been searching for. 'It's number 283,' she tells him.

'I'm going this way anyway,' he says.

And she does feel grateful.

'Visiting friends?' he asks.

'Not really.'

'Work?'

'It's a . . . building. I need to see it. An address, that's all. A friend of mine came here.'

She looks to one side and sees that his grey eyebrows are raised high.

'You're sure of the address?'

'Number 283. Yes.'

'Well, you're here.' He nods towards a large rectangle of grass, with paths and benches and young rowan trees. 'That was 281 back there and this up ahead . . .'

She follows him along the pavement to the front of the next building.

'. . . is 285.'

Tami finds that she is walking back towards the grass. There is a lump of pinkish stone, roughly cut but for one side, which is perfectly flat and into which an inscription has been cut. *Freedom Park.*

'Was it a factory, this place your friend went?'

'I don't know.'

She feels a sting in her tear ducts and she knows she is about to cry. She tenses up, trying to stop it. Once it has started she will have to let all the emotion pour out and there won't be any holding back the tears until it is done.

'It was,' he says. 'I remember it now. A paint factory.'

She digs a long thumbnail into the palm of her hand, pulling herself back from the edge. Her eyes are watery, but she turns to look at him anyway.

'It was years ago. But you don't forget something like that.' He must be able to read her confusion, because he adds: 'It was a fire. Half the city's fire trucks trying to put it out. There was so much paint in the building that in the end all they could do was pull back and spray the other buildings all around to keep them cool so they didn't go up as well. The sky was orange with it. They had drums of something in there that went off like a room full of landmines. A complete burnout.' He shakes his head. 'A miracle more people weren't killed.'

'So it's gone,' she says, knowing she is stating the obvious. She's travelled halfway across the country for nothing.

'Sorry,' he says.

She reaches out and touches the railings. She doesn't know what she would have done, even if it had been standing.

'Thinking about it,' the man says, 'it must have been ten years, maybe. Or maybe nine. The time just slips by when you're my age.'

Tami finds that she has turned towards him. Her hands are grasping the map book so hard that her knuckles look like marble. 'When?' she hears herself asking. 'What month?'

'That's easy. It was December. The week before Christmas.'

The library has the same atmosphere as the one she visited in London. The same smell. Tens of millions of pages of printed paper. The man behind the desk has pale-blue eyes and the kind of weathered face that would look more at home on a rock band's roadie than on a librarian. She asks him about copies of the local paper for the week before Christmas in the year Jack went missing.

'Aye, we do have them.'

She looks towards the rack of papers at the side.

'The old ones are down in the stack.'

'And?'

'It'd take me a wee minute to find them.'

He hesitates, as if giving her space to say that he shouldn't bother. But she's come too far for that.

He inhales slowly, as if the effort of breathing is all he can cope with today. 'You'd better wait here, then.'

She watches him go, then looks up to the wall clock. The long hand clicks forward an increment, moving towards the top of the hour. Her last train leaves at ten to five – in fifty minutes. The journey to Leicester will take her five hours. She should have enough time to shower and sleep and be up fresh, ready to clock on for the early morning shift in the sandwich factory.

She's trying to work out how far it is from here to Glasgow Central Station. Twenty minutes, perhaps. If she leaves by twenty past, she should still have plenty of time.

There's a question that has kept swimming about in her mind – about what she hopes to achieve through this research. It surfaces now. She doesn't think she wants to see Jack again. If she saw him walking through the library door, her impulse would be to run for the emergency exit. But neither can she put a lid on his memory and the emotions it churns up inside her. She needs to know the history of her separation from him. 'Discovering' that he'd been unfaithful and deserted her was like having a skewer driven into her flesh. Immediate, white-hot pain. Pain so strong that she happily watched the blood flowing from her own wrists in the knowledge that she would sleep without ever waking up. It wasn't a cry for help like they said. It was a leap towards oblivion.

Now she has been told that the old story was a lie.

She can't remember the pain directly but it is as if one of the layers of self-protection has been pulled away. The memory is still veiled, but not so heavily. She feels as if she has been woken suddenly but incompletely from a deep sleep. She wants to go back into sleep or to wake up fully. Anything but the confusion of this in-between world, with the shreds of old dreams snagged around her mind.

She hears the thump of a pile of papers dropping on to the desk. The roadie librarian is there, looking at her.

'Bring 'em back to the desk when you're through,' he says.

Tami doesn't have to leaf through the inner pages to find it. The picture on the Wednesday's cover is of a black sky lit with orange flame and a silhouette of the Glasgow roof-scape, with an arc of bright yellow and white curving up from the centre of the fire towards the left, looking like the launch of a ballistic missile. *Exploding oil drum*, the caption says.

It is clear from the article that the flames were still not out at the time of going to press. No one quoted seemed to think that there was any hope of salvaging the factory itself. The main question was damage to surrounding properties. Several cars in the street had been destroyed and another building fifty metres away had caught fire – though that had been put out very quickly. She turns to pages two and three and sees more photographs. A column of black and grey smoke seen from a distance over the landmarks of the city. A close-up of a fireman leaning against the pressure of the hose, directing a jet of water through a factory window. The articles mention possible causes of the fire. Bad wiring. A cigarette lit by a rough sleeper. Children playing with matches. Arson.

Tami glances at the clock again. She still has ten minutes.

The cover of the Thursday paper shows an image of the gutted building. Police tape stretches across the road. The sky is visible through the factory windows. Everything in the building seems to be gone – floors, walls, roof. The caption reads: *Factory fire: pictures inside.*

She finds an article on page three. The factory had been closed for two months because the company had gone into receivership. Though most of the windows and doors had been boarded up to stop thieves breaking in and stripping the place, it was clear that several rough sleepers had been using it to doss down in at night. The temperature dipped to minus four on the night the fire started. Anyone sleeping there would have wanted some kind of fire – just to stay alive. That was the direction the police investigation was going when the paper went to print. Police were treating the factory ruins as a crime scene and stated that it could be days before they could say for certain that no one died in the blaze. As for insurance cover – the value of the payout was thought to be in excess of £4 million. Tami can't find any reference to who the money would go to. The receivers, presumably.

She finds herself putting the Thursday paper to one side and moving on to Friday, aware that time is moving past her, knowing that she will have to run when she has finished. The story is back on the lead spot at the top of the front page. She feels her stomach clenching up as she reads the headline. *Factory Fire Body Found.*

This is the point where Tami could still make it to the train – physically it would be do-able. But she realizes now that it wasn't ever a real possibility – not since she looked at the park where the factory used to stand. She takes a last glance at the clock and continues reading.

The remains of a body – thought to be that of a male adult – were discovered under a fallen partition wall. No visual identification was going to be possible because of the fire damage. The police were appealing for information from rough sleepers in the area and from agencies that were working with them. Pieces of metal found near the body must have belonged to a primus stove – though fire investigators were saying that the blaze began in another part of the factory altogether. Arson had climbed to the top of the list of possible causes.

Tami finds herself taking the stack of papers back to the desk.

'Did you find what you were after?' the librarian asks.

'The next week . . . need to see the papers after this . . . I . . .'

She sees him glancing at his watch. But this time he doesn't hold out to be let off the chore. He jots down the details on a scrap of paper and strides away. She waits, trying to look as composed as the other users of the library. She opens a women's magazine that is lying on the desk and pretends to read an article on how to determine a man's character from his handwriting.

There is a monster circling under the surface of her thoughts. She can feel the turbulence in the wake of its movement. She knows it is there but dare not look directly at it in case her awareness brings it up to the surface.

A body. She wonders what remains of a corpse once it has been in a fire like that, whether it is charred flesh, or if only bone is left, or if perhaps it is just a pile of dust, something that mourning relatives could scatter from an urn in some favourite place. She doesn't know where she would like to have her own remains spread. Bradgate Park, perhaps. She used to go there as a child, before she met Jack.

Jack. She finds it hard to think of him right now. It is as if her mind gets foggy when she tries to recall his image. She feels herself drifting.

Jack. He came to Glasgow in the week before Christmas. Perhaps on the train, like she did. Or perhaps he drove. He walked down the same street. She sees it in her mind now, as if through his eyes. The buildings close-packed and tall. And it was winter. The blue sky is replaced in the image by grey, darkening towards dusk. And there is the factory, straight out of the *before* picture from the newspaper. She imagines the windows boarded. But the homeless man must have found a way inside somehow.

She sees one of the boards cracked, with a corner broken away. Big enough to clamber through. Into what? She doesn't know. Her eyes are slowly adjusting to the almost black. Just the thin light leaking in through the staved-in window. No heating. She sees her breath condensing in the air in front of her face. She walks forward into it, hands stretched out in front of her. A paint factory. Would she be able to smell the solvents? She inhales through her nose. Just cold, damp air. Concrete dust, perhaps. Idle machinery in front of her.

'Here you go, then.'

Tami jolts out from her vision, back to the here and now of the library. Her breath is coming fast. She finds that her eyes are looking at the far side of the reading room, though they are only now starting to take in the physical reality of the place.

'You feeling OK?' he asks.

'Fine. Yes. Thank you.'

She takes the pile of newspapers from the desk and

hurries back to the table, trying not to look as strange as she feels.

There is a photograph in the Saturday paper, a repeat image of the fire – the exploding oil drum. The police had upgraded their investigation to a murder inquiry. Tami reads how fire investigators had discovered solvent residues in the factory – mostly the kind of thing that would have been expected in connection with paint manufacture. But two of the samples taken had proved to be different. Someone had been splashing petrol around two windows on opposite sides of the building – possible entry and exit points. Petrol inside. Petrol outside. A deathtrap. Tami closes the paper. Her vision is tunnelled, seeing only the newsprint, unaware even of the desk on which the papers lie.

There is no paper for the Sunday.

Monday. The city working towards the holiday. Reports touching on the paint factory are buried on the inside pages. There's an article on homelessness at Christmas that mentions the factory. An opinion piece by a local clergyman quotes Jesus saying that the poor are always with us. There is an article on drug use among rough sleepers that suggests heroin may have been a motive for the murder. Tuesday. Christmas Eve. A thick paper, full of advertisements for January sales, some due to start on Boxing Day. Three-piece suites and dishwashers. The report of *nothing to report* in the murder investigation is tucked away on page five.

No newspaper on Christmas Day.

She leafs through the remainder of the week's news but finds nothing more. Everyone was moving towards the New Year. Starting afresh.

And Tami – she tries to remember what was happening to her when all this was going on in Glasgow. It must have been on the television news. She should have seen it herself.

It was her first Christmas in prison. Not yet at the anniversary of being inside. She was just managing to hold it all together. Rita was protecting her from the murderous Joy. She was looking forward to Jack's next letter. His next visit. But there were no more visits. She knows that she can't let herself move any further in this direction. There is a deep black pool of despair in front of her. She was immersed in it once before. She doesn't know if she could climb out a second time.

Jack.

She can't even picture his face now. She sees him walking away from her. The back of his head. His shoulders. She moves forward, trying to catch up, but he is always just out of her reach. She wants him to turn around. But he won't do it.

'Jack?'

No response.

'Jack!'

'Miss . . .'

The librarian is touching her shoulder with his hand, shaking gently. Her face is wet, tears running.

He eases the pile of newspapers from under her arm, pulls them clear and wipes a smudge from the top page. 'Closing time,' he whispers. 'Sorry, hen. If you come back another day, ask for me. The name's Pat. I'll do what I can.'

She wants to say something that will explain, but each time she tries to put the words together in her mind, they seem wrong. So she just nods her head.

Pat looks at her, his face full of concern. 'Where are you from?'

'Leicester.'

'That'll be the accent then. And you're reading about the fire?'

'Yes.'

He hefts the pile of papers off the table. 'You don't have to talk about it if you don't want to.'

'I . . . It's OK.'

'They never found out, you know.'

'Found what?'

'Who the killer was – the one who murdered the tramp.'

'It *was* a tramp, then?'

'Sure.'

'They know that for certain?' She stands up and faces him.

Pat shrugs. 'They never found a name. But it had to be a tramp, sure enough. No one else would be in a place like that.'

Early evening and, though the police station never really sleeps, it is quieter than during the day. Policing goes on around the clock, but the bits that can be scheduled ahead of time can usually wait for daylight. Frank makes a point of stopping to chat with the desk sergeant. Listening to the man's gripes with a patient smile. Making it seem like there is no great hurry. He keeps his hands in his trouser pockets. Less chance of the tremor being visible that way. The man doesn't even ask why he's working so late. Frank feels pleased with himself. Everything is normal. Everything is good.

He walks back into the building, through the quiet corridors. There are lights on here and there. A few ultra-keen officers. Mo would have been one of them. But she should be at home, eating a quick meal before heading out to the football stadium for the multiculturalism meeting.

Sure enough, the Community Relations office is dark. He steps through the door and looks around. His eyes are adjusting to the gloom, and he starts to be able to pick out details of the furniture. He can just see through the glass partition that separates off Mo's mini office. Her computer monitor is a grey rectangle against the ghost-white wall behind. He steps across the room, opens her door and sits in her chair. When he was here before, he noticed her scent in the air. But now, in the dark, he feels her presence more strongly, as if his sensitivity to her smell is made more acute because of what he is doing.

He presses the power button and the computer hums into life. The screen brightens, flooding him with harsh light. He glances back at the outer door, checking what he already knows – that he can't be seen from outside. Then he is back to the screen, fully focused.

There is a picture of Van Gogh's *Sunflowers* on the screen. He accesses the menu and clicks the mouse button, bringing up a list of Mo's files. She must have typed her memo on this computer. That means a record of it will remain on the hard disk. He searches for a likely-looking name in the file list. His eye settles on one called *Riot Memo*. He double-clicks it, and the contents open up on the screen. He rereads the phrases. *Thanks for listening to my warning about tension in the Muslim community.* Bingo.

Getting rid of the physical memo from her filing cabinet wasn't enough. While the digital file exists on the computer, she still has the evidence to protect herself. He selects *Riot Memo* and rests his finger on the DELETE button. His mind follows the track of logic he wore last night, reminding himself that this is for Mo's safety.

He wonders what else he will have to do to get her temporarily suspended. Removing her get-out-of-jail card isn't going to be enough. She will need another push. Some words to the chief constable. And perhaps something else.

He reads the file details on the screen and an idea comes to him. It is so simple and elegant that he wants to laugh out loud. His fingers move quickly on the mouse and the keyboard. First he makes a copy of the file, calling it *Temp*. Then he deletes the original. And finally he re-names the file he has created, changing *Temp* to *Riot Memo*. The result – nothing seems to have changed. Except the creation date. He checks the file details again. *Riot Memo* now looks as if it was written today – after the riot she was warning about. He checks his watch. Her meeting won't have started yet.

There is one more task to make the illusion complete. He prints off another copy of the memo, then slips it into the suspension file in the filing cabinet to replace the one he removed before.

He is about to power down the computer but holds himself back. There is one more thing to do. There's a place on the computer where a record of deleted files are kept. It's called the Recycle Bin. He double-clicks on it, opening it up on the screen. Then he deletes its contents. It is done.

The moment she tries to use the memo to defend herself, he will deny receiving it and it will seem as if she has been lying to try to protect her position.

A noise jolts Frank back into awareness of the room around him. Footsteps in the corridor. His hand jabs the computer's power button, turning it off. The brightness of the screen dies. He makes to stand, then freezes. A shadow moves into the splash of light near the outer door. It slows, then stops. Frank holds his breath.

'Hello?' It's a man's voice. 'Mo? Are you there?'

Frank recognizes the Asian accent. The man outside the door is Inspector Paresh Gupta from Race Crime. Frank forces himself to exhale slowly through his mouth and then take another breath, trying to calm his racing heart. Then the shadow shifts and pulls back from the doorway. He listens to the footsteps recede.

PART THREE

It is the same nightmare. Jack is running away from me, throwing his arms like a sprinter. And though his hair is blown back as he accelerates, and I feel the loss as he moves away, he never breaks free. He is always there at the point of leaving my life. The same bit of film played over and over.

I know I'm going to hear my voice calling his name. Just like every time. But tonight I am going to see his face. Tonight I won't be able to wake myself until I have seen too much.

He is turning. I see the side of his head. The hair is singed, crinkled to nothing by some vast heat. I want to close my eyes, but I know they are closed already. I am seeing through them, unable to keep out the image as he faces me full on. Black, charred bone where his face should be. Hollowed sockets for eyes. All flesh burned away.

Before I can scream, I am back at the start, with Jack running from me, throwing his arms like a sprinter. And I hear my voice calling to him again. I see him begin to turn.

Chapter 13

Tami never answers the bell these days without checking through her window first. The trouble is, Steve Lloyd has his face angled up towards her when she pulls back the net curtain. He alternates between ringing and hammering after that. The girl from the downstairs flat puts up with it for five minutes before going to the door and asking why he's running down the bell battery. Tami stands in the passageway biting her knuckle, listening to Steve Lloyd trying to sweet-talk his way inside, willing the woman not to let him through.

She feels trapped. She only got back from Glasgow an hour ago. All she wants to do is get back in contact with Superintendent Shakespeare and ask him to check the police records, to find out if the body in the ruined paint factory was ever identified.

Tami can hear her boss saying that she's been under the weather for the last few days and he's worried. She might be in some kind of trouble. It is a transparent lie. But Mr Lloyd is too sexy for it to fail.

'I guess it's OK,' the downstairs woman is saying.

'Thank you. You're a great neighbour. She's lucky to have you.'

'Thanks a million,' Tami whispers. It's not that she has anything against the man. But she's been through the emotional grinder in the last twenty-four hours and her boss's advances always leave her confused.

She listens to his footsteps climbing the stairs. She wants to tell him to go away. But to do that she'll need to open the door.

'Tami?' There is a tentative knock. 'Tami?'

She holds her breath.

'I know you're there.' His voice is quieter now, as if he is afraid the woman from downstairs is listening and might change her mind. 'We need to speak. I won't come in or anything.'

Tami moves her hand to the catch. If she could just hold herself together for a couple of minutes, she'd be able to get him to leave.

'It's work,' he says. 'I'm trying to help you save your job.'

She undoes the catch, but it is him who opens the door. He is wearing chinos and a pressed white shirt, open at the collar. He has a pair of designer sunglasses in one hand. His expression looks different from before – a frown of concern. 'Are you all right?'

She nods.

'I was worried.'

Tami feels brittle. She wants to be able to weep, to let someone else take over and make the decisions, even if it is just for a couple of hours.

He reaches out his hand. She takes it. He steps inside and leads her back into the flat.

'Are you sure you're all right?'

Another nod.

'If you were sick you should have let us know. We ended up short-staffed. And it's the second time.'

'Sorry. It's been difficult. I had to . . . I had to go away. I . . .'

'You should have told someone. We had to put it in the log.'

'You don't know what it's been like.'

'The company has a policy, Tami. One warning. Fired on the second offence.'

She closes her eyes, but that only squeezes out the first tears. The knowledge that she is now crying sends a wash of self-pity over her, turning the drops into streams. She wants to be enfolded. To be hugged and told that everything will be fine. It has been too many years since she could be like that with anyone. She leans forward and finds that she is taking a half-step towards him. His arms encircle her. She presses her face into his chest and smells the clean cotton and the warm skin underneath.

'I've fudged the paperwork,' he says. 'I might be able to keep it hidden. But it's not going to be easy this time.'

Tami's weeping is wetting his shirt. But it feels good to let go. She leans against him, feeling his hands stroking her back.

'I'm sorry,' she says again.

'I'll find a way to help you.'

His hands are moving in soothing circles, around the curves of her hips. The circles work lower, running over her buttocks. His embrace is firmer now, and she finds herself being held more tightly against him. There is contact all the way down the front of her body. Her breasts are pressed into his broad chest. The embrace has somehow become sexual, though she didn't notice the moment when the change occurred. She pulls back.

'What's the matter?'

'It's not right,' she says.

There is a flicker of uncertainty in his eyes, then he is smiling again. His arms are gathering her back to him. 'Don't be coy. I know you like me.'

'Yes . . .'

'And I like you. You know how much I've protected you. If it hadn't been for me you'd be out of a job already.'

'Yes, but . . .'

His fingers are massaging the small of her back, the pressure of his grip is easing her closer. 'You can be nice to me, like I've been nice to you.' He kisses her on the cheek, then on the neck.

She can feel his breath on her skin. It smells of spearmint. 'I'm not ready.'

'Just relax. It'll be fine.'

She wrests herself free of his arms and edges back. He steps forward, matching her movement but not trying to stop her.

'Come on,' he says. 'You'll enjoy it.'

'Not today. I'm all confused.'

She continues to retreat, but his eyes won't let go of hers. Feeling that she must be about to hit into the wall, she snatches a back glance. The bedroom door is right behind her. His advance is shepherding her towards it.

'I'm sticking my neck out for you at work. If I got caught showing favouritism . . .'

'I'm . . . I'm grateful.' Her voice sounds very small.

'I'm not asking much in return.'

He takes a big step and she finds herself retreating through the doorway.

'Please don't spoil it like this,' she says.

'It's you who's spoiling it.'

'No.'

'Come on. Be nice to me for once.' He catches her wrist in his hand.

'No!'

The bed is just behind her. Tami summons up her strength and snatches her arm from his grip. 'Get out!' she shouts.

'Don't be stupid.'

'I don't want you in here.' Her voice is quieter again, but with more authority.

She thinks she sees uncertainty in his eyes. Then it is gone. He smiles and puts his hands in his pockets. 'It's your loss.' He turns and saunters towards the door. 'You'll come round,' he says. 'You want it really. And you need me to save your job.'

A phone call breaks into Frank's uneasy dream. He wakes sitting up, the receiver already in his hand.

'Yes?'

'Sorry to disturb you, sir.' It's a man's voice. Frank's mind clears and he recognizes it as belonging to one of the sergeants under his command. 'I thought you'd want to be informed.'

'What?'

'It's Mo Akanbai. She's been attacked.'

It feels to Frank as if he has been plunged into a pool of freezing water. His idea of getting Mo suspended, of removing her from danger – it was pathetic. He hates himself for not warning her directly, for preferring his own career to her life. Vince has made his move already. So quickly.

He is vaguely aware of Julie sleeping next to him, of the bedroom, of the sergeant speaking through the phone.

'Sir? Are you there?'

'I . . . Yes.'

'She's OK, sir,' the sergeant says.

'Not hurt?'

'Nothing physical.'

The relief hits him as hard as the initial shock had. Frank lets the receiver rest on his shoulder while he catches his breath. When he puts it back to his ear, the sergeant is describing the incident.

'. . . a solo job. He chased her. She got to her car. He smashed the window but she got away.'

The initial panic should have gone now, but Frank's heart is still racing. His mind jumps. The thought comes to him that it might not have been Vince at all. He tries to measure his words as he speaks. 'Do we have a description of the attacker?'

'No chance. He was wearing a balaclava.'

'Not even his skin colour?'

'Well, he has to be white, doesn't he. There's racist graffiti all over her car.'

There is an amount of sleep loss beyond which Frank finds he doesn't get any more tired. He has a sense that his body is absorbing some more profound level of fatigue – but it doesn't become any harder to keep his eyes open. And after the phone call his mind won't be still. Thoughts are buzzing – even before he sits up. A swarm of darting anxieties and unanswered questions. Mo. Vince. Tami. The agreement. The blackmail. Mo again.

He looks at the bedside clock. It isn't yet five thirty. He lies down again and closes his eyes. Julie stirs, but only to turn over, then she is deep again. Frank knows that another hour of sleep would help him. But the more he concentrates on trying to let go, the crisper his thinking becomes and the more clearly he sees that this is a waste of precious time. He gets out of bed, lifts his dressing gown from the hook and tiptoes from the room.

First he makes a cup of coffee and sits himself at the breakfast bar in the kitchen. The more he tries to think about Mo and the danger she is in, the more confused his thoughts become. He knew Vince was interested in her. But how could he have said anything – short of confessing that he has ten grand of Vince's bribe money sitting in the boot of his car? There is no answer.

He looks into the bottom of his empty coffee mug. 'She wasn't hurt,' he whispers.

He gets up and walks out of the kitchen, wresting his mind away from Mo, filling his steps with purpose. He marches to the garage, to a shelf where rolls of spare wallpaper lie side by side. He tears off an arm's-length strip of plain backing paper and carries it to his study, rolling it in the opposite direction as he goes. By the time he reaches the desk he is ready. The paper is flat and his mind has shifted to a different problem.

He unlocks the drawer and takes out the blackmail photograph. Nine faces smile back at him. These are the only people he can be definitely sure were not holding the camera when the picture was taken.

He thinks back a couple of days to when he was standing by the roadside. The image on the table in front of him is stunningly similar to what he saw then. Almost nothing has changed. The hedges are perhaps slightly taller. The tree in the background is perhaps more bushy. He looks at the repair line in the tarmac that he saw on his visit. It is identical – so far as he can tell.

It is strange that the physical environment remains constant when the lives of the nine individuals have altered beyond recognition. Change seems to be a uniquely human condition. He wonders why God created man to grow and decay. Perhaps it is because of the fall from grace.

There is a relaxed self-congratulation in the nine faces. Each is oblivious to a future that has now come to pass. Frank feels a shudder travel downwards from his shoulders.

He busies himself with a marker pen, printing the word BLACKMAILER in the centre of the sheet of wallpaper. Next to it he writes the word PHOTOGRAPHER. Between these words he draws a connecting line. It may be that the two are one. But if not, there has to be a relationship.

Around this centre he prints the numbers one to nine, arranged in a circle. Starting at the top, working clockwise, he adds a name to each number.

1 *SUPERINTENDENT KRINGMAN*
2 *SERGEANT SHAKESPEARE*
3 *JACK STEEL*
4 *JOHN STEEL*
5 *GABRIEL*
6 *EDDIE PIPER*
7 *BILL ARNICA*
8 *RED OWEN*
9 *BIRD'S EYE*

There are other people connected to the photograph by implication. He remembers the names of three more police officers who knew about the arrangement. These he jots down in smaller writing, just outside the inner circle. Then there are members of the Steel family. Tami and Vera as well as a couple of brothers and a sister, now moved away. Eddie's wife – this in very small writing, as he can see no likelihood that she was involved. She always kept her distance from the business, seeming to pretend that she didn't know where the money came from.

Frank scores lines through the names John Steel and Bird's Eye – both died of heart attacks. That coincidence holds him up for a moment. But heart disease is one of the most common causes of death for men – especially of that age and generation.

Going back to the photograph, he notices that it was taken at a moment when all the men had their faces directed towards the camera. It is as if they had known their picture was being taken. In Frank's memory, they were huddled around in a circle. Perhaps there was a sound and they turned to look en masse. He might not remember a detail like that. Perhaps the photographer slipped where he was standing behind the hedge. If he'd been caught there would have been trouble. Frank touches the photograph, running his finger over the face of Gabriel.

There is a movement outside the study. Frank turns his diagram over, covering the photograph. The door opens and Julie looks in, her expression sleep befuddled.

'Did you come to bed at all last night?'

'Sure. Of course.'

She opens her mouth as if to speak, then closes it again and walks out. Frank folds his diagram and locks it in the desk with the photograph.

The children stayed at friends' houses again last night. Frank isn't allowed to call this a sleepover any more. The phrase became 'staying over' when the eldest hit fifteen. The house feels very quiet. No TV sounds. The bathroom is available when he wants it. There is enough hot water for a long shower.

When he comes downstairs the second time, he finds the table has been laid. White tablecloth. Cutlery perfectly placed. The breakfast plates are works of art. Two rashers of bacon, a fried egg, tomato, golden mushrooms. It's not just that everything is perfectly cooked; it has been arranged perfectly as well. Tuesday's *Times* lies folded on the table. Toast in the rack. Fresh butter in a stainless-steel dish.

Julie stands, watching him. Waiting for his reaction, perhaps.

'It's very nice,' he says.

She sits herself directly opposite him, not touching her knife and fork. She looks older, more like her real age this morning. The skin on her face seems drier, greyer, somehow – though he tells himself that this must be his imagination, or a change in her make-up. She is pouring two cups of tea.

He would like her to start eating. But the wasted passage of time is like a pressure building in his head, so he gives up waiting and forks a button mushroom into his mouth.

'I try my best,' she says.

'It's lovely.'

'I could do something different – but you've always asked for this.'

'This is what I like.' He watches her as he chews. 'You're looking worn out. Why not get the doctor to look at you.'

'Me? Me!'

The force of her protest takes him aback. 'Well, your skin . . .'

'It's you who should be getting a check-up! You've not been to bed in days.'

Frank is shaking his head. He opens his mouth to speak, but Julie gets her words out faster.

'You should look at yourself in the mirror. I've never known you like this. Even when you were going for your inspector's exam.'

She has her teacup clutched in two hands in front of her. Frank sees her arms trembling. He gets up and comes around the table to her.

'I'm fine,' he says.

'You are not fine, Frank Shakespeare!'

'It'll pass. I promise.'

He tries to put his arm around her shoulder, but she brushes it away.

'If it's another woman, I want to know.'

'No!'

'I told myself . . . I told myself I shouldn't ask. That it's better not to know . . .'

'I'm not!'

'So long as you weren't . . . weren't going to leave us.'

He puts his arm around her. She pushes him back but there is no real strength in her. He draws her in to him.

'I'd never leave you. There is no one else.'

She's still struggling, so he releases her. She pulls away and turns her liquid eyes on to him. Somehow she is managing not to cry. It must be taking a huge effort of will. 'Then tell me!' she shouts. 'I have a right to know!'

'Tell you what?'

'Whatever you're holding back from me. I can't take it like this any more!'

'There's nothing.'

'Where did the money come from?'

'I don't know.'

'And you're not sleeping.'

'It's work. That's all.'

Protecting Julie. Withholding information. Half-truths, then barefaced lies. Frank thinks back over the steps that have led him to this elaborate deception. Each was taken for her and the children. And perhaps for himself as well.

He built a wall to protect his family. Whenever it started to leak, he patched and reinforced it. But the pressure of the truth has grown behind that wall, and each leak comes through with more force. If he could dismantle it, he would.

But there is no way to do that now, without such an explosive rush that they would all be swept away.

And now he has to leave Julie. To step out of the door on his way to work. Pretending that everything is normal. She is still in the kitchen. She is washing the dishes by hand, though they have a machine. He calls to her from the hallway.

'I'm going now, love.'

She doesn't turn from the sink. 'Goodbye.'

He is caught between going and staying. Pulled towards the door and towards her with equal force. Her back is stiff and her movements abrupt. Saving his career is worth nothing in itself. He takes half a step away. Then he hurries back to her. He puts his hands on her stiff shoulders. The tendons of her neck feel like steel cables under the skin. He wants to tell her he loves her. But he has said those words so many times that they seem to have lost their meaning.

Instead he says: 'Remember that time in Scotland – when it rained every day and we ran out of dry clothes?'

He feels her neck loosening slightly as she nods.

'We walked along the beach,' he says. 'Remember? The rain was so fine, it drifted under the umbrellas and there was nothing we could do.'

'Yes,' she whispers.

'It must be, what . . . ?'

'Twenty years ago,' she says.

'We could go back. Have another holiday there.'

'Could we?'

'I could book some days.'

She turns to face him. 'When?'

The last time they went to Scotland it was for two weeks. That was the kind of thing they could do when they had more time than money. The drive alone had taken them two days.

'The next bank holiday weekend. We could fly from the East Midlands Airport. We could . . .'

But then the doorbell rings.

Julie takes hold of his hands. 'Leave it,' she says.

He nods, but the sound of the real world is interfering with the image that was building in his mind. 'We could take in some shows in Edinburgh,' he says.

She shakes her head. 'Let's go to Skye, like before. Please. I want to watch the waves with you. I want to get rained on and have a room with no TV. And nothing but seagulls and seals to watch.'

The doorbell rings again. For longer this time.

Frank's body twitches. He breaks off eye contact and looks at the buttons on the front of her blouse. 'I'll see what holiday I can book.'

'You never take all your holiday,' she says. 'But it's your right.'

Whoever is standing on the doorstep has now got a finger on the bell and isn't taking it off. Frank breaks out of Julie's grip.

'I'm sorry,' he says. 'I'll be right back.'

The ringing only stops when Frank starts unlocking the door. He removes the chain, flicks the catch, slides the bolt. He already knows it is a woman on the other side. He can make that much out through the dimpled glass. But it's only when he opens up that he sees it is Tami Steel.

'I'm sorry,' she says.

'What are you doing here?'

'I'm sorry. I . . .'

'Who is it, Frank?' Julie asks.

'It's uh . . . it's work.' He can feel her behind him. For a moment he keeps his body filling the gap. But she is going to see at some point. Better to be open. So he steps out of the way and swings the door wide. 'Julie, this is Mrs Steel. You've met before.'

'You'd better invite her in.'

Frank finds himself sitting in the living room with Tami seated opposite. Julie is positioning the occasional tables, placing coffee and biscuits in easy reach. His wife is smiling, but Frank knows her well enough to see that the expression is a veneer.

Tami is another one who seems to have aged in the last week. The skin under her eyes looks puffy, though whether that is from lack of sleep or from weeping he can't tell. She stares down into her lap, where her hands are working on each other.

'Should I leave you to talk?' Julie asks.

Frank glances at Tami but gets no clue from her. 'Just for a couple of minutes,' he says. He would like to add that she could leave the door open if she wants, but by the time he has thought this it is too late. Julie has gone.

'You shouldn't have come here,' he says.

'I had to. It's about Jack. Something's happened.'

Frank is aware of the switch in his mind. He moves from concern for his wife to excitement about the case he is following. He hates himself for letting it happen so easily. But he will have time later to wallow in feelings of his own shallowness.

'I know what happened,' Tami says. 'I . . . I think I know.'

He is sitting forward in his chair. 'Tell me.'

'He was after the man who . . . the man who framed me. He went to Glasgow. Years ago.'

Frank is gripping the arms of the chair. He watches, thinking she is going to start weeping. Her eyes look watery.

He keeps his voice level. 'What happened?'

'A fire. There was a body. They . . . the police . . . they never found out who.'

Her eyes are bright, the lower edges brimming, but still she doesn't cry. There is an intensity about her that he hasn't seen before. He listens to her story: a factory fire, an unidentified body, an unclosed case from nine years ago.

'Why did you come here instead of the police station?' he asks.

'I can't. Nothing official. My probation officer . . .' She shakes her head.

'What makes you think I'll keep your name out of it?'

She straightens herself and looks directly into his eyes. 'Everyone has to keep *some* stuff quiet.'

He's not sure what she knows. But she has certainly picked up something about his situation.

'Who've you been talking to?'

'Lots of people.'

The defiant light in Tami's eyes dims. It is as if all her energy has been exhausted. She bends forward until her forehead is on her knees, her hands covering her face. He's not sure, but he thinks she is crying now. He feels an urge to step across and comfort her. That's when Julie comes back into the room, knocking first but not waiting for a reply. She stands in the doorway for a second, staring at Tami, then she leaves the room, closing the door silently behind her.

Frank dials the number of a contact who works with the Strathclyde Constabulary.

'Hello?' he says.

'Shakespeare?'

'The same.'

'How are you doing, man?'

Frank automatically slips into his cover-all smile, even

though he is speaking on the phone and the other man cannot see him. 'I'm doing fine. Just fine. Listen, I was wondering if you could help me with something?' He relates some of the details of the case – the address of the factory, the date of the fire. But not the guess that Jack was lured there by his murderer.

'I remember it,' the man interjects. 'One dead. It could have been a lot worse.'

'There must be files on the case?'

'True enough. It was arson, you know. There'll have been a homicide inquiry. But I don't recall anything coming of it. They built a park on the site – did you know that?'

'Could you look at the files for me – unofficially, I mean?'

'Nope. But I know someone who can. If I tell him now, he might be able to call you later today. No promises, though. How does that sound?'

'I owe you one,' Frank says.

'You owed me more than one already. Would it be three now, or four? That's the trouble with the English – they never pay their debts.'

Chapter 14

Morning shift at the sandwich factory. Tami wanted to be early for it, but stopping off at Superintendent Shakespeare's house has pushed her timing back. And the morning snarl-up on the inner ring road is worse than usual. They're digging up the tarmac on Tigers Way and that backs up the traffic for half a mile. She tries willing the jam to clear, but it gets heavier instead. The engine temperature gauge is creeping up towards the red line.

By the time she does make it on to the industrial estate, there are no parking spaces on the roadside near the factory. She pulls the car up with two wheels on the pavement in a place with only one yellow line. She figures that she can move it later when she pretends to go for a ciggie break.

Assuming she does still have a job. Which depends on her facing down Steve Lloyd.

Seeing him isn't going to be pleasant, but it is necessary. If she were to be fired it'd mean serious trouble. Her Post Office account is already empty. But she can't quite believe that her boss really has the guts to follow through on his threats and risk an accusation of sexual harassment.

She runs from the car and slams through the front doors of the factory with her watch showing three minutes past. The other workers are heading from the lockers, already dressed for the food preparation tables. A couple of the women give her look-what-the-cat-dragged-in glances. Mr Lloyd is standing over in the far corner near the loading bay with a clipboard resting on one arm.

She turns her back so she doesn't have to look at him as she ties her apron strings and pulls on the hair guard. She is at the sink, washing her hands and forearms with an angular block of anti-bacterial soap. She knows he is approaching by the way the chatter in the room dies down.

'Miss Steel . . .'

'Tami,' she says, without turning.

'You are late on shift this morning.'

'No. Just on time.' She is drying her hands on a paper towel.

'It is five minutes past.'

'I was through the doors on time. You're stopping me getting to my place.' She turns and pushes past him, heading for the equipment table to pick up a vegetable knife. He follows.

'Miss Steel, I've already marked your time on the sheet.' He says this as if it is the final proof of her wrongdoing. 'And you've had warnings before.'

She turns to face him. There is a pen in his hand. She has a sudden all-consuming urge to snatch it from him and stab it into his cheek as Joy once did to her – just to see the shock and incomprehension on his face.

He is still speaking, saying something about an official letter. She watches his mouth move. The knives rattle against each other as she leans her weight back against the equipment table. Something clicks inside her head.

'Do you still want to have me?' she whispers.

His mouth stops working mid-word. It hangs open for a second. 'What did you just say?'

'You still want it?'

'It's too late for that.' His voice has dropped to match hers. There is uncertainty in his eyes. 'I can't back out. It's on the time sheet.'

'Never heard of Tipp-Ex?'

'Tami, I . . .'

'How bad do you want it?'

He wets his lips, glances to the side, as if checking there is no one within earshot. 'I could . . . I could suspend you for a couple of days and bring you back.'

'You're gunna fire me for being a couple of minutes' late. But not if I go to bed with you?'

'Keep it down,' he hisses.

'But that's it, right?'

He doesn't answer. He is frowning, casting his eye over her, as if she might have concealed a recording device about her person somewhere.

'Right?' she demands again.

'Go home,' he says. 'I'll come round later.'

She grips the edge of the table behind her. There is a shudder of stainless-steel blades jostling against each other. She stares straight at his face. 'You haven't answered.'

'Why do you want me to say it?'

'To see if you've got the balls.'

The frown drops from his brow, and she sees the flicker of a smile. 'Does this kind of game turn you on, is that it?'

'I'm waiting.'

He leans forward and breathes into her ear. 'Let me fuck you and I'll give you your job back.'

That is what she wanted to hear. The words that absolve her of the need for restraint. She jerks her knee up. There is a sharp exhalation as the air rushes through his wide-open mouth. His eyes are watering. He staggers back, bending more tightly from the waist with each half-step until he over-balances and falls to the concrete floor.

She lowers her knee, pulls off the hair guard and apron, throws them behind her and marches out towards the door. Suddenly everyone in the room is talking at once. Someone whoops. Tami turns to see a couple of the younger girls bending over him. Then she is out of the building, knowing she can't go back.

She wants to floor the accelerator, but the traffic is still heavy. She has to queue to leave the industrial estate, and she finds herself resenting the other cars, especially as the ones she is sandwiched between – a red BMW convertible and a black Mercedes – must have cost more to buy than she could earn in three years. Even if she had a job.

She flashes back to the moment her knee hit Steve Lloyd. It is the second time she has done that to a man in nine days. The first time it was the shock that made her do it. It was an unplanned reaction. But this time she wanted it. She looked for the trigger. But kneeing Steve Lloyd hasn't made her anger go away. It's brought it to the surface. Nothing she could have done to him would have been enough to cut away the feeling. She is disgusted by him, but more disgusted by herself for not seeing from the start how starkly one-dimensional his intentions were.

She has reached the inner ring road now, and the Mercedes is still right behind her. She knows she can't continue to rage against the world. When other people are wealthy it isn't an attack on her. If she wasn't so disturbed by her uncertainty about Jack, she might not have reacted so strongly to Mr Lloyd.

She glances at the speedometer and sees that she has been driving at close to forty. Ten miles an hour over the speed limit. She can't afford a fine. She eases down on the brake.

The car behind her slows to match her. She looks again in the mirror, suddenly anxious. She slows down further, giving it a chance to pull out into the next lane of traffic and overtake. It continues to hang back. That's when her heart jolts into a fast, heavy beat. She puts her foot down and pulls away, extending the gap. The Merc stays back this time. She is looking in the mirror as she turns off the ring road, heading towards her own street. It doesn't follow.

She has more important things to worry about. The petrol tank, for example, is almost empty. The temperature gauge was red-lining just now. That means a garage bill. She parks, turns off the engine, then sits still, watching the road.

Five minutes later she walks to the flat, scolding herself, mouthing the word *paranoid* over and over.

Rita is sitting in the living room, smoking. She doesn't seem surprised to see Tami home. 'Hi, babe,' she says.

Tami drops her bag and keys on the coffee table and marches to the kitchen. Her fingers are trembling as she fumbles for a strip of nicotine gum. There is only one left after this. She slots it into her mouth, feeling short of breath. Not daring to turn towards the fridge. The jar containing the packet of heroin is like a radio beacon, flashing its presence into her mind. Closing her eyes doesn't help. She doubles her rate of chewing, yearning for the sense of well-being to hit.

Rita's voice drifts into the silence. 'Someone called while you were out.'

Tami is back in the living room and in front of Rita in three long strides. 'Who?'

'Dunno.'

'A man?'

Rita drags on her cigarette. Her eyes are dreamy, the pupils dilated. 'It was a woman.'

'What woman?'

'Very straight. Grey hair'

'Miss Quick.'

Rita nods. 'That's the one. She's got a posh accent.'

Tami feels her life crumbling. 'What did she say?'

'Dunno. Something about the police. Left a note.' She points to a folded sheet of paper resting on top of the gas fire.

Tami pounces on it.

Dear Tami, Please call me as soon as you read this. A mobile phone number is printed underneath in the probation officer's careful hand.

'Good news?' Rita asks.

'What did she say? You have to think!'

'Wanted to know if an Aussie pig had been here.'

'An Australian policeman?'

'It was an Australian name. Inspector something. Bruce. Yeah – that's it.'

Tami swears under her breath. She only knows of one Bruce, and he was camped outside Gabriel's London hotel. The man who took the glass she'd been drinking out of. Picking it up so carefully. Not disturbing her fingerprints.

'You got nothing to worry about, sweetie,' Rita says. 'I didn't tell her nothing.'

'Nothing?'

'Just that I'm your flatmate.'

'Not your name?'

Rita laughs. 'You think I'm crazy? She asked, but I wouldn't tell her.'

Frank Shakespeare is in the office trying to act normally, not knowing any more what that would look like. He found himself shouting at his secretary earlier, but then, with the paranoia of the post-riot witch-hunt, that might well pass. He still feels bad about it, though.

'I'm going for lunch,' his secretary says.

There's enough force in the delivery of this announcement to warn Frank not to object, even though it isn't yet half-past eleven.

'That's OK,' he says.

She has already marched from the room.

It isn't just in his own office that the atmosphere is poisonous. Throughout the station, junior officers are keeping their heads down. All the senior officers are looking over their shoulders, waiting to see who is going to try to stab them in the back. There's been no announcement about Mo Akanbai being investigated by Complaints and Discipline, but something must have leaked out. People have been whispering. Everyone is keen to identify a scapegoat other than themselves.

Frank opens his desk drawer and looks at the blackmailer's mobile phone. There is nothing to see. Checking for messages has become a nervous habit.

There is a soft rap on his door. He pushes the drawer closed.

Mo Akanbai, the woman of the moment, steps into the room.

'What do you want?' he asks. He knows the words came out too harshly, but she is still smiling.

'The Race Crime Unit are doing a raid tonight,' she says.

'And?'

'And I thought I'd better check it with you first.'

'You want to go on it?'

She nods. 'I know you don't like me stepping on CID toes, but . . .' She flashes a winning smile.

'I won't complain – as long as the community relations work still gets done.'

'Thank you, sir.'

'Any other news?' He wants to give her space to talk about the attack on her car the other night. She hasn't yet spoken to him about it directly.

'Not really,' she says.

'Nothing at all?'

'Well, we're still looking for anyone who witnessed the beginning of the riot. No one was there, of course.'

Frank gives up trying. She'll talk about it when she is ready. 'What about the hospital A and E department?' he asks. 'Any burns cases from that night? They'd be suspects.'

'Five,' she says.

Somehow he isn't surprised that she has the answer. She's that kind of officer.

'They must have been at the riot.'

'They've been questioned already. Three of them said they had accidents fuelling up petrol lawnmowers. At night!'

'The other two?'

'Police officers.'

'Hell.'

'There are a few people left to question. But it's pretty much a wall of silence.' She reels off a few names. The usual suspects.

He asks some questions, pretending to keep his mind on the subject, but the conversation dwindles to an awkward silence. He is conscious that his actions towards her might seem like betrayal – if she were to find out. At the same time, he is anxious that Complaints and Discipline haven't started asking questions yet. She needs to be suspended – to step out of the public eye for a couple of months. For her own safety.

Unexpectedly, she says: 'Are you OK, sir?'

'Why shouldn't I be?'

'It seemed like something was on your mind.'

'No.' He waves a hand to dismiss her. 'Enjoy your raid.'

He watches her heading out and feels a sudden pinprick of curiosity. 'Where is it you're going?'

Mo turns. 'You know that racist, Vince the Prince? We're doing his house. It's on the St John's estate. Should be fun.' She closes the door behind her.

Frank has done things in the past that have been against the law. Offering to not press a charge when a suspect had information to bargain with. Doing deals with small criminals to drive out big ones. That is life in the real world – the treatment of crime rather than its cure. But Frank has never taken money for these misdemeanours – other than his police salary.

He was hoping that there would be nothing to report to Vince the Prince. That way he could hang on to the £10,000, use it as bait to catch the blackmailer, then return it – saying he'd changed his mind. Another forty-eight hours might have been enough. But now he has to choose. If Vince gets raided without being warned, he's going to know he's been betrayed. Honour and revenge are everything for a thug like that. Vince would be sure to try to take Frank down with him. Frank either has to return the money before the raid or warn Vince that it's going to happen. He rests his face in his hands, covering his eyes with his fingers. There was no way he would have helped Vince – even before the attack on Mo.

There is one bright thought – that perhaps Vince will get taken down. Once he is in custody, Mo will be safe. The irony is that she will be there on the raid that gets him.

It's not yet noon when Frank parks his car outside the White Ox. Too early to be in a pub. But the place is already busy. He steps out of bright sunshine and into the beery smog of the saloon bar. The chatter hushes, then drops to nothing. Only the barman seems to be ignoring him. Glasses clatter against each other as he loads them on to a tray.

Frank's eyes are slowly adjusting to the gloom. He has the momentary urge to look down at his clothes. He changed out of uniform only ten minutes ago. But clothes don't hide the truth. Every man and woman in the place will know he is a police officer. Best not to make a point of trying to hide it.

Vince is standing directly ahead of him, leaning backwards against the bar. It is a controlling position from which the man can observe everyone who comes into or goes out of the pub.

Frank advances, keeping his face stern. 'A word with you.'

Vince lolls back against the bar, a leery smile on his face. A study in insolence. 'Me?'

'Outside.'

Vince sweeps his eyes around the room, as if checking out who is watching, making sure that they know he knows. Then he nods, hefts his weight forward and follows Frank out into the sunshine.

The door swings closed behind them, and Vince's character changes. 'Shouldn't have come here,' he says, his voice quiet and controlled.

'This couldn't wait.'

'Next time, use the phone.'

'There's not going to be a next time. That's what I'm here to tell you.'

Frank is aware of a break in the rhythm of Vince's stride, as if he has tensed up.

'You can't go back on the deal.'

'It's off. I can't do it.'

They are in the car park now, still with their backs to the pub.

'You took the cash. Try and welsh out and I'll finish you.'

'I'm giving it back.'

Frank gets his keys out of his pocket. He unlocks the boot of his car. The two bundles of notes are in the Jiffy bag, just as they were when they came through his front door. He holds it out towards the other man. 'It's all there.'

Vince looks but doesn't take the package. 'Why?'

'I can't do it. That's all.'

'Scared?'

'No.'

'And why so urgent?'

Frank pushes the package into the other man's chest. 'Count it,' he orders.

Vince is smiling now. 'You're earning it,' he says. 'Keep it.'

'I can't help you.'

'Already have, mate. You doing this tells me everything. Means they're gunna follow me. Or I'm gunna be searched or something. And you being all previous like this tells me it's soon. Today, maybe.'

'I don't want your money.'

'Too late,' Vince says. 'You're in already. One of the team.' He winks. 'You keep my name out of things and we'll all be slick. If I don't go in for questioning, no way no one's gunna find out you took the money.' Then he turns and walks off back towards the pub. 'Thanks for the tip,' he calls.

Chapter 15

They are both waiting for her, each in their own way. Frank feels his blood pressure rising but isn't sure what he has to be tense about. He sits in the armchair flicking through the channels with the remote control but can't find any that he can settle on. He is stewing over the events of the day, the way he was cornered by Vince. The things he then did during the afternoon in order to keep Vince's name out of the investigation. But that, he tells himself, is another story. He has to keep his mind on track. He should be thinking about Tami's imminent visit.

Julie seems to be throwing all her energies into preparing the house, as if for an honoured guest. She cleans the already dust-free lounge, making Frank lift his feet so she can vacuum right up to the furniture. The smell of a slow-cooking casserole in red wine sauce wafts in from the kitchen.

Neither speaks to the other.

The doorbell rings just before six twenty-five.

'She's early,' Julie says.

Frank jumps out of his chair before the bell finishes ringing, but Julie still manages to get to the front door first. He sees her opening it and then stepping back, almost as if she was pushed. When she turns around, he sees she is holding a bunch of freesias.

'Thank you,' she says. 'You ... you shouldn't have bothered.'

'I'm sorry for all the trouble,' Tami says, stepping inside.

'You're no trouble. Really. I'll just go and ...' She hurries towards the kitchen, holding the flowers away from her body as if they were a baby crocodile.

They are halfway to the lounge when the phone rings. Frank glances at his watch before picking it up.

'Is Superintendent Shakespeare there?' It's a man's voice. An Edinburgh accent, Frank thinks.

'Speaking.'

'Oh. Hello there. I was a wee bit confused with the phone number they gave me.'

'I'm at home.'

'Oh, that'll be it, then. I hope you're not poorly or something.'

'No. No. It's just ... I'm making the enquiry for a friend. It's not really official.'

'A friend, eh? Righto. Well, I've dug out the papers you were asking for. I had to go all around the houses, though, because someone had filed them in the wrong place.'

'I'm sorry,' Frank says.

'There's not much to it. We have a couple of photographs. Half a dozen witness statements. A copy of the fire investigator's report. Were you looking for more?'

'The case is still open?'

'Officially, yes. But there's no more work to be done. It's one of those files. Can't throw it away. But it'll never be solved. Unless you've got something for us?'

'There are photographs of the body?'

'Well ... there wasn't much of a body. They found most of the skull, the long bones, a couple of vertebrae. The rest is just fragments. The pictures aren't the sort of thing you'd be wanting to stick on the bedroom wall.'

'Right.' Frank glances at Tami. She is standing rigidly, watching him. He wonders how much of the other side of the conversation she can hear.

'There were a few objects,' the man says. 'A belt buckle. A ring. Some bits of a camping stove.'

Frank rubs a hand back through his hair. 'If I give you my other number, could you run the pictures through the fax machine for me?'

'No problem. And if your friend sees anything she recognizes – you'll let me know?'

'She?'

'Just a guess,' the man says. 'With missing persons, it's usually the women who go on looking years after it happened. The men like to close their minds to it after a time. That's the way it seems to me.'

'Have other people looked through this file?'

'Someone must have. It didn't get misfiled by itself.'

Frank and Tami wait in the study next to the fax machine. She is looking at the objects on his desk, picking up the executive toys that his kids have given him for Christmas over the years. He doesn't think she is really seeing any of them. It is all displacement activity.

'How's the flat?' he asks.

'I'm sorry?'

'Your flat. The place you live. No problems with it?' He wants to distract her – to make the wait easier.

She blinks rapidly as if trying to focus her eyes. 'It's OK.'

'What about the rent?'

'A bit . . .' she shrugs.

'Steep?'

'Yes.'

'You could get a flatmate,' he suggests. 'Share the cost.'

'There's no room. I've got Rita staying.'

'Rita?'

Tami looks away. 'Just a friend.'

The fax phone rings. Frank tenses. There is a brief whistle and purr of electronic communication. The rollers start juddering. His machine is one of the old kind. A continuous sheet feed. He watches the paper emerging from the slot, the end curling downwards.

Bones and fragments of bone. A jumble. They show white on a dark background. He can make out a jaw in the high-contrast image. Teeth. A shoulder blade. Something that could be half of a long bone. This has to be a scene-of-crime photograph. The remains as they were discovered on the floor of the ruined paint factory.

The curled end of the paper falls over the edge of the table. The next photograph is emerging. The same bones and others, laid out on a table, each in its own place. The shocking thing is how little remains of the complete skeleton. Whereas the arms, legs, pelvis and jaw are almost complete, only a few fragments of the ribs remain. There are large gaps in the backbone. The top of the skull is completely gone.

The third photograph starts to emerge. This is harder to identify. A series of angular plates. Three blackened bars, hooked over at the top. Then he remembers what he was told over the phone. It is a primus stove, with the solder that once held it together removed. Evaporated.

He smiles to himself with the pleasure of a small puzzle solved. He glances at Tami to see if she has got it too. She doesn't seem to notice him. Her eyes are fixed on the paper emerging from the machine. She isn't blinking at all. Frank feels his own eyes watering in sympathy. He turns back to the strip of photographs. They have reached the fourth picture. A hoop of some sort. Metal, presumably, to have survived the fire. Only when it is half out does he recognize the coin that has been laid next to the object for scale. That makes the hoop very small. Suddenly he has it. A finger ring. It is shaped like a snake, wrapped round on itself, eating its own tail. There is an indentation for the eye, which might once have contained a stone of some kind.

The thump of something hitting the carpet makes him look down. Tami lies sprawled next to the desk, eyes closed.

It was the first Christmas that Tami and Jack had together as a couple. She was still living at home, but the friction between her and her parents had grown so strong that she was spending as little time in the house as possible. Coming in late, preferably after they were in bed. Staying in her room until she heard her father slam the front door as he left for work. Her mother would catch her over breakfast. There was always time for a little scolding. But she had her own money coming in by then. There wasn't much her parents could do. Her love and comfort were coming from Jack and his family.

Perhaps she gave them cause to be angry. She didn't take their orders. She stayed out late with a man they didn't like and didn't trust. The more she disobeyed them, the more they got to laying down arbitrary rules. Everything from length of hemline to style of haircut. The more rules there were, the more there were for her to disobey. Of course, at the heart of it all was the one rule they never spoke out loud. Don't let him take you to bed.

She'd been having sex with Jack for months. The main

enjoyment at first had been the disobedience itself. But Jack was getting closer to her just as her parents were cutting off their love. The more they isolated her, the more she needed him. And when he was inside her – those were the moments when his love felt the strongest.

Her parents would have had to be blind to miss the swagger in Tami's step, the confidence she felt oozing from her skin. One time she turned and caught her mother staring at her. It was as if the woman was searching for clues. Tami looked directly back, returned the gaze as an equal – not as the maiden daughter. It was woman to woman. Her mother must have known then, because she blushed crimson and hurried away. But whether her parents ever stated the obvious when they were speaking to each other, Tami did not know.

The point of no return came right at the end of the summer holidays. It was a Saturday. She was eating breakfast in the kitchen. Her mother came in and started complaining about the state of Tami's bedroom. She answered back. Her mother started shouting – which brought her father into the room. He waded in to the argument with a speech that sounded as if it had been rehearsed. There would be consequences, he said. She had to shape up or she'd be punished.

'Like hell.'

'And don't you use language.'

'You swear more than me.'

'You're still a child!'

'Only in your mind!'

That was it – months of argument boiled down to its most concentrated form. Two shouted sentences from which neither father nor daughter could back down.

'You're a child till you're eighteen. That's the law.'

'I'm old enough to marry.'

'Not without my permission.'

'And I'm old enough to have sex. I do, too!'

It was her mother who slapped her. And then it was over. There was nothing more to say.

When she came home that evening, she found that her mother had boxed up a load of her stuff and sent it to the charity shop. All her soft toys and posters. Some clothes she'd grown out of but had kept as mementos. Nothing of importance, really. But when she got to think about it, those few possessions had been the last thread that kept her attached to the house. It wasn't her home any more.

All that remained was a narrow bed. There was a wider, warmer bed waiting for her already. So she stuffed the last of her things in a couple of boxes, called a taxi and drove around to Jack's house. As soon as he saw her there on his doorstep he pulled her in and held her.

Jack wouldn't take any money for rent. When her wages started to accumulate, she asked him what he wanted as a present.

'Why?'

'You've been so kind to me.'

He shook his head.

'Just tell me what you'd like,' she begged.

But he wouldn't accept anything.

There was a stall on the market that dealt in old jewellery. Jack used to hang around there sometimes, when he had the time. He got on well with the owner. It was the kind of place where you had to ask for the prices of things. There were no labels. One day she saw Jack looking at a silvery ring laid on the black velvet. A snake, swallowing its tail. He picked it out of the display case and tried it on. It looked good and he smiled. But then he put it back again and closed the glass lid.

When he was gone, she asked the stallholder about it.

'He's had his eye on it for a couple of days,' the man said.

'I want to buy it for him.'

'Hmm.'

'How much?' she asked.

'Let me think about that.'

She went back the next day and asked again. This time he nodded. 'I don't want to cheat you,' he said.

'So how much?'

'Twenty quid.'

That was a lot of money for her, but it was the first thing she'd seen that she knew he liked and he didn't already have. So she bought it, kept it secret for a few days, then found she couldn't bear to wait for Christmas. She made him close his eyes and then slipped it on to his finger. The fit was perfect. She never saw him take it off after that. In her naivety, she'd thought it was silver with a ruby for an eye. But at that price it had to be steel and garnet. Like so many things from that time, it wasn't what it seemed.

Tami comes to, not sure how much time has passed. Shakespeare is bending over her. She feels his hands pushing her on to her side, pulling her uppermost knee forward so it rests on the floor. There is a low humming sound coming from just behind her head. Too regular to be the buzzing of an insect. Then she remembers the fax machine. It must still be going. She tries to get up, but the policeman has one hand on her shoulder, keeping her down.

'Take a nice deep breath,' he says. 'That's right. Now another.'

His hand comes off her and she rolls over so she is facing the ribbon of dangling paper. The end reaches the carpet as she watches. She can only have been out for a few seconds.

She sees the pictures of the bones and then the snake ring, right at the top.

When she was in prison, she used to wish for Jack to die. It was her way of coping with the recurring cycles of self-loathing and self-pity. At one time she even fantasized about killing him herself. But now she sees the evidence of his death, she feels neither happiness nor sadness. There is something – an emotion just discernible through the shock – but she can't put a name to it. It can't be loss, she thinks, because she went through that years ago.

'Did you bang yourself when you fell?' Superintendent Shakespeare is asking.

'No.' She uses the edge of the desk to pull herself into a kneeling position.

'Are you sure? You went down with a thump.'

She searches her head with her fingertips and finds a tender place just above her left ear. There isn't any blood on her hands.

'Don't look at the pictures now. Give yourself a break.'

'I'm OK.'

There is a typed page juddering after the snake ring photograph. She pushes herself on to her feet. She is aware that he is watching her. She catches a movement to one side and turns to face it. It is her own reflection in the window glass. Her hair is wildly unbrushed. Her face seems thinner than it should be. There's no colour in her at all.

'You recognize the ring?' Shakespeare asks.

She looks back to him and nods.

'Are you a hundred per cent sure?' He reads from the page of writing that has just come through the fax machine. 'A . . . ring in the shape of a snake . . . made out of . . .'

'Steel,' she says.

'. . . out of white gold . . . with fragments . . .'

'No!'

'. . . of stone in the eye socket . . . identified as . . .'

'It was junk jewellery,' Tami snaps at him. 'Twenty quid from the market!'

'It was a bargain, then,' Shakespeare says. 'The eye would have been a ruby.'

'No.'

She puts her hand on the desk to steady herself. The wooden surface feels warm and silky smooth. Shakespeare is looking at her. She can't read his emotions. She can't even read her own.

He clears his throat. 'You don't happen to remember which dentist your husband used?'

Chapter 16

Frank is standing on a bridge over the canal, looking down into the oil patterns on the surface of the dark water. He came here to get away. To wait for the call. But it is the wrong mobile phone that rings in his jacket pocket.

'Not at your desk, Franky?' Kringman's voice. Taunting as usual.

'It's my day off.'

'Makes a change, you taking your holiday. How's the arrangement with Vince going?'

Frank runs a hand back through his hair. He doesn't need the extra stress of Kringman's call. 'I don't have an arrangement.'

'Took the money though, eh?'

Frank doesn't want to engage in a needling match with the retired superintendent. Not today. He glances down at his jacket, making sure its line is still smooth, that nothing shows.

'The truth hurts, Franky.'

'He's a racist,' Frank says. 'A thug. I'm going to get him to take the money back.'

'Is that what's gnawing at you? Scruples? You still have those money problems, though.'

'Not for long.'

There's a pause before Kringman speaks again. 'I have

other contacts. People who might be in the market for information.'

'More bloody thugs?'

'Nothing that'll tax your conscience so hard. There's a businessman. No race views so far as I know. He'll pay for your help.'

'What kind of business?'

'He's a landlord.'

'Why does a landlord want police information?'

Kringman laughs. 'You've been too long out of the rented sector or you wouldn't have to ask. You're losing the common touch.'

'Why are you doing this?'

'Ever thought I might get a finder's fee?'

'Do you?'

'No'

'What, then?'

'Perhaps it's the satisfaction of seeing holier-than-thou Frank the bloody bard Shakespeare having to put his fingers into the shit of the real world for a change.' Then he hangs up.

Frank feels his insides shrink. He has the urge to throw the phone into the water. His hand shakes as he replaces it in his pocket. Feeling suddenly conspicuous, he walks off the bridge and down the steps to the towpath. It is cooler here, near the water, shaded by the masonry of the bridge itself. He relaxes, letting the smile drop from his face. Over on the other side of the canal a coot is swimming, bobbing its head as it goes.

He finds himself glancing down to check the line of his jacket again. He can feel the packages in his inside pockets as he moves. On the right side is an envelope containing £10,000. Vince's money. On the left, an identical envelope stuffed with paper cut from a magazine. He can't see the bulge of either packet through the fabric, but he smoothes his palms over them anyway.

He made the two packages to appear identical from the outside. That the one with the real money feels different against his chest he puts down to paranoia. The money doesn't belong to Frank, and somehow that makes him feel more anxious than he did on the occasion of the first payoff.

The real cash is there as a backup. The only reason he might need to produce it would be to lure the blackmailer out into the open. That would be enough. To see the man. One glimpse of his face.

He pulls the blackmailer's mobile phone from his outer pocket. He looks at the screen. No messages yet. The battery is down to half-power. Signal strength low. He walks out from under the stonework and it improves.

A cyclist is riding along the towpath towards him. A teenager without a safety helmet. Frank watches the boy duck low over the handlebars to avoid hitting his head as he passes under the bridge. The bike is passing, kicking up gravel. The boy shouts a string of expletives as he accelerates away. Designed to shock, perhaps, or frighten. But Frank's mind is on the phone in his hand. A message has just come through. Two words.

Leicester University.

It takes him half an hour to get to the campus. Five minutes for the drive across town and twenty-five minutes of blood pressure overload during which he searches for somewhere to leave the car.

He's standing now at the main gate. The Students' Union

building is on his right. The chemistry department is over to his left. He starts walking up the hill into the campus.

Then the mobile chimes again. He snatches it out of his pocket and is about to jab the button to read the message but holds himself back. His instant reaction to the incoming message was far too strong. He takes a deep inhalation, then breathes out. His heartbeat feels over-fast and over-heavy. Moving as casually as he can manage, Frank turns three hundred and sixty degrees. No one seems to be watching. The tremor in his hand is slight enough that no one else would notice. He presses the key to retrieve the message.

Attenborough. Floor 14.

Only after he puts the phone back in his pocket does it occur to him to wonder how the blackmailer knew to send the message at that moment – just as he was walking into the campus. He looks around him again. There aren't many people here out of university term-time. He looks up at the Attenborough Building in front of him. It is a tower block, the tallest of the three landmark buildings that mark the university out on the Leicester skyline. It's an off-white, late-1960s structure. There isn't much to recommend it as an architectural statement. The only touch of beauty is the sky reflected in its glass windows. The reflection makes it impossible for him to see if anyone is looking down from inside.

He walks in through the main doors and follows the signs through to the base of the tower itself. There are three ways of climbing the building. He could use the stairs – which have the advantage of being the method the blackmailer will least expect. But fourteen floors will wear him out before the chase really begins. The second option is a pair of conventional lifts. The third method is a strange contraption known as a paternoster.

The nearest parallel he can think of is an electric lift. But the paternoster isn't like any other lift that Frank has come across. For starters, there are no doors. He stands in front of the two openings in the wall, watching individual box compartments moving past in procession. On the right side they are moving up and on the left they are moving down. People stand in some of them. If they want to step out, all they have to do is time their move so that their foot comes down on the solid floor. It looks alarming, but it seems to require no more coordination than getting off an escalator.

Paternoster – someone told him once that it is the name of the Lord's Prayer when said in Latin, and that the lift got this designation because people have to call for Divine assistance when they step inside. But Frank knows different. Paternoster is also the name of a string of prayer beads.

He watches the next compartment rise into view and steps across the threshold. He is in and going up. It is as easy as that. He turns and looks out at the floors moving past. The floor numbers are marked on the wall. He keeps a count in his head as he passes the third, fourth and fifth.

And with each floor that passes, he gets a glimpse out of a window with a view of Victoria Park below him. Each time he is higher above the tops of the trees. Floor eight. Floor nine. Floor ten.

He touches the package of money through his jacket and then, on the other side of his chest, the package of worthless paper. He consciously makes his shoulders relax. Two deep, slow breaths. Floor eleven. Floor twelve. He steps out of the box he has been travelling in, on to the solid ground of floor thirteen. There is no one standing on this level. He listens to the hum and rattle of the paternoster for a moment before walking towards the stairs.

It is now that he notices how clear a view he has of the ground through the windows – but also how distant it seems. He would need binoculars to make out the faces of people walking on the pavement below.

Frank climbs the stairs slowly, placing his feet, keeping quiet. His eyes come level with the fourteenth floor and he sees a group of young people huddled together – research students, perhaps. Two women and three men, sharing some confidence. One of the men steps back with a broad grin on his face and the others erupt into laughter, clinging on to each other as if that is the only thing that prevents them from falling over. They stagger off in the direction of the paternoster, still supporting each other with arms slung over shoulders. Their voices become suddenly muffled, then they are gone.

Frank climbs the last steps to the fourteenth floor. He looks around him, absorbing the layout. There is a notice board on the wall. Windows looking out over the city on one side and the park on the other. The doors to the lift. Doors to offices. Plastic tiles on the floor.

Frank has followed the instructions. If the blackmailer has been tracking his progress, now is the moment when the mobile phone will ring. He is suddenly aware of his own isolation. The skin on the back of his neck tingles. He looks at the display on the mobile just as it begins to chime. He presses the button and reads the message.

Show money to webcam. Keep it in view.

Frank looks around and notices for the first time a tiny camera mounted to a wall bracket up by the corner of the ceiling. A webcam. If it is connected to the Internet, it could be watched from anywhere in the world. Anyone who has access to a computer and a phone could be viewing him at this moment.

Again, Frank scolds himself for underestimating the blackmailer. He listens. There is no noise other than the rumble of the paternoster. No one is near. He reaches into his pocket, pulls out the packet of cash, opens it slowly and fans the money out in front of the lens: £10,000 in £20 notes. Then he puts it back in the envelope.

A second later the phone chimes again. He retrieves the message one-handed.

Pin money to notice board. Keep in view.

Frank is thinking fast, trying to work out when he can substitute the cash for the dummy envelope. He turns slowly, keeping the package of money to his side at head height. He steps slowly to the notice board, pulls out a spare drawing pin and uses it to skewer a corner of the heavy envelope, holding it in place. He takes a half-step back and looks up to the camera.

The blackmailer could be viewing him from anywhere. But he is unlikely to be far away. There is too much risk of a passing research student looking in the envelope out of curiosity. The blackmailer has to figure on getting here within a couple of minutes.

Frank notices another detail now. The camera can't see everything on this level. The stairs, for example, are out of view. The openings to the paternoster should be visible, but the angle is too tight for a viewer to see into the moving compartments.

The phone chimes with another message.

Go down to fifth floor in paternoster.

Frank takes a step backwards, then another. He has no intention of getting far from the money this time. He turns to look at the paternoster openings, and then, making the gamble that the blackmailer will not remember which side is going up and which side is going down, he steps into an ascending box. He can't seem to get enough breath into him. He puts his hand on the wall of the compartment to steady himself. The fifteenth floor comes into view. He jumps out, then runs for the stairs, running down them in six huge strides, landing each footfall on his toes, making them as silent as possible at that speed. He emerges back on to the empty landing of the fourteenth storey, keeping close to the wall and out of view of the camera. Only a few seconds have passed.

Something is rolling across the floor. A tiny object. He stares at it as it comes to rest. It is a drawing pin. He looks at the notice board. The package of money has gone.

He is running before he has had time to think it through, only knowing he has been tricked again. He jumps into the descending carriage. The pin was still rolling. The blackmailer must have ripped the envelope from the wall a fraction of a second before he arrived. There's no movement in the lift – so the man can't have been trying to escape that way. And he can't be going down the stairs. Which means he is in the next paternoster car below the one Frank is standing in.

The floors pass. Twelve. Eleven. Ten. Frank listens, trying to hear any sound through the machine noise that might indicate that the blackmailer has jumped off. He knows he has fallen for another version of the same trick. The presence of the camera suggested to him that the blackmailer was some distance away. The truth is, he must have been in one of the offices on floor fourteen. That is the only way he could have reached the notice board so quickly.

Floor eight. Floor seven. Floor six.

Frank starts drawing a series of deep breaths into his lungs, oxygenating his blood, ready for the chase. The message told him to go to the fifth floor. He passes that, now, continuing down towards ground level. The carriage arrives and he is out, walking fast rather than running. He doesn't yet know who it is he has to chase. There is a scattering of people here in the wide corridor that leads to the main entrance. His eye is caught by a man, perhaps fifty metres ahead.

Loose jacket. Baseball cap. Jeans and trainers. He is walking too fast.

Frank starts to run. He has gone five paces when the man turns to glance back. He is wearing wrap-around dark glasses. The brim of the hat is low. Frank can't make out the face. The man starts to run. Frank accelerates. They are racing, flat out. The gap is down to forty metres but the blackmailer is out of the building already. Frank crashes the doors open and follows him into the blinding sunshine.

Other people are turning to look, getting out of the way. The man is pelting down the drive towards University Road. The gap isn't closing any more. Frank forces his legs to pump faster. The man ahead is too small to be Eddie Piper. Too young to be Kringman.

They are sprinting along the road. The blackmailer skips between the traffic to the other side. Frank tries to follow, but two buses are coming and he has to wait for a second for them to pass. The gap has widened again.

Frank sees a car parked on the pavement ahead, directly in front of the university bookshop. The blackmailer skids to a stop and clambers into the driver's seat. Frank tells his legs to go faster, but it feels as if the muscles have been replaced by lengths of lead.

The engine starts. It is moving away, bumping down from the pavement to the road. The exhaust pipe scrapes once on the tarmac. But the car is accelerating out of reach. The numberplate is pasted over with what looks like mud.

Frank clutches at his chest. He thinks of Mo Akanbai. Of Vince the Prince, whose money has now gone beyond his reach. The despair tastes like acid. He drops to his knees and throws up in the gutter.

Chapter 17

Red Owen doesn't seem pleased to see her. He stands in his hallway, conspicuously not inviting her in. He folds his arms, then refolds them. Finally he clasps his hands in front of him like a man about to view the body at a funeral.

Tami makes herself speak. 'Jack's dead.' It feels as if she is having to force her words into the silence.

'God.' Owen looks up, meeting her gaze. The shock seems genuine. 'I'm . . . I'm sorry.'

'We need to talk.'

He nods. 'Yes.'

'Can I come in, then?'

Another nod – that seems to be in answer to some internal question rather than directed towards her. Then he stands aside.

Time has changed them all. Superintendent Shakespeare has risen to prominence. Eddie has run to seed. Owen has transformed from the sly, greasy man she remembers to some kind of bank manager figure. Her own changes are too painful to name.

Owen ushers her into the living room and turns on the lights but leaves the curtains open. 'My wife isn't home yet,' he says, as if this explains something.

Tami sits on the sofa. 'Tell me about Jack.'

'I told you already.'

'There must be more. How was he when he came to see you that last time?'

Owen shakes his head.

'Was he scared, excited, what?'

'How was it he came to die?' Owen asks.

'A fire.'

'God. When was it?'

'The day after he left you.'

Owen blows air through his cheeks. He sits in the armchair. Several seconds pass before he speaks again. But when he does, it is as if the shock of what he has heard has uncorked the bottle and the story starts to flow out. 'Jack was all fired up, see. I do remember that. He was jumpy with wanting to get on with something. We hadn't been together for months before that, mind you. But he wouldn't stand around talking.

'And he wasn't properly shaved. So he had to have one of my disposable razors from the bathroom cupboard. And when he came downstairs again, he had a little cut.' Owen touches a place under his own chin.

'He was always doing that,' Tami says. 'Sensitive skin or something.'

'Well, it wasn't so bad. But when I asked him if he wanted to use my aftershave, he said he wouldn't. I took him to mean that he couldn't because of the cut.'

'Anything else?'

'He was fixed on doing something. Going somewhere. You know how he was when he had it in his mind to do something. There was never any distracting the man. I wanted us to go out, get an Indian or a Chinese or something. But he had to be going.'

'Going where?'

'I don't know. But he made me think it was Scotland he was heading for.'

'And he just came to give you that message? That's it?'

'Pretty much so. Yes. He did have the shave and a bite, of course. And he made a couple of phone calls, and then he was gone. I never saw him again.'

'Phoning who?'

'Come on, Tami. It was nine years ago!'

She stares at him. He seems to wither.

'He phoned John. I do know that much.'

'You were there when he phoned?'

'He sent me out but . . .'

'You listened through the door.'

'No.'

'Then how do you know who he called?'

'It was a long time ago, Tami. I was different back then. I was always on the lookout for information. That was the way my business worked. When the phone bill came, I looked through it to find the numbers he called.'

'So you don't know what he said to John?'

'No. And that's the truth.'

'You said he made phone *calls*. Who else?'

'The bank. And a solicitor. And somewhere else. I can't remember.'

'Try.'

He shakes his head. 'It's gone.'

'Which solicitor?'

'The same one Jack's family always used. They had an office in town.'

'The phone bill – you still have it?'

He snorts a laugh and just for a second Tami thinks she sees the old Owen again. A flicker in his eyes. 'I've got nothing,' he says. 'Nothing from that time. Everything was sold, lost, stolen or burned. It's all gone.'

Tami can't remember the solicitor's name either. They

look in Yellow Pages but there are none listed in the street where the office used to be. Without thinking, she starts dialling Jack's mother's number. She listens to the ringing tone, full of impatience. Only when she hears the click of it being picked up on the other end does her mind jump ahead to what she is going to say.

'Hello. Vera?'

There's a pause before the woman answers. 'I don't want to speak to you.'

'One question. Who was Jack's solicitor?'

'Why?'

Because Jack is dead – this is what Tami is thinking. And Vera will have to know. Eventually. But Tami says: 'I just need to know.'

'Are you getting a divorce?'

'I . . . no . . . I just need . . .'

'The name's Jenks,' Vera says. 'He's moved to Horsefair Street. Look him up yourself.' And then she hangs up.

Walking used to be a chore when she was a child. She would boil with resentment when her mum announced that they'd save the bus fare and walk into town. Then, when she was married to Jack, nothing was too good for her. They took taxis. He drove her in his car. She felt like the queen. But now – after all those years when a hundred metres was the furthest she could go in one direction before coming to a security fence – now walking is a luxury.

The journey into town is more than three miles. She has just about enough money in her purse, but she walks past the bus stop anyway. She's never walked three miles in her life and she isn't intending to do that now. A few stops will be enough for her to stretch her legs and save a few pence.

She marvels at how strange the process is. All those muscles need to be worked in coordination with each other. But the legs seem to do it on their own. The more she tries to think about it, to bring it under her conscious control, the harder it becomes. So in the end all she can do is give in to the hypnotically repetitive movement of placing one foot after the other. Letting the pavement pass under her. Letting the rhythm free her mind.

She's done a lot of thinking about Jack since his memory ghosted back into her life. A lot of remembering. Events that she thought she understood now seem unclear. The snake ring, for example. If it was made of white gold, why did the man on the market sell it to her for so little? He would have told Jack about her interest in it. The two men were good friends. Jack must have paid the bulk of the money for the ring, so she would be able to think that she was getting him the gift he wanted. She can't see any other explanation. He tricked her. That's one way of looking at it. Or he was being loving.

She learned about Jack's death yesterday evening. It hit her like a physical blow – but didn't touch her emotions, so far as she is aware. It felt like being thwacked on the head with a frying pan. She reaches her hand up and touches the spot above her ear where she hit the carpet. It is only slightly tender this morning. It seems curious that such an injury can heal so quickly.

She wonders why, if she isn't sad about her husband's passing, she isn't happy either. He's dead. That's what she used to want. But the harder she searches herself for an emotion, the more aware she becomes of the empty space inside her where that feeling should be.

Jack took her to a vehicle rally once. It was like a circus, with tiers of wooden benches for the audience. They had a team of painted minis instead of clowns and motorbikes in place of horses. For elephants they had two monster trucks, chained together, pulling in opposite directions in an outrageous tug of war. She remembers that now – the thundering growl of the drivers revving their engines. Diesel exhaust and raw power. And the chain lifting off the ground, tightening as the trucks took the strain. But neither vehicle moved more than a few centimetres. So long as the drivers revved at the same time as each other, the pull was perfectly balanced. That was part of the showmanship of the thing. And the longer it lasted, the closer to the edge of her seat she sat.

Tami wonders now, as she walks, whether her emotions are like those two trucks. Relief and despair perfectly balanced, with her standing in the middle, waiting to see which one will prove the stronger.

She arrives at Horsefair Street, unaware of the walk.

She remembers the solicitor now she sees him. Jack had her draw up a will when they were first married, and it was to this man they came to do it. Mr Jenks. He'd been working alongside his father back then. Now he has three younger solicitors working with him, all women. He smiles as he tells her this, though she doesn't detect any condescension in his voice. His hair is shockingly white, but in other respects he looks young and vigorous. His tan suggests a recent holiday.

'I need to talk about Jack,' she says.

'Very good. I haven't seen him for some years.'

'Nor have I.'

She tells him some of the history. Surface detail only. That her husband went missing and that his body has now turned up.

'I'm very sorry,' he says.

'Did he contact you nine years ago? It would have been in December.'

Mr Jenks laughs regretfully. 'My memory isn't up to that, I'm afraid.'

'It would have been a phone call.'

He shakes his head. 'We've moved offices since then. And my father passed away last year. But I could check the records.'

Mr Jenks comes back into the office with two green cardboard suspension files under his arm. The slim one has her name on it. The fat one is labelled Jack Steel.

'You will probably be wanting a solicitor to deal with probate. I would be happy to do that for you.' He opens up Jack's file without waiting for her to respond. 'Now, then. Let's see ...' He walks his fingers through the papers, extracts two and closes the file. 'We have a will. And a letter of wishes. Good.'

Tami watches Mr Jenks reading. It feels as if the heat in the room has driven out the oxygen. She takes an extra breath. 'I'm ... not interested in money. I just want to know ...'

'The money has to be distributed. Whether you are interested in it or not.'

'I just want to know what he said when he phoned.'

'My father has passed away, as I said. And Jack's father. Which leaves myself as the only surviving executor.'

Mr Jenks closes the will and puts it to one side. He then opens the other document and nods. 'December, you say? Nine years ago. I don't think we can know what your late husband said on the phone all that time ago. He was probably dealing with my father. But we could speculate that it was something to do with this. It is dated 7 December of that year.'

He must catch Tami's uncomprehending look, because he elaborates. 'A letter of wishes is a document phrased in less legalistic language than the will – intended to be helpful in the event of the death. It gives general guidance. A view of the overall intention of the deceased regarding the distribution of his or her asserts and property.'

Tami's throat has dried. It feels as if she has swallowed a handful of dust. 'That's normal – to have this letter?''

'Normal enough, yes. Though perhaps not as normal to die so soon after drawing up such a document. Statistically speaking. It almost implies an awareness of the possibility of death. Can I take it that the death was not from natural causes?'

Tami finds she can't speak, so she answers with a nod.

Mr Jenks draws air slowly through his lips. 'I'll need to know more of the details, though that can wait. The important thing for now is for you to be assured that everything is in hand. I know this won't make your loss any easier to bear, but all this—' he gestures to the documents on the table '—shows how much your husband was thinking of you.'

Tami tries to object but, again, her mouth seems disconnected from her brain.

Mr Jenks takes a box of pale-pink tissues from somewhere behind the desk. She finds herself wondering whether he has another box of pale-blue ones there, or if it is only women who weep in his office. For she is weeping now. That is another surprise, because she isn't aware of feeling sad. Mr Jenks is still talking. She concentrates on following what he is saying.

'. . . a bond, thus avoiding inheritance tax. And this doesn't have to wait for probate to be completed. If you can just get a copy of the death certificate to me, I'll be able to pursue that for you and you should get the money within a couple of weeks.'

'What money?'

'The bond that Jack set up for you that November nine years ago. Half a million pounds. That will be tax-free.'

Tami felt this way once before. A huge yawning void where her emotions should be. Her body reacting as if she was sad. Her consciousness drifting. Waiting. When the weeping ebbs and she thinks she will have enough breath to get through a phone conversation, she calls Vera and asks for directions.

'Why do you want to go there?' her mother-in-law asks.

'I just need to see.'

'It's nothing to do with you. And why all this interest now? What's happened? Have you heard from Jack?'

'Tell me how to find it!'

'No.'

'I'll keep calling.'

'I'll hang up.'

'I – need – to – see – him!'

There is a pause after that, filled with the faint hiss of white noise on the telephone line. Then Tami hears an uneven gasp of inhaled air, as if it was Vera who was holding her breath, or crying, or both.

'He's at Gilroes,' Vera whispers.

'Where at Gilroes?'

It seemed as if Vera's resistance is broken now, because she reels off directions without any more complaint. Tami grabs a Biro and copies them on to the back of a receipt. It seemed simple enough.

'Thanks,' she says.

Vera gasps for air again. 'Why see him now?'

Tami hangs up. She doesn't have an answer.

*

She walks, not daring to think, knowing that when the wave hits her she'll be unable to do anything. Her brisk pace slows as she progresses further in along the curving central drive from the main gate. She checks the writing on the receipt, though she remembers the instructions well enough. The ink lettering has smudged.

She turns off along the third path on the left. She's creeping forward at funeral pace now, counting off the memorial stones as she passes them. And then she's there. In front of a dark block of stone, highly polished, with the name of her father-in-law in large gold lettering. There is a pot for flowers, but it is empty.

'Hello, John.'

She addresses the memory of her father-in-law in a whisper, though there is no one else within earshot. It is as if she doesn't want the occupants of the other graves to hear, to gossip her words along the line, like so many workers in a factory.

'Why did you write that letter?' She waits for a beat, as if an answer might come. 'You knew it wasn't true. But I thought . . . I thought . . .'

She takes a series of deep breaths, getting herself back under control. 'It was worse than if he'd died.'

She is fingering her wrist, feeling the edge between smooth skin and irregular scar tissue. 'You bastard,' she says. 'You bastard!'

She first met John in the market. She served him coffee from plastic cups. He used to have three sugars. By the look of the man, it all went directly to his stomach. Tami remembers his hands, big enough to surround the cup with his fingers. And his smile, over the stacked boxes of tomatoes. He treated her well from the start. He gave his blessing for the marriage. And when her own parents wouldn't speak to her any more, he became a kind of father. It was John who paid for her legal fees. And when she wanted to plead not guilty to possession of the heroin, and everyone told her she was being stupid, he was the one who came round first.

'If that's what you feel, then that's what you have to do.'

He even talked Jack round to her way of thinking.

And when Jack stopped writing, it was only John who kept in contact. Then after a few more years even his letters stopped. No one bothered to tell her the old man had died.

She steps up on to the polished stone that covers the grave. She kicks the headstone. 'I believed you! You—' she kicks again, searching for pain to cover the emotions that are now boiling up to fill the void. '—bastard!'

She squats down so her face is level with the lettering. John Steel. Then she lets her eyes focus on the ghost of her own reflection in the shiny surface. She punches towards the image of her own face. Her knuckles slam into the headstone.

He lied to her. It was John who told her that her husband had got another woman pregnant, that he was going off to start a new life in Scotland. All lies. It was John who kept on sending letters, spinning out the deception, promising support. If he'd wanted to save her the suffering, he should have tried some other lie. The one he told her was more painful than anything else he could have chosen.

She spits at the stone. But it is not enough. She could dig up his corpse and smash the bones and swear at them and piss on them. But nothing would be enough to give expression to all the anger she is feeling.

Jack loved her. And then he died. And the man whose body is under her feet lied to her to make the pain ten times worse than any bereavement. She beats her wrists against the edge of the stone. Then she opens her mouth and howls.

Chapter 18

Frank's first problem is making up a story about how he came by the information. Simple is always best, he thinks. So he tells his contact in Glasgow that a woman came to him privately to ask about the disappearance of her husband. In a sense, it is true.

The Glasgow police seem to have mixed feelings about pursuing the case. The words they say are positive. But the way they say them suggests that the fire is an event that everyone would prefer to forget about. There is no chance of finding the arsonist at this distance in time. But Frank gives the details anyway. And they promise to get things moving at their end.

The second problem is that medical workers aren't supposed to give out information about their patients without their patients' permission. There are exceptions, of course. Where the patient is dead, for example.

That is the theory.

Frank is waiting with the phone receiver to his ear.

'Hello?' A man's voice. Elderly, but not excessively so, by the sound of it. White. Middle class.

'Hello,' Frank replies. 'You were Jack Steel's dentist?'

'My receptionist tells me you are calling from the police station.'

'Yes,' Frank lies. He is sitting in his office at home, having been careful to key in the three digits that instruct the phone company to withhold his phone number. 'You knew Jack well?' he asks

'And his father. Yes. Jack moved to Scotland, you know.'

'He's dead.'

'My goodness. I'm so sorry.'

'Yes.'

'He seemed such a vigorous young man.'

'So we need to see what paperwork you have.'

'I'm sorry?'

Frank smoothes his tie with his free hand. He could leave this for the Glasgow police to sort out, but that would take time. They didn't seem to be in much of a hurry.

Dental records aren't the only way to prove identity, of course. There is always DNA. A sample from Jack's mother could be compared with any genetic material they could recover from the bones. But that approach would be expensive and slow. And Frank is in a hurry. Every day, Tami's mystery seems more connected to his own problems.

'The body has been found,' Frank says, speaking slowly and clearly. 'We just need to see the dental records for confirmation.'

'So you don't *know* yet?'

'This is a formality.'

'Shouldn't there be a . . . a procedure for this? A death certificate or something? I don't want to . . .'

'This is the procedure. I'm a police officer. I need to see his records.'

'What was your name again?' the dentist asks.

To hesitate at this point would be a disaster. Instead, Frank hardens his voice. 'When did you last see Mr Steel alive?'

'Me? I . . . It would have been many years ago. I'd . . . I'd have to check.'

'We still don't know who killed him.'

'Killed?'

'Murdered.'

'Good heavens.'

'Your cooperation would be appreciated.'

'I'll . . . Yes, of course . . . Where should I send the records?'

'Fax them up to the Strathclyde police.'

'Yes. Thank you.'

'Don't mention it.'

Frank reads out the contact name and number, then gets the dentist to repeat it. He hangs up, sits back from the desk and rubs his face with his hands.

Jack was one of the original conspirators. He and his father thought up the agreement in the first place. And it turned out that they gained the most from it – in influence if not in money. They became the most powerful men on the St John's estate – not by force, but through respect and influence. And it seems to Frank as if they are the most likely ones to have had the photograph taken. It would have been their style – a precaution for possible later use. They might have put it in a safe somewhere. Another person could have found it. This is a conjectural connection between Jack and the blackmailer. Timing provides another connection. Jack's widow gets released from a long stay at Her Majesty's pleasure and within a couple of weeks hate mail is arriving through Frank's door – which develops into blackmail within three months.

Logic pushes Frank towards suspecting Tami herself. But his emotions don't agree. She doesn't seem like a liar.

Frank slaps a hand on to his cheek. 'Think,' he whispers. But the only thing that comes to his mind is Tami and her reaction to the image of the ring as it rumbled through the fax machine. That is the picture in his mind when the study door opens and Julie steps inside.

'Busy?' she asks.

'No.'

'You've been in here hours.'

'Sorry.'

'I don't want sorry. I want to see you smile again.'

Frank smiles for her.

Julie shakes her head. 'A real smile. Not like the ones you give at work. I can tell.' She walks over to the desk and kneels next to him, one hand on his shoulder. He feels her hand kneading the taught muscles. 'You should work on your bonsai trees.'

'I've watered them already.'

'We could book that holiday.'

'In a few weeks,' he says. 'I'll have more time then.'

'That's why you're like this. You never have time. Not for you or for us. Not even for the children. Do you know where they are right now?'

He shakes his head. 'I thought you . . .'

'Would be looking after them? Like I always do. They're out. At friends' houses.'

'Again?'

'What do they have here?'

Frank has no answer. He feels a surge of impotent self-loathing.

'Let's go to the cinema,' Julie says. 'We haven't seen a movie together for years.'

'We don't know what's on.'

'They have twelve screens. There must be something

we'll like. Anyway, it's not the film. It's the having time for each other.'

He opens his mouth to try again but she is already pulling him to his feet.

They head around the inner ring road towards Braunstone and the Warner Bros cinema. The schedule is filled with summer action blockbusters. Twelve screens of exquisitely choreographed violence. Frank chooses the one that looks the least formulaic. Julie leads him to the back, and they sit together in the dark. She puts her hand over his on top of the armrest.

Frank keeps thinking about the blackmailer through the opening sequence. He is aware of Julie glancing at him, so he pretends to watch the film.

The way he sees it, Jack must have believed Tami was innocent. Framed. A man like Jack wouldn't have been able to rest with that perceived injustice. He would have spent his time trying to work out who the guilty person was. That would have been safe so long as the person he was tracking didn't know. Then came the demand that Jack go to Scotland. The meeting in the factory. The fire.

But Frank can't see any reason why John Steel would give Tami the impression that Jack had run off with another woman. Unless it was true. Either John believed that Jack had just disappeared – which he would have surely followed up – or he knew about the murder. But unless John had a reason to hide the fact that Jack had been killed, he would have shared the information with his daughter-in-law.

Frank knows where these facts are leading, but the idea repels him. He has been a police officer all his working life. He has had to work with people so far down in the swamp of immorality that they have almost no hope of redemption. But this is somehow more upsetting. Tami isn't a bad person. He didn't feel comfortable at her trial. Someone should have told her to plead guilty. She might have been out in four years instead of ten. Even if she was innocent – and until now that thought hasn't really hit him – it would have been the best thing to do. And then to hold out so many years on the inside before admitting she did it.

He feels Julie's grip tightening on his arm and realizes he's been staring at the speaker on the side wall of the cinema. That's when the mobile in his pocket chirps. People in nearby seats turn to frown at him. Someone in front swears. He fumbles for the switch, trying to stop the ringing.

'I'm sorry.' He gets up and looks back at Julie. 'I'm sorry. I'll just . . .'

'Call them back later,' she hisses. There is a note of desperation in her voice.

He looks at his phone. The number displayed on the screen is one he doesn't recognize. The first digits are 0776 – which means the call is coming from a mobile. Julie is right. This isn't just about a second-rate action movie. It is about them spending quality time together. He sits again, clicks the phone to silent mode and puts it back in his pocket. He feels her arm link through his and her head come down on his shoulder.

'I love you,' he says, hoping the feeling will follow the words, trying not to think about who might be calling him.

The black cab slows to cross a speed bump. Tami clutches at her safety belt. She hasn't taken a taxi since coming out of prison. She hasn't had the money. She doesn't have it now. But the practical reality of having lost her job and not having an income any more – this has been washed away in a formless wave of emotion and the stark knowledge that the whole basis on which she has been trying to rebuild her life these last nine years has been false.

Jack lost his life trying to save hers.

The taxi is idling now. The diesel engine turns, making Tami's seat shudder rhythmically. She realizes that the driver is waiting for something. She looks through the window and sees that they are outside her own flat.

'How much?' she asks.

'Eight quid.' He speaks tetchily, as if it isn't the first time he's told her.

'Sorry, I . . :' She is fumbling in her bag, already knowing that she hasn't got that much cash.

He is drumming his fingers on the steering wheel. She sees him looking at her in the mirror.

'This is all I've got.' She passes a £5 note and change through the glass partition and watches him counting it.

He mutters something about calling the police, but jabs his thumb in the direction of the door. Tami clambers out. He mouths more obscenities towards her, then revs the engine and accelerates away.

She is left standing in the road, not taking in her surroundings. All she can see is the door. She stumbles inside, then climbs the stairs. It smells of cigarette smoke and old carpet. The door to her flat is unlocked, but she is too much inside her own mind to feel angry towards Rita.

She drops her bag in the passageway and stumbles through to the living room. It's there she sees them. Two men in grey suits. They are standing with their backs to the window, watching her. The one she recognizes flashes a smile.

'Inspector Bruce Lowrie, CID. We met in London. And this is Inspector Andrews.'

'You . . .'

'The doors were unlocked. It seemed like there'd been a break-in.'

'I didn't leave them unlocked.'

'There you go, then. And there's damage to the doorframe downstairs. As if it'd been kicked in.'

'That was the riot. Days ago.' She glances around the room, then into the kitchen. The fridge is still closed. Nothing looks to have been touched. 'You shouldn't be in here,' she says.

'What were you doing in London?' Bruce asks.

'I . . . why were you spying on me?'

The other officer chuckles.

Bruce licks his lips. 'It was drug trafficking, wasn't it? That's why you were in prison.'

'I didn't do it.'

'One kilo of heroin found in the boot of your car. Even a junkie like you couldn't use that much yourself.'

'I'm clean!'

'And now you're out. Visiting old friends.'

'He's not a friend!'

'You met him before.'

'No.'

'Then why go to see him?'

Tami opens her mouth, wanting to say that she was looking for her husband. But the words won't form.

'Was it to get drugs?' Bruce asks.

'No.'

'Something else?'

She nods.

'But you do admit going to see Gabriel.'

'She didn't say that!' It's Rita's voice, from the passage-way behind Tami.

'Who's this?' Bruce demands.

Rita steps across the room, dragging her leather jacket. She lets it fall on to the floor and drops herself into the armchair, so that she is facing the two men. 'Who are these bozos?'

'CID. Inspectors Bruce Lowrie and . . .'

'Got some sort of warrant?'

'We don't need one to . . .'

'She doesn't have to say nothing.'

'We could arrest her.'

'On what charge? What's she done? Spoken to someone in your bad books?'

'We can come back with a warrant.'

'Yeah, yeah, yeah. You're from London, right?' There's no answer, but both men look as if they're trying to kill Rita with their eyes. She nods. 'How long you reckon on spending in Leicester? She's not worth it. Doesn't know anything. Not gunna speak, anyway. May as well bugger off back south.'

'You don't know anything,' Bruce sneers. He turns to Tami. 'This woman will get you into trouble.'

'Go!' Rita says. 'You got no right being here.'

There's a second when Tami thinks they're going to stay. Then the two policemen walk. They slam the door behind them.

'Never talk to the cops,' Rita says. 'They can't do nearly so much as they say. It's all bluff. Just keep quiet and string it out and they give up ninety per cent of the time. She waits for a moment, as if expecting some explanation. Then she gets up and takes Tami's hand. There's a strange light in the woman's eyes.

'I met someone,' she says at last. 'We go way back. Best I don't tell you his name, though. Anyway – he said he'd set us up in business. It's all safe, I promise you. We just need to use the flat. He arranges everything else. And we never have to have more than a couple of grammes here. The punters order. We collect. We give it to them. So even if we were caught – and we won't be – it'd be just like small amounts. They could only do us for possession.'

Tami is shaking her head through this. 'Not drugs. Please.'

'Then what are you going to do for money?'

'Another job.'

'More minimum wage crap? Even if you get something tonight, they won't pay you for a week. No rent.'

'There's money. Insurance.'

Rita blows air through her mouth in disgust. 'On what?'

'Life insurance. Some kind of bond.'

'They don't pay out if you kill yourself, girl.'

'On Jack. He's dead.'

Tami's eyes have been on the carpet through this exchange. When Rita doesn't come back at her with another waspish remark, she looks up. The shock on Rita's face cuts through her own grief. The woman is shaking her head. Her mouth hangs slack.

'They found his body,' Tami says, not understanding why the impact of her words is so deep on Rita.

'It'll take time to get the full amount,' she says. 'But the solicitor told me I could get an emergency payment. A couple of thousand. We'll manage.'

The words that Rita is mouthing still have no voice.

Tami reaches out and takes her hand. 'I forgot you knew him. Sorry. But it was long ago for you.'

'You said he'd just died.'

'They identified the body now. But he's been dead nine years . . .' Another wave of self-pity breaks over Tami. Rita pulls her hand away. 'I'll get you some tea.'

Tami looks at her friend through the tears. She knows Rita has a hard shell. She has never seen it crack before. But whatever was exposed under the surface has now been sealed over again. Rita is back to her old self, and it is Tami who is breaking up.

'Get a grip, girl,' the woman says. 'You've lasted without him till now.'

Frank is lying on his back, staring at the ceiling above the bed. Julie lies sleeping beside him, breathing slow and deep. They gave up on the movie halfway through. Neither of them had been watching it properly. Then home. And when she invited him to bed with her it felt awkward – as if they were still dating. Each unsure of the other's feelings.

To not make love would have been unthinkable. It would have been to say that something was wrong with their marriage.

But the further they got, the more he found himself searching her eyes, trying to understand what was going on behind them, and the more he saw that she was searching his. At the end she turned her head sideways on the pillow and cried out. He pretended to climax then rolled off her and lay panting and depressed.

At least she was able to go to sleep. He envies her that.

The upstairs windows are open, but the air in the house hasn't cooled. The curtains hang still and heavy. Julie's shoulder twitches. Trying to figure out what is going wrong with their relationship seems only to make his mind work more slowly.

But as soon as he starts thinking about Jack's death, he finds his thoughts clearing. He never saw himself as a friend of Jack's. But he knew the man well enough to have a fair idea of how sharp he was. He was easy-going as well, but too street-savvy to walk into an obvious trap, like meeting in a deserted factory in the middle of the night. But that, it seems, is exactly what he did. The puzzle is well enough defined for Frank to know that he isn't going to be able to find an answer without getting more information.

Julie twitches again and moans. Frank edges away from her and gets out of bed. There is no point in him trying to sleep. He goes downstairs barefoot, starts heading for the kitchen, then detours to take his mobile from the table in the hall. He remembers it ringing in the cinema. He forgot to turn it back from silent mode when he came home. So he clicks it on, ready to reset it.

There is a new message waiting for him. It is from his contact in the Strathclyde police force.

What next?

Nothing else. No explanation. He reads the message again, noting the time it came in. Three hours ago. He would have been leaving the cinema. He tries to think what his contact in the Strathclyde police force would do if he failed to get in contact by phone.

Frank turns on the spot and enters his study. It is there – a strip of paper hanging from the fax machine. Two standard teeth diagrams, annotated in handwriting, followed by a page of single-spaced typing.

He tears the paper off and steps back to the hall, where the light is on. His eyes jump between the two diagrams: molars, incisors, fillings. Areas of one diagram are shaded off as missing.

He doesn't understand what he is seeing, so he skips down to the bullet points in the page of conclusions. The teeth in the jaw fragments found in the factory belonged to a male in his twenties. He would have been a man with poor dental hygiene who had not visited a dentist in more than a year prior to the time of death. The teeth do not match the record of treatment outlined in the notes provided by Jack's dentist. The body is definitely not that of Jack Steel.

Frank knows that there must be a logical cascade of information to be had from this fact. He needs time to think. But first, and more urgently, he has to contact Tami and let her know – before she does something they might both regret.

Chapter 19

The point of no return for Tami comes at some time between one and two in the morning. Up until then she could still pull back. There is the possibility of sleep, of letting go.

But the longer she keeps awake, the more tense she becomes. The more tense, the more she thinks of Jack and the way she misjudged him. The feelings turn around on themselves, like a huge circular current.

Up to a point she understands the process that is happening to her. It was the same in prison in the hours before she tried to kill herself. The psychologist explained it all to her afterwards.

They kept her on some pills they called antidepressants after that. The medicine didn't stop her feeling depressed. It just slowed her mind down to the extent that she couldn't keep the self-destructive spiral going.

That was years ago. Now she is without the sea-anchor effect of those drugs. Nothing is stopping her drift. She can see the whirlpool ahead. She can hear it roaring. She knows she should turn around and swim the other way. Fight against the current.

But she doesn't want to.

In a right state of mind she would not be able to harm herself. Even in her present distress it would be impossible.

But somewhere up ahead – not far now – is a maelstrom. There, no thought will be possible. There, she will take her own life. She lets herself drift towards it.

By three in the morning she can no longer see what is happening to her. She is gripped by the crashing cycles of sorrow, self-pity, despair and self-loathing. By four in the morning she is starting to self-harm, hitting herself against the wall – sometimes her fist, sometimes her forehead. But even that isn't enough. The only thing that brings relief is the thought of killing herself. There is a rightness about the idea. It is like finding the last piece in a puzzle and fitting it in place.

When she tried to kill herself before, it was by smashing a window and putting her hands through, raking the wrists from side to side across the jagged edge. But that was painful and ultimately it didn't work. This time she has the perfect tool.

She goes to the kitchenette, opens the fridge and pulls out the pickle jar from the back of the shelf. She unscrews the lid and tips out the contents on the work surface. She bought the heroin knowing there was enough for three doses. The needle is new. She doesn't have a cigarette lighter, so she uses the flame from the gas ring to heat the spoon, to cook up the heroin. The sealed plastic wrapper crinkles as she releases the hypodermic needle.

At this point her mind feels perfectly calm. She fills the syringe, concentrating as if she was painting the fine detail in a picture. She holds the syringe up to the light. The liquid is golden.

It is beautiful.

She carries it through to her bedroom, sits cross-legged on the bed and wraps the strap of her bra tight around her upper arm, flexing her hand and slapping the skin to make the veins stand proud. Then she slides the needle home. It has been years since she last did this, but the routine still feels natural. She presses the plunger, watching the liquid disappearing into her body.

Frank is still sitting in his study an hour after reading the message about the dental records. He has a fresh cup of coffee on the desk along with the sheet of fax paper – held flat with a pen resting on each end. He isn't reading the paper, but having it there seems important, as if some secret will be unlocked by its presence.

He starts with two bits of information that, for now, he will take as true. The ring found with the body was Jack's. The body was not. Jack could have planted his ring on the body to make it look as if he had died. Or the owner of the body might have obtained Jack's ring before being killed in the fire. But each new thought brings a cascade of further possibilities. A third party might have taken Jack's ring and planted it on the body. The fire victim could have found Jack's ring on the floor, or stolen it, or been given it, or bought it.

Frank turns his coffee cup slowly on the table, watching a lick of steam rising. There is another way of looking at the puzzle. Two possibilities. Jack could be dead, or he could be alive. Dead is easy to understand. He walked into a trap – knowingly, perhaps. He was killed. Perhaps a tramp found his ring and was later caught in the fire. But to postulate that Jack is still alive would require an explanation for why he has not shown himself all these years – even to his wife.

Tami.

Frank still doesn't understand what is going on in the woman's head. She saw the picture of the ring and collapsed on the floor. But when she regained consciousness – after a few seconds – she seemed composed. If it wasn't the early hours of the morning he would go and see her immediately, convey the news, find out if she is surprised or not. It is still possible that she knows more than she is saying.

The world spins. Tami can't see much. She can't think much. Her breath is so shallow that she can't feel it herself. She only knows that she is dying from the overdose. And that brings a sense of peace. Or it should bring peace. But there is something wrong as well. Something she can't remember. She should remember it. Perhaps it is something she has to do. Or a thought she has to think. It has been so many years since she shot up, but the experience is still fresh in her memory. A rush of elation and well-being. Deeper than warmth, more aware than anaesthesia, faster than alcohol, more intense than sex. It was all a long time ago. Too difficult to think of it now. Easier to let go. To let the sleep drag her down.

At four thirty in the morning Frank clicks the kettle on. He unscrews the lid of the instant coffee, breathes in the smell and finds to his surprise that it doesn't give him a kick. The water rumbles to the boil next to him. He breathes in again and knows he is drinking too much of the stuff. He looks at the draining board. There are already three used teaspoons there. That would make this the fourth cup since getting out of bed.

What he wants to do is drive across town to Tami's workplace and speak to her. He feels close to some discovery. It is in the air around him. Invisible but tangibly present. If he could only force himself to think that little bit more clearly, the secret would surely reveal itself. If he could only wring a few more drops of logic out of his jumpy brain.

He paces back to the study, hands deep in his pockets, shoulders hunched. There are several copies of the Bible on the shelf. The New International translation. The Jerusalem Bible, including the Apocrypha. There is also a copy of the Good News version, which he bought some years ago out of a sense of duty and has never read. But it is an old King James he now pulls down. It has a black leather cover and gold lettering. It is heavily embossed. When he flicks through the foxed pages, a musty smell wafts up at him. He balances the volume on the desk, spine downwards. Then he removes his hands, letting the covers fall outwards. It spills open at the Gospel of Matthew, Chapter 24; vs. 43–44:

> *if the good-man of the house had known in what watch the thief would come, he would have watched and would not have suffered his house to be broken up. Therefore be ye also ready . . .*

Frank closes the book. The pages come together with a dull thump. He walks to the window and shifts the curtain to look outside. All he can see is blackness and the reflection of the room. He paces back to the desk, touches the Bible and screws his eyes closed.

When he makes the decision, it is in a rush. He snatches at the phone on the desk, jabs his fingers on the keypad and clenches his fist as he waits for the unhurried voice of the directory enquiries operator to finish his sentence. He knows it won't do Tami any good to have a police officer calling the place where she works. But events are moving too fast for niceties.

It is a man who answers the phone at the factory.

'Hello?'

'I'm looking for Tami Steel.'

'Who is this?'

'I'm a police officer. Do you know her?'

'Sure. But she's not here. What do you want her for anyway?'

'When will she be back?'

'She won't. I fired her. Could I ask your name, please?'

Frank hangs up. He looks at the clock, then starts moving towards the door, not having decided but starting anyway. He grabs a pair of tracksuit trousers, a T-shirt and some underwear from the ironing basket and dresses in the utility room. He leaves a note in the kitchen where he knows Julie will find it in the morning.

He closes the front door, turning the key in the lock so that the latch won't spring home with a click. He might still be able to make it home soon enough for no one to know he was gone. That would be one more set of lies he could avoid saying. He knows he will have to hurry, though. The sky is starting to turn grey already. The air still smells damp, but it will change soon, heating up towards another arid day.

He drives towards the city along the Glenfield Road, empty of traffic, keeping it slow and steady. Tami won't mind being woken. She's used to the night shift. He turns the headlights off. Sidelights are enough now the morning is coming. There is a milk float ahead of him. He overtakes it smoothly, thinking only of the road ahead.

There are a few cars moving by the time he gets to Tami's street. He slows over the speed bumps and pulls up in a parking space just in front of her door. Some of the windows here have been repaired since the riot. Others are boarded. He steps on to the pavement and looks up at her window on the first floor. There is a sheet of cardboard over the broken pane. He pushes the street-level door and finds that that hasn't been repaired either. It swings open.

There is a yeasty old-carpet smell inside. Dampness. He listens, hears nothing. He climbs the stairs to her landing and listens again. He imagines her sleeping inside. He touches the door with the fingertips of his right hand. Only now he starts to think of the emotional impact his news is likely to have on her. He's had to break bad news to people before. It's part of the job. But when you go to tell a woman that her son is dead, you are operating on well-known ground. There are established procedures for such things. He's done the training. Telling a woman her husband might still be alive is different. Frank doesn't think there is a course for that. He remembers the way she kneed him between the legs when he first spoke to her, telling her he was a friend of Jack's. He still hasn't fully untangled that puzzle.

A mobile phone chimes, and Frank pulls his hand away from the door. His first thought is that it must be the blackmailer calling again. Who else would send a message at this time in the morning? But Frank left that phone in his uniform pocket. It is hanging in the wardrobe in his bedroom. He pulls his own personal phone from his jacket pocket and retrieves the message.

It is from Ricky at the phone company. *He turned it on again.*

Frank half-runs down the stairs, out on to the street. It's discernibly lighter than when he went inside. A car eases over the speed bump outside Tami's house.

Frank keys in Ricky's number. It takes a long time for him to pick up.

'It's me,' Frank says.

'That was quick,' Ricky purrs. 'Thought you'd be tucked up in bed.'

'He turned the phone on?' Frank prompts.

'Yes. He's a night owl, too. If it is a he.'

'You have a location?'

'Mmm. A pretty good one. It was half an hour ago. He only kept the phone on for two minutes and fifty seconds. He sent one text message and switched it off again.'

Frank finds that he is scraping his heel over a bit of gravel, grinding it against the paving stones. He makes himself drop his shoulders. 'Where was he?'

'Near Humberstone Road. Do you know it?'

'Yes'

'I looked at the map. It could have been from any one of eight properties.' Ricky reads out the addresses while Frank marks them in Biro on the back of his hand.

Ricky clears his throat. 'About our arrangement . . . ?'

'I'll post the money tomorrow.'

'I could come and collect it. Put a face to the voice.'

'No.'

'I don't suppose you want to tell me what it's about?'

'No.'

The addresses that Frank was given are divided between two streets of terraced houses, the rear yards of which back on to each other. Four mid-terraced properties on Perry Street and four on Moorland Street. A mobile phone text message was sent to him from somewhere in that block. He is surprised how small the area is. At the same time he is daunted by the task of presenting himself at the door of each of those houses, out of uniform and without any official identification.

It might be better to wait and watch. But it is impossible for one man to watch two streets at the same time. Which is all assuming the blackmailer wasn't just walking down the road past these houses as he sent the text message.

Frank checks his watch. It is five minutes to eight. He

goes to the first house and knocks. He hears a woman's voice through the door. She is shouting something. There is a clicking of locks and the door opens wide. Frank finds himself looking directly into the front room where a boy of perhaps ten years stands, head on one side. There's a smell of stale tobacco smoke and burned toast.

'Yeah?'

'I'm a police officer. Is your father in?'

The boy turns and yells back into the house. 'It's the cops, Mum. They're after Dad.' He calls this in the kind of voice one might use to say the post has arrived.

A woman in a short dressing gown stalks into the room, arms crossed. Frank tries not to look at her legs.

'What's he done now?' she asks.

'I'm just following up reports of a disturbance near here early this morning. Was anyone up at around five a.m.?'

'You gotta be kidding me! There's always a racket out there.'

'Does anyone else live here?'

She shakes her head. 'He's working down in London. Now let me get on – unless you want to take the kid to school yourself?' Then she closes the door and Frank is alone again.

The door to the second house opens with a waft of different smells. Indian cooking and fabric conditioner. An elderly Muslim man stands looking at him, grey eyebrows raised. Frank tries the same routine, but the man just shakes his head.

The third house is occupied by another white family. This time the husband is at home, but Frank doesn't recognize him. The final door yields no answer. The inside of the windows is covered in newspaper. He looks through the letterbox and sees bare floorboards and a pile of junk mail.

The morning traffic is starting to build. The occasional sounds of doors slamming and distant engines turning over have started to blend in with each other to become a background rumble so constant that Frank can only hear it when he really concentrates. His own household will be up by now. Julie will have found his note.

He reaches the first address on Moorland Street. He doesn't need to knock to see that this one is empty. The windows are vacant. There is no furniture inside. The paint is peeling from the door and an estate agent's board sticks out from the wall. He walks along the road. The next three houses all have rangoli patterns chalked on the doorsteps. That means Hindu families. Not the home of the person he is looking for.

He checks his watch. He should go back and talk to Tami. He should go and see what message the blackmailer has sent to him. He won't manage both of those tasks and still get into the police station in time for the start of work. He has a uniform in the boot of the car. He tries to think through all the possibilities. But this location still feels like the strongest clue he has had to date. He isn't willing to give up on it so easily. The empty house has a side passage. The door that must have once blocked the way through is leaning unhinged against the wall.

Frank edges past a wheelie bin and through towards the back. The yard is paved, though weeds have somehow managed to colonize the cracks. Thistles stand knee high. There is no sign that anything here has been disturbed in a couple of years. He peers in through the kitchen window, but all that he can see are dead flies on the inside sill and sheets of yellowed newspaper on the floor.

He steps back into the centre of the yard, stands on tiptoe and looks across to the neighbouring plots. Most of the

Asian households have paved over the back gardens. One has an array of flowers in tubs. He looks across to the houses on the road behind and sees the same pattern. Except for the empty house. It takes him a couple of seconds to consciously register what it is that seems wrong about it.

The upstairs room at the back. Probably the bathroom. A frosted-glass window. The small upper section of the window is open. Just a crack. He only noticed because of the slightly deeper line of shadow beneath it. But now he has seen it, the house doesn't feel quite so deserted.

One minute later he has crossed to the other street and knocked on the front door again. Still getting no response, he clambers down another bin-choked side passage into the rear yard.

Everything but the bathroom window is closed. There is paper over the windows downstairs so he cannot see in. Everything is locked. He gets down on his knees, puts his nose to the crack under the door and inhales. He can smell concrete dust and damp woodwork. And other things. A faint scent that might be a woman's perfume, or perhaps some kind of soap. And fainter still, a cooking smell. Last night's evening meal, perhaps. The scent of occupancy.

He has seen enough break-ins to know all about how it is done. He has seen every trick in aftermath. But this is the first time he has picked up a broken brick and used it to shatter a window himself. It proves easy. Even the sound of the glass breaking is quieter than he expected. He reaches a hand inside and finds a door key on a nail in the wall.

His first thought is that he must have made a mistake. The only floor covering downstairs is a layer of dust and dead bluebottles. And, worse, the stack of junk mail behind the front door is so deep that it reaches almost to the letterbox. Frank turns around and looks at the door through which he has just entered the house. Other than the fragments of broken glass, the floor there is clear.

'Hello?' he calls. 'Anyone home?' If there is anyone in the house, they would know he is here. Better to make it open, to play it innocent as far as that is still possible. He steps on to the stairs. The boards creak.

'Just checking the houses on this row,' he calls, making it up as he goes along. 'There's been a gas leak.'

As he climbs, his eyes come level with the landing. Bare floorboards. But dust-free, with a curving mark that might have been made by a damp cloth being wiped over the surface. He takes the last five steps.

'Hello?'

There are three rooms upstairs. It is dark in all of them. He pushes open the nearest door with his foot, then reaches in and clicks the light on. The first thing he sees is the window, covered completely in what looks like aluminium foil. Then the camp bed beneath it. A backpack on the floor.

Frank does a quick search of the other rooms and finds them empty. All the windows have had the same treatment. Newspaper on the outside, aluminium foil on the inside. Even with the lights on, no one would be able to see a thing from outside the building.

He returns to the backpack, kneels next to it for a moment, aware that his heart is beating faster than it should and that his face is hot. He feels like an over-pumped balloon.

Then he starts working through the contents, pulling them out and laying them on the floor. Toiletries: spray-on deodorant, a roll of tissue, toothbrush, toothpaste, towel and flannel. Next out are two pairs of neatly folded jeans, one black denim, the other blue, two grey T-shirts and a burgundy-coloured fleece top. He lays one set out on the floor, to get some idea of the size of the man who might have worn them. It looks somehow wrong, so he readjusts the way the shirt lies over the jeans, reducing the overlap to nothing. With that done, it is easier to imagine the man who might fill the clothes. But even with the readjustment, he would have to be a fair few centimetres shorter than Frank. Shorter than Red Owen. Thinner than Eddie Piper. Bill Arnica might well fit into them, but it is hard to believe he would ever take off his tie, let alone don denim.

Frank continues to search the pack. He finds fifteen £20 notes in a side pocket – uncreased and smelling new, as if they have just rolled out of the cash point machine. There is nothing smaller. No loose change. Nor are there any bus tickets or receipts. No driving licence. No chocolate wrappers. No postcards or pebbles or badges or any of the curious keepsakes that usually inhabit the forgotten corners of travellers' bags. When he finally has the backpack empty, with all its contents laid out on the floor in front of him, Frank still hasn't found anything with any individual personality. It is an assemblage defined by what it does not contain.

With this pattern in his mind, he starts thinking about the items that would be needed in a stripped-down existence, squatting in a disused terraced house in Leicester. He tries to visualize the sequence of events in his own routine. There are no pyjamas – but not everyone wears them. The weather is hot. The windows are covered. Perhaps he walks to the bathroom naked. He uses the toilet. He washes. He dries using the towel. He gets dressed – except that there is no underwear.

Frank already knows the backpack is empty, but this omission seems so inexplicable that he dives his hand back into it again.

Nothing.

He gets up and steps over to the camp bed – the only item of furniture in the room. Behind it is a carrier bag that he had not noticed before. He turns it out on to the floor next to the other objects.

And there in front of him is the missing underwear, but not as he was expecting it. He stares at the pile, realizing that there was another item missing from the bag. No shaving equipment. He reaches down and runs his fingers over five pairs of white socks, five identical pairs of pink cotton panties and two white bras.

The answer is close now. He feels sure of it. He remembers Tami. He started out by suspecting her. But she somehow managed to insinuate her way into his trust. Now he sees these women's clothes, he thinks of her again. She is the only woman he knows who is connected to the blackmail photograph. And she would certainly fit into them.

He had been going to break the good news to her before going to work. But there isn't any time now. He has to get back home to check out the blackmailer's mobile. Tami will have to wait until lunchtime.

Tami is lying on her back with her eyes open. She can't see anything now. Or what she can see somehow isn't reaching the last pocket that remains of her conscious mind. There is pain here, but it is far away, as if it belongs to someone else. And movement – her head rolling as a hand slaps her face again. She even thinks she hears someone call her name.

Then blackness. No feeling. No thought. Just a sense of the part of her that has been there all the time, through every change from child to rebellious teen to happy wife to convict, to suicide.

Then that, too, fades. All dimensions disappear. She is the last spot in the centre of the television screen after the power has been disconnected. Hanging for a moment, then fading to black.

PART FOUR

They are playing 'Leila' at the end of the disco. I cling to Jack, pressing my face into his neck. I don't know if it's the Bacardi or his smell that is making me dizzy. His hands are on me, and I'm letting him touch where he wants. He could have any woman in the club, but he's chosen me.

That guitar is banging out the same notes over and over – in time to the spinning of the room. Eric Clapton's voice, calling for his love like she's the one thing he needs. Like the needing her is driving him insane. Like the craziness is what makes him what he is.

If Jack and I have a song, this is it. I close my eyes and let it happen.

Chapter 20

Frank is touching forty as he heads back out of the city towards Glenfield. He sees the white markings on the road too late and has to stab at the brake pedal. There is a blue-white flash as the speed camera goes off. He swears out loud, at the camera, at the cars in front, at the road. Three points on his licence – unless he can argue somehow that he was on emergency business. Another lie. He swears at himself.

He hits the gravel parking space in front of the house just as Jem emerges from the front door, dressed in school uniform.

'Where you been, Dad?'

Frank tightens his mouth into a smile and ruffles his son's hair. 'Work. You know.' Another lie. 'I'm in a rush. Sorry.'

He's in the house and running up the stairs, cursing himself for not taking the extra second for a proper goodbye.

'Frank?' It's Julie calling from the kitchen.

'Yes, love.'

He's in his wardrobe, burrowing through pockets for the blackmailer's mobile.

'Where were you?' Julie asks. He can hear her coming up the stairs.

He is stepping through the phone's menu. He presses the button to read the new message.

Thanks for the money. I will call again soon.

Julie comes into the room. He drops the phone into his jacket pocket, wheels to face her. Heartbeat making it hard to think. Mind trying to switch from one mode to another.

'Frank?'

'I'm fine,' he says, unasked. 'Rushing, though. Sorry.'

She puts a hand on his chest. 'Where were you?'

He steps back from her touch and turns to the wardrobe again. 'I'm running late. You know. Talk later. OK?'

The door slams behind him. He jerks around but Julie has gone.

He gets to the police station twenty-five minutes late. No one will say anything. He's too senior for that. But he's aware of the way they are looking at him. He smiles at them and nods greetings as he marches towards his office. He tells himself that he is still in control.

When he gets to his office, two men in grey suits are waiting for him. One is tall and broad in the shoulder, the other short with a face as wrinkled as a raisin. Both are standing though there are seats they could have used.

The larger man extends his hand. 'Inspector Roger Ericson, sir. Complaints and Discipline. This is Sergeant Thelps. Forgive the intrusion, but your secretary said you'd have a few minutes for us.'

Frank knew this moment would come. Now it is here, he is glad the men who have come to question him are of lower rank. He smiles briefly at each of them, then gets round to his side of the desk.

'You've had my statement about the riots?' he asks.

Ericson nods. 'I have seen it.'

'Well?'

'Our investigation isn't connected with that directly. We're looking in to the matter of a complaint made against one of your officers by a member of the public. Inspector Marjorie Akanbai. It's a minor matter. I don't think there is really any issue for her to answer. But in the process – looking through the papers – we came across an inconsistency. While we were about it, we wanted to clear it up.'

'Mo's a good officer,' Frank says.

'Inspector Akanbai stated that she sent a memo to you on Friday afternoon regarding the Muslim community. But you are on record as saying you received no warnings of any sort.'

The smaller man, Thelps, has been silent all this time. Now he sits forward. 'Explain that,' he says.

Frank is so taken aback that a junior officer should use this aggressive tone with him that for a moment he sits with his mouth hanging half-open. 'I received no such memo,' he says.

This is what he has planned to say. To get Mo into just enough trouble so she is pushed out of the picture for a couple of months. But now the words are out, he feels a wave of guilt.

'Where did it go?' Thelps demands. 'She's given us a copy of it.'

There's no way back now. Frank's lie seems to have a momentum of its own. 'Perhaps she wrote the memo after the second riot,' he says. 'To cover herself.'

'That's a serious accusation.'

'You asked for suggestions. I'm not accusing anyone.'

But he knows that they know that is exactly what he is doing.

Ericson smiles again. 'Well, we'll have to leave it there for the time being. I'm sure the issue can be resolved.'

The two men leave. The door slams, and Frank is alone again. If he could change anything, it would be to get Mo free from all this. She is tangled up in his story, and it isn't her fault. He has tried to do what was right at every stage, but underlying all his decisions was a flaw. He cared too much about his own reputation. If he could only get the money from somewhere – another of Kringman's criminal contacts, perhaps – he'd be able to pay back Vince. Then he could really work at making things right for Mo.

The ceiling. A light bulb – very bright. Then a face, blocking it out. Rita's face. Rita's hand flashing in front of her eyes. Sounds that become words, then fade into sounds again.

'. . . fucking get it together, girl . . .'

Then Rita's face is gone and the light bulb is out.

It doesn't feel as if she is coming round from unconsciousness. Her conscious mind has been there all along. It's just that time has slowed to nothing, and there is no dimension in which she can think of anything.

Rita's face. More sounds. '. . . to a doctor, if you . . .'

Rita's hand flashing past her eyes again. This time she feels herself blinking.

'. . . try a bit, girl. I'm not doing it for . . .'

A hand on the side of her face, tipping her head to the left so that a column of wood comes into view. She stares at it. More sounds. Thumping feet getting fainter.

Time must be flowing to some extent because one moment the thing in front of her eyes doesn't have any identity and then it becomes a leg of furniture. She is looking at her bed sideways on, her head on the floor.

She finds herself rolling on to her front, then climbing up

the quilt, over the corner of the mattress. She has no idea if she is moving slowly or fast, only that once she is in bed she will be able to sleep and that everything will be better.

When she wakes, it is to the knowledge that she is breathing and that something is pressing against her mouth.

'. . . up and you can go back to sleep again. Come on.'

She opens her eyes and sees Rita holding a cup in front of her face.

'That's a girl, Tami. Drink up.'

'What's happening?' Tami whispers.

'You're scaring me half to death. That's what.'

Death. She hears the word and remembers. '. . . should be dead.'

'I'm not doing this another time, you hear. Try and top yourself again and I'll let you.'

Tami drinks. It is sweet tea. Lukewarm. The effort tires her and she lets her head back on to the pillow. 'Why aren't I dead?' she asks.

'Sleep,' Rita says.

And she does.

Tami wakes again to the smell of toast. She still feels woozy, but not like before. Now she has some kind of awareness of herself. She stumbles through to the kitchen and finds Rita peering under the grill at two slices of bread.

'Stale,' Rita says. 'Only way to eat it is toasted.'

'I should be dead,' Tami says.

Rita shrugs. 'Did you want to be?'

'I injected enough to kill myself twice over.'

'Must have been cut with something.'

'It was pure!'

Rita pulls the grill pan out and rests it next to the sink.

Drops of water on the draining board hiss into steam. She plasters margarine on to the toast with a knife. 'It's never pure, girl.'

'You cut it with something,' Tami demands. 'Didn't you!'

Rita stares at her toast.

'What was it?'

No answer.

'Well?'

Rita wheels towards her. 'Why did you want to be dead? I've saved you often enough, girl! You don't even have a habit no more. You're straight. Think of me for a change! I was going cold. I had to get some. It was your stash or go sell myself.'

'What did you cut it with?'

'Diazepam, paracetamol, some other stuff.'

'Shit.'

'You're alive, aren't you? What more do you want?'

Rita picks up a slice of toast. Tami watches drops of melted margarine falling on to the vinyl floor as the other woman eats.

'You got a letter,' Rita says through her mouthful. 'From that cop Shakespeare.'

Tami stumbles back into the lounge. The letter is on the coffee table, already opened.

'The body wasn't Jack's,' Rita says. 'Jack must have made it look like it was him – but it wasn't.'

Tami picks up the sheet of paper and reads the words.

'*Now* you can thank me,' Rita says, 'for saving you. Again.'

Chapter 21

Tami can't sleep these days unless she is dressed. She wears a shirt and thin jogging trousers. It isn't comfortable, but when she wakes, as she does several times through the night, she doesn't have to scramble into clothes before checking the flat.

She is awake now, lying in bed, looking up at the ceiling. She is sure this time that she has heard a noise from somewhere outside. A metallic clatter. It could be a cat or a fox knocking something over. She is gripping handfuls of the sheet. She makes her fingers open, releasing it. Then she rolls out of bed again. Her feet land softly on the carpet. She pads to the window and puts her eye to the crack where the curtains haven't properly closed.

The moonlight seems unnaturally bright at first. She sees the sloping slate roof of the outhouse, the weeds in the back yard, the rear wall with its gate open. It was closed when she looked out yesterday. Through it she can see the walkway between the gardens and, further back still, the next row of houses behind. Everything is black and white. Everything is still except for one shadow. She sees it through the open gate. It shifts across the rubble and fly-tipped junk. It moves once and then it, too, is still.

Even now she has fixed on it, she can't resolve what she is looking at. She stares, trying not to blink for fear that she might lose it amid the pattern of shadow and moon-light. Her eyes are stinging from the effort. It feels as if that tiny span on which she is focused has grown to fill her vision.

Then it happens. The shadow moves again, crossing behind the doorway and disappearing behind the wall. It is human. Man or woman, she can't tell. But in the blink of it passing it turned its head and looked straight up at her window.

Tami draws back from the curtains slowly. She feels sick. And when the doorbell rings it makes her jolt so hard that her arm cramps. She rubs the muscle, trying to loosen it.

The person at the door can't be the same one she just saw out of the back window. There hasn't been time for them to get there. The bell rings again. She runs to the front window and looks down to the street. There is a man leaning on the wall. She can see only his shoulder from this angle, but she recognizes the bulk straight away. It is Eddie Piper.

Eddie stumbles in, bringing a waft of stale body odour and fresh alcohol. She closes the door, double-checking that the deadlock has engaged properly. There is a dull thud from the living room. He has collapsed into the armchair. His feet are splayed in front of him. His chin rests on his T-shirt.

'I'm sorry,' he mumbles. 'In a mess.'

Tami doesn't turn the light on. She hurries through to the kitchen and looks out to the rear yard, checking for movement from this different angle. There is nothing to see, but that doesn't mean there isn't anyone there.

Having Eddie in the flat doesn't make her any safer if he is as drunk as this. She spoons coffee granules into a mug and boils the kettle. The smell of it hits her as she pours the boiling water. She wants some herself, but her heart is already racing. Extra caffeine would push her over the edge.

She has to shake him by the shoulder before his eyes open. 'Don't sleep.'

He takes the cup, flinching as a few drops of the scalding liquid slop on to his leg. He blinks a couple of times then puts his face over the mug and inhales the steam.

'Come on, Eddie.'

His eyes are closed again. 'So sorry.'

'Wake up!'

He pushes his feet against the carpet, working himself further up in the chair.

'Now drink.'

He does as he is told, slurping over the lip of the mug. It sounds as if he is taking in more air than liquid, but his eyes snap wide open and he straightens himself further.

She checks the windows and doors again while he drinks. There is still no sign of life. This time, when she comes back she turns on the small lamp. It doesn't look as if he has changed his clothes since she last saw him. Stained jeans and T-shirt. His stomach hangs over his belt, and his face is angled down into his coffee. Tami stands in front of him, clutching her hands. She looks back over her shoulder, making sure her shadow isn't falling on the curtain.

'Did you see anyone outside?' she asks.

'Christ,' he says. 'What time is it?'

'Four in the morning. Did you see anyone out there?'

He waves his arm bluntly in her direction. 'I'm sorry.'

'What are you doing here? Did you come with someone else?'

'Want to talk. This thing I didn't tell you,' he says.

She looks into his face. The awareness seems to be coming back to him. The mug is half-empty. 'Keep drinking,' she says.

He slurps, swallows, looks down at the carpet. 'Wasn't

your business. But now . . . Hell, I'm a shit. Hate myself, you know?'

'Tell me,' she says.

'You knew me before. I was OK. People liked me.'

'You're still OK, Eddie.'

'Was different then. Didn't think about stuff. Didn't need to. Money was easy.'

'Times change.'

'I was straight with our side. Always. You know that?'

'Drink the coffee.'

He drains the mug, then leaves it balanced on the armrest. 'They trusted me. Jack trusted me. I never blabbed. I got jobs. You know . . . easy money.'

'Jack liked you,' Tami says.

He looks up. 'Really?'

'Yes,' she says, though she isn't sure how true it is.

'We had good times, me and Jack. It's not the same since he's gone.'

'Why are you here?'

He takes a deep breath, then says: 'Want to know what happened to me?' He doesn't wait for her to answer. 'I did this house in Stoneygate. Done the same kind of job hundreds of times. Soft 'n' easy.' He's speaking as if rushing to get the story out.

'When was this?'

'Years back. You'd only been inside a couple of months. Job like that should be a cakewalk. But the owner was there. He hears me, comes downstairs screaming. Telling me to drop it all. He's an old bloke. White hair. Wild-looking.'

Eddie pauses for breath. The further he goes with the story, the more alert he looks. He is sitting up properly, his words hardly slurred. And Tami senses, even though she doesn't understand the reason, that this story is part of the reason Eddie has come to see her in the middle of the night.

'I drop the stuff,' Eddie says. 'I don't want any trouble. But the old bloke lifts his arm. He's got a gun. An old revolver or something. His hand's shaking. I turn and leg it, but he shoots anyway. The bang's so loud in that room, it's like being smashed over the head. And I'm thinking he's got me. I'm gunna die. But I'm running anyway. There's bullet holes in the back door. I'm through and out into the garden. He's still shooting. Empties the gun at me.' Eddie dries up as suddenly as he started. He clenches and unclenches his fist.

'If he hit you he'd have gone to prison,' Tami says.

Eddie shakes his head. 'Maybe.'

'But he didn't hit you.'

'Would've been better if he had.'

'You don't mean that.'

'It didn't happen to you. Or you'd get it.' He rubs his face with his hands, as if trying to wake himself up.

'Get what?'

'I still did houses. But I was jumpy after that. Like the old bloke was gunna be there. I got nightmares, you know? Me! Couldn't sleep. Was worse each time I went breaking. Then I couldn't hack it no more. Stopped breaking. Then everything went bad.'

'You've got a problem,' Tami says.

He shakes his head. 'I'm just shit scared.'

'I knew one girl on the inside who was the same,' she tells him. 'Her husband beat her up. Even when she left him, she got nightmares about it. Each day she was more afraid. In the end she couldn't go out of the house.'

'Why was she in prison?'

'The husband came looking for her. She killed him.'

'I'm not a head-case.'

'There are medicines to help. Antidepressants and stuff.'

'I'm not a head-case,' Eddie says again. 'Just lost my bottle.' He is staring at the carpet.

It feels to Tami as if she's just heard some kind of confession and that she is expected to absolve him. But there isn't any connection between Eddie's story and her own life so far as she can see. And she instinctively rejects his self-hatred.

She angles the high-backed dining chair towards Eddie and sits. She is glad he's with her now. Her fear of the creeping figure outside in the moonlight is receding as he begins to sober up. When she glimpsed the man through the bedroom window she was convinced he was spying on her. Now it seems more likely that it was just some drunk finding a dark corner to relieve himself in.

'You can get over it, Eddie,' she says. 'You can get over anything if you really want to.'

'Didn't mean to tell you all that,' he says.

She waits for him to explain. He takes the empty mug and turns it in his hands. 'It was after that time. I was real low. No money. And I was drinking. When he came and asked me to do a job – I said yes.'

'Who?'

'Bird's Eye.'

Tami remembers the old man. No one had liked him, but everyone did business with him.

'He tells me to meet him that night. I turn up and there's him and another bloke. And they've got . . . got spades and a pick and torches. They want me to help them carry the stuff out into the grass.'

'Where was this?'

'Western Park. I do it all like they say. Follow them out so far that we can't see the road. There's just this path and bushes and trees. And I get the shakes and need to drink. They're saying I'm useless. But I do keep going. We go way out into the real thick bushes. I have to duck down low and then crawl. And then we start to dig.

'I'm freaking out. It's a deep hole, and they're looking serious. And I'm thinking what they might be planning on burying. Then I get so bad that I can't do it. They were so frigging angry, I thought Bird's Eye was gunna hit me with the pick and put me in the hole. It looked like a grave. They have this bad argument about what to do with me. Then they send me away. I just run. I run all the way back to the car.'

'Who was the other man?'

Eddie shakes his head. 'Can't tell you.'

'Would he hurt you?'

Eddie nods. A tear runs down his cheek.

'I wanted to know what was up. So . . . I hid and drank the rest of the bottle. And I waited. They . . . they came back all muddy from digging. And they . . . opened the boot. There was a plastic sack.'

'What kind of sack?' Tami is sitting forward in her chair.

He shakes his head, as if voicing an answer would be too much for him. 'They dragged it . . . out into the park . . .' He is sobbing now. He holds out one hand towards her as if he is a rugby player fending off a tackle. With the other hand he covers his face.

'When did this happen?' she asks.

'After . . . after Jack disappeared. It's only now . . . now everyone's looking for him . . . I didn't think it before. I would have told someone. Would have told you. I'm sorry.'

He staggers out of the chair and towards the door.

'Eddie. Come back.'

But he clatters away down the stairs. 'I'm sorry,' he says. 'I'm so sorry.' Then the front door slams.

Frank flinches when the phone starts to ring. He reaches for the TV remote control, resting on the arm of the chair, but Julie's hand covers it before he can get to the mute button.

'Leave it,' she says.

It rings. Frank clenches his' jaw muscles. The ringing stops. He relaxes.

'This is our night,' Julie reminds him.

But when the ringing starts again, Frank is out of the seat in a blink. Through to the phone in the hall. He closes the door behind him.

'Yes?'

For a second there is no answer. Then he hears a wheezing breath. 'Frank?'

'Speaking. Now who is this?'

The breath turns into a laugh. 'On edge tonight, boy?'

Then he recognizes the voice. It is Superintendent Kringman – though not sounding quite the same as before. 'Are you all right?'

'It's you that you should be worried about, Franky. What is it they call you? The Bard?' He laughs again.

'Have you been drinking?' Frank asks.

'Wouldn't that be nice? You could blame it all on the demon drink. You Methodists are all the same. Killjoys.'

'You don't sound yourself. I was worried, that's all. And we're Anglican.'

'Well, Bardy boy. You should be worried with the Russian in town.'

'Gabriel?'

'Don't play all surprised. I know you put him on to me.'

Frank listens to Kringman's wheezing breath. It sounds as

if he is laughing again. Only after the line clicks dead does it hit him that the old man could have been crying.

He keys in Kringman's number from memory. It rings for a long time before the old man picks up.

'I've had nothing to do with Gabriel,' Frank says.

'Methinks you protest too loudly, Franky boy.'

'Why is he in Leicester?'

'Blood,' Kringman says. 'Or money. They're the same to him.'

Frank knows that Kringman is like this on purpose. Evasive. Winding people up as if it was his only pastime. 'Have you seen Gabriel?'

'Rattled your cage, have I?'

This time, the breath at the end of the sentence is definitely a laugh. If it wasn't for the old superintendent's daughter, Frank would be sure the man was drunk.

'I need answers.'

'That's what he said, too.'

'So he did speak to you?'

'You remember that heroin haul in St John's? What was it – seven years ago?'

'Ten.'

'How much did we get?'

'Eight and a half kilos.'

'That must be why they promoted you, Bardy boy. Useless facts stick to your brain like shit to a shoe.'

'What about the heroin?'

'Mardy Bardy – you know that's what we used to call you?'

Frank didn't.

More papery laughter down the phone line.

'Tell me about the heroin. Was it Gabriel's?'

'Everyone knew that.'

'So?'

'So he hasn't forgotten. He remembers grudges like you remember your National Insurance number.'

All the personal insults are part of the process. Frank knows that. The old man wasn't so cranky when they worked together. But Frank has been promoted since then. And Kringman has sunk into diabetic retirement. This exchange is a trade-off. Letting the old man have the pleasure of winding him up in exchange for a few morsels of information. The trouble is, Frank doesn't know if he's got it all yet. The crumbs he's been given certainly don't make a whole picture.

'Gabriel wants to know who grassed him up all those years ago. Is that it?'

'Maybe.'

'Maybe?'

'How much heroin did you say we recovered, Franky?'

'Eight and a half kilos. Plus the extra kilo from Jack's wife's car. Total nine and a half.'

'Nine and a half.' Kringman repeats. There is a pause, as if the old man is catching his breath. 'But what if Gabriel shipped twenty kilos? You were always good at maths. How much did someone skim from the haul?'

'Ten and a half.'

'That's right, Mardy Bardy. Ten and a half kilos of unfinished business. Plus interest.'

'But why now?'

Kringman doesn't answer.

Chapter 22

It is a hot night again. But Tami has taken to closing and locking the windows before she goes to bed. All but the once-paint-sealed window, which has no catch. She tried using a wedge-shaped strip of wood, jamming it in the side runners, but it fell out with only a little joggling. A serious intruder would have no problem with it.

She stands now reading the instructions on the tube she bought from Wilkinsons. No contact with eyes or skin. Do not swallow. The irony of the final instruction might have made her laugh in a different situation – only use in a well-ventilated space. She snips the end off the nozzle and squeezes out a line of clear glue. By the time she has run the length of the window crack the tube is empty. The instructions say that it sticks in under ten seconds. She waits twenty before trying to haul the window open. It is stuck firm.

Instead of wearing panties to bed, Tami pulls on a pair of cotton shorts. She slips her bra off without removing her T-shirt, then lies on the bed. Rita is still out, presumably selling drugs to make enough money to feed her addiction. It is almost as if the difficulty of getting by and maintaining a habit is what keeps the woman going – the struggle giving her some kind of purpose. Perhaps that is no less logical than living to work to have the money to live.

Tami closes her eyes and tries to stop thinking. But thoughts keep coming. They start as little things. Like the words Jack used when he came to see her that last time in prison. It seems important to remember them now, but she can't. Perhaps there was a message in them for her. A hint. Part of her mind is trying to recall them. But another thought is starting to form – that there is no point in Jack pretending to have died in the fire if no one was going to find out. If he planted the snake ring on some tramp, then it would be important that whoever he was trying to hide from saw it. But only the police had access to the evidence.

She is so tired now that thinking is making her feel nauseous. But she can't stop. The thoughts keep coming at her. Attacking her. And she finds herself defending against each one.

It is a rattling window that wakes her. The sound is coming from the kitchen. She finds herself sitting up in bed. She stumbles into the unlit kitchen, pulls the long, broad blade of the vegetable knife from its slot, then backs herself against the wall. Her breath is coming in short gasps, but it still feels as if she can't get enough oxygen. The room tilts. The window rattles again. She forces herself to advance towards it, holding the knifepoint out in front of her.

Then the window rattles again. Down in a garage courtyard, perhaps fifty metres away up the street, a van is reversing. The engine revs and the window resonates again. The tension falls from Tami so suddenly that she almost lets go of the knife handle. She carries it back to the bedroom and puts it on the floor near the wall – so that she can reach it if she feels the need.

This time she falls into a deeper sleep. For once there are no dreams to disturb her.

When Gabriel used to come to Leicester, back in the days of the agreement, he'd stay in a cheap place on the edge of Waterfields. It called itself a hotel, although it was nothing more than a bed and breakfast that did a sideline in letting out rooms by the hour.

He had the money to stay anywhere he wanted. But the grand hotels were never his style. It seemed as if living out of grubby rooms with stained carpets was a kind of virtue to him. He did it because he could and others couldn't. And, of course, his customers didn't look so conspicuous in that part of town.

If Gabriel had been dealing cocaine to stockbrokers, he would have needed a more grandiose setting. A big hotel in the centre of the city. Somewhere with real art on the walls instead of Athena prints. But that was never going to be a market he could tap. There was too much raw menace about him to maintain a network of that kind.

Frank slides his car into a slot fifty metres from the back entrance of the hotel. He turns off the engine and listens to the silence. At first he thinks there is no one on the street, then he sees a movement at the corner up ahead. A prostitute shifting her head to one side, getting into a better angle to look down the road towards him.

Frank sits still, knowing he is invisible with his face in the shadow. She goes back to her corner. He doesn't move. He is taking his time, examining each of the cars on the other side of the road. He isn't sure what he is looking for. But ten minutes waiting can't hurt.

A car crawls down the road and away. A group of young people spill out from a side street. Men and women dressed for clubbing. They pass his car without looking in. He watches them recede in the rear-view mirror, their laughter going with them. He waits until the dashboard clock has moved on past the quarter-hour. Then he gets out, slips across the road and into the shadows of the hotel's rear car park. He stops here and looks back at his own car and the others parked on that side of the road. They are all empty. The only one that concerns him is a white van twenty metres away. The rear window is silvered on the inside. He watches it, looking for any movement in the suspension. Something that would indicate the presence of people inside. After five more minutes of watching, he gives up and walks into the hotel.

He steps through the rear door and inhales cheap air freshener and stale tobacco. It brings back the memory of the last time he was here. That was ten years ago in the aftermath of a drugs raid. It looks as if the decorations haven't been changed in that time, though it is hard to see much because the lighting is a couple of hundred watts short of adequate. There is no one at the front desk. He hears a TV somewhere in a room behind. Late-night soft porn from Channel Five. There is a bell on the counter. He reaches over it and takes the guest register book.

Business seems to have been poor lately – though the hourly guests probably aren't asked to put their details down on paper. Nothing written for wives to check up on – or for Her Majesty's Inspector of Taxes.

There are eight names registered as having checked in during the last three days. Of those, four have checked out already. Frank examines the remaining four. He remembers something about the Russian from all those years ago. It comes back to him now as he sees the writing on the page. Gabriel's hands may be as hard as meat tenderizers, but they are dexterous. One of the four possible residents is a Mr Henseling, registered in room number fourteen. The name looks German. The handwriting is fine and regular, sloping to the left, just as Frank remembers it from years ago.

Room fourteen is at the back of the building on the second floor. The corridor is wide, though the dim lighting and dark wallpaper make it feel narrow. Frank walks down the left side, placing his feet close to the wall, trying to avoid any creaking floorboards. It is a hopeless task. By the time he reaches the door, he has made enough noise for someone like Gabriel to be ready.

Frank knocks softly. No answer

'Gabriel? I need to speak to you.'

There is a sound from inside the room. A muffled crash, perhaps a foot catching a chair leg.

He knocks again, more firmly this time. He tries the handle. It turns. The door isn't locked. Frank opens it and sees a woman. Thirty, perhaps. Wearing a short black skirt and holding a red blouse over her chest.

'Get the fuck out of here!'

Frank steps inside. 'Where's Gabriel?'

'Don't know anything. OK? I'm going.'

Frank sees a flash of pale breast as she pulls the blouse over her head and worms her arms into it.

'The man,' he says. 'Who is he?'

She glares at him. 'Don't know names.'

'Where is he?'

'Said he had business to do. And the room's paid for, OK? I was just sleeping a bit.'

She is squeezing her feet into a pair of high-heeled boots as she says this. He watches her pull up the zips.

'When did he leave?'

She picks up a glossy black handbag. 'Got no right pushing in here when I'm undressed.'

'Tell me when he left!'

'Half an hour. An hour. What's the fucking difference?'

'Where did you meet him?'

Glaring at Frank, she moves towards the door. 'I'll scream if you try and stop me.'

He steps aside and she is gone.

The first thing Frank does is put his head through the open window and check that he has clear access to the fire escape. Then he sets about trying to lock the door of Gabriel's room. But the only way to do it would be with the room key, and that is missing. So he heaves the chest of drawers across the door, forming a kind of barricade. Doubtless Gabriel would still be able to force his way inside, but it would take enough time for Frank to make his escape.

And since he is standing next to the chest of drawers, that is where he starts his search, working as quietly as he can, opening the top drawer, finding it empty then pulling it out all the way and feeling around the outside surfaces. He doesn't know what he is searching for. Anything would do – drugs, money, documents. But if there was something really incriminating, Frank doubts that Gabriel would leave it here. A weapon, for example, he would carry with him. Especially if, as the girl said, he was out on business.

You can't feel pain when you are asleep. So it's not the knifepoint tracing the skin of her neck that starts Tami waking but the shifting of the mattress as the man sits himself on the edge of her bed.

In that fraction of a second before she snaps her eyes open and sees the silhouette of his head against the pale ceiling, she already knows it is a man. It is the body odour.

Slightly sour. Intensely male. The knife pulls away. She opens her mouth to scream. But a fist thumps into her stomach, knocking the air from her lungs in a voiceless exhalation. Then his hand clamps over her mouth with a force that presses her head into the pillow.

'No noise,' he whispers. The accent is foreign. She doesn't need to think to know who it is.

She tries to fill her lungs, but the muscles of her chest won't pull. She tries to curl, but her head is still being held in place. Her knees come up to her chest. The air is rushing in through her nose now. Gabriel's face is low over hers. This time she can see his eyes as they catch the faint light from the window. The knife comes into view between them, then his head withdraws.

'No noise.'

She feels the pressure of his hand release. Then it is gone, and she is trying to drag more air into her lungs.

'You visit me before. Now I visit to you.' He turns the knife in his hand, looking at the blade as if it is the first time he has seen one. 'You are a nice girl. Don't want to hurt you. So just tell and make it easy, OK? That way we stay friend.'

She manages to nod.

'Good girl. Now you tell me where is Jack.'

Tami's eyes shuttle between the knife blade and Gabriel's face. 'He went to Scotland.' Her voice sounds papery thin.

'For what? For woman? For drug deal? For kill someone?'

'I don't know. He said it was for woman. I mean . . .'

'So he go. And a fire get him. Right?'

She nods.

He slaps her so hard that her head jolts to one side. 'Lying bitch.'

First there is shock, then a stinging pain, then tightness and heat in the skin of her cheek. She can taste the blood where her teeth have cut into the inside of her mouth. She thinks she should be crying but somehow her body isn't reacting in that way. There is a kind of hyper-clarity to the situation. Her mind has jumped ahead, seen that Gabriel is testing her honesty, that he has inside information.

'There was a fire,' she says. 'A body. All burned.' She is spitting the facts out as quickly as she can manage, guessing that he knows most of it already, feeling for where the edge of his knowledge lies. 'It had Jack's ring on the finger. The one I gave him. But the teeth don't match. It isn't Jack.'

'And?'

'And that's all I know.'

He slaps her again. The same cheek. Jerking her head around in the same direction. 'Lying bitch. Tell the rest or I cut you.'

Which is where Tami's fear becomes something more animal than human because she has nothing more to say. 'I don't know anything!'

He slaps her, harder than before. This time she rolls with the movement, tumbling off the mattress on to the floor, in the gap between the bed and the wall. He gets up and comes around to where she is lying. 'You want to play, then we can play. But you will not like the game.'

He reaches down towards her, as if he is going to grab her by the hair. But her hand has found the handle of the vegetable knife, lying where she left it. She slashes it upwards, cutting the air. It makes contact with something and she loses her grip. It drops point first to the floor, landing a finger's width from the side of her head.

Words and spittle explode from Gabriel's mouth like the scatter from a sawn-off shotgun. He has pulled himself back. His left hand is dripping blood. There's a fraction of a second when Tami thinks he is going to launch a kick at her. She reaches for the knife again, grabbing the blade by mistake, fumbling for the handle, aware that it is wet.

Gabriel stands to his full height. He looks from her face to the knife. Then he opens his mouth and laughs. 'Fucking bitch. You cut us both.'

Tami has the knife above her as she lies on the floor. She already felt the trickle down her arm inside her sleeve, but assumed it was Gabriel's blood. She changes focus and sees the red slash on the side of her thumb. The Russian is still chuckling. He holds out his hand. 'Get me cloth to wrap this.'

Tami eases back to the wall, keeping her eyes on him and the knife in front of her. She pushes herself upright. All the fighting tension seems to have gone out of Gabriel. He has turned so his back is almost to her, but not quite. His unwounded hand pulls open a drawer, plunders through her underwear and pulls out a pair of white cotton panties. He holds them towards her for a moment, not quite asking for permission, more showing her what he is about to do. Then he wraps it three times around his wounded left hand, finally looping the elastic waistband over the fingers, holding the rest in place. A bloom of red seeps outwards through the cotton, but there are no more drops of blood falling on to the carpet.

'Go,' Tami says, jabbing the knifepoint towards him.

He drops himself on to the edge of the bed and sighs. The only way she can get out of the space between the bed and the wall is by walking right past him or clambering over the duvet.

'You got cigarette?' he asks.

'No. Get out.'

'That's not a way to speak to me. We are brothers now.' He gestures with his bloody hand towards hers – as if that offers some kind of explanation. 'You got some booze, then?'

'In the kitchen,' she says.

It looks as if he is waiting for her to go and fetch it. When she doesn't move or lower the knife, he hauls himself off the mattress and lumbers out of the room. Tami follows behind, keeping well out of range, tensed for the moment she is sure will come, when he will wheel and spring at her.

He opens the fridge door, spilling yellow light into the room. There is a clink of glass and he pulls out half a bottle of cheap supermarket white that Rita left there. 'Where you keep the strong stuff?'

'That's all there is.'

'Then we make do with it, yes? I show you a trick.' He slides the bottle into the icebox and closes the fridge again. 'Now we wait.'

He goes back to the lounge, turns the big armchair so that it faces the passage leading to the front door, then he sits, his dark bulk taking possession of it. She doesn't turn the light on. Instead she places herself on the edge of the hard dining chair, not quite facing him straight on. And there she waits, though she doesn't know what she is waiting for.

She still has the knife, but her hand has started to ache and she finds it is impossible to grip the handle firmly. She watches him as best she can in the gloom. She hasn't noticed his expression changing, though there now seems to be a suggestion of a smile. She wonders if it is just her projecting her expectations on to his blankness.

The dark stain on his makeshift bandage does not seem to have expanded further. She can see his eyes on her. When at last he speaks it is casually, as if he is passing the time of day.

'My great-grandfather killed Communists.'

'What?'

'They put him in prison camp. You know these stories? Siberia. So many hundred thousand men. So many million. He was one of them. They put them in the camp, and then everyone can know there is something worse than being dead. But my great-grandfather was strong and clever and he stayed alive.' He speaks this last sentence as if it is ironic. A joke.

Tami peers at him through the gloom, but his face gives away nothing.

'They used to tell me every day the story of great-grandfather. How he was a true patriot. The Communists would all be killed in the end. They would have a tsar again from somewhere. And my great-grandfather would be recognized. This is what I had to live every day. Lies and dreams. Stories of how he ate rats so he could live. How he escape and was found again and put back. All this Russian hero crap. They love to tell it. Like it would make the filthy bread on our table taste better. Only one story is good. That is the one I show you tonight.'

He lapses into silence again. Tami can feel the pulse in her injured hand. A dull pain pulsing under the surface of her skin.

'Why kill Communists?' she asks, trying to keep him talking.

'Why kill Communists?' he echoes. 'Sure. Good question. The tsar kills so many million. Stalin is just the same – like another tsar. It has no meaning.' Gabriel nods towards the vegetable knife in her hand. 'How many men have *you* killed?'

'None.'

He laughs. 'You try to kill me.'

'I was afraid.'

'Was?'

She knows she has to keep focused, but the dark and the stillness and the passage of time are lulling her. Fatigue flows through her body. She loosens her grip on the knife handle. 'You could have killed me already,' she says.

'Yes. Good. You are smart.'

'Why are you here?'

'To find Jack. Just like I told you.'

'Why find Jack?'

He doesn't answer. She tries to tighten her grip on the knife again. The pain is so sharp that it cuts into the heavy sleep that is resting on her mind. She grips harder. The minutes pass. Five, ten. It is hard to keep track in the gloom.

It feels as if a pressure is building inside her. 'Why?' she says again. She doesn't expect an answer. But she feels as if she needs the sound of a voice in the room. Anything to stop the silence roaring.

'Jack stole from me,' Gabriel says. 'Long time ago.'

'Then why look for him now?'

'I didn't know it before.'

'How do you know?'

'Someone steals from me. Something very, very big.'

'Heroin?'

He shrugs, as if the answer does not need to be spoken out loud. 'Some is in your car. Some the police find. The rest—' he spreads his hands, turning the palms upwards '— it vanish like . . . just like Jack.'

'It wasn't us. Jack hated drugs.'

Gabriel doesn't answer. It seems though he has accepted the fact that she has nothing more to tell. The silence lengthens. Ten minutes. Half an hour. Tami has to grip the knife handle again, making the pain sharpen her mind, keeping her awake. Her backside is going numb from the hard dining chair.

'What are you waiting for?' she asks.

He takes a long breath, so deep it is as if he is smoking a joint. Then he blows air and shakes his head. 'No more waiting. It is time.'

He stands, coughs into his fist, then heads to the kitchen. Tami watches the light from the fridge shine out. The wine bottle clinks. Gabriel holds it up, inspecting the contents. 'It is good,' he says. 'Half is ice. Now we drink.'

Tami watches him pouring from the bottle into two mugs. Much less than half a bottle of liquid flows out. He steps towards her, offering one of the mugs. She strengthens her grip on the knife handle but takes the mug. He steps back and grins.

'We drink to finding Jack.'

He tips his head back and takes a long swallow, then wipes his mouth on the back of his hand. Tami sips from her own mug. The liquid is so cold that she can hardly taste any grape flavour. She gets the hit of the alcohol, though. Very strong. More like a spirit than a wine.

'Good, yes? This is the one good story from my great-grandfather. The only one I believe. They made some kind of vodka this way in the winter. Potatoes mashed in water. It ferments. Then they put it outside so it freezes. They melt off the alcohol into bottles. Throw the rest away.'

'Why are you still here?' Tami asks.

'Like I say. To find Jack.'

'I don't know where he is.'

'Maybe.'

He turns his head, touches a finger to his lips, indicating that she should be silent. There is a noise from the stairs outside. A creak. Then another.

'It's no one,' Tami whispers. 'Just a friend. Don't hurt her.'

Gabriel has crossed the living room in two long, silent strides. He waves her back with one hand.

Metal scrapes and taps on the other side of the door. Tami holds her breath, thinking of Rita. This isn't her fight. She knows nothing about Jack. Gabriel's hands spread and clasp, spread and clasp, as if he is warming them up, ready for action. More fumbling then the click of a key at last finding the hole and slotting home. Gabriel leans forward slightly from the waist. The key turns. Tami flings her mug. Ice-cold liquid splatters on her throwing arm. The mug smashes on the wall next to Gabriel's head. He flinches, as if stung. There is a fraction of a second of stillness. Gabriel looking at her, a dark trickle down the side of his face. Silence from the landing. Then Rita's footsteps crashing back down the stairs and Gabriel gone, pounding after her.

The sky is indistinguishable blue, so bright that Frank has to shield his eyes to look at it. Below it is a wall of mottled brickwork, heavily stained. Near the base the pointing is marked out by lines of dark moss. Then there is the culvert of oily water. If it is flowing, the movement is too slow to discern. There is a tyre lying here, half-submerged. On the near side there is a sloping concrete apron scattered with litter – Styrofoam cartons, advertising fliers, shredded strips of polythene.

All is still. And then there is the body.

She lies on her back, eyes almost closed as if she is squinting into the sky. He wonders what she saw in her last moments.

A CID inspector squats next to her. He is a keen man with a thin nose. And though he is wearing shoe covers and gloves, it is clear that he isn't particularly worried about preserving the crime scene.

'Time of death?' Frank asks.

The man glances up, irritation showing in his eyes. 'Why do you ask?'

'Professional curiosity.'

'She wasn't here yesterday afternoon. That's all I can tell you.'

'Not even a guess?'

'After midnight. Before dawn. There won't be any witnesses. There never are for this kind of thing.'

Frank looks up again and tries to imagine the sky black. She may have been looking at the stars, but she can't have been aware of them.

The inspector gets back to his work. He bags up a cigarette lighter, a spoon and then a syringe. 'Do you know something about this?' he asks. 'What's brought you down here?'

'I was passing.'

The truth is, Frank heard about the body on the police radio. A drug overdose so close to Tami's flat. It might have been her.

'You have a name yet?' he asks.

'Nothing definitive. Just a personalized key ring. If it's hers, then the name's probably Rita.'

Chapter 23

The chimneystacks of the opposite terrace are silhouettes against the pale blue of the evening sky. Tami turns on the lamp and crouches down on the floor of the living room.

Rita is dead. Tami can't understand why the news should feel like a surprise. Everyone in the world seemed more vulnerable than Rita. Yet any statistician could have said that at forty-eight the woman was already beyond her life expectancy. A smoker and boozer. A heroin addict. Unemployed. The only time she had money was when she was selling junk. Homeless.

It was Superintendent Shakespeare who came with the news. Other officers might come and ask some questions. Or not. Thinking back on it, she remembers what she didn't notice at the time – that he was watching her, observing her reaction as he said those words.

Tami takes a plastic carrier bag – part of Rita's caravan of worthless treasure. She pulls out a chunky necklace. Pink crystals, each as big as a fingernail. It is heavy. The sort of thing that someone half Rita's age might have got away with wearing. She delves into the crinkly plastic again and pulls out a miniskirt, two small towels, a salt pot and a sheaf of letters held together by an elastic band.

Tami walks her fingers through the envelopes, passing

over the typed official communications. She has her own stash in a drawer in the bedroom. She comes to a sheet of notepaper with a message scrawled across it in Biro. She knows the hand. She blinks twice, trying to clear her vision so she can read.

Rita. Here is the money. Don't spend it all at once. Jack.

Tami rubs the paper between her finger and thumb. She knew about the arrangement – that Jack paid Rita to act as her bodyguard in prison. This confirmation should be no shock. But somehow it is. Perhaps it is the fact that Rita kept the note for so long.

Tami takes the plastic bag and upends it on the carpet. She sifts the glittery junk, searching for more traces, finding none.

It hits her now that the arrangement with Jack must have meant more than a financial transaction. Rita continued to protect Tami – in her own way – long after Jack was gone. Her last act was to run from the flat, drawing Gabriel after her.

Tami realizes now that, however irritating it was, Rita's presence did protect her. That protection has now gone. She looks to the window. The sky is blacker than the chimneystacks now. She gets up to close the curtains. The street outside seems empty. She walks through the empty flat to the back and peers out on the yard. She can't make out anything in the gloom.

This is the first night in recent weeks that everyone will know she is alone. It is as if she is standing under a spotlight in a darkened room, waiting for whoever is out there to do what they will.

The sandwich factory is closed to her. She doesn't have

the money to stay overnight in a hotel. Nor does she know anyone whose floor she could sleep on. There is only one person who she can think of to call. She gets out her phone and keys in Miss Quick's number.

'Hello?' The probation officer's voice sounds guarded.

'I'm in trouble.'

'Tami?'

'Someone's after me.'

'Is it the woman who was in your flat?'

'Rita's dead. It's the man who killed her.'

There's a pause before the probation officer speaks again. 'Stay calm, Tami, and tell me the full story.'

'He . . . he knows where I live.'

'Are you certain?'

'He's a drug dealer.'

'Oh my God.' For a moment the crisp efficiency drops from Miss Quick's voice. 'Do you think . . . is he near you now?'

'Don't know.'

'You'll need to get your things together. There are a couple of hostels that might have beds. And a women's refuge. I can ask after we get you out of there.'

'My car's out of petrol.'

'Then walk. Just leave the house. Head down the main road towards town. I'll drive out and pick you up.'

Tami feels a rush of relief. 'Thank you. Thank you so much!'

She grabs one of Rita's empty plastic carrier bags, runs to the bedroom, scoops in some underwear and a few clothes. The bathroom yields a toothbrush and towel. Handbag and mobile from the lounge. Within thirty seconds she is stumbling towards the door, carrying what she needs but leaving everything she cares about behind.

Her nerves are still tight, so she jerks herself back to the window for a final check. She parts the curtains with the flat of her hand and looks down to the street.

It's then that she sees Gabriel getting out of a large black car. There is another man with him.

Death by overdose. In this case alcohol rather than heroin. A socially acceptable drug. And as if to prove the difference, this death scene has been picked over by three scene of crime officers as well as a CID inspector. All are decked out from feet to face in white. They stand now in a row, job done, gloved hands clasped in front of them as the chief constable enters, followed by his deputy and another colleague. Frank has just brought up the rear. It feels as if he has entered a church rather than a garage and as if he is facing an altar instead of a model train layout.

Superintendent Kringman's body lies curled on its side on the floor, half underneath the table. His face is away from them. Frank is thankful for that. This is a very different experience from seeing Rita's corpse. Kringman he knew in life. He talked to him less than a day ago. He has a sudden pang of anxiety that the phone records will throw up the connection.

It is the chief who breaks the silence. 'All done?'

The inspector nods.

'Your guess?'

'Heart attack, sir. But it *is* only a guess.'

'Time?'

'The daughter was the last to see him alive. That was—' the inspector turns back the pages of his notebook '—yesterday at twenty-two thirty. She drove to a friend's house, where she stayed the night. She came back in this morning and found him.'

'She didn't touch him?'

'No.'

'Anything else?'

'Just this.' The SOCO points towards a half-empty bottle of clear liquid heavily dusted with white powder. 'He'd been drinking.'

'He didn't drink,' Frank says, instantly regretting it.

The chief turns. 'Explain.'

'Superintendent Kringman didn't drink. It was . . . it was on medical advice. Apparently.'

'How do you know?'

Frank can feel the chief's eyes dissecting him. 'We used to be colleagues. Or rather, I worked for him. He wasn't allowed alcohol. I thought it was . . . common knowledge.'

The dark eyes stay on him for a moment longer, then the chief turns away. 'Very good. Toxicology will clear it up.'

'But if he didn't drink . . .'

'What is the drink?' the chief asks.

'Vodka, sir,' says the inspector.

'Then half a bottle should do it,' the chief says. 'Be tactful in the report. He had a fine record. We need role models.' He turns and marches out. The others follow him in line. Frank is left alone with the body.

Rita could have overdosed on heroin at any time in her long addiction. But her death happened within a few hours of Gabriel's arrival in Leicester. The juxtaposition makes Frank as certain as he can be that it was murder dressed up to look like an all-too-easy-to-believe accident. Now Kringman dying during the same night. In a sense, Frank finds this death easier to accept. Kringman knew he didn't have long left. Gabriel might not even have had to force the alcohol into his mouth. It might have been enough to place the bottle in front of the man and tell him to drink.

The real question is – if Gabriel is on a killing spree, getting revenge on the people he thinks might have been involved in stealing his drugs all those years ago, who will he turn on next? Frank can think of two possibilities. Himself and Tami.

He takes a last look at Kringman's body, then follows the others out of the garage and into the harsh sunlight of the afternoon.

Tami knocks on the door of the downstairs flat. The girl who answers it looks puzzled to see her.

'I need to come in,' Tami says. She doesn't wait for an answer, but pushes inside.

'What's happening?'

'Just keep your door locked.'

Tami hurries through to the back. She opens the door, steps out into the yard, then closes it silently behind her. She hears the distant sound of her doorbell ringing. She looks up to the rear windows of her flat. The light is still on. Then she is away, stepping across the paving to the rear walkway. Fearing that someone is going to reach out to grab her. Not able to see into the shadows. She steps forward anyway, knowing that going back would be worse, more certain.

She is in the walkway and running, not able to see the ground in front of her, raising her knees high with each step, trying not to trip over anything that might lie on the ground. The thump of her feet is too loud. The echoes slap back at her off the buildings to either side. There is a dull clatter as she catches an empty can and sends it skitting across the slabs to crash against the wall.

And then she hears more footfalls. These are behind her. Heavy. Pounding hard. One pair or two. The echoes make it impossible to tell. They are crashing through the litter. Gaining on her. She can see the light ahead where the walkway issues on to the street. Seventy metres. Too far. She isn't going to make it to the end. She half-turns to look back, catches her toe on something and goes tumbling forward. The ground hits her chest. Her head bounces on the concrete. She sees lights flash. Her ears are ringing. Then her feet are being pulled, twisted, so she flips over on to her back. There is a man standing over her. His face catches the streetlight from the end of the walkway. It is Gabriel's man from outside the front. He has a knife in his hand. Broad-bladed and long.

'Gotcha,' he whispers.

Then there is a noise that doesn't seem in place. A wooden sound, almost like a musical note. Gabriel's man stumbles. Half a step forward. His knees bend. Then he's folding. Falling like a heap of clothes dropped from a hanger. A gurgling snore escapes from his mouth.

Tami takes all this in with a glance. But her attention is sucked to the figure of another man, holding a wooden baton in his hand. He is standing half inside one of the gardens, wearing a hooded sweatshirt so that his eyes are shadowed. He drops the baton. His hand flashes out and grabs her by the wrist, and she is being pulled through the gateway. She is on her feet and stumbling through the dark, junk-choked back yard towards a dead house. She trips on something, a brick perhaps. But his grip is firm and she finds herself lurching forward instead of falling again.

There's a noise behind her. A scrambling and a groan. Gabriel's man is getting up. The hand gripping Tami's wrist stops pulling and she finds herself being pushed sideways into a dark corner. A hand presses over her mouth and a body presses into hers. Very close to her ear she hears a hiss.

'Shh.'

Gabriel's man is on his feet, looking up and down the walkway, testing the side of his head with a careful hand. He stumbles off in the direction of the road.

Tami is concentrating on her breathing. Taking shallow inhalations through her nose, exhaling through her mouth. Scenting the air. There is a smell of dried sweat from the man next to her. It is familiar. The seconds pass and the feeling hardens into a queasy recognition. She doesn't need to be able to see his face to know who it is. The smell of his garment is enough. She pulls away and speaks his name: 'Jack.'

'Shhh,' he hisses again.

He opens the back door of the house and pulls her inside, into the deeper dark. He still hasn't let go of her wrists. All she can make out is the pale rectangle of glass over the front door, but he leads as if he can see in the dark. She stumbles along behind him until they are next to the front door. She pulls her hand back but he doesn't let go.

'No time,' he whispers.

She twists her hand down below his wrist and then up past it on the outside, forcing the grip to break. 'No!'

'They'll be back. Gabriel and his people.'

Jack says this as if it is enough. As if he expects her to be satisfied, to hold back patiently until some more convenient time. She wants to tell him how wrong he is, but the gulf between his apparent assumption and the place where she finds herself standing is so vast that she can't find any words to bridge it. So she launches her fist towards him, a swinging roundhouse punch to the chin. There is an explosion of pain in her hand, as if she has just punched a brick wall. But Jack is stumbling away from her. She hears the sound of him hitting the ground. She can't see his body in the dark room.

She doesn't need to or want to. She fumbles for the door handle. It is unlocked and she is on the street, stumbling, then running away from the house, towards the main road where Miss Quick said she would come to rescue her. It is the only place she has to go.

Chapter 24

It is Friday morning and Frank is in hell. His mind jumps from self-hatred to yearning for non-existence and then on to increasingly frantic plans to rescue his morals and save himself from public exposure as a corrupt police officer. Then he is back to the self-hatred.

Mo was attacked again last night. At her home this time. She's alive but with facial bruising. If the patrol car hadn't arrived when it did . . . He can't even bring himself to think about it directly.

The door to Frank's office is closed. He puts his forehead on the desk and closes his eyes. If he had only returned the money to Vince right at the beginning. If he hadn't given in to the first blackmail demand. If he hadn't gone along with Kringman all those years ago. Each step along the path seemed right as he took it, done for motives that seemed pure at the time.

He presses his hands over the sides of his head, covering his ears, blocking out the sound of the building and replacing it with the roar of turbid blood flowing in his own veins.

It isn't his fault that Complaints and Discipline are so slow, that Mo hasn't been suspended from work already. If she had been, she'd be out of the public eye, the attack might not have happened. But now Vince has gone for her at her home – is it too late? The man knows where she lives. Frank immerses himself in formless self-loathing again.

It is the ringing of the desk phone that breaks the spell. His hands come away from his head. He sits up and snaps his eyes open. His heart is racing.

He grabs the receiver. 'Hello?'

'Mr Shakespeare?'

'Hello?'

'It's me, Mr Shakespeare. Ricky.'

Frank rubs his forehead with his hand, trying to focus his thoughts. 'Ricky from the phone company?'

'Bingo! I knew you wouldn't forget me.' There is a childish delight in the voice.

The switch in Frank's mind takes no time at all. His thoughts are ordered again. Vince is gone. The blackmailer is back in focus. 'Has he called again?'

'No.'

'Did my payment arrive?'

'Thank you. Yes.'

'What is it, then?'

'It's just that I came by some more information that you might want. Something else.'

'Tell me.'

'Okey-dokey. But it will cost a little bit more money.'

'I don't have more.'

'Oh.' Ricky sounds disappointed. 'I can sell it to someone else. But I'd like it better to be able to sell it to you, Mr Shakespeare.'

'Who would you sell it to?'

Ricky giggles. 'That's half the secret. But I'll tell you anyway. There is a man called Gabriel. He'd pay me for it.'

'How much?'

'He'd give me a thousand. But from you . . . If you gave me

half that, I'd be happy. I like policemen.' Ricky pauses, then adds: 'And you can pay me next month if that will help.'

Frank takes a deep breath. 'OK.'

'I'm so glad. Here it is then – you gave me that number and asked me to tell you when the phone was switched on. Well, this man Gabriel – he's a big man, leather jackets, foreign accent – he gave me the exact same number and asked for the exact same service. I did it, of course. But I didn't tell him about you. And I won't now that you're paying me.'

'What did you tell him?' Frank asks.

'You know Gabriel, then?'

'Did you tell him the locations?'

'Of course I did. Just the same ones I gave you. So if those places are special in some way – you should know that Gabriel knows about it too.'

Miss Quick was as good as her word, picking Tami up on the main road into town. There were no places in the homeless hostels but they found one in a women's refuge. It was available for only one night. But no one asked any questions.

When the probation officer was leaving, she turned and said: 'We'll have to talk about it, you know.'

'Yes.'

'And where will you go tomorrow?'

'I don't know.'

Miss Quick flashed the briefest of smiles. 'Sufficient unto the day. Try to have a good sleep. Things will look different in the morning.'

It is noon the following day when Tami returns to her flat. The front door is unlocked but not broken. Nothing has been trashed. But there are signs that Gabriel's people have been through everything, searching her possessions. The furniture is not exactly where it was. A drawer is open a centimetre. When she pulls it fully open and looks inside, she sees that her clothes have been moved, taken out and replaced.

She feels nauseous. That might be from fatigue – she was awake all night. Or it could be because her space has been defiled. Or because Gabriel will return. Or because she knows that Jack will come back and try to talk to her.

Jack doesn't arrive straight away. She lies on the bed with her eyes wide open, looking at the ceiling She knows that if she does allow them to shut, she will see his face in her mind's eye. Every few minutes they start to close and with an agony of self-will she forces them wide again.

She lies like this, waiting for three hours before hearing it. A low rattling noise. She walks to the kitchen doorway. Jack is outside the window, trying to get in. He was the one – she sees that now – who has been entering her flat while she was out. Leaving nothing out of place but subtle vibrations in the air – a trace of a memory of a scent. He is standing on the outhouse roof. It must be an easy climb for him, up the drainpipe and along the line of ridge tiles to the wall. And from there to the old window – easy to lift once he had broken the paint seal. Until she glued it closed again.

She steps into the room and he looks up. She can see the mark on his jaw where she hit him. For the first time in nine years she looks into his eyes. They are the same. But his face has aged. He puts his palms on the glass and mouths some words. She can't make them out. She doesn't need to. The expression tells her everything. It is so harrowed, so pregnant with longing that she has the urge to give in, to open her arms and her heart and beg him to come back. It would be so easy. It would be like the first time, letting him lift her off the floor, letting him take away her trouble. She allows the feeling to come forward, to occupy her mind. But only for a moment.

'Go round the front,' she says.

He shakes his head. This time she manages to make out the word he mouths. 'Gabriel.'

She leaves him there, strides to the front window and looks through the net curtain to the street. There is a dark van parked on the other side of the road. In a road where each of the residents has their own car, it is easy to spot a newcomer. And Tami has never seen this van before. She marches back to the kitchen, waves him away from the glass, then she jabs the point of the big vegetable knife into the crack where she squeezed the superglue and starts to lever it back and forth. The blade sinks into the spongy wood and the leverage is gone. She pulls it out, moves along a few centimetres and tries again. This time she finds an unrotted section. The blade bends as she increases the pressure. Then, with a sharp splintering sound, the window starts to move.

Jack pushes upwards from the outside. The narrow crack turns into an opening and he is clambering through.

They stand looking at each other. There is an expression on his face somewhere between pain and longing. He steps towards her, arms spreading. She steps back. He stops, frowns, seeming confused.

'Go,' she says.

'It's a shock. I'm sorry.'

'Go away.'

'I wanted it to be different. But Gabriel . . . I had no choice.'

'Get out of here!' She is shouting, pointing to the window.

He puts a finger to his lips. 'He's outside. You can't stay here. You shouldn't have come back. In a couple of minutes his men will be here.'

'Then you go your way, I'll go mine.'

Jack is shaking his head as if he can't understand what she's saying. And it hits her that by sending him away, she is reacting. Displaying a reflex rather than a choice. She closes her eyes and takes a deep breath. And when she opens them again she asks: 'Why did you tell me there was another woman?'

'There isn't time. We have to get out.'

'Unless you answer, I'm going to the front window and calling him up here.' She can see the doubt in his eyes. She steps back from him, then wheels and marches through the living room towards the front window. She is a step away from it when he catches her around the forearm and pulls her back.

'What the hell are you playing at?'

Tami's wrists are itching. She wants to expose the scars for him to see. She wants him to know what he did to her.

'I never told you that story,' he hisses. 'That was Dad's idea. I told him not to, for Christ's sake!'

She tries to wrest her arm free, but he has it tight and there is no strength in her.

'It had to look real – your reaction. I said he should let you know, that you could act it. He only told me after what he'd put in the letter. It was to protect you. It was all for you.'

Tami twists her arm around again. This time Jack's grip breaks. A car is moving down the street outside. A black

Mercedes. It pulls up in front of the house. Jack moves around her so he can look at it. A car door slams.

'We're out of time,' he says. 'They're here.'

Jack makes her go first, backing out of the kitchen window. Her feet kick in the air before finding the outhouse roof. Then he is following, pulling the window closed. She crawls on hands and knees along the roof ridge, then slides down towards the gutter. One of the slates cracks and a fragment slips and tumbles over the edge. She lets herself down after it. The final drop is only half a metre, but her ankles jar as she hits the ground. He drops cat-like next to her, takes her hand and leads her through the yard to the walkway entrance where she was chased the night before.

There is a bang from the front of the building, sounding quiet against the hum of the daytime city. It is the outside door being broken through. In a few seconds they'll be in her flat. She lets Jack lead her along the walkway, then left on to the street. Tami can feel the breath rasping at the back of her throat as they run. Jack leads her along Green Lane Road then down Perry Street. He stops so suddenly that she bumps into his back. The house in front of him has old newspaper stuck on the inside of the windows. He unlocks the door and pushes it open, ploughing back a small mountain of junk mail.

She follows him inside. The door closes behind her.

'Why?' she asks.

He frowns as if he doesn't understand the question.

'Why did you make me think there was another woman?'

'I told you. It was Dad, not me.'

'You could have let me know.'

'I was following the man who framed you. He said he'd

kill you. There was someone on the inside and she was going to do it as soon as he said the word.'

'Joy?'

He nods. 'When she attacked you, it was a warning for me to back off.'

Tami raises a hand and touches the place where the pen went into her cheek.

'I'm ninety per cent sure it was Gabriel,' Jack says. 'But I never found out for certain. Whoever it was, he started sending threats. I had to go up to Scotland to meet him.'

'The paint factory,' Tami says.

Jack glances into the building. 'Can't we talk about this later?'

'I need to know!'

There's a pause before he answers – as if he is reluctant to cross some internal barrier. 'It was a paint factory. Yes.'

'Tell me what happened.'

'I went there like he told me. In through a window – the place was all boarded up. I knew he'd try to kill me – whoever he was. But I thought I'd at least get a sight of him. I'd dodge the bullets – if that's what it was going to be. If I got out alive, I'd know who it was.'

'And if you didn't?'

'Then I'd be dead and he'd leave you alone.'

Tami feels her stomach constrict. She has changed her mind. She isn't ready to hear more. But Jack is telling it anyway. And with each sentence he seems more certain of what he is doing.

'I thought he'd be waiting for me. Or maybe he'd follow me in. But he just poured petrol and torched the place. I heard it start. It was like a handclap. I went back through the rooms to find out what it was. But it was well ablaze by then. All I could do was go searching round the building, trying to find another way out. A window maybe. But they were all boarded. There was smoke everywhere. And things exploding upstairs.

'Then I found a room that wasn't on fire but it looked like a bomb had gone off there. Something had blown in the room above. A gas cylinder or an oil drum or something. There was a hole in the ceiling and the window boarding was blown out. And I knew I could escape. Then I saw the body – some guy sleeping rough. He was dead already.' Jack shakes his head. 'I left the ring so they'd think I was dead.'

Hearing Jack's confession is like having a tooth drilled by the dentist. Hearing the drill. Feeling the grit of broken enamel mixed with blood and saliva. But not feeling any pain. Not yet. Tami is afraid that if he goes too deep, the pain will start to come. But she asks anyway: 'Why didn't John tell me you were dead?'

'Would that've been better?'

She wants to say yes, it would. A thousand times better than being left to believe she'd been betrayed.

Jack runs a hand through his hair. 'Look. If he'd told anyone I'd gone to meet someone in that factory, then the police would have done tests on the body. They would have found out it wasn't me. The killer would have found out. I had to just go missing. The killer had some inside track with the police. I knew that already. I knew he would see the evidence. That's why Dad made up the story about another woman. Easy for people to swallow. No missing person file. No one would connect me with the body – except for the man who told me to meet him there. And so long as he thought I was dead, he wasn't going to threaten you any more. You were safe.'

Jack looks down. 'I didn't want it to be this way – when I met you again. But it all got out of control. I'm . . . sorry it happened like this. It must be a shock. But I'll make it up to you. Now we're back together, everything is going to be different.'

Tami is shaking her head. He is talking about a different universe from the one she's inhabited for the last nine years. 'Why didn't you tell me later?'

'I wanted to – but it wasn't safe.'

'I had a right to know!'

'I was protecting you.'

'Did I need it?'

'You were inside. I couldn't protect you properly in there.'

'You think I'm so fragile?'

'It was dangerous.'

'Why not when they released me, then? I've been out for months!'

'I was watching over you. You were safe. And I sent Rita to be with you. It was only once you were out of prison that I could start to stir things up – to find out who it was that framed you.'

'Stir?'

'It has to be someone from the agreement. Once you were safely out, I started sending them anonymous letters. I wanted them to panic, to make mistakes.'

'Everyone? Gabriel too?'

'Everyone. And then I pushed more. I demanded money. Threatened to expose the agreement.'

'Blackmail?'

'It was for you, Tami. To find the person who framed you.'

'You waited all this time to tell me you were here!'

'It had to look real. But I was watching, in case he moved on you. And then he did. And now we *know* it was Gabriel.'

'You don't know anything.'

'Tami.' He steps towards her, arms opening again, like he did in the flat, as if he thinks he's said enough to make up for it. She springs back out of his reach.

'Tami?'

'No way!'

'Tami!'

'I'll scream if you touch me again.'

'You need me now.'

'I do not!'

'Please.'

'No!'

Then very quietly he says: 'I need you.'

She turns her back on him.

He steps around so that he is facing her again. But this time he doesn't try to touch her. 'To beat Gabriel we need to help each other.'

There is truth in this. She would prove nothing by running away. 'I will help,' she says. 'But that is all. Nothing more. And when it's over, it will be over. I won't be seeing you again.'

The pain intensifies in his face.

She looks around her at the bare room. 'What is this place?'

'A safe house. I . . . I set it up for you in case we had to run.'

'Who knows about it?'

'No one. There's nothing to connect this place to you or me. We really are safe here.'

He doesn't try to grab her arm this time, but walks ahead, looking back like a child to see that its parent is following. He leads her upstairs. The floor is clear of dust here. The windows are dark, covered in layers of newspaper and aluminium foil. He switches on the lights and shows her into a bare room with a camp bed and a backpack. She sees a set of androgynous clothes laid out on the floor and a plastic bag spilling women's underwear.

'You bought this for me?'

When he doesn't answer, she looks round. There is shock on his face.

'Someone's been here,' he says. 'It was all stowed in the backpack.'

It takes Jack less than a minute to find the entry point. A broken pane of glass in the back door. 'They unlocked it and just walked inside,' he says.

'Local kids?'

'Perhaps. But they would have stolen the gear upstairs.

'It's not the kind of stuff they could have sold.'

Jack shakes his head. 'We'd better get you out of here.'

'Me?'

'Us.'

'Is it safer outside?'

Jack snaps his head around.

'What?'

'Did you hear that?'

Tami didn't. But now she does. A faint grating sound from the back. The wheelie bin being moved. Jack makes to grab her hand, but she pulls it away. She doesn't need him to lead her any more. She springs through to the front of the house, getting to the door before him. So she is first to know that they are trapped. A man's shadow falls on the newspaper that covers the front window.

There is a crash from the back. Gabriel strides through the broken door. His arms hang by his side. Relaxed. His left hand holds a gun.

'Don't try,' he says.

Jack seems like the very opposite of Gabriel. Tensed. Edging backwards in half-steps. Elbows bent. Fists balled but empty.

Gabriel waves the barrel of the gun, indicating that they should move. 'Upstairs.'

Tami finds herself following the order. It is as if all the willpower and volition that she has built up since confronting Jack has suddenly been sucked away.

Jack looks as if he is about to spring forward.

Gabriel shrugs. 'Be stupid and the woman . . . You know.'

Jack moves after that, but jerkily, like a puppet fighting against the man holding its strings. Gabriel follows three paces behind. Up the stairs. Across the landing. Into the bedroom. He leans his shoulder on the wall next to the door, flicks the gun barrel down. Tami drops to her knees. Jack follows a second later.

'Good. Now you talk.'

'Let her go,' Jack says. 'And I'll tell you everything.'

'I let her go and you tell nothing.'

'I promise.'

Gabriel laughs. 'Where you hide it? Tell me that and I let her go.' He pushes himself off the wall and paces around the edge of the room until he is directly behind them. 'No answer?'

'That's because I don't understand the question.'

'And the pretty wife? She too?'

'She doesn't know anything.'

Tami feels resentment mixing with her fear. But still she doesn't speak.

'One rat squeals to police. They find eight and a half Ks of Afghan white. The pretty wife has one K in her car. Ten and a half Ks missing.'

'It was ten years ago,' Jack says, his voice pleading now.

'You think the stupid Russian forget so easy?'

Tami hears a sharp smack and Jack is falling forward. He hits the floor, eyes rolled up. Tami shrieks. She feels the gun barrel jabbing into her side. With his free hand, Gabriel grabs Jack by the belt and drags him across the floor towards the radiator. She starts getting to her feet, but the Russian switches aim from her to Jack, pressing the gun into his kidney. There is a metallic click. Though she didn't notice them before, Tami now sees the steel glint of a pair of handcuffs. In two movements, Gabriel has snapped one side on Jack's right wrist and the other on to the radiator pipe. The whole process took less than thirty seconds.

Jack is coming round, groaning and blinking, shifting his head from side to side. He swears under his breath. He pulls his hand tight against the chain.

Gabriel straightens himself. 'Good. Now you tell. Who is the rat?'

'Not me,' Jack says. 'And not her.'

'Where is the ten and a half Ks?'

'Someone . . . the rat . . . must have sold it.'

'No. This is rare shit. Very pure. They sell it and I will know.'

'Then I haven't a clue.'

Gabriel walks around the room to the window. He peels back a corner of newspaper and aluminium foil and peers down to the road outside. Tami hears his footsteps on the floorboards as he moves up behind her, but she can't bring herself to turn her head to watch, so Jack's cry is the only warning she gets before he hits her. She is on her face on the floorboards and her head is ringing. There is a weight pressing on the small of her back. Something angular. His knee perhaps. She tries to roll but the pressure increases. Then his hand is running through her hair, down her neck, caressing her skin. His fingers slip inside the neck of her blouse.

Jack screams. 'No!'

Tami feels the hand pull back.

'You remember something to tell?'

'It wasn't her. Nor me. I swear it.' She can't see his face, but she can hear the animal panic in Jack's voice. The handcuffs clang against the radiator.

Gabriel grips the fabric of her blouse just behind her neck. There is a pause, then he jerks it down her back. The neckline slips over her skin, coming abruptly tight around her throat. She feels the pressure on her windpipe. She can't breathe. The fabric starts to rip over her left shoulder and the pressure releases. Gabriel pulls a second time, tearing the blouse off her other shoulder. The sense of exposure is suddenly overwhelming. The handcuff chain clangs on the radiator.

'I'll tell!' Jack shrieks.

'Talk then.'

'It was . . . it was the policeman. Shakespeare. He . . .'

'No,' Gabriel cuts in. 'A lie.' Tami feels his fingers looping around her bra strap.

'Please . . . Bill Arnica, then . . .'

'No. More lies.'

'I know,' Tami whispers.

She feels Gabriel's hand stop. And now she's spoken the first words, she feels strength coming back into her. 'I know where they put the heroin.'

'Where?'

'In a secret place.'

'You took it?

Tami feels Gabriel's knee pulling away a fraction, releasing the pressure. She raises her head and turns it so she is facing

Jack. He is on his feet, but his back is bent and the handcuff chain is taut between his wrist and a pipe near the floor. He is looking at her, his eyes pleading. And it hits her for the first time that in his attempts to protect her Jack has been no different from her parents all those years ago. It is as if she is too young, too innocent, too fragile to protect herself. He is shaking his head, mouthing *no*.

'You took it?' Gabriel says again.

'I lost everything,' she says. 'Husband. Home. Everything. You think I'd care if it was a hundred tonnes of heroin? No. I didn't take it.'

'Then how you know where it is?'

'I know because someone told me.'

'Who take it?'

'Bird's Eye. And he's dead. I know this is the truth.'

There is a pause. A moment when she doesn't know how Gabriel will react. She is telling him that the one who double-crossed him is beyond vengeance. Beyond even Gabriel's reach.

Then Gabriel hits her on the side of the head with the pistol. It is so unexpected that she doesn't start to feel the pain until seconds later.

'No!' Gabriel shouts. Then 'No!' again and another blow.

She must be unconscious for a few seconds after that. When the room comes back into focus, she sees blood pooling on the floor near her eye.

Jack and Gabriel are shouting at each other. Their voices are coming from the other side of the room. The weight has gone from her back. She looks up, blinks focus back into her vision. Jack is kneeling now. One of his eyes is puffed up, almost closed.

Gabriel is lining up a punch, fists in boxer pose, one guarding his face, the other doing the damage.

'She doesn't know!' Jack hisses, bloody saliva trickling from a corner of his mouth.

'You tell, then.'

Another punch. This one to the body.

Tami looks for the gun and sees it in the outside pocket of Gabriel's leather jacket. She wouldn't know how to fire it, even if she could come up behind him and take it. She starts to crawl forward anyway.

'Bastard,' Jack shouts.

Another left-hand jab, this one to the mouth. 'Shut up!'

'Bastard!' Jack spits at Gabriel's face. He starts roaring now. Incoherent. Making noise. And Tami knows that he has seen her, that he is covering for the dry scrape of her skin over the floorboards. For a second his eye catches hers. He flicks his gaze to the open doorway.

Then Gabriel is landing punches on his chest and Jack is gasping.

Tami has reached a point directly behind Gabriel. She lifts herself on to all fours and inches forward. She is reaching out her hand. Her fingers touch the metal.

Gabriel launches another punch and the gun swings away from her. But when it swings back she is ready. She grasps it, intending to pull it clear in one easy movement. But she has never held a gun before and isn't ready for its weight. It spills out of her fingers.

Gabriel is turning. Lashing his fist around towards her. The gun lands on the floorboards. She dives to grab it and the fist passes over her head. There isn't time to aim. No time to pretend she could fire it. So she summons all her panic and anger into one last act and hefts it towards the window. Glass breaks. There is a sudden jagged opening and natural light is streaming in. Someone shouts in the street.

Then there is the whoop of an approaching police siren.

Gabriel swears. He kicks, catching Tami on the hip, raising her feet momentarily off the ground. She lands on her side, doubled up in pain. He is at the door, backing out of the room.

'Talk to the pigs and you die. I promise.'

Then he is gone. The police siren stops close outside. The back door slams.

When Frank arrives at the building, there are already two police cars in the road. Two uniformed officers are keeping a small crowd of civilians back.

'Well?' Frank asks.

They look at him with what seems to be respect. 'How did you know?' one asks.

'Contacts,' he says. 'Tell me what you found.'

'A gun. There's a woman in the house threw it out. She's been beaten up.'

'Tami Steel?'

The respect turns to something more akin to awe. 'Yes, sir.'

'Anyone else?'

They shake their heads. 'It's a mess inside. The radiator's been pulled off the wall. There's rusty water everywhere. And blood. Looks like there was a fight.'

'Is the woman talking?'

'Not a word. But I guess you already know what happened, sir.'

Chapter 25

Tami doesn't speak but her fingerprints shout. They, along with Gabriel's, are on the loaded firearm that was found in the street. She is only out of prison under licence and is certain to be sent back inside if she doesn't offer an explanation. She spends one night in the police station cells before cracking.

Gabriel was there, she says. He threatened her with the gun. He beat her up. There are marks on her face to match the story. She doesn't know why he did it. And she doesn't have any idea about the blood spatter marks found on the floor and wall. DNA analysis shows that they came from another man. Not Gabriel. As for the radiator – Tami says Gabriel pulled it off the wall to show his strength.

She is released on the same day that CID corner Gabriel in London. Inspector Bruce Lowrie is the arresting officer. Gabriel is hauled off to the cells, swearing in a language presumed to be Russian.

The charge is possession of a firearm and GBH. And since the media are on a crusade against the spread of guns, and since Gabriel is such a prize for the police anyway, there is a suggestion that he might be put away for several years. Frank hopes that Tami can find a way to live safely – whatever it is she isn't telling. And he hopes also that with the jailing of Gabriel the blackmail demands will stop.

Gabriel's lawyer requests that he be released pending trial. If his passport is taken away, she says, he won't be able to go anywhere. The police argue it the other way. He has contacts in the world of people trafficking. He has money. And he is dangerous. Bail is refused.

The surprise is that Gabriel's passport, offered at court, turns out to be British. It emerges that he was born in Bristol but moved at the age of three to Estonia to stay with his maternal grandmother. She died when he was thirteen, and he came back to England to live in a sink estate. His long criminal record started a couple of years later. Whether the Russian accent is put on or genuine, no one seems sure. But the hint of serious contacts in the East must have been useful in his business. Easy for him to bully or to tempt.

On the Wednesday after Gabriel's arrest, Complaints and Discipline finally get round to investigating Mo Akanbai's computer. They decide that her prophetic memo wasn't written when she claimed. The creation date recorded on the hard disk proves it. It follows that she has lied to protect herself and to incriminate a senior officer. The chief constable has no choice but to suspend her.

Everything has happened as Frank planned. She should be out of the picture. Away from Vince's gaze. And it is only temporary. In another couple of months she should be back on active duty. Plenty of time, Frank thinks, for him to find the money to pay off the racist, and then to find a way to take him down.

But events are happening outside Frank's control. Other people's stories impinging on his own. The long-awaited multiculturalism conference arrives on the following Saturday. It brings with it a travelling circus of anti-fascist demonstrators and neo-Nazi racists, all up for the fight. Bricks and bottles on the streets of Leicester.

Vince is there, still dreaming of his white super-race. Mo is there, too, trying to stop him. And somehow, in the middle of the battle, witnessed by hundreds of people, Vince is killed. No one saw a thing, of course. No one is charged with his murder.

A huge weight is removed from Frank's conscience. His luck has changed. The risk of exposure is suddenly reduced. And the danger of being drawn into further illegality.

The days pass and no further blackmail demand arrives. At first, Frank checks the mobile every morning. Then it is once a week. The summer fades. The leaves turn golden-brown.

Now he has other things to worry about. The inquiry into the riots is grinding on. His bravery on the street has been recognized. But an expert has examined Mo Akanbai's computer and stated that her memo to him was tampered with. No one has been able to prove it was him. But he has been suspended from duty while the matter is investigated further. On full pay but on the brink of public disgrace. The only thing that makes the situation easier to cope with is the knowledge that Mo herself is in the clear.

He tells himself that this is like a holiday. He will be able to do all the jobs that he has been putting off. Replacing the washers in the kitchen taps. Clearing the guttering of moss. Treating the patch of rot at the back of the garden shed. And at last he has time to give proper attention to his bonsai trees.

He tells Julie that it will all work out fine, that he has done nothing wrong at work. She doesn't ask any questions. There is a distant sadness in her eyes that he finds hard to look at.

By mid-winter he is out every day in the garden. He buys a paraffin heater for the shed and moves some of his gardening books down there.

Then, one afternoon in early January, he gets an official letter. The Complaints and Discipline department are holding back pending the report of the external inquiry into the riots. He will have to wait another few months for a conclusion to be reached about his own case.

But the truth is, he doesn't think he can face the investigation.

He reads the letter twice. The blackmailer's photograph comes to his mind. And the mobile phone – unremembered and unchecked in months. He takes it out of the locked drawer in his study, turns it on.

There are no messages waiting.

Tami knows about prison. It doesn't deal with problems. It freezes them. Gabriel is locked up on remand but when they finally release him – in a day, a month, a year, ten years – his drive for revenge will be as fresh as when he walked inside.

Jack phones her once a week through the summer. He says it is to discuss Gabriel's upcoming court case. But there is never anything to say on that subject, so he talks about the things he is doing instead. He asks about her. She has found a job in another food preparation factory and started studying towards an NVQ. Her new boss is a woman, and the atmosphere on the production floor is better. He listens. They talk. It is always her who breaks the call, saying she has to go.

With Christmas on the way, the shops start piping seasonal music and the crowds in the city centre jostle with frantic acquisitiveness. The factory puts on an extra shift to cope with demand. Tami works right up to Christmas Eve. The manager gives each of the workers an envelope as they leave. A card with two £20 notes inside.

Jack calls round on Christmas Day. It is the first time she

has seen him face to face since Gabriel's attack. He is thinner than she remembers. His eyes have lost something. She can't say what. She stands on the doorstep, talking to him for five minutes. Then she says goodbye. Back in the flat, she turns the TV on to drown out the silence. She flicks between the channels. The Queen's speech. A cartoon. A movie. The Queen's speech again. She watches for five minutes, then leaves it on and goes to the kitchen to make a cup of coffee. She doesn't cry.

He doesn't phone her for a month after that, and then it is to report that the trial has been set for a date in April. They chat for a minute. He tells her about his job. He is working for a furniture wholesale business. Cash in hand. She tells him about the NVQ, her first qualification. He says he is pleased. Then he says goodbye. She hears no more from him after that.

Until today.

It is her morning off, so she sleeps late. She pulls on some clothes and wanders out to the shops. Milk and the local paper. Speckled bananas to chop up and mix in with her cornflakes. A breakfast treat. She eats slowly, showers, then reads the news over a cup of coffee. An article tucked away on page seven reports that Superintendent Frank Shakespeare has resigned from the force. The inquiry into his conduct hasn't even got under way. A spokeswoman for the police said it brought the matter to a close. There was nothing more to be done internally and no criminal case to answer. Superintendent Shakespeare was a popular officer who contributed much to law and order in the city.

It is eleven thirty when Tami's phone rings. Jack's voice on the other end of the line. He sounds frantic.

'It's the trial.'

'Doesn't start till tomorrow,' she says.

'No. There's not going to be one.'

'I thought . . .'

'There was a problem with the evidence. They've dropped the case.'

Jack's voice is crackling with near panic, but Tami doesn't feel anything. She knew this moment would come.

'When does he get out?' she asks.

'He's out already. They released him this morning.'

Tami puts down her mug, still half-full. She gets up.

'Where are you now?' From Jack's voice she can tell that he is holding the phone to his ear as he walks.

'I'm just leaving the flat,' she says.

'You've got to get everything together. Money. Cheque-books. You can't go back.'

She stoops on her way out, picking up a sports bag that has been waiting near the door for the last eight months. 'I'm packed already.'

They meet on the industrial estate outside the sandwich factory where Tami used to work. She gets out of her car and sees him hurrying along the road towards her, a supermarket carrier bag hanging from one hand.

'You'll have to get rid of that,' he says pointing at the Fiat.

'And then?'

'Get a new one. Something blue or grey.'

'And?'

'You know what you have to do.'

'Leave Leicester? Change my name?'

'All of that.'

'What colour should I dye my hair?'

He passes her the carrier bag. Inside she finds four cans of coke, two pork pies and two triangular boxes of sandwiches of the kind that she once assembled. And at the bottom, under all the food, is an envelope stuffed thick with money.

'Twelve thousand pounds,' he says.

She closes the bag and looks up at him. 'I've given up meat.'

'I'm . . . sorry.'

'The money?' she says.

'It's for you. To help you get started again.'

'I can't take it.'

'It's what's left from the blackmail money. It's yours by right.'

He looks down, as if embarrassed, and it hits her quite unexpectedly that they are not just estranged. They have become strangers.

She drives them to the petrol station. Jack tries to get her to let him do the work, but that isn't right any more. The sun is shining. She looks back to the filler nozzle. The air around it is shimmering with petrol fumes.

'All OK?' Jack asks.

'You think I can't manage?'

'I'll pay, then.'

'No.'

'I wish you'd let me help.'

'It's your money I'm paying with.'

She drives. Jack doesn't ask where she's taking them. She wouldn't know what to say if he did. She leaves the ring road at St Nicholas Circle, heading out of town along the A47.

'I'm leaving Leicester,' she says.

'Good.'

'And you've got to leave, too.'

'I can't.'

'He'll kill you if you stay,' she says.

'He'll follow us both if I leave.'

'You dying is going to make it better?'

'At least then you'll be safe.'

'Don't you lay that on me, Jack Steel!'

'It's true. The only reason he'd go for you is to make me suffer. If I'm dead . . .'

'I'm the one who grassed him up.'

Jack shakes his head.

Tami sees the entrance to Western Park on her right. She makes a snap decision, jabs the brake and throws the car into a sharp turn.

'Tami . . .'

She pulls up by the roadside just inside the park gates, turns off the engine and rounds on him. 'My parents thought I'd not grown up. That's why I left them.'

'I know.'

'You don't know anything! You're just the same. You think you need to protect me. Like I'm a child or something.'

'This is different. Gabriel is a killer.'

'It's just the same. What you're saying with all this—' she waves her arm towards the carrier bag of food and money '—is that I can't look after myself. If it's really got to be finished now, then I'm staying with you.'

His eyes widen for a second.

She shakes her head. 'Not as your lover. We'll finish this business together. But then I'm out of here. Alone.'

He turns his face away from her. 'Right.'

There's a long silence after that. When he turns back to face her, his eyes seem colder. 'Eddie told you that he came here – to Western Park – with Bird's Eye and another person. They buried something in the middle of the night.'

'I told you all this,' she says.

'And you said he thought they were burying my body.'

'So?'

'So – I'm not dead, in case you hadn't noticed. It must have been something else in the hole.'

'Or someone else.'

Jack shakes his head. 'Gabriel's missing heroin. The Afghan white. Someone planted one kilo in your car. What happened to the rest?'

'You don't bury heroin,' Tami says. 'You sell it.'

'Could Bird's Eye do that? Would he know how? And Gabriel said no one had sold it – that he would have known if it'd hit the streets.'

Tami runs a hand through her hair. 'Russian bravado.'

'He's not really Russian.'

'Then common bravado,' Tami says, getting out of the car.

Jack follows her. 'If Bird's Eye had Gabriel's drugs – then he must have been the one who planted the packet in your car. Him or the other man.'

'Eddie never said it was a man.'

'It's got to be.'

'Why would Bird's Eye want to frame me?'

Jack laughs sourly, as if the answer is transparent but distasteful. 'Bird's Eye made his money in lending and repossession. My Dad helped people out when they were in trouble.'

'So?'

'Bird's Eye hated my family. You being caught with the heroin ruined our reputation. Trust was all we had. Nothing worked after that.'

Tami pulls at her sleeve. The skin of her wrist is itching. The motive may be obvious to Jack, but to her the logic is clouded by pain.

'But Bird's Eye is dead . . .' Jack seems to be voicing his thoughts as they come to him. He is staring at a distant oak tree. 'He was dead soon after you went inside. A heart attack. The other man is the one we're after.'

'It's Gabriel who wants to kill us,' Tami says. 'That's what you said before.'

'Only because he thinks we took his heroin. But the man Gabriel's after is the same one that we're after – the one who framed you. He's the one who tried to burn me alive in the paint factory. He's the one who had you attacked in prison.'

Tami shakes her head. 'How do you think any of this is going to help? Gabriel is out there, looking for us. He's not going to hang round this time. No time for talk.'

'So we need to find the man who stole his dope.' Jack pulls a mobile from his pocket and clicks on the power.

Tami steps closer and watches him keying in a text message. 'Who are you sending that to?'

'Eddie Piper. Red Owen. Shakespeare. Gabriel. Everyone from the agreement.'

'No one will come.'

He presses the SEND button. 'They all will.'

Frank is staring at his display of bonsai trees. Each of them is perfectly watered, trimmed and fed. There is nothing more he can do with them for now. He has his hand in his coat pocket, feeling the rubberized handle of the clippers. He takes them out and steps towards the fifteen-year-old oak. He snips off a couple of twigs from one of the lower side branches. With that done, he needs to balance the tree by removing one from the other side. Then another. When he steps back and examines his work, he knows he has gone too far. For it to be made right he will need to take off more wood higher up the tree.

He feels a sudden prickle in the corner of his eyes. It's not until the first tears start to form that he recognizes what is happening. He hasn't cried since he was a child. He turns his face away from the house and uses the back of one hand to wipe away the evidence.

Next week he will start looking for work. Security companies sometimes take on consultants. The media have been known to hire people in the know to comment on criminal cases. And if nothing comes up at first, he could always find some charity work. It would get him out of the house. Make him useful again.

Julie was pleasant towards him over the months of his suspension. But the love had cooled. They seemed to be acting out their marriage for other people's benefit – the neighbours, the congregation, the children. In the times they were alone together there was nothing.

When he told her he had resigned, she just nodded. Nothing more than that. He counts the years forward until their son, Jem, leaves home to go to university. That's how long their marriage has to run.

He hears her now, opening a window. He checks his face with his hand before turning. Her hair is speckled with white these days. He hadn't really been aware that she was dying it before. She beckons him over.

'It's been on the news. That Russian man you put in jail . . .'

'Gabriel? It wasn't me, really.'

'They've released him.'

Frank's mind flashes back to Tami, the blackmail photograph, Vince, all the agony he went through.

He closes up the clippers and starts walking back to the house. He is hurrying by the time he reaches the side path. He throws off his boots next to the back door and runs to the study. It takes him three attempts before he manages to fit the key in his desk drawer. He tries to click on the blackmailer's mobile phone, but there is no battery power after all these months. The charger that came with his own mobile fits, so he uses that, plugging it into the mains. The screen on the blackmailer's phone lights up. The message icon is showing. He clicks the button and reads.

Highest bidder gets all. Negatives. Drugs. Auction on Western Park. Tonight. 1.00 a.m.

'Is everything all right?'

He jolts around to see Julie standing in the doorway.

'Yes, love.'

It is only after the light in her eyes has dimmed that he realizes it was there at all. She turns and walks back into the house. He hears the vacuum cleaner roar into life.

The road into Western Park is barred by old iron gates at night, so Tami and Jack drive a few extra metres to the car park of Environ, the local environmental charity. It is getting dark already. Lights are on in the nearby houses, shining warm yellow through the trees. But Tami's car is distinctive, even in this gloom. Gabriel, Shakespeare and the rest can't fail to recognize it if they come in this way.

'That should draw them in,' Jack says.

'To where?'

He points to the corner of the tarmac area, where a concrete path leads up an incline into the park proper. Streetlamps are spread along its line, close enough to each other so that their light is continuous. But they serve only to intensify the darkness further away.

Tami feels as if the skin on her body is tightening. She shudders. They spent the afternoon going over the plan. She felt less certain each time they talked it through. But Jack's enthusiasm grew to make up the difference.

She goes through the logic in her mind again. Gabriel was shipping twenty kilos of high-grade heroin. He told them that much. He was storing it in Leicester before distributing it around the country. He must have thought he knew what was going on in the St John's estate. He never tried to sell any of it there and, according to the agreement, he would have been warned if the police were planning anything.

But someone must have known what he was doing. They stole just over half his stash and then told a police officer who wasn't involved in the agreement about the remainder. Kringman and Shakespeare were out of the loop. The police raided and, though Gabriel wasn't convicted, he lost his safe place.

Whoever the informant was had another trick to pull. He left one kilo in the boot of Tami's car, carefully seeded with forensic evidence. Tami had no possibility of avoiding prison. The Steels were the agreement's honest brokers. With them discredited, it was all over.

Then come the unknowns – this is where Tami starts to worry. If Bird's Eye was one of the people who took the drugs – if he was burying it that night in Western Park – then the person he was with – the person Eddie refused to name – is the one who has been in the background all this time. He's the one who Jack was trying to track down, who used threats against Tami to warn him off. He is the one who finally tried to burn Jack to death in the paint factory. Or it could be a she. There are too many unknowns.

'What if the person who framed me arrives first?' Tami asks.

'Then he'll go straight to the place where the drugs are buried.'

'If it is drugs.'

'We've been through all this!'

'And if Gabriel gets here first?'

'He'll find your car then go into the park, looking for us.'

'And Shakespeare – why call him in?'

'They're all involved. We throw them together and the truth's going to come out.'

'And if . . . ?'

'Look,' Jack cuts in. 'It doesn't matter what order they arrive. They're all going to come because they all want to finish it. But once we have Gabriel and the man who framed you together in the place where the drugs are buried . . .'

'Gabriel kills him,' Tami says.

'Would that be so bad?'

'And if he tries to kill us?'

'It's night. We'll get away.'

This last statement seems like self-deception to Tami. But that doesn't remove the choice she has to make. She can run away and restart her life under an assumed name, always looking over her shoulder. Or she can face all her fears in one go.

'It might work,' she says.

Jack nods. She can see the excitement in his eyes. She can see that the thought of failure hasn't entered his mind.

'Go if you want,' he says. 'I can manage.'

But she would rather die here tonight than live through more years of uncertainty – not knowing if he is alive or dead. And that reaction is a surprise. She doesn't understand why it should matter to her what becomes of him.

There are some items that Frank didn't return to the station on the day he formally retired. He still has his uniform, though he is sure he will never wear it again. There are some computer disks, backups of letters, lists of contacts that he thought might be useful when it came to looking for work. But now he has moved on, he doesn't want to open up any of those documents again. Neither can he imagine being able to destroy any of them. That would be an admission of defeat.

In the bottom of the box of oddments from that time is an item that he knows he should definitely have returned. A can of pepper spray. He somehow managed to put the illegality of its possession out of his mind. Until now. He takes it out and slips it into his coat pocket alongside a heavy-duty torch with a handle long and sturdy enough to be used as a club should it be needed.

He is wearing an old navy-blue sweater. And a pair of old black shoes. Everything is dark enough for the task ahead. The blackmailer has ruined his life. The way he sees it, there is nothing really left to lose.

The children are in bed already. He stands on the landing listening to them breathing. Julie comes out of the bathroom, brushing her hair. She catches him, he thinks, in a moment when he is experiencing the full magnitude of what has happened. She stares, as if shocked. He is expecting her to ask where he is going, dressed like this. He will have to tell her that he is going for a walk. It looks like rain. He doesn't want to get his other clothes wet and muddy. But she turns away without speaking and steps into the bedroom.

'I've made a mistake,' he says, after her. 'I'm going to lose my job. It's my own fault.' This is his final confession – his lowest point. There was no moment in the process of them drifting apart when he has felt this lonely and wretched.

She comes back to the door, weeping. There is an expression in her eyes that he doesn't understand – an intense longing. He feels her emotion cut into him. He was expecting anger. Neither of them speaks. Then he turns and hurries away down the stairs and out of the house, trying to forget what he just saw.

He walks into the night, lengthening his stride, forcing his mind back on to the immediate task. It is a quarter to midnight. There are a few stars showing through gaps in the rapidly drifting clouds. He gets out his car keys, then changes his mind. Better to walk.

It takes him ten minutes to reach the westernmost edge of Western Park. He clambers up the earth ridge, designed to keep out travellers' caravans. Then he stumbles down the other side and across the open grass, jogging away from the streetlights.

After a hundred metres he has to slow down to an uneven walk. It is so dark here that he can't see the ground under his feet. The soil is rutted with wheel tracks. He stumbles and has to put in a quick extra step to find his balance again.

The last of the stars are covered now. The only light is the dull orange of the city, backscattered off the blanket of cloud. Silhouetted against it, he can see the outlines of young trees. The way ahead seems barred by a bank of close-growing branches and thin trunks. He knows from memory that there is a break somewhere along the line, but it takes him another minute of blind stumbling to find it.

The ground is sodden. His shoes feel heavy with clay. His socks are wet. He squelches through the gap, into the interior of the park. Ahead is a wide grassy area surrounded by drifts of bushes and trees. It is a place that would be obscured from the outside world even during the daytime.

It is still three-quarters of an hour before the time the blackmailer instructed him to turn up. But only a fool would leave it to the last moment.

Instead of moving across the grass, Frank now skirts the open area, keeping close to the bushes so his own silhouette will not show against the skyline. The park is a network of enclosed areas like this, connected by openings in the hedges and sometimes by narrow paths through dense drifts of trees. It is an easy place to get lost in at any time of day.

He finds another gap and steps through it, placing his feet carefully, quietly – though the breeze has strengthened and the leaves around him are rustling loud enough to drown out any small sound. He surveys the next area of open ground. Searching.

He sees the light for a fraction of a second before it blinks out, and then only on the periphery of his vision, but it is enough. He swivels his head around to the left, looking down the slope, focused on a patch of impenetrable black, a shadow within a shadow. After five minutes he hasn't seen any more, so he starts to work his way around the edge of the trees, keeping low. He grips the torch in his hand, knowing he can't turn it on but finding the weight of it reassuring.

It isn't until he is halfway to the next gap that he gets the next indication that he isn't alone. A momentary flash of dull green light, silhouetting a face. It is perhaps thirty paces ahead there for a second, then gone. But Frank is left with the image in his mind. A man illuminated in the light from the display of the mobile phone he is holding to his ear.

He strengthens his grip on the torch handle and advances. It is the blackmailer – that is what he is thinking. The man who has destroyed his career and his marriage. He imagines raising the torch and bringing it smashing down on the back of the man's head. Afterwards he can think, make decisions, decide what to do.

He is breathing fast. Landing each step brings another

moment of risk. A dry twig or a loose stone. He is so close that he can smell the stale cigarette smoke on the other man's clothes. Frank draws back his arm, ready to strike.

Whether it is sound or smell or some kind of instinct isn't clear. But the man jolts around as Frank swings his arm. He ducks under the torch and dives forward. His head knocks into Frank's stomach, sending him tumbling backwards on to the wet ground. The man is on top of him. Frank manages a half-swing of the torch handle. There is a dull thud of impact and the other man falls sideways, crying out and cursing. It is a voice Frank knows. Shrill and insistent. He rolls free and clicks on the torch, shining the beam on to the figure on the ground.

'Arnica?'

'I'll kill you!' Bill Arnica snarls.

Frank turns the torch on himself. 'It's me.' Then he turns it off.

'What are you doing here, Shakespeare?'

Frank drops his voice. 'Same as you.'

Arnica swears some more under his breath.

'Look,' Frank whispers. 'We should help each other. It's the same man blackmailing us both. Together we might catch him.'

'And then?'

Frank doesn't answer.

Arnica makes a sound that could be a grunt of satisfaction. 'Then we see what Shakespeare's made of.'

Chapter 26

Tami is sitting in the darkness in the same position she has occupied since leaving Jack earlier in the evening. She has a raincoat spread underneath her, and her back is resting against a tree. It is a dewy night – not freezing, though the cold has managed to work its way through her clothes and skin as the hours have passed.

To her right is the lighted path across the park. To her left she can see the Environ offices. The car park is straight ahead. Her Fiat is out of view below the downward curve of the ground. She draws her knees up close to her chest and hugs them.

An hour ago a car drew in and parked. No one got out so she crawled forward for a closer view. It was parked in the far corner, rocking on its suspension – just enough for her to know that there were people inside. It drove away ten minutes later.

She thinks about it now as she waits – about what sort of people they might have been. Young, probably. Teenagers with no bed to share. Ten minutes seems like too short a time. She feels a sudden pang of regret for her own loss.

Below her, another car is pulling in. It turns, ready to head out again. But then it stops. The engine cuts. Two figures get out of the front. Men, to judge by the way they move. They circle the car, looking outwards, searching for something. Then one of them taps his hand on the roof and the back doors open. Two more men get out. One of them is larger than the others. He says something and strides off towards the path across the park. Two men follow him. The other gets back in the car.

For a few seconds the men are out of view below the curve of the hillside. Suddenly she feels exposed. Picking up the raincoat, she retreats further into the darkness, keeping her head low.

She stops and looks back in time to see the group emerge from below the slope. They are not on the path, but have come to her side of it and are walking three abreast. Though they are in comparative darkness, the path lights still touch them. She waits until they have passed her position, then takes the mobile phone from her pocket and autodials.

'Yes?' It is Jack's voice, muffled by the roar of wind passing over the mouthpiece.

'Gabriel's coming your way,' she whispers. 'He's got two men with him.'

There's a pause before he answers. 'Stay there. Keep watching.'

'There's three of them,' she says. 'We didn't plan for that.'

'It doesn't change anything.'

Tami says: 'I'm going to follow them.' She cuts the connection before he has time to object.

It is easy at first. The three men have fanned out into a line, with perhaps sixty metres between either end. Gabriel is in the centre occupying the flattest ground. His men have to pick their way. Tami hangs back, keeping to the darkest places.

The problem comes when the man on the extreme right moves off into an area of darkness as deep as her own. Now she has a choice. She can drop back even further and risk the others getting out of her field of view. Or she can trust that the hidden man is still walking at the same pace. She will have to decide quickly, because the next thirty paces will bring her level with the place she lost sight of him.

She can feel the mobile in her pocket pressing into the side of her leg. She could call Jack and ask him. The wind would cover the sound of her words. She touches the phone through the cloth, then draws her hand away. She will follow.

There is a cry up ahead. A man's voice calling in pain or surprise. Angry shouts. Crashing in the undergrowth. Tami runs forward. There is a flash of torchlight in the distance. Voices raised. Another cry. Definitely pain this time. A fight. Two voices. A warning shout. Tami comes over the rise of a hill and they are there in front of her, in no deeper shadow than her own. She is exposed. She drops to the mud.

Two figures, circling each other like boxers. One is Gabriel's man. He throws a punch and the other – a heavier figure – ducks under it, then sends out a blow of his own which catches the first man on the chest. A third figure – the other of Gabriel's men – lies sprawled on the ground. Then Gabriel steps in. He is holding a gun.

'Stop,' he says.

And they do. They turn and Tami sees the bulky man's face. It is Eddie Piper. He is scared. The prone figure clambers to his feet. There is a cut on his forehead. He wipes the blood away from his eye.

Gabriel circles Eddie. 'Not lost it,' he says. 'Good fists still.' When he is directly behind Eddie, he releases his own fist at the ex-boxer's lower back.

Eddie collapses on to his knees, but he doesn't shout out.

'Me too, Eddie. Not bad fists, eh?'

Eddie nods.

'Where you go, then, Eddie, tonight?'

'Nowhere.'

Gabriel launches another fist.

Eddie grunts with the impact. 'Someone told me to come,' he says.

'Who?'

'Dunno.'

Another punch. Then Gabriel steps back, massaging his fist. He beckons his men to take over. They wade forward and start taking it in turns to punch. Eddie raises his hands to guard his head, but he can't stop all the blows.

'Who told you?' Gabriel asks again.

'Dunno!'

Eddie is bleeding. A cut on his cheek and another under his hair somewhere.

The Russian steps forward and holds the gun to Eddie's puffy face. One eye is almost closed already. He pushes the gun barrel into Eddie's mouth, jerking it hard forward at the last moment. There is a crack of metal on teeth. Eddie chokes.

'Where you go in this big park? You go somewhere, yes?' Gabriel pulls the gun back. 'You show me where.'

Eddie coughs, spitting out blood and broken teeth. He may still punch like a boxer, but Tami can see the weakness in his eyes even from here. It comes from inside. He nods to Gabriel.

From the bottom tip of the park to the top corner is a walk of three-quarters of a mile. The width isn't much less. The slopes, hollows, trees, bushes and occasional buildings would give enough cover to conceal a regiment in the daylight. At night, brigades might pass each other without knowing.

It is now nearly one in the morning and Frank's toes are numb from the cold. His feet squelch with each step. Bill Arnica is stumbling along in front of him. The man grumbled and nagged until Frank gave in and let him lead. That was fifteen minutes ago. The task seems impossible whichever path they follow.

'There,' Arnica hisses.

Frank can't see enough to know which way the man is pointing. 'What?'

'A light. Didn't you see it?'

'If I'd seen it, I wouldn't be asking.'

'Over there!'

Frank moves his head directly behind Arnica's shoulder. With his eye he follows the black line of the man's arm. 'You're imagining it.'

Arnica sets off in the direction he was just pointing in. 'Come on.'

Within twenty paces they reach a bank of young trees. The spaces between the trunks are filled with a crisscross of branches and brittle, scratching twigs. Arnica gets down on to the sodden turf and starts worming forward.

Frank mouths: 'You're mad.' But he crouches anyway, then goes down on his belly and tries to follow. He is bigger than Arnica and makes more noise. The water is seeping though his trousers, but the further under the trees he goes the drier the ground becomes. By the time he has crawled three metres, the number of side branches has diminished to the extent that he can get on to his hands and knees again and shuffle forward more comfortably.

Arnica stops dead. Frank raises himself up, trying to see what it is. The wind drops for a moment and it is suddenly quiet. Then Frank hears it – a metallic clang of metal on stone. He closes his eyes to listen, but the wind is blowing again, rushing through the branches above his head. He opens his eyes and sees a flash of torchlight and, silhouetted against it, the crawling form of Bill Arnica.

Frank catches up with him at the lip of a small hollow. Now he can see directly – the young trees are less thickly planted here. A low-powered torch is lying on the ground, seeming to cast more shadow than light. Two men are digging with spades. Frank recognizes one of them as Eddie Piper. Two more men are standing by. One has his arms folded. Frank can't see the depth of the hole in the ground, but they must have been working at it for some time to judge by the mound of earth.

Only when the man with the crossed arms speaks does Frank realize it is Gabriel.

'Go faster.'

'Too many roots,' Eddie says. 'Wasn't like this before.' His voice sounds strangely slurred.

'Is the right place?'

'I think so.'

'How deep to go?'

'I . . . I can't remember.'

'So maybe you dig your grave, Eddie. If you're wrong.'

Only when Gabriel uncrosses his arms does Frank see the handgun. He taps Arnica on the shoulder, then starts crawling backwards, over the lip of the slope and out of Gabriel's view. The wind is continuous now, and he has no fear of being overheard. But still they back off twenty metres before risking a whispered conversation.

'Gabriel is the blackmailer,' Arnica hisses.

Frank doesn't buy this. 'What's in the hole?'

'Drugs. Or a body. It doesn't matter. If we bring the police, he'll get caught. He'll go to prison. No more blackmail.'

'How do you know he's the blackmailer?'

'He called us here. Believe me. I'm going to phone the police.'

'Why not use your mobile?'

'I can't be connected to this,' Arnica growls. 'Nor can you. There are payphones in the New Parks estate. I'll use one of those. You stay here.' Arnica crawls back towards the edge of the thicket. Within a few seconds he has been swallowed by the dark and the wind.

The hole is noticeably deeper when Frank gets back to his viewing place under the trees. Eddie is standing thigh-deep. Gabriel and both his men are on the edge, looking in. Perhaps Eddie is below the tree roots now. The earth mound is growing. The spade clangs on something. Eddie bends, pulls out a lump of stone and hefts it on to the pile. Then he is bending again, scooping out earth with his hands.

Gabriel says something that Frank can't hear. His men nod and one of them walks away, pushing through the tree branches, out of the glimmer of torchlight.

'I've got something,' Eddie says.

As the wind increased, Tami found she could follow Gabriel with less fear of being detected but could hear no more of the conversation. The only certain thing was that Eddie was leading them to a place where something was buried. Gabriel sent one of his men off into the darkness. He returned half an hour later with two spades – though whether these were stolen or had been put in the car earlier, Tami has no idea.

Then there is the question of Jack. He should be here somewhere, in the park. If he hasn't stumbled across this place, he might still be groping around in the dark, searching. Or he could be as close as a few metres away, looking in at the men digging in the hollow, just as she is. She wouldn't know.

She has the mobile phone in her pocket set to silent mode, as is his. She could text him but there would be no point. It isn't just that describing the location would be impossible. If she did make contact, he'd only tell her to get out of danger.

From where she now lies she can see Eddie and Gabriel's remaining man taking it in turns to climb into the hole and pull out handfuls of earth. They have given up on the spades and it seems as if they are working around some embedded object, trying not to damage it.

Gabriel is pacing, like a wolf. Twice she sees him get out a cigarette, put it in his mouth, then remove it and throw it down on to the ground.

Tami feels a drop of water touch her face. She looks up and feels more raindrops. The branches and leaves are black against the dull and dirty orange of the clouds. They whip as gusts of wind pass overhead.

It happens when she looks back to Gabriel. There is a bright flash of torchlight that turns everything yellow. She sees the shadow of her own head on the ground in front of her. She tries to roll to one side. But too late. The torch falls. A weight presses down on her back. Hands are holding her arms. Legs kneeling on her legs, pinning her to the ground. She has been caught by the man that Gabriel sent out into the dark a few minutes ago.

The weight lifts off her and she feels herself being dragged over the earth, pulled forward into the hollow. Gabriel is swearing. She tries to twist free. He steps up and kicks her in the side. Something cracks in the wall of her chest. A rib. Perhaps two. She is doubled over, trying to breathe, in agony with every inhalation.

'What you do here? Bitch! Tell me!'

She can't get enough air into her lungs to say anything.

Gabriel rounds on the others. 'Dig, fools. There's no time now.'

Tami opens her eyes and sees across the ground surface to where Eddie and one of the men are hauling something out of the hole. Black plastic sheeting. Heavy-duty polythene. Water pours as it is pulled free. The package thumps down on the earth next to her. She inhales the sulphurous smell of anaerobic decay. The foul water is seeping through her coat, soaking into her sweater. She can't move to get out of its way.

Gabriel is on his knees next to her. She sees him pull a knife from his pocket. He dips the blade into the plastic sheet and incises a line. The reek of decay is suddenly stronger. He uses the blade to open up the slit. Then he curses again. He reaches into the hole and pulls out a smaller plastic-wrapped packet. Loops of binding tape hang loosely from it. Gabriel crushes the packet with his hand. Dark water pours out.

'This was mine!' he says.

The others have crowded close around. All Tami can see is a ring of heads and flashes of yellow light when the torch beam passes over her face.

'It is ruin! All shit and ruin!' Gabriel stands and points the gun at Eddie. 'Why you do this?'

'Wasn't me!' Eddie is backing away. 'I just dug the hole. Didn't know . . .'

'You!' Gabriel points at his men. 'Back to the car.'

One steps over Tami; the other goes around her. She is aware of them leaving. The sound of breaking branches recedes and is swallowed by the wind. Her face is wet with fine rain. Gabriel is pacing, as if waiting for them to get far enough away.

'They are gone,' he says. Then he shoots.

The bang and muzzle flash are so strong that for a moment after the shot they fill Tami's senses. She tries to get up, but the pain in her chest stops her rising any higher than a low crouch. Eddie is down, clutching his thigh. He still hasn't cried out, but his bloodied face looks as if it is about to scream. There are another two explosive flashes and black wounds appear in Eddie's other thigh and in his knee.

Frank crouches in the darkness, paralysed by uncertainty. Bill Arnica should have put his call through to the police by now. Even if they didn't believe him straight off, a gunshot echoing over the park will surely be reported by someone. Eddie lies bleeding from a bullet wound to the thigh. Tami is down as well. Neither injury looks life threatening in the short term.

At the same time he is trying to work out what has happened. Eddie can't have sent the blackmail message. He's been pulled in unwittingly. Gabriel has forced him to show where a stash of heroin was buried. That's all Gabriel was after. But the blackmailer – Frank still can't see the connection.

Two more shots slam Frank back into the immediate world. Two bullet wounds in Eddie's other leg. There's too much blood. Eddie won't last long. But the police can't be far away.

There is a movement on the other side of the hollow. Gabriel swivels, gun pointing. Jack Steel steps out of the darkness, hands raised.

'Let the woman go,' he says.

Gabriel's gun hand drops and he laughs. 'Jack. It's been long time no see, right?'

'Sure.'

'You come to the auction? Like me?'

'I called the auction. I sent the message. Let the woman go.'

Gabriel laughs louder this time. It sounds forced. 'I thank you. You make things so easy for me.' He raises the gun, pointing it at Jack's head.

'Tami did nothing.'

'Maybe.'

'Let her walk.'

'Sorry, no. You understand.'

In the darkness, Frank is straining his ears for the sound of approaching feet. Jack was the blackmailer. If Gabriel pulls the trigger there will be no more threats and extortion. Tami, Eddie and Jack will be gone. Gabriel will disappear. Only Bill Arnica will know – and he will keep quiet for his own sake. There is no more time for the police to arrive. All Frank has to do is turn away and his problems will be over.

The rain has soaked his coat through. His hair is plastered to his forehead. And he finds that he is weeping, though he doesn't understand why.

'Wait!' he shouts.

Gabriel spins around and backs up to the edge of the light. He sweeps his gun, as if searching for a target. 'Come!' he shouts.

Frank doesn't move. 'Kill them and I'm a witness.'

Gabriel fires. The shot passes over Frank's head.

'Policeman Shakespeare? It is you, right? Then I kill you, too.'

Frank flattens himself to the ground. 'You won't get us all in the dark. Kill me and Jack escapes. Kill Jack and I escape. Either way there's a witness.'

Gabriel turns the gun and shoots Jack in the leg. It is the

casual ease with which he does it that shocks Frank more than anything. One moment Jack is standing. Then he shouts – more in surprise than pain. He falls like a puppet with cut strings.

Frank has had no time to react or think or try to second-guess Gabriel. Such banal violence seems beyond any logic. The Russian is advancing on him already, gun barrel first.

There is only one hope now – help arriving. If he tries to run away through the thicket, Gabriel will hear him and shoot. He feels a huge wash of regret that he isn't one of the policemen rushing through the night to this place to sort out some other people's messed-up lives.

He stands and steps forward, hands raised. 'Think before you shoot,' he says. 'You were set up. Kill these people and you'll never know who did it.'

'No.'

'Yes. He'll get away and be laughing at you.'

'Shut up.' Gabriel turns the gun to point at Eddie. He shoots him once in the head. There is a jerk of impact. A small entry wound just to one side of the nose. Eddie has no time to cry out. He is dead.

The gun barrel is pointing back at Frank before he has a chance to move. 'Now you.'

Frank thinks he sees a momentary tremble in Gabriel's hand. 'Everyone will laugh.'

'You stole the drugs.'

'No.'

'The other police. Kringman. He did it.'

Frank shakes his head. 'We were happy the way things were. The agreement was working.'

'Eddie, then.'

'Eddie was a fair boxer but he couldn't have planned something like this.'

'Him.' Gabriel gestures with a flick of the head towards the place where Jack lies moaning.

Frank tries not to focus on the barrel of the gun. He makes his eyes meet Gabriel's. 'Whoever took your heroin also framed Tami. It ruined Jack's reputation. And his dad's.'

The gun is still pointing at Frank's chest, but Gabriel's eyes have changed. They look down and to the side. 'You know who?' he asks.

'If you shoot us, the secret dies here. No one will know except the person who did it. And he'll be free.'

Gabriel lowers his arm. 'Then tell me how to find him.'

But here Frank has no answers prepared. He says the first thing that comes into his mind. 'Whoever did it will know how to find this place – just like Eddie did.'

'Who?'

Which is when the truth hits Frank. In this huge park at night, who could possibly have stumbled across the one place where the hole was being dug? Yet one person did find it. He opens his mouth to say the name, but it doesn't come out. There is a bang and a muzzle flash, and he looks down at his body to see where the bullet has struck. He can see nothing. Then Gabriel falls forward and lands on his face. There is a bullet wound in his back at kidney height. The gun fires again. Gabriel's neck blooms red.

Bill Arnica steps into the torchlight. He is holding a handgun.

'Why?' Frank asks.

Arnica wipes the rainwater from his face with his free hand. He doesn't answer. He raises his gun.

'Why?' Frank asks again.

Again, no answer.

'Was it to take down Jack and John Steel?' Frank can hear

the rising pitch of his own voice. He is trying to stretch out his last few seconds.

Arnica lowers the gun by a few degrees. 'They weren't the heroes you think,' he says.

Frank nods. 'But they were like kings when the agreement was going.'

'They did it for themselves. No one else.'

'So you framed Tami to ruin them. Is that it?'

Arnica raises the gun again. 'You wouldn't understand. Goodbye, Shakespeare.'

Tami lies curled in the mud. She hasn't moved from her place next to the stinking packets of ruined heroin. The pain is less now that she is keeping her breathing shallow. But the will to fight has gone out of her. In part of her mind she knows that all she has to do is keep still and wait and it will all happen for her. There is nothing more to do. No more decisions to try to make.

Jack's plan has failed. The person who framed her did not arrive to be confronted by Gabriel. It is her and Jack and Eddie whose lives are forfeit. The guilty men are going to go free.

All she needs is passivity and she will slip into death. Oblivion. It is all she desires. To switch off consciousness and have the screen reduced to that single point again, then to nothing. She has heard everything. She knew from the moment when Gabriel sent his men away that there would be no path out of the trees for her. Even for a man like Gabriel, the fewer witnesses to a murder the better. Jack could have escaped, but he exposed himself in a useless bid to save her. Typical male bravado. Except that this particular man was offering his life for hers.

An explosion of sound. A muzzle flash.

She doesn't move. Perhaps the next shot will be for her. She hopes so. Then Gabriel falls. His legs land on top of hers. His torso crashes on to the mess of plastic and stinking water next to her side. She feels a stab of pain as his arm bounces off her back. It lands on the ground in front of her.

Then another shot. Gabriel's blood splashes her face.

She hears Bill Arnica's voice. It is only now that she understands. Jack's plan did work, after a fashion. The man who framed her – it was a man, it seems – has turned up. The text message brought him and Gabriel together over the remains of the missing drugs. Only in one detail did the plan go wrong. Arnica killed Gabriel rather than the other way around.

She listens to Arnica and Shakespeare. They are talking about the agreement, about her, and Jack and John. She thinks of the suffering of the last ten years. All that black sorrow and madness coming from a power struggle to decide who would be king of a sink estate – a place that no one would choose to live in if they had the resources to get away.

It makes no sense to her. But it doesn't matter. She knows who it was – the name of the man who ruined her life. That is something, at least, before she dies.

She finds she is staring at an object that has fallen out of Gabriel's hand. She is so far back in her own mind that it seems to be a minute or two before the thought comes to her that she could pick it up. If only she had the will-power, the volition. She inches her hand towards it. She knows how heavy it will be. But it is vastly heavy. She raises it anyway.

She points it at Arnica. Then she pulls the trigger. The gun jumps in her hand but she holds tight, pulling the trigger again and again until there are clicks instead of explosions. It is Superintendent Shakespeare who eases the gun out of her hand.

'You've done it,' he says. 'He's dead.'

Chapter 27

Tami's lung was not punctured by the broken rib, but there is the possibility of other internal injuries and the doctor tells her to stay in hospital for observation. Then begins a series of interviews with CID officers, all of whom manage to arrive outside normal visiting hours. She's not sure if this is by design or if it is just bad luck, but the nurses don't keep their displeasure hidden.

None of the CID men look comfortable in the hospital. They sit at her bedside, straight-backed, asking their questions. Always the same questions, but each time in a different order. Even if Tami had the desire to deceive them, she wouldn't be able to. All her willpower was used up when she fired the gun.

She tells them everything. All the things that happened to her and all the things she now understands. John and Jack Steel set up the agreement and unwittingly became the hub of the St John's estate. They took away Bill Arnica's influence just as he was fighting to keep his seat on the city council. He framed her to kill the agreement, to discredit the Steel family and to regain his lost power. He was helped by Bird's Eye, another enemy of the Steel family. If Jack hadn't tried to track down the culprit, the matter would have ended there. But the harder Jack pushed, the more force Arnica used to push back.

Inspector Bruce Lowrie travels up from London to speak to her – with a different colleague this time. He asks his questions and notes down her answers. She can't read anything from his face. But when he's finished he gives her a nod. 'Job done,' he says.

Miss Quick comes to see her on the second day. She doesn't say much, but Tami can sense the woman's anxiety.

'Am I going back inside?'

The probation officer shakes her head. 'I don't know.'

'I killed a man.'

'It's with the police. They wouldn't tell me – even if I asked.'

It is on the third day after her admission that the doctor comes and tells her that he is content for her to be discharged. She dresses behind the curtain. Her chest hurts when she puts her arms into the sleeves of her jumper. When she emerges there is a WPC waiting for her. Tami is expecting to be arrested, but the woman just tells her that because she is a witness to a crime she'll have to let them know if she is planning on being out of the city. Then she smiles and says: 'They should give you a medal for what you did.'

'And Jack?' she asks. 'Will they charge him?'

'For what?'

'Blackmail?'

'If someone complains. But it doesn't look like that's going to happen.'

Tami's flat is cold and smelling of damp. She turns on the gas fire in the living room and goes to make a cup of tea. There's no milk. For a moment she thinks of going out in the rain and buying some. But it is easier to drink it black. She sips, and it occurs to her that most decisions for most people are that way – a balance of pulls in different directions, taking the course of least resistance. She has only swum against the flow once or twice in her life. But that doesn't mean she is any more powerless than anyone else. And giving in to what she wants doesn't have to be a bad thing.

Jack turns up a couple of hours later. His leg is in plaster and he is leaning on a pair of crutches. It takes him a long time to climb the stairs.

'I won't stay,' he says. 'I just wanted to see you. To say I'm sorry.'

'There's no need.'

They sit opposite each other, drinking black tea.

'I'm going to Ireland,' Jack says. 'Once the plaster's off. A new start. The pay's not bad over there. Or that's what they say.'

They each sip their drinks and stare into the glow of the gas fire. It is Tami who breaks the silence. 'Who did it?' she asks.

'Did what?'

'Took the photograph you used to blackmail them. You must have had someone else there hiding behind the hedge.'

He chuckles. 'There was no photograph. I went back to the lay-by this year – after you came out of prison. I took a picture. Then I went through the old photo albums. I had hundreds of snaps from the 90s of all the people. Party shots, mostly. I took them to this man in a photo studio, paid him a few hundred pounds and he did it for me. It's all digital. He scanned them into a computer, made it look as if they were all standing there. It's just a matter of cutting and pasting.'

Tami shakes her head. 'Nothing was what it seemed.'

'Except us,' he says. 'We were real.'

'Were we?'

'Yes.'

'I was just a child. I didn't know anything.'

He shrugs. 'It doesn't matter now, either way. We'll need to do the divorce thing, I guess.'

'Or,' she says, 'we could try to start again.'

Jack peers, as if trying to work out if she is serious.

'I don't mean move in.'

'Then what?'

'Go out together. Somewhere.'

'Like a date?' Jack struggles to his feet.

'A first date.' She holds up her hand, flat palm towards him, stopping his advance across the room. 'I'm not the girl you were married to ten years ago.'

'Then let me take you out for a meal.'

'No. We go fifty-fifty. I'll pay my share.'

The joyful surprise on his face softens into understanding. 'That's not easy for me.'

'I know.'

'I'll try,' he says.

'That's good enough for now.'

She steps forward, closing the gap between them. It's not wrong, she reminds herself, to do what feels good. She turns her face to one side and leans forward, offering him her cheek. She thinks he is going to kiss her straight away, but instead he holds himself back a fraction and she hears him inhale through his nose, deeply, as if he is filling his lungs. She can feel the warmth radiating from him. And then he touches his lips to her skin.

She lets herself feel it. After all the insanity of her search, when she was longing to regain what she had before, it is strange to discover that she has found something quite different, or perhaps that the pain has changed her into someone different and that she is, for the first time in her life, content.

Frank can't kneel or he'll get his suit muddy, so he squats next to the flowerbed, scooping compost into a hole in the soil. Everything is prepared. He takes his bonsai oak and upturns it, tapping the bundle free of the pot. There isn't much soil. Even with all the clipping he has done over the years, roots have grown to fill the space available. He teases out some of the fine hairs with his fingers, then rights the plant and lowers it into the hole. With his free hand he scoops in the pile of loose earth.

He is so focused on the task that he doesn't hear Julie approaching until she is level with his shoulder.

'Won't it grow big,' she asks, 'if you plant it out like that?'

'Yes.'

'Then it won't be a bonsai any more.'

'If I have to go away . . . Well, it needs caring for. This way it has a chance.'

'And me?' she asks. 'How will I manage if you go to prison?'

'I'm sorry. For everything.'

She nods, as if taking in his apology.

'When this is all over,' he says, 'would you come on holiday with me?'

'Will we be able to afford it?'

'We could do it cheaply – in the off-season. Drive up to Scotland. They've got a bridge these days. You don't need to use the ferry to get to Skye.'

She crouches down next to him. 'If you got in trouble again, would you tell me at the start or make me wait to the end?'

It is an easy question to answer. All Frank has to tell her

is that it would be different, that he has changed. But lies aren't as easy as they were. 'I don't know,' he says.

She looks down and presses her hand on the soil next to his, helping to firm in the bonsai oak. 'You told me you were sorry for everything,' she says.

'Yes.'

'I'm not. Not for everything. In the end, it might just save us.'

There is the beep of a car horn from the front of the house. 'It's your taxi,' she says. 'Are you ready?'

Frank gets to his feet. 'Yes,' he says. 'I'm ready now.'

Acknowledgements

I would like to express my gratitude to the following people for their help during the writing of this book: the members of LWC, particularly Liz, for their critical comments, encouragement and expert advice, Pat for lending his name and his ear for dialogue, Kate and Fuan for advice, friendship and editorial input, and Stephanie for her unfailing support.

**POCKET
BOOKS**

Also by Rod Duncan

Backlash

A vicious campaign of terror has left Leicester's ethnic communities shocked and scared. As riots break out, police community relations officer Inspector Mo Akanbai watches her painstaking bridge-building work going up in smoke. At the same time, she's suffering the bitter aftermath of a secret romance with fellow officer, Paresh Gupta.

In the course of the investigation, Mo believes she has uncovered a terrorist conspiracy that reaches well beyond the race-hate gangs. But with enemies inside and outside the force, she doesn't know who to trust. Aware of the dangers, Paresh urges her to leave the city. Instead she stays to fight.

An idealist in a world of compromise, Mo makes an original and memorable heroine. With its compulsive style and gripping plot, brilliantly evoking the dynamic mix of the inner city, *Backlash* marks the debut of an outstanding new British talent.

ISBN 0 7434-5019 1
PRICE £6.99

POCKET
BOOKS

Also by Rod Duncan

Breakbeat

Retro-punk Daz Croxley is profoundly dyslexic and perpetually
unemployed. Society expects nothing of him – and he's happy
to oblige. But when he chances on a handful of stolen
banknotes, he becomes the focus of attention from criminal
gangs and police – all demanding information he doesn't have.

Daz's only hope is to play his pursuers off against each other in a
deadly game of bluff and double-bluff. To survive, he must draw
on all the strengths of his quirky, unconventional mind. And to
find the missing information, he will need the help of friends like
Patty, the aging misanthrope, and Kat the claims advisor, whose
sexy green eyes he can't stop thinking about. His greatest
challenge however will be to change the way he views himself.

'An action-stuffed tale of crime, intrigue and murder'
Zoo Weekly.

ISBN 0 7434-5020 5
PRICE £6.99

POCKET BOOKS

This book and other **Simon & Schuster/Pocket** titles are available from your bookshop or can be ordered direct from the publisher.

| 0 7434 5019 1 | **Backlash** | **Rod Duncan** | £6.99 |
| 0 7434 5020 5 | **Breakbeat** | **Rod Duncan** | £6.99 |

Please send cheque or postal order for the value of the book, free postage and packing within the UK; OVERSEAS including Republic of Ireland £2 per book.

OR: Please debit this amount from my VISA/ACCESS/MASTERCARD:

CARD NO: . . . .

EXPIRY DATE: . . . .

AMOUNT: £ . . . .

NAME: . . . .

ADDRESS: . . . .

. . . .

SIGNATURE: . . . .

Send orders to SIMON & SCHUSTER CASH SALES
PO Box 29, Douglas Isle of Man, IM99 1BQ
Tel: 01624 677237, Fax: 01624 670923
Email: bookshop@enterprise.net
www.bookpost.co.uk
Please allow 14 days for delivery. Prices and availability
subject to change without notice